INHERITED DANGER

Inherited Danger
Book Two of The Dawning of Power trilogy
By Brian Rathbone

Copyright © 2008 by Brian Rathbone.
White Wolf Press, LLC
Rutherfordton, NC 28139

The Greatland

Sylva

Northern Wastes

Isankland

Westland

Faulk

Adderhold

Inland Sea

Mundleboro

Astor

Eastland

Southland

Prologue

Impenetrable darkness shrouded the cold caves, and Wendel Volker shivered as the freezing dampness crept into his bones. His persistent cough rattled in his chest. Though he had gone to his bedroll hours ago, his mind refused to quiet. His troubles demanded attention, demanded he find some way to act, some way to set things right. He had thought of little else for days, but no answers were revealed to him, only feelings of guilt, anger, and despair.

Catrin was gone, and he would probably never see her again. For all his strength and devotion, he had failed to protect her, just as he had failed to protect Elsa, and now they were both lost to him. Like a coward, he'd hidden in the cold caves when Catrin had needed him most. He had relied on Benjin to stand in his place. He'd been a fool. Perhaps Elsa had been wrong all those years ago; perhaps she should have chosen Benjin instead.

Balling his hands into fists, Wendel tried to drive the thoughts from his mind, but memories of Catrin would not relent; they flooded him with guilt and remorse.

When he turned his thoughts to his present situation, there was no relief. Catrin had left behind a troubled land. Though he knew she had done the best she could and was immensely proud of her, her actions had not been enough. To achieve peace under these circumstances was more than any individual could accomplish, and Wendel wondered how the Godfist would ever overcome the turmoil threatening to consume them all. General Dempsy's men still held the harbor, and no one could know what they planned to do next. Headmaster Grodin was succumbing to age, and he ruled over those within the Masterhouse only in name. It was Master Edling and his followers who truly held sway, and their stubborn arrogance only exacerbated the problems. By refusing to grant amnesty to the Zjhon soldiers who defected, they had divided the citizens of the Godfist.

Though the tribes of Arghast had helped defend those in the cold caves, their presence had only served to confuse matters. Once it seemed the Zjhon no longer presented an immediate threat, they claimed to have fulfilled their oath to

Catrin but left a force of thirty mounted men behind to guard the cold caves. It was difficult to believe they had come in the first place, especially since they claimed to be bound to Catrin.

Perhaps he just couldn't accept it, Wendel thought. Even after witnessing some of the events in the harbor, he could not convince himself that Catrin was the Herald of Istra. It just seemed too surreal. She was his little girl, not a harbinger of doom. He made himself believe it was all a coincidence, that Catrin had nothing to do with the bizarre occurrences. Either way, it mattered little now. The Godfist was caught up in a three-sided war, and he doubted he would ever see his daughter again.

The thought of leading a revolution had no appeal for Wendel, yet he found himself caught in that position. His attempts to relinquish power had been fruitless; no one was willing to take his place. Even when he threatened to step down and leave them leaderless, no one volunteered.

Exhausted and ill prepared, he struggled to find a solution. If he surrendered to the will of the Masters, then the Zjhon defectors would be cast out with nowhere to go, and the bloodletting would begin again. Wendel could not accept that.

Jensen insisted they retake the farmlands and highlands, but Wendel was loath to leave the protection of the cold caves. Here, at least, they had the benefit of natural fortifications. If they retook the countryside, then they would be spread too thin to adequately defend themselves. It seemed a puzzle with no solution, and his thoughts ran in circles.

Their supplies were dwindling, and soon they would have no choice but to leave their shelter despite the danger. Sighing, he tried once again to put the problems from his mind. Hoping some revelation would come to him in the morning, he rolled onto his side and continued sweating despite the prevailing cold.

Shades of darkness shifted in his room, moving as if specters lurked in every corner. Chiding himself for letting the stress affect him in such a way, Wendel rolled to face the cave wall and squeezed his eyes shut.

When a foul smell reached his nose, it was already too late to escape. Even as he cried out, a cold blade parted his flesh.

Chapter 1

Hope can be foolish or in vain, but without it, all is lost.
--Ebron Rall, healer

* * *

The seas behind the *Slippery Eel* churned in her wake and left a visible wash of turbulent water. The ephemeral trail gradually dissipated in the distance, where, once again, the waves became nearly indistinguishable before another ship churned them anew. The *Stealthy Shark* remained within sight and kept pace with the *Slippery Eel,* but she did not close the gap. The two ships were evenly matched when in top condition, but the *Eel* was heavily damaged and wallowed sluggishly. She had been taking on water since before leaving the harbor, and the crew had been unable to stop all the leaks. The bilge pumps were the only things keeping them afloat.

The loss of men during their flight from the Godfist left Kenward severely shorthanded, but clear skies, fair winds, and calm seas were a boon to the crew and made their work a bit easier. Catrin, her hair cut short, stood alongside Kenward at the stern, both watching the ship that trailed them.

"I don't understand it," Kenward said. "The *Shark* is in much better condition than the *Eel;* she should've overtaken us long before now. Fasha and her crew are definitely not aboard. The *Shark* is being sailed by boilin' *amateurs,*" he continued, knowing his sister and her crew were either dead or stranded on the Godfist.

"I'm sorry," Catrin said, touching his arm.

"Fasha's the most stubborn and tenacious person I've ever known," he said with fierce pride. "She'll swim her way back to the *Shark* if that's what it takes."

His obvious pride in her made Catrin smile, and she thought again, as she had so many times before, of what it would be like to have a brother or sister. Chase was the closest thing she had, and she shared Kenward's loss. That thought led to her wondering again how her father, Benjin, and the others had fared. Wanting desperately to see them or at least know they were well, Catrin despaired. That knowledge was beyond her reach, taunting her. She had no illusions about the journey ahead of her, and she accepted the possibility that she might never see any of them again.

"There, you see?" Kenward said suddenly. "The rigging's all wrong. They're already blowing off course. If these fools catch us, it'll be no one's fault but mine." He walked away, a sour look on his face. Catrin matched his stride, following him to the helm.

"What can I do to help?"

"You've done enough already. Without your magic, I don't think any of us would've escaped the Godfist. Those of us who live owe our lives to you."

"And I owe my life to you and your crew. You risked yourselves to save us, and I'll always be grateful." His mention of magic sent a chill up her spine. She had never considered her powers to be *magic,* and the image disturbed her.

"Well, I hadn't thought of it in that way," Kenward said. "And we could certainly use you. Bryn has been promoted, since Jimini, the bosun, was lost in the storm. Jimini was a good man--the best, but Bryn is deserving of the post. Ask him to show you what you can do."

After searching much of the ship, Catrin located Bryn, who was high above her head, methodically examining every part of the rigging. He checked line, pulley, and sail for damage. Glancing down for a moment, he noticed her, and she waved.

"Can we talk when you have a free moment?" she called up to him.

"No more free moments for me. I'm 'fraid," he shouted in response. "I'm comin' down." His movements were slow and methodical compared to his previous acrobatics. "M'head still hurts; my balance is off. I feel like a bumbling fool."

"It'll pass, and then you'll be back to yourself. I know you're busy and short of hands. What can I do to help?"

He looked dubious for a moment then winked as she put her hands on her hips. "The first thing you must learn is how to tie knots. All of them."

"Is that all?"

Bryn chuckled and retrieved a small canvas and a length of supple line. He handed them to her. "Come back when you have them all mastered," he said, and Catrin accepted his challenge.

Spreading the canvas out on the deck, she held it in place with a couple of spare pulleys. Painted with fine illustrations, depicting each knot and its name, the canvas was intimidating. She hadn't known so many different types of knots existed. This was indeed a test.

Determined, she began with an easy knot. It was a simple pattern, but the line twisted in her hands and seemed to resist forming even the simple bowline loop. Still she persisted and was proudly admiring her first knot when Nat approached.

"I think we should talk."

"I suppose we should," Catrin replied, not liking the look in his eyes or his tone.

"I'm sure Benjin planned to tell you certain things," he said. "I hope he has already discussed this with you. Do you remember your mother?"

Catrin turned sharply and stared at him. She had not expected such a personal question, and in response, she nodded sadly. Memories of her mother were faded, more like gauzy images, but when Catrin thought of her, she felt warm and safe and often smelled roses. Her mother had loved roses.

"Did your father ever tell you about your mother's family?"

"No. He doesn't like to talk about it, and I never wanted to make him unhappy, so I never asked," Catrin replied.

"Did Benjin tell you about his relationship with her?" he asked, looking somewhat disgusted.

"Benjin and I have never discussed my mother for the same reasons," she answered.

Nat sighed. "They should've told you, but since they did not, I will. I'm sorry. It would be better if this came from Benjin or your father."

Catrin grew anxious, uncertain she wanted to hear what he had to say. "I think . . . I don't . . . I don't think I want to know," she said, but her imagination was already conjuring frightening images that continually grew worse.

"I'm sorry, Catrin, but your destination is the Greatland, and your life may depend on this information," he said firmly, and she nodded. "You've probably heard that my father was deranged, and people say I inherited his disease. My father had visions. He saw things that urged him to take one course of action over another. They were not always specific things. They were more like overpowering intuition." He watched for her reaction.

She had heard the rumors, but she judged Nat for herself. After all, he had given her information that had been instrumental in her escape from the Godfist. Without his help, she might never have gotten away. She owed him her life. Thinking of what Kenward had said, she realized they all owed their lives to each other. None of them could have survived alone.

"How did you know what to write in your letter?" she asked suddenly. "Where did those words come from, the part about land and water? How could you see the future?"

It was Nat's turn to be dumbstruck. "See the future? I can't see the future. Those words just occurred to me as I wrote. Now that I think about it, I'm not even sure what they mean." He looked thoughtful for a moment. "Were they somehow prophetic?"

His words had seemed strange when she read them because they had made no sense. Yet when she needed inspiration, they rang in her mind.

Water shapes the land.

His strange poetry had changed the course of history. As she recounted what happened on the plateau, his eyes grew wider with every detail.

When she finished, he sat, staring at his hands. "My letter changed the face of the Godfist and killed hundreds of men."

"I'm not proud of it," Catrin said a bit defensively.

"A thousand apologies. I know you did your best. I was just taken aback by the effect of my spontaneous words. You were protecting your homeland, and you are a true hero."

Catrin didn't consider herself a hero. She was a scared little girl, unprepared to face the challenges ahead. Kenward and Bryn, who'd been watching the *Stealthy Shark* wander farther off course, approached before she had a chance to sort out her feelings.

"I don't think they have the skill to catch us, sir," Bryn said. "They've made up no time during our repairs, and now that we can make more speed, we could lose 'em."

"We need food, and now's the time to fish," Kenward said. "If we fill our hold, we'll not starve crossing the barren seas, but it'll slow us down. If those fools ever figure out what they're doing, they could catch us."

"We could jettison the fish if'n they catch a miracle wind, and I, for one, would rather not starve," Bryn said.

Kenward smiled. "Drop the lines, men. Let's fish."

Large trawl tubs were prepared with multiple lines, hooks, and bait. Catrin gasped as an emerald green carpet began to cover the waters around the ship except for the trail of dark water in her wake.

"It's from the storm," Kenward said. "We call it a storm oasis. The force of the storm dredges up nutrients from the seafloor, and large amounts of plankton flourish in the normally barren waters. The plankton fields lure fish, and they draw more fish and birds." He pointed off the starboard side, and Catrin strained to see. An enormous creature suddenly rose up to the surface, and she jumped back in fear.

"Whales. There'll be more. Keep your eyes to the seas, and you'll see things you've never imagined."

Catrin watched the whales, afraid they would attack the ship. Kenward assured her they posed no threat, but she was still anxious around such massive creatures. Porpoises played in the ship's wake. They chittered at Catrin and the crew, entertaining with their antics. Some jumped high into the air, while others walked across the water on their tails, and the natural beauty took Catrin's mind from all that was troubling her.

Later, when the crew hauled in the first of the trawl tubs, they were energized as they strained to work the windlass, and they let out a cheer when three massive tuna were pulled onto the deck.

Large coffers of salt and pine boxes were brought from the hold. Cleaned fish were placed in the boxes and packed with dried sea salt. The salt would draw the moisture from the fish and prevent spoilage. Catrin and Nat helped as much as they could. After seeing Nat filet fish with efficient and skillful strokes, the crew seemed to look at him with newfound respect. Soon they were laughing with him and patting him on the back while exchanging tales and techniques.

Catrin had no skill for gutting fish and little desire to learn, so she settled for packing salt around the fish. The salt supply dwindled rapidly, but the crew was already boiling off large pots of seawater in an effort to replenish their supply. It was a slow and tedious process.

Kenward watched intently as Catrin and the others worked alongside his crew. "I'd like to welcome the new members of the crew. They may not yet know bow from stern, but they work as if their lives depend on it," he said, smiling broadly, and Catrin thought it an odd compliment, but the crew hooted and stomped their feet. Catrin flushed but was glad to have earned their respect. She was also thrilled to see Nat working as part of the crew. Never before had he seemed so happy.

The seas yielded a bounty, and at the end of the day, nearly half the hold was filled with salted tuna, round eye, and shark. Grubb, the ship's cook, prepared a feast of fresh fish for the evening meal, and the aroma from the cookhouse had mouths watering.

Catrin felt good for her efforts. Hard work had always helped keep her from worrying over things she couldn't change.

After stowing the rope and canvas in her cabin, she sought out Nat. Their conversation was unfinished, and she needed to know what else he planned to tell her. His cabin door was closed, but she could hear him moving within. She knocked lightly and waited.

11

Nat opened the door and sighed when he saw her. "Come in. I suppose you want to hear the rest," he said while pulling himself into his hammock. He stared at the ceiling as he spoke.

"When your father, Benjin, and I were about your age, my father had a vision. He was convinced the Zjhon would attack the Godfist. I did not believe him then. As far as I knew, our people hadn't encountered any others in hundreds, if not thousands, of years. I'd begun to see truth in what others said about him. I thought he was stricken by madness.

"He tried to convince me to go to the Greatland to search for information. I refused. I wanted only to court Julet and convince her to marry me. He said terrible things would happen if I did not go, but I was young, stubborn, and foolish," he said, his voice overlaid by the waves of anxiety that poured from him like a wellspring.

"He gave up on me and approached your father. Wendel was proud and brash and would do just about anything to prove his bravery. When my father challenged him, your father took the bait, hook and line. There was nothing anyone could do to dissuade him, not that many knew of the situation." He drew a deep breath before continuing. "Benjin thought the quest was a delusion, and he argued with your father, but somehow Wendel convinced him to go."

Nat's tone had gradually changed until he seemed to be talking to himself, having forgotten she was there, consumed as he was in his own memories. "Father made the arrangements. Benjin and Wendel boarded a small pirate ship along the southern shores of the Godfist. They were supposed to travel to the Falcon Isles but somehow managed to travel all the way to the Greatland aboard that small vessel. It's a wonder they did not perish." Nat grew quiet, his hands balled into fists, and Catrin thought she heard a growl escape his throat. He started to speak several times but had to stop to regain his composure.

"I tried to forget about them and my father's warnings. I pretended none of it was real, telling myself they were all mad, but then sweet Julet died." He sucked in an unsteady breath before he went on. "She was bitten by a glass viper, which are extremely venomous and usually only found in the desert. How it came to be in her bedding is still a mystery, but it cost me everything. All my hopes and dreams died with Julet, may her soul be free."

No words could adequately express Catrin's condolences, and she could think of nothing to say that wouldn't sound trite. Instead, she chose to put her hand on his and give it a gentle squeeze. She gave him a few moments to grieve. When he had composed himself, he continued.

"My father blamed me," he said haltingly. "He said I had affronted fate, and fate had treated me in kind. In a desperate attempt to convince fate to return my Julet, I tried to set things right. I knew it would never work, but that didn't stop me from trying. I could no longer stand the sight of my homeland. Everything reminded me of my failure, of how my actions had killed Julet," he said, smashing his fists against his thighs. "I left the Godfist in a small fishing boat, hoping to find Wendel and Benjin. It was a terrible journey, and it took me over a year to find them. When I did, I met your mother.

"It was a difficult time," he said, looking her in the eye for the first time since he had begun speaking. "I'm sorry to have to tell you this," he said, and he paused as if he were unsure he should continue.

"Your mother captured both Wendel's and Benjin's hearts. She seemed truly unaware of their feelings, and the tension grew. Wendel and Benjin became bitter toward each other and were both miserable. One day they told Elsa she would have to choose between them, but she cared for them both and refused. Eventually the tension was too great, and Benjin challenged Wendel. They argued at first, but it escalated, and they fought like madmen, nearly killing each other. Elsa and I pulled them apart, and we were both injured in the process. They fought us blindly and did not thank us for our interference.

"After the fight, Elsa tended Wendel's wounds. I'm not sure if it was the loss of his friend or Elsa's silent choice that drove him, but Benjin left without a word. Your father was saddened by his departure but did not go after him."

13

Catrin could feel her heart breaking as she listened, unable to bear the thought of her father and Benjin fighting. "Why are you telling me this?"

"I'm telling you because there are many in the Greatland who will remember your parents and the events surrounding their departure from the Greatland. You see, your mother was the daughter of a very wealthy noble, a prominent member of society." He paused a moment to look at Catrin. "And you are her mirror image."

Tears blurring her vision, Catrin could bear no more and fled the cabin.

* * *

Nat wasn't proud of himself, but he'd begun to do what was right. Still, he dreaded what would come next and doubted any words would make Catrin understand. With a deep sigh, he tried to sleep. It would not come. A haunting but familiar sensation grew steadily, and he braced himself. The taste of blood filled his mouth as his muscles clenched and the vision overwhelmed his senses.

The land shivered under the weight of an ill, green light. A foul demon with eyes of ice sundered the air, and the skies caught fire. In the demon's path, Catrin stood, abandoned and alone, her arms cast wide and power flowing around her. Roaring as it came, the demon engulfed her in its flames, and she disappeared into the conflagration.

Nat sucked a deep breath as the seizure released him, and he felt himself being ripped apart, torn among the visions, duty, and the wrath of men long dead.

Chapter 2

The past is indelible, but our every action weaves the fabric of the future.
--Enoch Giest, the First One

* * *

Catrin avoided Nat for the next few days and kept herself busy practicing knots. Mastering all of them gave her great pride, and she sought out Bryn. He watched her demonstrate.

"Not bad," he said, "but on a ship, you have to be able to tie them without thinking or even watching what you are doing. Come back when you can do them all with your eyes closed."

Disappointment was overwhelmed by the need for success. Refusing to fail, Catrin squatted on the deck. Her eyes closed, she found her other senses heightened. Things that normally complemented her visual image were now her only source of awareness. When Nat walked across the deck, she knew him from the rhythmic click of his staff against the deck. The sound grew closer and stopped, and she was not surprised when he spoke.

"I'm sorry, Catrin. I didn't want to hurt you."

"Then why did you? You could have simply told me I looked like my mother and people might recognize me!" she said, realizing even as the words left her mouth that she was being unreasonable. Nat was not to blame for the pain his message stirred within her.

"I'm sorry," he said.

"No. I'm the one who owes you an apology. I reacted poorly and have been acting like a child. Please sit with me," she said, motioning to the spot next to her. Nat eased himself slowly to the deck, grunting as he settled himself.

"I'm gettin' old."

"I've been meaning to ask you something," Catrin said. "How did you manage to swim and hold on to your staff at the same time?" She remembered her own terrifying plunge into the sea.

Nat's back stiffened and his face grew stony. "I had to choose," he said. "I had to choose between my life and my father's last wishes. I knew I couldn't swim with the staff in my hands, at least not very well. But to drop the staff would have been to betray my father. I would not allow the consequences, not again--I couldn't." The venom that poured from him, as if she had lanced a festering wound, surprised Catrin. "They said I was crazy to hold on to the staff, that only a madman would try and swim with an iron-shod stick," he said with an angry, hurt look toward the crew.

"I see," Catrin said, looking him in the eye.

It was Nat's turn to feel foolish; he seemed to realize the crew could not have known how that would hurt him. He shook his head. "I must have seemed crazy to them, risking my life to save a piece of wood and metal. There was no way they could have understood. I would have died without their help."

He sighed. He looked down at the deck, breaking eye contact with Catrin. "It pains me to trouble you more, but I must. You left before I could tell you the rest. I cannot go with you to the Greatland," he blurted.

Catrin sat back so quickly that she smacked her head on the deckhouse. Unable to formulate a response, she just stared at him in shock.

"It's not that I don't want to go. Please understand. I know I swore to protect you, and I will for as long as I can. But I cannot go to the Greatland. It was forbidden to me. I have known this time would come and have dreaded it, but now it has arrived and I shall do my duty to my father," he said.

Catrin was not sure how much more she could take.

"On his deathbed, he made me swear I would never again set foot on the Greatland. He said that if I did, something far more dreadful than Julet's death would occur, and I cannot allow that to happen."

He looked directly at Catrin. "It seems I've taken too many vows, and now I must choose, for I cannot obey them all. Will you, Catrin Volker, Herald of Istra and my dear friend, please release me from my vow?" he asked, kneeling and placing his forehead on the deck before her.

"I cannot," she said forcefully, and his head jerked up from the deck. He could not contain his utter dismay, and his face went slack. He looked into Catrin's face and was confused when she smiled back. "You can keep *both* vows. There is no need to choose. I am flexible, you see. You don't need to come with me to protect me and my interests; I'll need someone to look after things on the Godfist."

Nat smiled when he realized she had cleverly solved his dilemma, allowing him to keep his word *and* his pride. Catrin, though, had an icy feeling in her stomach. She would go to the Greatland with only Vertook to guide her, and she was not yet certain how Vertook felt about the journey. She might have to face the Zjhon alone.

"Your passage from the Falcon Isles has been paid, and I have gold for you. Members of the Vestrana should be available to help you on your quest once you reach the Greatland."

"Thank you," Catrin said, nodding, but things had changed between them. Knowing he would not accompany her, their relationship felt thin and strained. Nat sat for a while in uncomfortable silence then excused himself. It was a strange parting, and Catrin was saddened by the tension. She tried to wish Nat well, but she kept seeing herself alone in a strange land where everyone wanted her dead.

A sudden wind threatened to blow away the canvas and line. Catrin quickly gathered them up and ran to her cabin. When she stepped inside, she heard muffled shouts from the deck and the sound of men running. Throwing the line and canvas aside, she rushed back to the deck. Several crewmen ran by her on their way to the stern. When Catrin arrived, most of the crew was already gathered there, trying to get a good view.

She could see nothing at first, but Bryn saw her dilemma and hoisted her onto his shoulders. Finally able to see above the other men, Catrin saw the *Stealthy Shark* on the horizon, listing badly and riding too low in the water.

"They're gonna sink her."

"It's a trick."

17

Kenward watched in tortured silence. Unable to stand still, he paced back and forth. The *Shark* listed sharply, driven by the growing wind. Part of her rigging struck the water and snapped off, and it became clear this was no ruse; the *Stealthy Shark* was foundering and beginning to sink.

"Turn this ship around!" Kenward shouted. "Set a course for the *Shark*. I'll not let her sink this day."

The crew sprung into action, arming themselves as they prepared the ship to come about. They all seemed to know that Kenward was doing this for his sister. He might not be able to save her, but he could save her ship. The *Eel* turned slowly, and Catrin urged it forward, as if her desire might somehow propel the ship. The *Stealthy Shark* had fallen far behind and looked as if it might sink before they arrived.

As the *Stealthy Shark* gradually grew larger on the horizon, her crew became visible. One man waved his arms frantically, and the others struggled to move about the deck, clinging to the rails. The ship was out of control, and the men seemed barely able to hang on. Catrin's knees buckled when they grew close enough to see the men's faces. It was Strom who waved.

"Strom!" she screamed, and everyone aboard the *Slippery Eel* looked at her. "Those are my friends. Help them!" All this time they had been right behind her, and now they were in mortal danger.

Kenward could not pull his ship alongside the *Shark* for fear of colliding with it. The seas were choppy, and unpredictable winds gusted at gale force, so they had to lower the small boats into the water. Men scrambled down, and Catrin saw Kenward begin his descent. Without another thought, she leaped over the railing and shimmied down one of the ropes. The boat below was overfull, and the waves tossed it as Catrin wedged herself between two men.

As they approached the sinking ship, men threw ropes onto the deck. Catrin spotted Benjin and called to him as he grabbed one of the ropes. He tied it to a pair of sturdy bollards on the deck and stopped just long enough to smile and wave to her. Within moments, they were all aboard the *Shark,* the crew scrambling to assess and repair the damage.

Vertook climbed on deck, went straight to the bilge pump, and began to crank it.

"Kenward!" Benjin shouted. "Do you have any pyre-orchid?"

"Not in many years," Kenward replied.

"Dreadroot! Have you any dreadroot?"

"Bring back dreadroot on the next trip," Kenward yelled to a sailor.

"Now! The need is urgent," Benjin insisted, and Kenward ordered the man to hurry.

Catrin had never heard of pyre-orchid, but Benjin's request for dreadroot terrified her. The only use for dreadroot she knew of was to treat severe infections, and it was only used in cases where the infection was out of control and likely to cause death. Dreadroot could wipe out rampant infections, but it was so powerful, it also killed many of the people treated with it.

"The hole in the hull is far too large to be repaired with oakum alone, sir. We'll need to patch it and then seal it," a crewman reported.

"Get the shelves from the cabins and use those to patch it," Kenward ordered. "We'll need more oakum from the *Eel*."

Benjin appeared stricken as he realized the materials needed to repair the ship had been onboard all along. "Boil me, I wish I'd thought of that. I had hoped the oakum would hold long enough to catch you, but it blew out with no warning, and I knew we were in trouble. Thanks for coming back for us."

Trying to account for all of her Guardians, Catrin searched the ship. She had seen Strom already, but in the chaos, she could no longer locate him. Osbourne appeared for a moment but was then lost in a flurry of sailors. Men struggled to repair damage at the helm; Benjin and Kenward rushed to their aid before Catrin could ask who needed the dreadroot. Praying it wasn't Chase, she decided to have a look in the cabins and moved toward the deckhouse.

Checking each cabin, she found them all empty, and when she reached the last door, she wondered where else to look, but the smell told her she had found him. Covering her

19

nose and mouth, she entered the cabin and sobbed when she saw Chase, pale and shivering, an open wound on his right shoulder. Angry flesh, mottled red and purple, surrounded the wound, and Catrin could feel the heat radiating from it without touching him.

He did not stir, even when she blotted the sweat from his forehead. His breathing was shallow and labored, and Catrin feared he was already lost, too far into sickness to ever recover. She cursed fate for its cruelty. All this time the herbs Chase needed had been just out of reach. If only she had known her friends were aboard the *Stealthy Shark,* then Chase would be safe.

The rough and unpredictable motions of the ship caused the hammock to sway wildly at times. Chase's body was dead weight, and Catrin winced as it soundly struck the cabin wall.

Benjin charged into the cabin, carrying a small vial and a flask of water. The dreadroot Kenward had provided was not in its usual powder form; instead it was concentrated oil. Benjin used extreme care in applying a single drop to Chase's tongue, knowing a larger dose would almost certainly kill him.

Chase did not react at first, but then his face wrinkled and he looked as if he wanted to spit. He shook his head back and forth wildly, trying to swallow. Benjin poured water over his lips, but Chase swallowed very little and sprayed most of it across the cabin as he coughed. After a moment, though, he drifted off, settling back into unconsciousness. His breaths were short, and Catrin encouraged him on each one, fearing it would be his last.

She was distracted when she noticed Benjin having trouble closing the vial with one hand, his left arm hanging limply at his side. Catrin moved to him and reached for his shirt, but he pulled away.

"I'm fine," he said. "Right now I need to help Kenward and the others attend to the ship. Stay here with Chase, please. Shout if his condition worsens." He rushed from the small cabin, not waiting for a response.

Holding Chase's hand, Catrin watched his chest rise and fall. Physical contact gave her the distinct impression of heat and corruption, and she could sense his life forces slipping away.

Uncertain of what to do but unwilling to do nothing, she placed one hand on his forehead and the other on his chest. After synchronizing her breathing with his, she began to concentrate on his getting well. Love and friendship poured through the physical bond, and her hands grew warm. A tingling sensation thrummed in her palms.

Energy swirled from her hands and into Chase, and she focused on the foulness raging within him. The infection gave her the impression of immense hunger and single-minded reproduction. It would consume him. She could not tell if the dreadroot was having any effect, for the infection seemed to remain strong, overcoming his body's weakened defenses.

Soon, though, his breathing became more regular, and Catrin decided to try something different. Holding both hands over his wound, she concentrated on the inflamed flesh. It repulsed her, but she refused to pull away. Energy poured into the diseased flesh.

A small trail of blood seeped from the wound, and Catrin grew alarmed, but the blood seemed to cleanse the area, carrying away foul contaminants. She sensed Chase's body beginning to fight the infection forcefully.

Kenward entered with a cloth and a basin of diluted wine. "Can you hold him in place while I do this?"

"I can do it," Catrin replied.

Kenward nodded and began to cleanse the area around the wound first. Chase moaned and thrashed, but Catrin held him fast. Kenward wiped the wound directly then applied pressure around it, forcing the foulness out. Chase shouted incoherently, but Catrin held him, speaking soothing words in his ear, her tears mixing with his sweat.

"That's all I can do for now," Kenward said after bandaging the wound. "Get him to drink water if you can," he added as he left.

Catrin helped Chase drink whenever he woke, and several times, she woke him just to give him more water. The ship's motion became more stable, and the listing subsided. In the hours before dawn, she leaned her head against the cabin wall for a moment of rest, and her eyes closed. She was asleep before she drew another breath.

Chapter 3

On the cusp of life and death stands a veil of gossamer, and those who behold it are forever changed.
--Merchill Valon, soldier

* * *

A terrified cry woke Catrin in the dawn hours, and she fell out of the chair she had been sleeping in. Pulling herself from the floor, she checked on Chase and drew a sharp breath. His body was covered in an angry rash. Every part of him was discolored and inflamed.

"I'm gonna die, Cat. I don't wanna die," he said through swollen lips as Kenward and Benjin arrived. Holding his breath, he endured while they inspected his wound, checked his temperature and pulse, and listened to his chest.

"I think you are going to make it," Kenward said with a smile. "The rash is not life threatening. It's one of the least deadly effects of dreadroot."

"Dreadroot? You gave me dreadroot? Are you mad? Were you trying to kill me?" Chase asked, incredulous. He tried to sit up quickly but immediately fell back to the hammock.

"You were near death, Chase. We had no choice," Catrin whispered, and he nodded slowly, asking with gestures for water. Once his thirst was quenched, he asked for food; the return of his appetite boded well for his recovery.

"Some great sorceress you are, Cat. We were behind you all that time, and you couldn't tell us from the enemy. What use are you anyway?" he said with a tired and forced smirk, which made her certain he would recover.

"Perhaps you should've thought of that before leaping on someone's sword," she said. He laughed a bit too hard and winced from the pain. "You relax." She kissed him on the forehead. "I'll get you something to eat."

"Are you having any trouble breathing?" she heard Benjin ask as she slipped out of the crowded cabin. She left the door open to freshen the air.

Approaching Farsy, one of the crewmen she recognized, she asked if they could get broth for Chase. Farsy winked and pulled a polished piece of metal from his pocket. He then began sending signals to the *Slippery Eel*. It took a moment before anyone responded, but when they did, the ensuing conversation of flashes was surprisingly short.

"The signal language is quite intricate," he said. "We can convey many things quickly, as long as both people are well trained. The skill has saved many lives."

Catrin watched as two men from the *Slippery Eel* scrambled into a boat and rowed toward the *Stealthy Shark*. When they arrived, Farsy threw down a line, and the men below secured a heavy basket. Once it was on deck, Farsy opened it and revealed a surprisingly large amount of food.

"You didn't think he was the only one hungry, did you?" he asked, seeing her look of surprise. "No sense making a trip for a mug of broth, I'd say. Besides, I knew Grubb would take care of us--he feeds us, and we keep him afloat. It's a fair bargain for all."

Catrin's stomach agreed with Farsy, and she thanked him. He nodded his reply, his mouth full of salted fish. Grabbing the covered mug of broth and some food for herself, she walked carefully back to Chase's cabin. The air in the cramped quarters was less foul when she returned, and a crewman had mopped the floor before throwing down some dried reeds.

Chase slept, but the rich aroma of the broth soon brought him from his stupor. He accepted it with shaking hands and sipped it, savoring the flavor. He thanked Catrin and she nodded, her mouth full of hard bread. Feeling much better after eating, she was thankful Farsy had thought to get enough for everyone.

Chase emptied the mug and handed it back to Catrin with mumbled thanks. He was asleep as soon as the hammock cradled his head. With Chase cared for and her fears for him diminishing, Catrin sought out Benjin. He stood near the helm with Kenward and Nat, and they seemed to be discussing plans for the rest of the voyage, but they fell silent when Catrin approached.

"Chase is doing better. He's had some broth and is sleeping again," she said, and the tension lessened slightly. She stood for a moment, watching Benjin, her emotions spanning the gamut. She could not decide if she was more glad, hurt, angry, or scared. The overwhelming circumstances made it difficult for her to maintain her focus, and when Benjin met her eyes, the words that left her lips surprised everyone.

"Why didn't you tell me you were in love with my mother?" she blurted, regretting the words as soon as she spoke them.

Benjin was dumbstruck, and Nat looked as if she had physically assaulted him. A dreadful silence hung in the air, broken when Benjin spun fluidly. His face contorted in rage, he struck Nat as quick as a snake. Catrin barely saw him swing, but a sharp crack echoed across the water, quickly followed by the thud of Nat's body against the deck.

Roaring in anger, Benjin spun away from Nat, and another crack resounded. Benjin's head snapped back, and Catrin stood, fists clenched, trying to decide if she needed to hit him again. Blood welled on his lip. The sight of it was too much for her, and she retreated to Chase's cabin. No one on deck uttered a word as she fled, and tension continued to hang heavy in the air.

Chase was awake when Catrin returned, and her distress must have been obvious.

"What's going on out there?" he asked without waiting for her to sit. She let out a sigh and shook her head. It took her a moment to compose herself before she could speak. Her voice wavered as she told the tale, and he listened in relative silence, though he let out a low whistle when she told him about her father and Benjin fighting over her mother. As she finished, she felt as if she had just poured her soul onto the cabin floor and left herself completely vulnerable.

"Things will be fine," Chase said optimistically, and his cheer in the face of his condition shamed Catrin; she had crumbled under the weight of much smaller problems. The things Nat said had brought her pain, but they also brought her a greater understanding of her circumstances. She realized her question must have been a shock to Benjin, and probably brought him enormous pain. Again, she regretted her insensitive words.

A brief meditation calmed her mind, and she considered seeking him out. Part of her wanted to avoid him, but she needed to make amends, knowing she would have no peace until she did. She found him at the bow of the ship, glowering out to sea and leaning heavily on the rail. Catrin read his posture: he wanted to be alone, but she decided not to honor his unspoken request for privacy. She approached him and placed her hand on his shoulder.

"I'm sorry," she said softly. He made no response for a few moments; he just continued to stare out at the endless waves. When he reached up and patted her hand, he left his hand covering hers, and she relaxed a bit.

"No more sorrys from you," he said, but his voice was husky with emotion. Catrin put her arms around him and laid her head against his back. They stood quietly for a while, neither of them willing to break the silence. They had unpleasant business ahead of them, but they silently and mutually decided to enjoy a few moments of peace together first. The stillness was broken when Bryn called for all hands on deck, and everyone aboard the *Stealthy Shark* gathered near the bow, where Kenward awaited them.

"Your efforts have paid off," he announced. "Both ships have been repaired sufficiently. We are ready to raise our sails and ride the wind." A cheer rose up from all those assembled, and the crew aboard the *Slippery Eel* answered in kind.

Kenward began the difficult process of dividing his crew and the inexperienced travelers between the two ships. They would be hard pressed to man both ships adequately, and everyone would have to work double shifts. Catrin and the others were assigned to experienced crewmen, to act as assistants and runners. Glad to be paired up with Bryn, Catrin would remain on the *Stealthy Shark,* where Benjin would serve as partner to Farsy.

Despite her repeated requests, Benjin refused to let her examine his wound. "It's healing well," he said. "I'll have no trouble performing my duties. Don't you worry any more about it. I'll be fine."

Strom, Nat, and Osbourne were assigned to the *Slippery Eel*. They exchanged quick hugs and farewells with Catrin. Even though they would be nearby, she missed them even before they departed. She hadn't yet had a single moment with them since they had been busy helping the crew. They left with promises of many tales when they could be together again. Catrin noticed Benjin talking with Nat and became alarmed, but she was immensely relieved and proud of them both when they shook hands.

The crews of both ships prepared to make full sail, and the new members of the crew were initiated in a frenzy of activity. Commands were issued, and admonitions abounded when mistakes were made. Praise was hard to come by, but when it was given, it meant a great deal more for its rarity. Catrin had helped a little during the first part of their journey, but now she was expected to act as a part of the team, and her actions could determine another crewman's fate.

Bryn did not tease or challenge her as he had with the knots; instead, he very seriously instructed her on which tasks were the most dangerous. She gave him her full attention and tried her best to complete each task, but many of the terms he used were unfamiliar to her, and he often had to do the work himself. Catrin watched closely, and she was proud that he never had to perform the same task twice. Once she had watched him do something, she was able to do it herself the next time. Even when struggling, she stubbornly insisted she needed no help.

The days and nights were exhausting, but the crews found a rhythm and began to operate almost efficiently. One day, Kenward returned from the *Slippery Eel* for a surprise inspection. After scrutinizing every part of the *Stealthy Shark*, he called for all hands on deck, and the crew gathered quickly. Bryn stood nearest to Kenward, waiting for the verdict. The ship had been under his command, and it appeared he would take this evaluation as a reflection on himself.

"The condition of this ship is surprising," Kenward said with obvious disappointment. Bryn did not hang his head, but the muscles in his jaw tightened, and Catrin knew he had hoped for better. Kenward smiled, no longer able to hold on to the lie. "Considering the circumstances and the shortage of hands, you've done an exceptional job, and you are all to be commended for your efforts. I can expect no more from you, but I will continue to expect no less," he continued, and the crew let out a cheer. "Catrin and Benjin will join me on the *Eel* for the rest of the day. I'll return them on the morrow."

Catrin was a bit surprised by the summons. She felt bad leaving Bryn, but he assured her that her efforts had already reduced the backlog of work, and he would manage until she returned. She was still trying to determine if he was being sarcastic as she climbed down to the boat waiting below.

On arrival, Kenward took them directly to the galley. Catrin was pleasantly surprised to see Strom, Osbourne, Nat, and Vertook already seated in the large room, which held them all comfortably. Kenward gave them some time to greet one another, and the room was soon filled with the buzz of several conversations, along with the delightful aroma of the special meal Grubb was creating.

Given their limited provisions, what Grubb provided was a feast. The honored guests were presented with a filet of tuna coated with herbs and spices and wrapped in a thin layer of seaweed. The filets were so large that they hung over the edges of the ship's largest wooden plates. Catrin noted with some interest that Benjin's filet was the largest by a significant margin, and she did not miss the sly wink Grubb gave him. The galley grew quiet except for the sounds of eating and groans of pleasure.

"As fine a meal as I've ever had," Kenward said. "A thousand compliments, Grubb."

"Will you eat with us?" Catrin asked, noticing that Grubb did not eat. "I have plenty to share if you would like some."

"I thank the lady for the invitation," he replied with a smile. "She is quite considerate, but I only eat when everyone else has been fed. Please, enjoy." He said it as if it were a simple fact and not a matter of preference, so Catrin let it drop. Still, it bothered her to have someone watch her dine, waiting for her to finish before he would eat. She wasn't sure she could consume such a large portion, but the meal disappeared more quickly than she would have imagined.

Grubb cleared the plates and brought bowls filled with dates, prunes, dried apples, and a few sugared lemons. Everyone tried a little of each kind of treat, and they all commented on the quality of their feast, knowing it had taxed their stores. Their stomachs full, most leaned back and found comfortable positions to relax in, while Grubb served a deep red wine in small wooden mugs.

"Friends," Kenward said after clearing his throat. "I've asked you here to discuss our common goals and dangers. I've known some of you for many years and others for a much shorter time, but we've already been through a lot together, and I consider us friends and allies. After all, we all owe each other our lives in some way or another. Now we must share what we know with one another. I fear we'll need all the knowledge we possess just to survive this struggle." Looks were exchanged as Kenward spoke, and Catrin noticed Benjin shifting in his seat. She respected and trusted Kenward, and she listened intently as he continued.

"I must begin by asking if anyone here has secrets they feel they must keep from the rest of the group. I want you to really think about this and be honest with yourselves. If you have any secrets you would not reveal to anyone in this room, even if their lives depended on it, then speak up now," he said and waited patiently to see if anyone would respond. Catrin mentally sorted her deepest and darkest secrets, including things she had trouble admitting--even to herself. It was not a pleasant process, but if it would keep her companions from harm, she would reveal them all without another thought.

Kenward let the silence hang while he refilled everyone's wine mugs. Catrin was surprised Grubb did not protest, but he was now happily eating his own meal, which made her feel much more comfortable.

"Good," Kenward said when no one responded. "So it is safe to say we all trust one another. I know it's not always wise to reveal everything you hold in confidence, but we need to divulge anything relevant to this conflict. I'll be the first to reveal information I hold in confidence, as a show of faith.

"There are Zjhon ships in the Falcon Isles, and my family has been trading with them openly. The last I knew, my mother's ship was commissioned to make supply runs for the intermediate forces stationed there. She bought time by claiming they needed to wait for the next cutting of herbs in order to satisfy the quantities required by Archmaster Belegra, which was a very convenient truth. I don't know if that relationship bought safety for my sister, but it is a possibility. I can only hope.

"The *Stealthy Shark* and *Slippery Eel* could not be seen in association with the legitimate trade fleet, and we departed as soon as the Zjhon arrived. We suspected the ships were chasing us, and we fled to the cove on the east coast of the Godfist. We've had no word since we left the Falcon Isles, and I don't know what has transpired there.

"We'll be approaching the isles soon, and we'll need to make the last part of our journey quickly and under cover of night if we wish to remain undetected. We'll be traveling to a cluster of remote islands, and there we should find a message from my mother. It'll tell us which anchorage is currently safe, and where to meet. Once we drop anchor, we'll take boats to the meeting place, and from there we can smuggle you aboard the *Trader's Wind,* my mother's ship.

"The journey to the Greatland is long and arduous under normal circumstances, but you will be confined to private chambers, where you can travel unbeknownst to the others aboard. The solitude and confinement will be a trial, but it is your best chance of making it to the Greatland undetected. Fortunately, the *Trader's Wind* will be well supplied and you should not have to fear starvation. Do you have any questions?" It took a few moments for them to digest the information.

"Where will we go once we get to the Greatland?" Strom asked, and Kenward gave others the chance to answer before he spoke.

"The *Trader's Wind* will be bound for New Moon Bay at Endland, that being the largest trade port on the east coast of the Greatland. There should be many merchant ships there from different parts of the Greatland; perhaps you could disappear into the crowds. It would be a perilous venture. If you decide on a different destination, though, you need not go all the way to port aboard the *Trader's Wind*. There are ships much like the *Slippery Eel* that work around that area. Once you are within the range of those smaller ships, we can arrange passage to just about anywhere on the coast and a few places where large rivers run inland," Kenward said, producing a large map of the Greatland, which he rolled out on the table.

Catrin studied the map and was dismayed by the size of the landmass so colorfully depicted. Gauging by the number of cities, rivers, and mountain ranges, the Greatland dwarfed the Godfist. The thought of such an enormous place intimidated her, and she wondered how they would decide on a suitable destination. Nat and Benjin had mentioned the Cathuran monks, but she had no idea where they would be found.

She considered asking, but then she realized Benjin had not uttered a word, and he did not look at the map. He remained where he was seated, occasionally rubbing his shoulder and looking grim. Catrin was puzzled by his manner until Kenward spoke again.

"I think your destination depends a great deal on what happened in Mundleboro seventeen summers ago, and there is only one person here who can give a firsthand account of those events. I hate to draw you out of your silence, my old friend, but I've waited many years to hear this tale, and the telling is long overdue," he said, looking at Benjin.

Cursing herself for not understanding sooner, Catrin sympathized with Benjin. Kenward had set a trap for him, and he walked into it, knowing it for what it was and allowing himself to be snared nonetheless. It was obvious he had no desire to relive those memories, but he must have decided it was indeed relevant, for he cleared his throat. Before he began, though, he walked to where Kenward stood.

"You may have a few gray hairs, but you've not changed a bit," he said in a low voice.

Chapter 4

Before we can truly understand our role in this life, we must first admit our reliance on every other life form.
--Hidakku the Druid

* * *

Benjin stood before the assemblage and spoke as if they did not exist. "Wendel and I spent most of our childhood trying to outdo each other, and when old man Dersinger started filling Wendel's ears with talk of the Greatland, there was no stopping him. Somehow, I knew his grand adventure would be dangerous and possibly fatal, but Wendel failed to see it. He was convinced we would take the Greatland by storm--just the two of us. We would save the world," he said in a rhythmic cadence. He seemed to have left the present, and the past poured from him.

"I didn't even know what we were supposed to be searching for. 'Clues about Istra' was all we had to go on, but Wendel seemed to think it was enough. Old man Dersinger sent us through the Chinawpa Valley to the Arghast Desert. We skirted the desert to the south and eventually arrived on the beaches, battered by storms all the way, and we feared we were too late. We saw no sign of the promised ship, and for nine days, we waited.

"When the ship finally arrived, though, Wendel became more determined than ever. When we met Kenward, I knew things were going to get worse." He paused as Kenward involuntarily choked, temporarily breaking the spell, and Benjin seemed to realize, once again, to whom he was speaking.

Catrin's sudden desire to smack Kenward must have shown on her face, for he nodded a silent apology to her.

"Kenward was on his first solo voyage with his new ship, the *Kraken's Claw,*" Benjin continued. "He and Wendel seemed to fuel each other's fires. Kenward's mother, Nora, had given orders to deliver us to the Falcon Isles. Wendel challenged Kenward to disobey those orders and sail directly for the Greatland. Kenward knew it was too long a voyage

33

for a ship as small as the *Claw*, but Wendel fed his ego, and it was more than he could resist," he said.

Kenward rolled his eyes, but when he noticed Catrin's glare, he assumed a neutral posture and tried to look innocent.

"I'm grateful that the crew proved themselves to be some of the craftiest and most resourceful sailors ever to set sail. It took every bit of their ingenuity and tenacity to survive the suicidal voyage. We almost starved and were nearly caught several times by patrolling military vessels, but Kenward and his crew found a way to escape each time," Benjin continued, and Kenward puffed his chest out.

"His seemingly endless luck drove Wendel to believe they were both invincible. When we reached the Greatland, Wendel walked in like he owned the place, and may the gods bless him, he pulled it off. He acted as if he truly belonged there, and no one questioned him.

"Somehow, he got us passage with a caravan and even got them to let us ride in one of the new carriages they were delivering. Wendel enjoyed the ride and played his part as if it were true. In contrast, I constantly feared someone would call his bluff, and then they would hang us both. We made the entire trip to Mundleboro without anyone giving us more than a second glance, but as the caravan waited in the tariff line, the trader rushed us out of the carriage. His customer had ridden out to meet him." He paused a moment and seemed to be reliving his memory.

"She sat atop her horse in leathers and a fur-lined coat, and her brow furrowed as Wendel and I climbed from the carriage that bore her family's crest on the doors--a pair of intertwined roses. Her eyes afire, she dismounted, moving like an angry cat. She demanded to know who we were and how dare we ride in her commission. The situation got worse when Wendel told her to mind her own affairs and added that her father would understand the needs of men. It was a stupid thing to say, and I'm still not sure exactly what he meant, but it enraged her.

"She grabbed him by the arm, swung him around, and demanded he explain himself and pay for a thorough cleaning of her carriage. He refused, of course, and brushed his hands over the seat cushions, as if that would satisfy her, or perhaps he did it because he knew it would infuriate her. I could never figure those two out. They argued until after dark. I finally told them I was leaving and would rejoin their argument in the morning." Benjin looked at Catrin, a silent apology in his eyes, and she knew before he continued that he would not coat the truth with honey.

"When Wendel said he had no more to say to 'Miss Self-Important' and would join me, she said her name was Elsa Mae Mangst, and he would do well to remember it. They started arguing all over again, and somehow he argued her into having dinner with him. They voiced their conflicting opinions over cold food for hours. As I said, I never understood those two.

"I tried to convince Wendel to move on quickly and escape the unwanted attention that his relationship with Elsa could only bring, but he insisted she was the key to our quest. She was highborn. She would have access to important information and would have contacts at her disposal. It didn't help matters that the Zjhon were waging war along the coasts, and the Mundleburins were building up forces along the border with Lankland. There had already been skirmishes, and the long-standing feud between the Mangst and Kyte families had begun anew. No one could remember what caused the original feud, but times of peace never lasted long.

"On the day of her majority, Elsa claimed independence from her parents' rule and took command of a border-patrol unit. The event caused quite a stir, but no one attempted to stop her. She had been well trained, and she assembled a force of elite fighters and rangers, those who could be as stealthy as they were lethal. Somehow, Wendel convinced Elsa we should be part of her force, and I think she agreed only for the opportunity to humiliate him. We trained alongside the veterans and did our best not to look like rank amateurs. Wendel succeeded more so than I, but I completed all the exercises. When we set out on our first official mission, we left through a fanfare that lined the streets of Mundleboro's capital city, Ravenhold.

"I'd thought Kenward and Wendel were the worst possible combination, but that was before I saw Wendel and Elsa fight together. They were brazen and reckless, taking careless risks that were just not necessary. Several good men were wounded in the first sortie, and the veterans chastised Wendel and Elsa for their foolish behavior. The journey back to Ravenhold, the ancestral home of Elsa's family, was downcast and subdued. Word of the events spread fast. Elsa's mother promptly bribed each member of Elsa's patrol to seek reassignment. Most accepted eagerly, not wishing to die while Elsa proved something to herself.

"Wendel refused the bribe, and he urged me to do the same. In the end, though, Elsa abandoned her service in the patrols. She said she wanted to be an independent ranger, a one-woman elite force. What Wendel did then was one of the stupidest things I've ever witnessed: he told her everything--our entire story. I thought she'd have us hung, but she surprised me and was lured by the danger and excitement, especially the possibility of reclaiming ancient knowledge. It wasn't long before the three of us began our journey across the wilderness in search of clues.

"We wandered aimlessly from hamlet to farmstead, listening to legends and fireside tales, but we found nothing that struck us as significant. They were pleasant days for the most part, with the exception of the incessant bickering between Elsa and Wendel. I often wondered why two people who irritated each other so much would choose to spend their time together.

"Elsa was kind to me and never let me feel left out of conversations, but Wendel seemed to forget I existed. Elsa was beautiful and strong and high-spirited. She was exciting, and I fell in love with her. It wasn't something I did intentionally. I even made myself find things I disliked about her, but even her flaws endeared her to me. I was hopelessly smitten, and neither of them saw it. They were blind, and so was I," he said.

Catrin was lost in his story. She felt as if she were there with them, living through Benjin's memory.

"One night we sat around our fire discussing the Zjhon and their recent conquests, and Elsa told us of their strict

36

religious beliefs. As they conquered new lands, they quoted spiritual doctrine and forced the people to join their faith or face death. Wendel realized the Zjhon scriptures could hold a treasure trove of clues, if only we could get a copy.

"Elsa said the common folk didn't have complete copies. They had to write them down or commit them to memory as sermons were read. The only places that had pristine copies were churches and the Masters' homes. Not satisfied with getting just any copy, Wendel and Elsa decided to steal one from the cathedral at Adderhold. They were convinced such a prestigious site would have a very old copy of the scriptures and, hopefully, one that had not been transcribed too many times.

"When we reached the hills along the shores of the Inland Sea, Elsa asked me to stay at camp and guard the horses, but I knew they really just didn't want me along. I could not deny her request and watched helplessly as they walked away, intent on sneaking into the Zjhon center of power to steal holy documents. I didn't think we'd escape the Greatland once such a high crime had been committed, knowing the Zjhon would be relentless in their search." Benjin stopped speaking long enough to drink from his mug. People shifted in their seats, but they waited quietly for him to continue his tale. He took a deep breath and began speaking again in a soft voice that some strained to hear.

"The alarm bells woke me the next morning. I hid in the hills and waited. After seven days, I nearly left. Patrols had been scouring the countryside, and I had to keep moving to avoid them, but still I waited, hoping they would return. One afternoon, as I was hunting in the hills, I saw a man stumbling through the narrow valley. It was Nat. Not the most pleasant company, for either of us, I suppose, but we waited two more days together.

"When Wendel and Elsa finally returned, they were all smiles. They were triumphant and ready for a pleasant journey home, but when we approached the Lankland border, we found it heavily guarded and patrolled. Wendel's plan was to simply act like we belonged there and march straight through the border check. 'Just act like you belong

37

here and we'll be fine,' he said. 'The guards look tired and bored, so we'll just blend in with the other merchants.'

"I thought it was a terrible plan, but Elsa sided with Wendel again. Nat and I had to either play along or stay behind. Everyone else played their parts well, and I did my best to hide my fear, but my nervous sweating nearly gave us away. Wendel convinced the border guards I was sick, and they rushed us along so they would not catch my illness. When we made camp within a secluded patch of forest, Wendel and Elsa celebrated their victory. He swept her up in his arms, and then he kissed her," he said, looking as if every muscle in his body were contracting. His hands were balled into fists, and his back was hunched. Catrin hated to see him relive such a painful memory, but she supposed it was necessary.

"I was young and foolish and in love," he said with tears in his eyes. "I confronted them and told them I was in love with Elsa. She said nothing. She just stood with her hand over her mouth in shock. Wendel laughed. It was the final insult. I could take no more. Something inside me snapped, and I attacked him. I took out all my fears and frustrations on him. I beat him mercilessly. He landed blows of his own, but neither of us would give up the fight. Nat and Elsa separated us, and we scorned them for it.

"When it was all over, Elsa ran to Wendel's side. I was left with the sympathies of Nat. I ran as far and as fast as I could and never looked back. Eventually, I found my way to Kenward and negotiated passage back to the Godfist. We sailed to the Falcon Isles, where I was to board a smaller ship. Elsa and Wendel arrived in the Falcon Isles not long after, having posed as traders and traveled in luxury on a larger ship. We traveled back to the Godfist on the same, smaller ship. I avoided them. Elsa sought me out once, but I pushed her away. She was hurt, I know, but no more than I was.

"I avoided them still when we returned to the Godfist, and the news of Elsa's pregnancy burned my soul. It was not until her death that I chose to go see their child, and I've not been the same since. I hid in the trees and watched Catrin and Chase play in the mud. Catrin was a tiny and perfect

38

little replica of Elsa; she stole my heart away." He glanced at Catrin with pain in his eyes. "I made amends with Wendel, and over time, we became friends again. I stayed close to him and kept my eyes on Catrin and Chase. We knew Elsa and Willa's deaths weren't natural despite the lack of any proof, and we were constantly alert for danger," he said, his voice hoarse.

Catrin was captivated by his tale but felt a terrible weight of responsibility. She could not help the pain brought by her resemblance to her mother, but she felt guilty nonetheless.

"There. I've told you the story and revealed many of my secrets. I've no more to say this night," Benjin said as he stood to leave. Kenward did not try to deter him. Instead, he dismissed everyone, saying they would meet again after they had sufficient time to reflect. Catrin was grateful for the respite, unsure she could take any more revelations this day. She retired to the quarters of a man who was on duty and fell asleep almost as soon as she was in the hammock.

* * *

In the dim lamplight, Strom looked much older, and when he spoke, there was something new in his voice, something Osbourne couldn't yet define.

"Listen, Osbo, I gotta know what you think. How are we ever going to be able to help Cat? We're powerless in all this. I'm no soldier or guard; I know how to stable horses, and you're a pig farmer."

"Without pig farmers, there'd be no bacon."

"Yeah, Osbo. I know. I do," Strom said under Osbourne's glare. "Lighten up."

"I don't know how to help Cat either," Osbourne said, feeling small and insignificant. "I don't know how to help any of us. I'm scared."

"Don't you worry, Osbo. Just stay with me; we'll figure out a way to have some fun before this is done."

"Now you're really scaring me," Osbourne said, his grin finally returning. "Your idea of fun usually ends up getting someone hurt."

"You only get hurt if you don't do it right," Strom said with a wink, and Osbourne sighed. "I guess, as far as helping Cat goes, we just do the best we can. Agreed?"

"Agreed."

"We better get some sleep. I've a feeling we're going to need it."

* * *

In the morning, they ate a quiet breakfast in the galley before Catrin and Benjin departed for the *Stealthy Shark*. Kenward waved as they climbed down to the boat. Catrin halfheartedly returned his wave.

The next two weeks passed slowly. The mood aboard both ships was somber and strained, despite making headway. The time spent in barren waters taxed their food supply, and they were down to minimal rations. Tired and overworked, they performed their tasks as best they could. Catrin checked on Chase regularly, and his condition continued to improve. Once he was no longer confined to his hammock, his recovery became more rapid.

"When we reach the Falcon Isles, you can finish healing and then return home," Catrin said as they stared out to sea.

"And leave you to have all the fun? I wouldn't wager on it," he said.

She shook her head. "We both know this is probably not going to end well. This may be your last chance to save yourself. I wouldn't blame you. There's much that needs to be done on the Godfist, and I wouldn't keep you from it," she persisted.

"Leave it be, Cat. I'm coming with you, and you'll like it. End of discussion," he said with a firm nod, and she let him win the battle.

"Nat will be staying in the Falcon Isles," she said, unsure what reaction to expect.

"How d'ya feel about that?" Chase asked, giving no indication as to how he felt about it.

"I wish him well, but I'm glad I won't be going to the Greatland alone," she said, and he simply nodded, apparently unwilling to say any more. Strom and Osbourne also insisted

40

on continuing on to the Greatland and would not be dissuaded.

"Nat is doing the right thing," Benjin had said when she had spoken with him earlier that day. "Staying behind was probably the harder path to choose, and I think he truly fears for you more than he does for himself."

Catrin didn't know how to feel. Nat had his own circumstances and reality, but he had proven himself both brave and honorable, and she decided to believe he was making a sacrifice instead of seeing him as a deserter. She was still trying to decide what she would do upon her arrival in the Greatland when the lookout called from the crow's nest: "Land ho!"

"These are not populated isles," Bryn said. "There're hundreds of islands that make up the chain, but only the larger ones are inhabited, and these are among the most remote."

As they approached a small cluster of rocks that jutted from the sea, Catrin noticed several objects floating in the water. Kenward saw them as well, and he set a course that would take the *Eel* dangerously close to the rocks. The floating objects were actually large pieces of lightwood attached to something below the waves with coarse rope.

"Crab pots," Bryn said. "The local fishermen use colorful markings to indicate ownership," he added with a wink, and Catrin realized this was the message from Kenward's mother. Her thoughts were confirmed when Kenward contemplated the markings for a few moments before declaring their plans.

"We'll remain here until dark and hide in the shadows. Hopefully no one will spot us. Once night falls, we'll make our way to safe harbor to meet my mother's men," he told his crew, and his words were conveyed to the *Stealthy Shark*. Both crews took advantage of the downtime, and most sought food and drink. Their supplies were low, but with land in sight, they worried less. Others sought their hammocks. Catrin took the opportunity to arrange a meeting with Nat. Bryn rowed her to the *Slippery Eel,* and she found Nat in his cabin.

"I've spoken with the others, and we'll all be continuing on to the Greatland. I'm sorry to leave you alone," she began, and he nodded silently. "I have no specific tasks for you. You're free to do as you wish. If you find any way to help my cause, however, I expect you to act. Agreed?"

"Agreed. I've been thinking about staying in the Falcon Isles for a while. Things on the Godfist will be what they will be whether I'm there or not. Perhaps I can learn more here. To be honest, I find the thought of living where no one knows my past quite appealing."

"I hope you find happiness. Farewell, Nat Dersinger. Thank you for all you've done and endured. May fate be kind to you," she said with a sad smile.

"Thank you, Catrin. You are kind and gracious, may the light of Istra and Vestra shine on you," he said formally and bowed deeply. "Before we part, I have a gift for you. My father said there'd come a time when someone would have greater need of this than I, and I believe that time has finally come. My family has guarded this staff for ages untold. The knowledge of its origins has been lost to time, and I can only hope our efforts have not been in vain. May it support you when you need it most." He held his staff out to her, and she accepted it hesitantly.

"Thank you, Nat. I'll take good care of it," she said, not knowing what to say. As she held the staff in her hands, she noticed for the first time that the metal heel bore a subtle engraving of a serpent head with empty sockets for eyes. It was disconcerting to look upon, as if it were yearning for something.

"I must say a few more farewells--if you'll excuse me. May we meet again someday," Nat said, and she was glad they were able to part without ill feelings.

Catrin thanked each crewman individually for risking his or her life to save her and her companions then returned to the *Stealthy Shark* to visit with those who'd been her shipmates. Those who share such experiences are never forgotten; even if the names fade with the years, the mental images remain indelible.

When they raised anchor again, the skies were clear and a nearly full moon shone among the stars. Catrin saw no comets and sighed; disappointment filled her whenever she looked and did not find them. Oddly, they brought her comfort, and she missed the feeling of security they gave her. A part of her worried there would be no more comets, no more energy for her to revel in, but she pushed her fears aside. What would be would be, and worrying over it would do nothing but sour her stomach.

The crews of both ships demonstrated their abilities as they navigated the many small islands, sailing generally north and west, and eventually a large landmass emerged from the night. Into a narrow channel they sailed with only lanterns to light the way, and they followed it to a small, natural harbor. Catrin could see no sign of anyone else about until lanterns opened aboard several small boats that drifted along the shoreline. No one made a sound, and Catrin kept her mouth shut. She waited for some instructions from the *Slippery Eel,* while she assisted Bryn and the crew in dropping anchor as silently as they could. Afterward, Benjin helped her strap Nat's staff to her back so she could carry it with both hands free.

Kenward signaled with a lantern, and Bryn quietly ordered one of the small boats dropped. He guided Catrin and Benjin to the rail and told them to climb down. He sent some men to help Chase, and he followed them. While Chase struggled to climb down with one arm, Catrin sat in the boat, wondering what life would throw at her next. She was about to embark on an extended voyage to a massive, foreign land whose inhabitants considered her the enemy. As they approached the small gathering of boats, she wondered if her life would ever be normal again.

* * *

Osbourne sat in the boat with his knees pulled to his chest, wondering at how quickly his life had changed. What had always seemed permanent and unchangeable was gone in an instant, and now he wandered through a new and frightening world, one where childhood friends wielded devastating powers.

Still unable to find calm within the chaos of his mind, he clung to the hope that Catrin would always be Catrin deep down and would never become one of the monsters that haunted his dreams.

Chapter 5

Expectations can be surpassed only by the unknown.
--Mariatchi Omo, philosopher

* * *

The boats that awaited them were far smaller than those from the ships, and the climb from one to another was treacherous. Vertook nearly panicked as he stepped into the small boat and lost his balance. One man steadied him while others countered his movements in order to keep the boat from capsizing. Once those bound for the Greatland were aboard the small boats, they rowed into the narrow channels that snaked through the coastal marshes. Like a natural maze, there were many dead ends, but the experienced men navigated them without difficulty.

As they glided across the still waters, no one spoke--the need for stealth understood. Mists swirled above the water, and clouds of biting insects appeared from nowhere. Kenward motioned them to stay down and be quiet. Soon after, distorted voices echoed across the water, and lights backlit the reeds and marsh grasses. The channel emptied into a large harbor, where several ships were moored. One of the ships was the largest vessel Catrin had ever seen. Dwarfing even the Zjhon warships, it made the *Slippery Eel* look like a rowboat.

It was to this ship the men steered while trying to remain hidden. Deep shadows on the seaward side of the ship swallowed them. The ship stretched high above them. Once alongside it, the men laid down their oars, and a rope ladder dropped from above. Kenward silently instructed them to climb one at a time, sending Catrin up first.

The rope ladder twisted and turned in her hands as if it had a life of its own, but she made the climb quickly. The ladder took her to a small access door on the side of the ship, and she was glad she didn't have to climb all the way to the deck. Hands reached out and guided her into a lavishly furnished apartment. Her staff caught on the opening, and she struggled a moment to free it. Two men helped her in then tugged on the ladder. While the others took their turns climbing, Catrin explored the spacious quarters, wondering to whom they belonged. It was certainly finer accommodations than she and her companions expected.

Thick carpet, stitched in delicate patterns of flowers and birds, covered the floors. Unwilling to soil something so beautiful, Catrin removed her boots and walked around the room with them in her arms. Rich, hardwood doors lined two walls, each with an ornate brass knob. Another, smaller door stood on the inner wall. Elaborately carved tables and chairs dominated the interior. The chairs looked comfortable, covered with embroidered cushions of varied design, but Catrin was drawn to a set of shelves recessed into one wall.

There she found a marvelous treasure: books of every description. Leather-bound volumes with gilded titles and designs on their spines stood beside books bound in colorful cloth. One especially intriguing tome appeared to be bound in some sort of tree bark. Afraid to even touch the precious volumes for fear of damaging them, Catrin just stared in awe; she'd never seen so many books in one place. She heard the others as they entered the room, but she was engrossed in the titles of the volumes, many of which were in foreign languages. When she stood from examining the bottom rows, Kenward stood beside her.

"I'm sorry. I didn't mean to pry," she said. "I'm fond of books, and this is a wonderful collection."

"Think nothing of it. Those're here for your enjoyment during the long voyage. I fear you'll find the collection insufficient before your journey ends. Incidentally, you can put your boots on the carpet; it's not a problem," he said.

Still self-conscious, she took off her jacket and laid it on the floor, placing her boots atop it.

Kenward just chuckled and shook his head. He asked everyone to gather around. "Welcome aboard the *Trader's Wind*. This ship was designed specifically for the long journey between the Greatland and the Falcon Isles, and she's well provisioned. She's still being loaded with the bales of dried herbs that are her main reason for being here, but she should set sail within two or three days. We were fortunate the rains delayed the harvest, or we'd have come too late.

"These rooms will be your quarters for the next half a year, and I'm sure you'll tire of them, but your attendant will try to make your stay as comfortable as possible. You must not leave these quarters for any reason. There are many merchants and their men aboard this ship, and we can't guarantee everyone's loyalties," Kenward said.

Catrin was shocked to realize these elaborate quarters were reserved for her and her party; the others appeared impressed and pleased as well.

"You'll need to double up in the sleeping quarters, but you should find them well appointed. It's not often the *Trader's Wind* has this many discreet travelers in the same group," Kenward continued with a smirk. "I'll meet with my mother and then return with your attendant. I'm sorry she won't be able to come herself, but we must maintain secrecy. The captain is rarely alone, and it can be difficult for her to explain sudden trips belowdecks. I'm sure she'll arrange for a meeting during your journey. In the meantime, I assure you that you're in good hands."

After lighting a lantern, he left by the door that stood opposite the hatch; it opened into a dark and cramped hallway. He closed it behind himself, and they were left to get acquainted with their surroundings. The sleeping rooms were relatively large; each held two hammocks and a feather bed along with two wooden chests. They quickly picked their rooms. Catrin chose a room to share with Chase, and Strom and Osbourne selected another, which left private rooms for Benjin and Vertook.

The arrangement suited them all, and they were still standing around when Kenward returned since none of them was comfortable sitting on the furniture in their dirty clothes. Kenward knocked before entering and was followed by a shy-looking young man who did not raise his eyes.

"This is Pelivor," Kenward said and introduced the young man to each individual. Pelivor's smile was warm and friendly. When he was introduced to Catrin, he shook her hand, only then raising his eyes to hers.

"Pelivor is fluent in High Common and Zjhonlander, as well as the Old Tongue and High Script. He'll help prepare you to blend in once you reach the Greatland. He'll be your only contact with the crew and will visit you periodically to assist with any needs you may have," Kenward continued, and Pelivor nodded.

"I must leave you now; my duties await, but before I leave, I have joyous news. We got word that Fasha and some of her crew have survived and escaped during the destruction of the Zjhon fleet. The *Slippery Eel* will leave for the Godfist with the dawn, and we look forward to reuniting the *Stealthy Shark* with her crew. Her missive mentioned something about a group of fools stealing the *Shark,* but I'm sure she'll forgive you," he said with a mischievous grin. "May the winds be fair and your journey swift, and I hope we meet again someday." He finished with a bow, and Catrin gave him a kiss on his cheek before he could escape through the hatch. He smiled and waved farewell.

Pelivor was nervous and unsure of himself. He was slight of build and seemed to shrink under their scrutiny, but then he noticed Catrin's boots sitting on her jacket, and he seemed braver for the sudden remembrance of his duties.

"I'll bring basins for washing. There are various articles of clothing in the chests. I'll be happy to care for your garments. Just leave them in a pile after you've changed," he said, nodding and walking backward toward the door. He slipped out without another sound.

Within the chests, they found neat stacks of garments. Other than size, they were all very similar, made with a light, soft material Catrin could not identify, whose color ranged from white to tan. She raided the other chests for garments in her size, and she soon had an ample wardrobe stored in her chest. The others had similar success, but the search had left their quarters in disarray--the pristine cabin suddenly looked as if a storm had struck. Catrin was just about to start cleaning up when Pelivor returned.

He carried four clay water basins, a large wooden pitcher, and a stack of soft, white towels. He nodded to Catrin over the towels as he set them down. She was impressed he managed it all in one trip, but the mess also embarrassed her. Pelivor's face registered no surprise, though. He immediately began folding and stacking the piles of clean garments. Catrin rushed to help him, but he seemed shocked.

"Please enjoy yourself. I'll just tidy these up. No need for you to bother with it. Would you like me to bring a washbasin into your room?" He walked to the basins, filled one, and questioned Catrin with his eyes as to which room she had chosen. He placed the washbasin in the room she indicated, handed her three soft towels, and returned to folding clothes.

The others, except Chase, who waited for Catrin to finish, were pouring water for themselves as she closed her door. It felt wonderful to get clean, and the moment of privacy was a luxury in itself. She took longer than she should have, but she felt refreshed and renewed when she finally emerged. Comfortable in her snug-fitting trousers and lightweight shirt, she had no more qualms about using the furniture.

"Thanks for being quick about it," Chase said with a twinkle in his eyes and a playful swat at her shoulder. Wrinkling her nose, she kept him at a distance. He smirked and went off to get clean.

Pelivor made several more trips, bringing them platters of fresh fruit, cheeses, and hard bread. Another trip yielded a case of the deep red wines favored by Kenward and his family. The rest of the evening was the most pleasant time Catrin had spent in far too long: she was clean and comfortable, her stomach was full, and she was relatively safe. The possibility of being discovered gave her some anxiety, but it seemed unlikely, and she put it from her mind.

Loaded with empty platters, Pelivor excused himself for the night, saying he would be back in the morning. No one said much for a while. They were content to relax or nap on the comfortable cushions and feather beds, though Chase said he had grown accustomed to the hammock and retired to their room.

* * *

49

Soon the novelty of leisure wore off, and the group began to systematically read all the books written in High Common. Catrin had been confused at first, having never heard the language she spoke given a name.

"Most nations speak High Common," Benjin said. "In the past, it was only the Zjhon who spoke Zjhonlander, but their influence has spread, and most people of the Greatland now speak both languages. Very few people understand the Old Tongue or High Script. Pelivor is quite a rarity."

Pelivor would accept no credit for his accomplishments. He would only say he was fortunate to have received a fine education. His self-effacing attitude annoyed Catrin. She could not stand to see such a bright and talented person think so little of himself, and she was determined to convince him of his self-worth. He seemed to sense her desire and was unnerved by it. She asked him pointed, personal questions and watched as he squirmed uncomfortably while attempting to formulate suitably humble responses.

Benjin and the others almost seemed to have sympathy for Pelivor, and they gave him advice on how to handle women. Their advice, however, seemed to disturb him more than Catrin's constant probing, and he often appeared to be fleeing as he departed their company, which seemed to amuse the men.

Catrin enlisted Pelivor's help in getting herbs for Chase. His shoulder still pained him, and Pelivor happily accepted the task. The next day he arrived with a special tea for Chase. Catrin would have preferred the herbs themselves, but she decided to trust Pelivor's judgment. However, she kept a close watch on Chase's condition just as a precaution.

"We should set sail by nightfall," Pelivor said on his next visit, and excitement rippled through the cabin. The journey ahead would be long, and everyone was anxious to be under way.

Pelivor became slightly bolder over time, and he spent most of his days helping them learn different languages. He concentrated on Zjhonlander, which Catrin found quite easy to learn. She made a mental mapping of each word in High Common and its Zjhonlander equivalent. It was easier for her to learn proper sentence structure, verb conjugation, and other linguistic nuances when she already knew many of the words and their meanings. Still, Pelivor insisted she learn to speak in three different ways, depending on where she was.

"There are many dialects and accents," he said. "If you wish to fit in wherever you go, you must not speak like a Southlander when in northern Mundleboro."

Before long, Catrin could speak passably with each accent, but some of the others struggled. While Pelivor worked more with them, Catrin picked up a book written in Zjhonlander but found it depressing. The other Zjhonlander books had a similar effect on her. They seemed to be written with the intention of making her feel inadequate and unimportant. More like propaganda than stories, they told her she should be thankful her betters were in control of her life and destiny.

One, in particular, raised her ire; it was among the newest and most recently written. On the cover, an embossed image portrayed Istra and Vestra in their immortal embrace. The now familiar symbol of the Zjhon triggered her initial anxiety, but the words within infuriated her, defying everything she'd ever been taught. Descriptions of the Statues of Terhilian made them sound as if they would be the salvation of mankind, if only they could be found. Everything Catrin had been taught about the statues portrayed them as terrifying weapons disguised as gifts from the gods.

"What do you know of the Statues of Terhilian?" she asked Pelivor, but he seemed hesitant to answer.

"I know very little about them," he said after a long pause, "but I know a great deal about what other people believe to be true. The statues are the source of the greatest and deadliest debate our kind has ever known. It would be presumptuous of me to offer any information as fact. Some believe the statues will destroy the world; others believe just as strongly they will save it. I remain unconvinced by either argument."

"Another unanswerable question," Catrin said as she put the book aside.

Disgusted with Zjhonlander writings, she convinced Pelivor to help her learn High Script. "In ancient times," he said, "the spoken language was much different from written language, and even in those days, High Script was understood by only a very small part of the population. We will concentrate on the written." He taught her how to form each of the symbols, and the sheer number of them, many of which were only slight variations of others, discouraged her.

"You mustn't make the strokes in the wrong direction; it distorts the character," Pelivor said as he watched over her shoulder. Over time, she came to see that it did.

It took much longer for her to grasp the intricacies of the archaic language, and many of the concepts seemed foreign to her, but she persisted nonetheless. Once she gained a rudimentary understanding of the language, she attempted to read books written in High Script, but they were confusing. Most contained accounts of family bloodlines and little else. Often, when she asked Pelivor what specific words meant, they were names of places, people, or families.

The books written in High Common were a luxury; most were tales of adventure and intrigue with happy endings. Nothing in them would help her prepare for the Greatland, though, so she pressed on with her studies.

Strom and Osbourne both gained passable knowledge of Zjhonlander, but Vertook steadfastly refused. He had tried at first, but no one spoke his native dialect; thus, it was much more difficult for him to learn. Catrin doubted Vertook would ever be mistaken for a native of the Greatland, and it probably didn't matter anyway. If they kept him disguised, perhaps he could be convinced to remain mute.

Boredom plagued the men. They didn't share her passion for books and needed some other way to occupy themselves.

"Any chance you could find us some dice?" Benjin asked Pelivor one afternoon.

"I suppose there's a chance. I'll make some inquiries on your behalf."

In the meantime, he brought a new stack of books for their entertainment; most were in High Common, but a few were in High Script. Those in High Common were soon divided among the others, and Catrin supposed more ancient lineage wouldn't kill her. She picked up a badly faded and ancient-looking tome and was pleasantly surprised to find it actually told a story.

It was an impossibly difficult text to translate, and she often had to read a passage several times before she had even a cursory understanding of what it meant. Even when she thought she made sense of something, she wondered if she weren't misinterpreting it. Based on her best guesses, she surmised that there had been two warring factions: the Om and the Gholgi, and the Gholgi were very powerful. Some passages seemed to indicate that the Om were forced to live underground in order to avoid the Gholgi. This confused Catrin, and she was almost certain she was reading something incorrectly, but she continued, hoping to find something to confirm or deny her assumptions.

"What do these two words mean?" she asked Pelivor.

"I don't know what Gholgi means. I apologize for my ignorance. This book is from the captain's personal collection, and it is probably the oldest text I have ever seen. Based on the ancient form of High Script, I suspect this is a relatively recent transcription of a much older work. Some of the words it contains may have never been translated before or may have no translation. The other word you asked about, Om, could be similar to Ohma, which means men."

"That makes no sense either, unless the men were fighting women. Perhaps Gholgi is the word for woman," she said.

"I doubt that. Uma is the more modern form of woman. Perhaps the old form was Um," he speculated, and Catrin scanned the pages in hopes of confirming his guess. She was almost disappointed to find the word Um used later in the text since that bit of conjecture only made the rest of the puzzle appear more complex.

The further she read, the more confused she became, and she eventually set the book aside in frustration. Pacing the cabin relentlessly, she was like a caged animal. She

53

needed answers, not guesses, but all she had were feelings and assumptions. Her confinement became like a tangible thing; it trapped her and prevented her from getting the answers she sought. She knew, deep inside, it wasn't true, but frustration overwhelmed her good sense. She stewed in her uncertainty and anxieties until she worked herself into a frenzied state. The men seemed to sense the rising storm, and they exchanged glances, as if wondering where she would strike.

Fears and concerns overwhelmed her, and she realized not all of the worry was hers. She could sense the others, and their moods were influencing hers. And she wondered if she could remain sane while trapped with so much emotion in what now seemed like small quarters.

Pelivor broke the tension when he brought dried fruits and walnuts soaked in maple syrup. Everyone gathered around him and sampled the unexpected treats. The mood lightened, and soon they laughed while licking their fingers. Chase and Strom told tall tales along with more than a few true tales, and Pelivor laughed so hard he nearly choked. Chase patted him on the back, and as soon as he was breathing again, they launched into a series of humorous anecdotes that nearly killed the young man.

Vertook surprised everyone when he told the tale of an adventure with his horse, Al Jhadir. He was somber at first, and Catrin could sense his pain, but she was also glad to know Al Jhadir's name; she would never forget him.

He said that he and Al Jhadir were once caught in a tremendous sandstorm, a storm so terrible, his love feared for his life. They limped back to camp barely alive and bearing a mighty thirst. The first thing they came upon to drink were jugs of whiskey. Laughing so hard that tears ran down his face, he had trouble finishing his tale. He finally managed to tell them that he and his horse nearly drank themselves to death, and his lover threatened to leave him after she found him passed out, his arms around Al Jhadir. Pelivor fell from his chair laughing.

The sight of Pelivor enjoying himself lightened Catrin's soul, as she felt somewhat responsible for his new confidence. It was Chase, though, who sent Pelivor over the edge. His rendition of their trip through the marshes sent Pelivor into fits. Even those who had endured those trials found Chase's comical reenactment too humorous to resist. When Chase got to the part about Strom realizing he had mistakenly used the leaves of a poison plant for personal purposes, Pelivor's eyes grew very large and he covered his mouth. He could not make a sound as he pointed and stared at Strom, tears streaming down his cheeks.

Claiming his stomach hurt from all the laughing, Pelivor excused himself, and they were all sorry to see him go. His mood had been infectious, and they all felt better for it. The silence he left behind seemed to lend itself to quiet reflection, and Catrin found herself reviewing many of the good times in her life. The silence held as if everyone in the room were enamored with it, and Catrin wondered who would finally break the spell.

All of them nearly jumped from their skins when there came a loud knock on the door just before it opened. A motherly looking woman gracefully entered the room and addressed them. "Greetings, friends. I'm Nora Trell, captain of the *Trader's Wind*. I welcome you aboard, even if it is a bit late," she said as she looked each of them over, and she smiled brightly when she got to Benjin. "Ah, so there's a storm cloud aboard one of my ships again. Benjin, you scoundrel, it's good to see you again."

Benjin approached her, and they exchanged a brief hug.

"This one nearly let my Kenward and your father get him killed," she said while pinching Benjin's cheek and arching her eyebrows at Catrin. "Kenward has said many a time that sailing with Benjin was like sailing with a thunderhead. I'm guessing it's still true," she said and laughed as Strom and Osbourne nodded vigorously in agreement. Benjin shot them a good-natured scowl, but Nora looked at Benjin seriously. "I still owe you a debt, Benjin Hawk, for helping to keep my fool son afloat. I would repay that debt now," she said, and she pulled a small bag from within her stout robe.

An assortment of brightly colored dice rolled out when she emptied it onto one of the tables. Benjin sucked in a breath, for these were not ordinary dice; each one was carved from a different type of gemstone, and they sparkled in the light. The faces of each die bore detailed designs, along with the etched value of that face. They ranged from four to eighteen sides, with several variations of each. Catrin didn't know the value of the stones themselves, but each of them was a work of art. Gauging by Benjin's reaction, she guessed they were very valuable indeed.

"It's too much, Captain Trell. I cannot accept such a generous gift, even if it is in the exact form I desired. I thank you, though."

"Nonsense," she replied. "I insist you take them, as they are not for you alone. Miss Catrin saved the *Slippery Eel* in rather spectacular fashion, I'm told. I hope to repay part of that debt this day and satisfy my curiosity. I'm not certain I wish to see anyone rip the clouds from the sky, as Kenward described your attack on the Zjhon, but the description creates a vivid image. He's an excitable boy, and he tends to exaggerate, but he seemed sincere in this?" she said, making the statement a question and looking at Catrin for confirmation.

"I wouldn't have used those words, but I cannot say his description is inaccurate," Catrin replied as humbly as she could. Benjin and the others nodded in agreement, and Nora was duly impressed.

"Truly powerful indeed," she said. "You have your mother's look about you. I hope you have a more conservative disposition than she did, given the power you wield." Captain Trell seemed to realize how harsh her words sounded. "I'm sorry, my dear; that was insensitive of me. Sometimes I forget when I'm not speaking to a member of my crew. Please forgive me. Your mother was a lovely young woman, and I was very sorry to hear of her passing."

Catrin nodded in silent acceptance of the apology.

Captain Trell broke the uncomfortable hush and changed the subject by asking Catrin if she had been able to read the books she sent with Pelivor. Catrin was downcast as she admitted she had grown frustrated with the old book, but Nora was sympathetic.

"Don't let it bother you. I've had several scholars examine that book, and they could tell me very little about it.

Mostly they said the writings were so old, they were written in a language that preceded High Script. I cannot remember what they called it now," Nora said, and she looked thoughtful as she shuffled through her memories. "It was a long time ago, but I believe one scholar thought this book told of the discovery of the Greatland."

Catrin was unsure what good the information would do her, as she doubted she would ever be able to fully translate it, but she tucked the knowledge away.

* * *

In a tangle of vines, Nat's long knife became wedged. Sweat dripped into his eyes while he yanked on the handle, trying to pull the blade free. Frustrated and tired, he prepared for a final yank when a hand rested on his shoulder.

Neenya moved his hand from the handle and stepped in front of him. Taking the handle, she moved it up and down as she pulled, and it soon slid free.

"Thank you, Neenya," Nat said, letting her, once again, take the lead. Her long knife seemed to sail through the undergrowth, but when he had tried to lead, he found it impossible to do. Neenya was a gift from the gods.

Among the villagers, he was seen as something special. It was impossible to know what it was they really thought since he did not understand their language, and even worse, none would dare speak to him. Even the village elders would only nod, shake their heads, or point. When they pointed, they almost always pointed to the same place: a high peak on the far side of the island, which was often obscured by clouds. It was there Neenya would take him.

As soon as Nat had shown the slightest interest in reaching that mountain, Neenya had stepped forward and the elders rushed them to start their journey. Since then, Neenya had been leading him deeper into the jungle, and Nat began to wonder if he would leave it alive. Snakes, lizards, and even frogs were threats here. Whenever a threat was near, Neenya would make a sharp hissing sound and point.

Despite the danger, Nat did want to see what the villagers thought was so important about this mountain. Something was there, waiting for him. Whenever they gained a clear view of that narrow yet majestic spire, he would stand in awe, overwhelmed by a feeling of anticipation.

Nat found himself staring at the still distant mountain and realized he'd stopped again. Neenya had continued to clear a path through the underbrush, and he jumped at the sound of her sharp hiss.

Chapter 6

Wager your coin only when you know something the rest do not.
--Hidi Kukk, gambler

* * *

Captain Trell's gifts provided days of entertainment; Benjin taught them to play a game known as pickup. He drew a grid on the back of a piece of leather and drew a number in each square. Players put their bets on the squares they wanted, and the dice would be rolled. They used a combination of dice whose maximum was equal to the number of squares on the grid, which made every roll a potential winner. If the number you bet was rolled, then you got all the bets on the grid.

The group had very little in the way of coinage, which made it difficult for them to play, but Pelivor solved their problem. He brought them a long strip of rawhide that he said they could cut up and use as pretend coinage. The idea was an instant success, and Pelivor even joined them for a few games. Benjin was an experienced player, and he tried to teach them the nuances of the game. Each player could bet more than one square per roll, but no more than one coin per square. They took turns placing bets until everyone passed on their chance to bet or until the grid was full.

The game could be frustrating at times; especially when they could not remember who had placed bets on which squares, but they had fun learning.

"Many places in the Greatland have elaborate pickup tables with colored betting chips for each player that make it much easier to keep track of, but this is better than boredom by far," Benjin said, to which they all agreed.

Catrin played on occasion, but most of the time she returned to her book, which she now thought was entitled *Men Leave*. This at least made sense given what the captain knew of the book. Even with the additional knowledge, she had few revelations. The latter part of the book seemed to describe the shipbuilding process, but she was unsure, and there were no illustrations to help her. The information

Captain Nora provided was inconclusive, and Catrin began to wonder if it was influencing her attempts at translation. Perhaps, she thought, she had been better off before finding out what someone else thought the book was about. At the times when she could no longer take the frustration, she talked with Pelivor or played pickup with the men.

Her games of pickup grew fewer as the intensity of the games began to increase. Benjin was no longer the most experienced player, and Vertook surprised them all by consistently winning. They asked him how he won so often, and he always gave them the same obtuse reply: "Patterns." This answer served only to infuriate the rest of them, as they sought to see these magical patterns Vertook used to beat them. Each time they played, they were more determined to win, and they demanded rematch after rematch, even after he had taken all their bits of rawhide numerous times.

"What do you mean by 'patterns'?" Catrin asked when she cornered him one day.

He just shrugged. "Patterns all around, but you must learn to see them. Some things more likely than others, and when one pattern happens, probably not happen again. Patterns not always right, but better than no patterns."

Catrin was not sure she understood his logic, but she began looking for patterns in everything, as Vertook suggested, and in many ways, she found confirmation of his words, not the least of which was his obscene winning streak. Despite her efforts to duplicate his feat, she was never able to see the patterns in relation to pickup, as Vertook did.

* * *

When they were near the end of their ocean journey, Pelivor brought them a large map of the Greatland that he rolled out onto one of the tables.

"Captain Trell wishes to know your desired destination, as she needs time to make the arrangements for the final leg of your journey. She does not recommend you land at New Moon Bay; the security will be tight, and you would stand a good chance of being discovered. It would not be the first time the *Trader's Wind* has been searched from top to bottom before being allowed to enter port."

The months aboard the ship had dulled the group's sense of urgency and allowed them to become complacent. Catrin had been able to forget some of her fears and anxieties, while the seclusion and comfort had fostered the illusion of security. With the map in front of them and the decision upon them, the thin veil of perceived safety vanished. Catrin trembled as a sense of foreboding weighed on her until she thought she would be crushed. Her eyes rested on the soft clothing she wore, and she felt the need to regain her edge and vigilance.

Determined to completely shatter the illusion, she excused herself, retreating to her quarters to don her leathers and homespun. Pelivor had cared for them well, and her garments were in considerably better condition than when she arrived. Her borrowed garments had been designed specifically for comfort, and Catrin found her utilitarian clothing rough and binding in comparison. The effect helped to remind her of the seriousness of her situation, and she visibly shifted her posture and attitude. The effect was not a complete regression to that which she had been before boarding the *Trader's Wind,* though; her new persona was better educated, more confident, and better mentally prepared.

When she returned to the common area, she found the atmosphere completely changed. Gone were the reclining figures garbed in white and tan; in their place, she found adventurers. The abrupt shift appeared to unnerve Pelivor, and he looked as if were surrounded by predators. Catrin could understand his unease; she, too, was disquieted by those who paced the apartments like angry beasts, despite being one of them. Her attempt to reassure Pelivor came out as a shrill demand that he not look so meek. He seemed uncertain of how to respond and quickly excused himself.

Benjin was the first to speak. "We'd best prepare ourselves for the rigors that await us. This journey has provided respite and opportunity for recuperation, but it's also softened us. Let's approach our next decision with wisdom as well as caution. Let's discuss the best possible

61

place to disembark the *Trader's Wind* as well as our ultimate destination. Let us consider our decisions well before we act," Benjin said, and his formal words struck their hearts.

Catrin nodded and joined the somber group around the map.

Benjin produced the bag of dice and poured a few into his hand. He placed them strategically on the map. The dice were a perfect metaphor for Catrin but one that struck too close to the truth for comfort. She imagined the dice rolling, her fate decided by patterns she failed to perceive. Benjin looked thoughtful and placed one last die on the map.

"I've marked these locations for a number of reasons. On the southeastern tip of the Greatland, we have Drascha Stone, one of the oldest Cathuran strongholds. We could land on the southern tip of Mundleboro and travel east to Drascha Stone. Far to the north, in the Northern Wastes, there is Ohmahold--thought to be the first stronghold on the Greatland. It's remote and surrounded by deep snow for much of the year.

"There are other, less significant Cathuran outposts in the remote parts of Sylva and the Westland," he said, motioning to the three smaller dice. "We'll be approaching the east coast, and traveling all the way to the west coast by ship would be risky. The Southland and Mundleboro have been occupied for only a few years, and the Zjhon influence has less hold there, but the southern coasts are brutally hot. Landing on the shores of the Southland would be difficult, as there are several key ports along the peninsula, and that area will likely be patrolled heavily."

"What about landing along the Northern Wastes or northern Endland? That would make for a relatively short journey to Ohmahold," Chase asked.

"Endland is densely populated, and the Northern Wastes are aptly named; they are barren and lifeless, and they can be deadly to cross. Autumn is nearly upon us, and the winter snows will soon cover the Wastes. I think we'll be best served by going south to Drascha Stone," Benjin replied.

After much deliberation, it was agreed that Benjin's plan was the most sound. His knowledge of this foreign land was far greater than what Catrin and the others possessed. When Pelivor returned, Captain Trell accompanied him. She greeted them briefly before getting straight to the point. "Where will you go?"

Benjin looked as if he would speak, but Catrin beat him to it. "We'll travel to the southern coast of Mundleboro, presuming the arrangements can be made."

"Your choices are few, and all of them dangerous, but I assume you are well aware of that. My options are limited in these dire circumstances, and I'm afraid your accommodations will be much less comfortable from here. There's a ship that should do this deed for me since her captain owes me his skin, but he is not the most trustworthy fellow. You are certain of your course, are you not? I'll not be able to change these arrangements once they are set. Please consider your options wisely. I'll send Pelivor for your answer on the morrow," Captain Trell said before she left.

None of them came up with a better plan, despite hours of contemplation, and on the next day, they gave Pelivor confirmation of their desires. Catrin had hoped she would feel better once the decision was made, but instead she found her anxiety increasing. Life was about to start moving at full speed once again, and she was afraid she'd lost her stride--if she had ever truly had it.

The months spent in close quarters had taken their toll. It seemed the group had run out of things to say, and each moment seemed to drag on. Having been reminded of the dangers ahead, Catrin and the others dearly wished to just get on with it.

Three days later, Pelivor brought them a large meal and word to prepare to change ships. "Your passage was difficult to secure, but Captain Trell bribed a mercenary ship to carry you to Mundleboro. The *Nightfist* should arrive after midnight. I'll let you know when they are prepared to receive you," he said then excused himself. He returned a short while later laden with packs, bedrolls, and a rather large coin purse. "Compliments of Captain Trell. She sends you luck."

Benjin accepted the gifts and weighed the purse in his hand. He looked as if he wanted to return it, to say it was too much, but then he seemed to swallow his pride. Catrin was glad he mastered himself. They would need coin during their travels, and now she had one less worry.

"You may keep the clothes that fit you, and I'll be happy to pack them if you wish," Pelivor said.

"Thank you," Catrin replied. "That is a generous gift, and we'll gladly accept it, but we can pack them. It'll give us something to occupy our idle hands." Thinking about the journey ahead, she could not decide if she was more excited or terrified; the two emotions churned in her gut, and she began to feel ill. A big part of her wished to stay aboard the *Trader's Wind* and hide for the rest of her life, but she knew she could not.

Chase and Strom tried to appear confident, but they could not hide their trepidation from her; she could feel the anxiety radiating from them. Her senses had become more attuned to her companions during the long voyage, and she felt much closer to them all, if not too close. She could sense that Benjin was reliving old and painful memories, and Vertook was terrified of boarding a smaller ship again, but she could also sense his desire to reach dry land.

"Get some sleep while you still can," Benjin said. "We'll want to be well rested when we board the *Nightfist*."

While Catrin agreed, she found it impossible to sleep. Knowing she was not alone in her insomnia did nothing to console her. When Pelivor finally arrived, Catrin yawned and had trouble keeping her eyes open. The rush of excitement had worn off, and she was drained and exhausted. Cursing herself for not sleeping while she could, she pulled herself from the comfortable chair and watched as the others rose no more quickly.

"I want to thank you all for your kindness during this journey," Pelivor said. "Thank you for including me in your games and storytelling. I enjoyed it very much. Captain Trell sends her thanks as well." Pelivor presented each of them with a gift. His gifts were simple, but the thought behind them was without price. To Vertook he gave a carving of a horse; the mighty steed it depicted was in full stride with its mane and tail flying in the wind. Vertook marveled over it and shocked Pelivor by embracing him in a bear hug.

When Pelivor turned to Strom, he produced a small canvas painted with brightly colored depictions of several plants. "This canvas can be used safely in an emergency," he said with a straight face, "but the plants drawn on it should be avoided." Strom flushed, but when Pelivor cracked a smile, he laughed aloud.

Next, Pelivor made his way to Chase and presented him with a small herb kit, complete with notes on which herbs to use for various ailments. "I hope your shoulder heals well, but in the meantime, this should help," he said, and Chase thanked him for the generous gift, shaking his hand firmly.

Osbourne clearly didn't know what to expect, and Pelivor had a sly smile on his face as he approached. He handed Osbourne a small stone vial filled with clear liquid. "This perfume is guaranteed to win the affections of any woman who smells it," Pelivor said loudly. Osbourne flushed and looked extremely uncomfortable. Catrin asked for a sniff, and Osbourne quickly but carefully stashed the vial in his pocket. Catrin laughed, and Pelivor winked at her.

Benjin stood with his arms crossed and stared down his nose at Pelivor, managing to look somewhat imposing. Pelivor hesitated for a moment.

"You deserve whatever you get, Benjin Hawk," Catrin said, "especially after the way you teased him about women."

Benjin let a small smile play across his face but maintained a defensive posture. Pelivor presented him with a hand-painted pickup grid. The lines were precisely drawn and the text beautifully penned. "Thank you, Pelivor. You are kind," Benjin said, patting him on the back.

Catrin wondered what Pelivor could possibly have for her. His smile was bold and impish as he moved to stand before her. "There are three gifts for you," he said then walked to the bookshelves, where he located the books Captain Trell had sent for her. The last item he held was a satchel that consisted of wax-coated layers of leather. He placed the books in the water-resistant case and handed them to Catrin. "The captain insists you take these. She only asks that you inform her of anything you learn of them. The last gift is from me," he said, and his face flushed. He hesitated for a moment but then seemed to realize this was his last opportunity. He put his arm around Catrin's waist, dipped her back, and kissed her firmly on the lips.

The others had to suppress their laughter and hooting for fear of making too much noise at such a crucial time, but the moment would never be forgotten. Catrin was befuddled by Pelivor's kiss, and she was speechless when he stood her back up. He ran his hand across her lower back as he released her, and she felt a chill run down her spine. Weak-kneed, she waited to see what would happen next.

Pelivor walked away without another word, opened the exterior hatch, and secured and unrolled the rope ladder. Catrin dreaded climbing out of the hatch backward, especially with her staff slung across her back, but she set her jaw and prepared herself. Pelivor helped her climb out into the darkness, and she groped in the air with her toes, trying to locate the next rung. It was a frightening climb, but she reached the boat that waited below. Her eyes were slow to adjust to the darkness, and she could not make out any details of the men in the boat. No one spoke a word.

Each of her companions made their stealthy descent, and Catrin was pleased to note that Chase had little trouble with his climb, though he was out of breath when he reached the boat. He had healed well, and now he could regain his stamina.

The sound of the oars stroking the water gave an eerie quality to their mute departure, and it felt like a dream. Catrin gazed back at the *Trader's Wind* and would always recall the memories of their journey with fondness, but she feared what lay ahead. The path before her was perilous and filled with uncertainty. She tried to harden herself in preparation.

The *Nightfist* appeared, at first, as a shadowy silhouette that became more solid and distinguishable as they approached. It looked dark and oily, and it gave Catrin the shivers. The crew dropped a boarding net that Catrin and the others climbed easily. The rough and mean-looking men on deck were no friendlier than those in the boat. Most wore vicious sneers on their faces. Several of them eyed Catrin in a way that made her very uncomfortable, and she was relieved when a man stepped forward, grunted at them, and

66

motioned for them to follow him. He led them to a room that resembled a cell more than it did a cabin.

Catrin entered the dark room with trepidation and was grateful when Benjin refused to allow the man to close the door behind him. They were left alone, cabin door slightly ajar. Two benches were the only items in the room, but she and the others made themselves as comfortable as they could. Chase, Strom, and Osbourne unrolled their bedrolls and rested on the floor. Benjin and Vertook sat, leaning against the walls, and Catrin reclined on one of the benches. Eventually Vertook moved to the other bench and slept.

"I don't trust these men," Benjin said. "I'll be much happier when we've parted company. I'll keep watch if you want to sleep."

Catrin tried to remain vigilant, but her eyes drooped with exhaustion as the subtle motions of the ship lulled her.

* * *

The ship's movements became abrupt, disrupting Catrin's sleep, and she nearly rolled off the bench as the ship executed a full turn. Benjin and the others felt it as well and were soon on their feet. Opening the door, which had slammed shut, Benjin peered into the darkness, and Catrin worked her way to his side, but all she saw were furtive shadows sliding in and out of the darkness. Whatever the crew was up to, they were doing it in utter silence.

Benjin tapped Catrin on the shoulder and pointed to the south. It took her a moment to spot the distant lights, but then she saw a great many as the ship crested a swell. Benjin closed the door and motioned for everyone to gather around.

"There are Zjhon ships to the south. I'm guessing the *Nightfist* will head to open water and try to skirt the patrols. Our current course argues against that logic, but I may be disoriented," he said, and they had to put their faith in the strange men who controlled their fate.

The hours passed in excruciatingly slow fashion; each moment seemed endless as they waited in silence. Catrin wanted to go out on deck to assess the situation, but the

67

mercenaries had made it quite clear that she and her companions were not welcome there.

In the last hours before dawn, the man Catrin presumed was the captain entered the cabin and motioned for them to follow. When they reached the rails, a couple of the crewmen laughed, leering at Catrin, but she concentrated on their surroundings. A rocky shoreline, where waves pounded against jagged formations, was visible in the distance. She looked down, expecting to see a boat waiting below, but instead she saw only dark water lapping against the *Nightfist*. She screamed as hands grabbed her from behind, lifting her from the deck. They groped her everywhere at once, and she heard her companions shouting. Hands pulled at her staff, but it was held fast by the straps around it.

In a sudden panic, she tried to draw on her powers, but she was not quick enough. After a sudden thrust, she fell with a shrill scream, plunging into the water. Others hit the water as she regained the surface, and she wiped her eyes just in time to see Benjin land a solid blow on the captain's nose before he leaped over the railing.

Vertook was Catrin's first concern; he could not swim, and she feared he would panic. Her fears were confirmed by the loud splashing noises he made as he thrashed in the water. Hampered by the weight of the staff, she reached him shortly after Strom and Benjin did. Vertook landed several solid blows on his would-be rescuers before they could get him to stop flailing. Benjin assured him he would not let him drown, and Vertook went limp in his arms.

Chase swam ahead with an awkward stroke and looked for a safe place to gain the beach. Though he slipped several times on the algae-covered rocks, he found a relatively clear path. Vertook was overjoyed when they reached shallow water and he could feel the sand beneath his feet. Benjin appeared glad to have the large man supporting his own weight again. Slowly they made their way across the treacherous rocks.

When they reached the sand, Catrin sat down, trying to contain her anger. How dare those men just dump them in the water?

"I don't know about the rest of you, but I always feel refreshed after a good swim," Chase said in an effort to lighten the mood; Vertook threw sand at him.

Chapter 7

We appreciate most that which we have lived without.
--The Pauper King

* * *

Shivering as the wind chilled her wet clothes, Catrin walked along the rocky beach in miserable silence, still stewing over the way the mercenaries had dumped them in the water--and not even at their desired destination. They'd given no explanation and had afforded them no indication of where they actually were.

"I believe we're in northern Endland. Perhaps a day or two walk from the Wastes," Benjin said. "We've little choice now but to brave the snows and make for Ohmahold. The lands to the south are too heavily populated for us to cross safely."

Ohmahold was by far the closest Cathuran stronghold if he were correct about their current location, and no one could argue his logic. They trudged along the coastline, covering as much distance as they could before sunrise, knowing they needed to be away from inhabited lands before the sun rose or they would almost certainly be discovered. Catrin had known the comforts of the *Trader's Wind* would soon be behind them, but she hadn't expected such an abrupt return to the world of cold and wet.

The sun rose on the weary group, and the mountains of the Northern Wastes loomed in the distance. The land became progressively steeper as the rolling hills grew in size.

"We'll need to turn inland eventually, but I think we should go as far north as we can first," Benjin said, but then he stopped as if just remembering something. He patted his belt and jacket then began to curse. "Boil me. What a fool I am. Now I understand what all the fuss was about when we were thrown overboard. It was a distraction. The coin Captain Trell gave us is gone--thieving sons of jackals. Now we have only the small amount I kept in a separate purse."

Catrin's opinion of the mercenaries sank even lower, and she vowed to inform Captain Trell of their treacherous actions.

In the midafternoon Chase spotted sails on the horizon. Fearing they had been seen, Benjin urged them into the hills, but the ship continued along its course. They skirted the hills for the rest of the day, walking until it grew dark, and they were exhausted by the time they finally struck camp. They ate some salted fish, decided who would take each watch, and those not on watch fell quickly to sleep.

Late in the night, Benjin walked to where Chase and Catrin slept. He woke them gently for their watch, but as he stood, he froze. "Be alert," he whispered. "I see a fire through the trees. I'm going to check it out. You two stay here. If anything goes wrong, wake the others."

"Take Chase with you," Catrin said.

"It'll be better if I go alone. I won't be long. Stay here," Benjin said, and he disappeared into the night. Catrin and Chase took up posts at either end of their camp, and Vertook stood watch with them, apparently awakened by his instincts.

"I sleep when Benjin returns," he said.

Catrin jumped when she heard a sharp snap in the woods, but nothing emerged from the darkness, and other noises followed, leaving the sentries on edge. When Benjin did return, he did so silently, which startled Catrin as much as the noises had. It wasn't that she was surprised by his stealth; it was just that seeing a figure suddenly materialize from the darkness could give one quite a start.

"There're two monks camped a few hills over, but they're in a drunken stupor, and I didn't want to frighten them. Better to approach them in the morning. Perhaps they can help us on our journey to Ohmahold," he said in a whisper then retired to his bedroll.

Vertook seemed satisfied and went to his bedding as well, leaving Catrin and Chase to keep watch. The rest of the night was uneventful, but they were vigilant nonetheless. Benjin rose before the false dawn and woke those who slept.

"During the night we discovered two monks camped nearby, and I'm going to go speak with them. Chase, come

71

with me; the rest of you, stay here. Remember that we're in hostile territory; remain alert. I don't know if anyone else frequents this area, but we can't be too careful."

"Hurry back," Catrin said, the suspense gnawing at her. She had spent her entire watch wondering if the monks would be friendly. Her recent luck caused her to fear the worst possible outcomes, and she envisioned a thousand different ways things could go wrong. Strom and Vertook paced with her, expressing their own helplessness with muttered curses.

As the sun rose, its warmth raised a heavy mist from the ground, which concealed the irregularities of the land and made the act of pacing difficult. Catrin nearly lost her footing a number of times, but she couldn't seem to stand still. The mist had dissipated by the time Benjin and Chase returned; they looked relieved but not ecstatic.

"They're friendly," Benjin said. "Their names are Gustad and Milo. I'd never met either of them before, but we have a common acquaintance. Many years ago, while searching for Kenward, I met a Cathuran monk named Gwendolin. She was gathering and researching some rare herbs that grow only in remote parts of the Southland, and I shared her interest in herb lore. She helped me a great deal, and I shared some of my knowledge with her. Gustad said Gwendolin is at Ohmahold, which should help our cause. He was reluctant to discuss her, which I suppose is natural; the Cathurans are a secretive lot.

"There's one other thing, though. The monks came here to gather materials for something they are working on. They've got far more than they can carry, and they seem to have lost their mule. They were going to make several trips, but they dallied too long, and the first winter storm could strike at any time. Since we just happened to be destined for Ohmahold as well, I, um, volunteered us to help carry the materials." He looked as if he were prepared for a negative reaction, but everyone agreed it would be worth the effort to have the aid of the monks. Catrin was just glad someone was willing show them the shortest way to Ohmahold.

After breaking camp, they hiked to the where the monks waited. The distance passed quickly in the daylight, and the camp soon came into sight. Catrin was shocked to see two of the dirtiest men she had ever encountered, surrounded by more than a dozen large, leather bags. Each man was completely covered in soot and ash, and their eyes stood out in stark contrast. The bags themselves were filthy with accumulated ash, and every step stirred small clouds. A bowl of land cradled the remains of an enormous fire, much of which still smoldered.

"We must put out the fire before we can leave," one said to the other as they approached.

"Yes, I suppose we must. Tiresome work, I say. Tiresome indeed. I'm grateful fate has afforded us some helpers."

"Brother Gustad, Brother Milo, allow me to introduce my companions," Benjin said, and he introduced each of them in turn. The monks placed both hands around the hand of each person they met. It was a show of honor, but the black stains left behind lessened the effect. It didn't take long, though, until those minor stains were of little consequence. Almost immediately, Gustad began issuing orders.

"Empty the bags of dried sand into a pile, refill the bags with sand or dirt and dump it on the fire. Repeat, until we can walk over this area. Don't empty the bags filled with ash, only those filled with sand," he barked, and Catrin was taken aback by his manner, but the monks were not lazy. They worked alongside the rest, dumping the dry sand in a tidy, cone-shaped pile. Armed with empty bags, they sought more sand, but the soil around the camp was covered with grass, and the beach was on the other side of a steep hill.

Dry sand was lighter than wet, but it was hard to find on the saturated coast, and damp was the best Catrin could find by her second trip. Gustad attempted to carry water back to the fire, but his bag leaked and he had only about a third of what he'd started with by the time he reached the fire. Steam rose into the air as the coals hissed and snapped, but his efforts covered only a small area, and he went back for more sand.

"Maybe next time you could build your fire pit a little closer to the water," Strom said, his tone dripping with sarcasm, but he could not have known the debate it would spark.

"Would take longer to get the fire started out in the wind," Gustad said.

"Less cover in case of a storm," Milo said before Gustad even finished.

"We wouldn't have to sleep by the fire."

"The tide could put out the fire for us."

"Before we're done. What good is wet ash?"

"Might be better if we made ash bricks while it's wet."

"Sand would contaminate the ash."

The argument continued and transcended human understanding. The monks loudly and simultaneously expressed strong opinions on the merits and flaws of moving the fire pit. It wasn't that they ignored one another while they spoke; it was a barrage of verbal communication that only they appeared to fully understand. Feeding off one another, they spoke ever more rapidly. Each statement made by one influenced the next statement made by the other, and somehow they seemed to keep track of everything said. To Catrin, it was like someone beating her with a flower to show her how it smelled. Strom walked away, shaking his head in disbelief.

It took four trips each before Gustad could be convinced the fire was completely out. Even then he threw fistfuls of dirt to cover a few remaining coals. Satisfied, he instructed them to refill the bags with the dry sand. Catrin and the others did the best they could to reclaim it all, but it was an impossible task. Milo looked critically at the bags that held close to a third less than they had before, but he said it would suffice.

Gustad, Chase, and Benjin went off to find saplings, and they returned after a short time with a fresh-cut shaft for each of them. Catrin placed the sapling over her shoulders; then she asked Chase and Strom to place bags on each end. The bags were heavy, but balancing them made the load easier to carry. Still, her shoulders began to ache almost immediately, but she used her staff for extra support, and it lent her strength.

On a northwesterly course, they marched through the hills. No path or trail guided them, and this did not appear to be a trip the monks made with any frequency. Hiking with the bags balanced across her shoulders proved treacherous, and Catrin concentrated on the ground ahead of her. They stopped often to rest, but their urgency increased as banks of dark clouds crowded the horizon. A frigid wind descended upon them, and they feared they would be stuck in a snowstorm. Breaks grew shorter and less frequent as the air continually grew colder and the storm clouds nearer.

"We've a long walk ahead of us still," Gustad said during one break, his breath visible as he spoke.

Catrin thought she saw a snowflake fall from the sky. She had no desire to be stuck in the Northern Wastes in the middle of a blizzard, and she expressed her desire to keep marching. Gustad, Benjin, and Milo all agreed that waiting could be deadly, and they pressed on as fast as they could manage. Catrin counted the number of steps she took between seeing snowflakes. At first, it was ten or twelve, but then the snow began to fall in earnest. Bearing a biting chill, the wind picked up, and soft snow turned to stinging sleet and hail, only occasionally changing back to snow.

With darkness upon them and the storm raging, Catrin wondered if they were going to make it. Gustad and Milo suggested abandoning the bags of ash and sand, but Benjin and the others did not put them down, they just kept plodding along, not wanting to give up after having come so far. Sleet and snow clung to Catrin's face and hair, and she felt as if her head were encased in ice. She and the others were near exhaustion, and as they struggled up a steep incline, she considered just lying down and letting the snow cover her. But at the crest of the hill, she raised her head as she heard the others exclaim.

A massive sprawl of sporadic lights stood before them. The brightest and closest were torches that burned on either side of the natural crevice that led to Ohmahold and warmth. The ancients had chosen the location well. The crevice and surrounding mountains made for excellent defenses.

75

"Mighty Ohmahold has stood for over three thousand years, but there is speculation that it was inhabited long before then," Gustad said. "The natural defenses have been reinforced over the eons, but one of Ohmahold's best defenses is currently falling around us. It won't be long before the lands surrounding us will be completely impassable."

Cold and tired, they struggled to cover the last bit of distance between them and safety. The sight of their destination gave them heart and quickened their steps despite their exhaustion. The storm worsened steadily. Snow became so thick at times that it completely blocked the torches from view, and the footing was deadly slick in places. When they finally reached the winding crevice, they gained meager shelter from the wind and ice. As soon as they entered the crevice, Gustad motioned them to rest. He walked to where a large metal sheet hung and retrieved a mallet from a hook. The metal sheet rang a discordant note as the mallet struck it, and the echoes distorted its call even further. Three times he struck it; then he waited.

"Let me do the talking," Benjin said to Catrin and the others, and they nodded their agreement. "May I use your staff, li'l miss?"

Catrin wasn't sure what he wanted it for, but she didn't bother to ask. Instead she just handed it to him. As they waited, less than patiently, in the cold, they concentrated on keeping warm. Soon, though, a man appeared around the corner and nodded to Gustad and Milo. He regarded Catrin and the others with mild interest, but, after he spoke with Gustad for a moment, he ran back toward the fortress.

"It's safe now. We can enter the main gate," Gustad said, retrieving his load. He and Milo began another of their arguments, and Benjin led the others on.

The number of manned armaments they encountered higher along the narrow defiles alarmed Catrin, but she supposed these were dangerous times. The natural defenses combined with the man-made additions were seemingly insurmountable, and Catrin could not imagine a force mighty enough to conquer such a place.

As a small horse cart approached, Catrin and the others squeezed themselves against the crevice walls to let it pass. The cart was not moving at high speed, but the angry look on the driver's face inspired them to move, and they heard him shout as he approached Gustad and Milo.

"What happened to Penelope? You best not have lost my mule!"

". . . must have wandered off," was all of Milo's response they heard before the other man launched into a tirade.

Benjin took the lead as they rounded a corner, and another impressive sight waited. A single, massive gate, made of entire tree trunks, towered above them. A natural formation of stone jutted out on one side, and stonework fortifications secured an enormous hinge. The opposite side of the crevice was blocked by the largest man-made structure Catrin had ever seen. Huge stone blocks were stacked on top of one another to form an impenetrable wall that encased the locking structures. Standing at attention before the gates were three armed men, and the man in the center stepped forward as they approached.

"State your business."

"We are travelers from afar, and we seek refuge. I'd also like to renew my acquaintance with Sister Gwendolin, if she is indeed here," Benjin said, and Catrin noted how little information he revealed to the guard. She and Benjin were both surprised when the guard gave him a disapproving look.

"*Mother* Gwendolin is quite busy and does not have leisure to greet wayward travelers," he said, looking down his nose.

"A thousand apologies, sir. It has been a long time, and I was unaware of her appointment."

"What's your name, then?"

"Benjin Hawk."

"I'll alert Mother Gwendolin to your presence. Perhaps she'll send some correspondence, but I wouldn't hold out my hopes. I presume you'll be lodging at the First Inn?" he asked archly, and Benjin simply nodded in response. "You must leave all weapons here. You may not enter with swords, knives, bows, arrows, maces, pole arms, spears, or any other deadly implement. We'll return your belongings when you depart Ohmahold."

Catrin and the others created an alarmingly large pile of deadly implements in the crate he provided, and he looked at them with suspicion. He ran his hands lightly over each of them, checking for concealed weapons, but he found none. Benjin leaned on Catrin's staff and made no move to turn it over.

"Your staff, sir."

"You'd deprive a man of his walking stick?" Benjin asked. The guard was taken aback by the question and stood in confusion for a moment, but then he gave the command to open the gates, and Catrin wondered if Benjin's mention of Mother Gwendolin was what swayed him. He scowled at them as they passed through the gate, as if he knew Benjin's limp was contrived.

Hoofbeats echoed from behind, and Catrin stepped aside to let the horse cart pass. The man driving looked like a storm cloud, and he slapped the leather lines on the horse's rump to get more speed. The wagon bounced and shook as the driver seemingly aimed for every bump.

Gustad and Milo rode in the back of the wagon and were thrown several hand widths in the air with each jolt. The bags of ash and sand spewed their contents with every landing, and the two men calmly bounced along in a cloud of ash, all the while arguing over who had been responsible for watching the mule.

As soon as Catrin and the others were inside the gates, men used horses to pull on massive ropes that attached to the gate on the other side of equally large pulleys. The horses strained against their harnesses as they strove to move the tremendous weight, and the gate slowly began to swing closed. Catrin paused to look when she heard the command to hold the gate, and she watched in disbelief as a very angry and icy mule charged through the gate, braying the entire way. Catrin smiled, assuming Penelope had found her way home.

A small city huddled within stout walls, and beyond the walls lay the inner city and temples. Even in the distance and relative darkness, the architecture was spectacular. Wondering where the First Inn would be found, Catrin turned a questioning gaze to Benjin, who looked slightly embarrassed.

"I'm not really sure where the First Inn is. I just couldn't give that horse's rear the satisfaction of asking directions. My apologies," he said. Catrin laughed and patted him on the back.

Small buildings and shops crowded against one another in the limited space. The streets were little more than narrow strips of cobblestone, most not wide enough to walk three abreast. Almost all the buildings were dark and closed up tight. Finding the inn turned out to be as simple as looking for lit windows, and in truth, it was difficult to miss. Constructed entirely of whole tree trunks, it was one of the largest buildings in the outer city, and a rosy glow emanated from cracks around the doors and shutters. The massive size of the trunks indicated they had come from ancient, and most likely virgin, forest. Double doors, hewn from a single tree, made for an imposing entrance. A large sign hung above the doors, depicting a tree with doors in the base of the trunk, and black metal lettering read, *The First Inn.*

Benjin pulled one of the doors open against the force of the wind, and a blast of warm air rushed out. After ducking inside, Catrin basked in the warmth, and the others wasted little time joining her. Tables crowded the large common room, and a cavernous fireplace took up most of one wall. Evidence of a large fire remained in the form of glowing coals.

At a corner table, three men sat conversing in hushed tones, paying Catrin and the others little mind. A man sitting near the fire slept in his chair, his head lolled to one side and his hand still holding a mug of ale. In a darkened corner, another man sat silently, and Catrin thought his gaze a bit too direct. She noted his presence but refused to look directly at him again, and whenever she cast him a sidelong glance, he seemed to be appraising her.

A rotund woman emerged from the kitchens and made her own appraisal of Catrin and her companions. She wrinkled her nose at their filthy appearance, making Catrin self-conscious. The woman, who was obviously the keeper of the First Inn, simply shrugged. "The baths are out back. You'll have to clean up before you can eat or lodge, agreed?"

"Yes, baths will be most welcome. We found ourselves helping a couple of monks with some rather dirty business," Benjin replied, and the innkeeper seemed to warm to him a bit. She warmed even more when he paid her for the baths along with advance payment for a hot meal.

"I am Miss Chambril. Welcome to the First Inn. I'll send Wonk to the bathhouse with water and towels in a moment. You can leave your bags here if you wish," she said as she walked into the kitchen. Catrin sifted through her pack in search of the soft clothes she had packed from the *Trader's Wind,* looking forward to being warm, dry, and in comfortable clothes. She sighed, realizing the time aboard the *Wind* had completely ruined her. In days gone by, she would have judged clothes by how tough or water resistant they were; now comfort was a definite consideration.

Wanting to get clean and dry as quickly as possible, she and the others hurried to the baths. Wonk turned out to be a man in his middle years, and he seemed like a pleasant sort of fellow. He brought a stack of towels on his first trip and asked if any of them needed a robe. Catrin and the others declined the offer but appreciated it nonetheless, and they were grateful when he returned with a basin of lukewarm water. He said he would be back with more, but they descended on the washbasin with intent purpose.

Catrin filled her cupped hands and splashed her face repeatedly. Each time, gray water seeped into the corners of her eyes, stinging and burning. When Wonk returned with another basin, Catrin stuck her entire face in the warmer water even before he had settled it on the stone bench. Using one of the towels, she dried her face and frowned when she saw how dirty the cloth came away. It seemed she might never get clean, but Wonk tirelessly brought fresh basins of water.

Eventually, the cold drove Catrin and the others from the baths, and they sought that warm meal. Miss Chambril did not disappoint. Bowls of steaming stew emerged from the kitchen even as they seated themselves. Catrin noted that only the sleeping man remained in the common room; the rest had apparently gone to their beds. The stew smelled fantastic, and Catrin blew on a hot spoonful, waiting less than patiently for her first taste. It was worth the wait. She tasted salty beef and tomato with onion, garlic, and celery. Large pieces of carrot were a treat, and she ate the carrots from Osbourne's stew as well.

Miss Chambril brought soft bread still warm from the oven, and they used no restraint when spreading it thick with apple butter. Catrin thought it might be the most delightful thing she had ever tasted, and she told Miss Chambril so. The innkeeper took the compliment in stride and brought them more bread and apple butter.

"What is that aroma? It smells wonderful," Benjin asked, sniffing the air. "Is that a brisket?"

"You've a discerning nose for such a dirty little man."

"Could I beg a shaving or two? It'd be an honor to sample your work in progress," he said with sincerity.

Miss Chambril visibly reappraised him. "I suppose that would be acceptable," she said. "Wonk will show the rest of you to your rooms when you've finished your meal," she continued, motioning Benjin to follow her into the kitchen. "I don't normally let strange men into my kitchen."

"Not to fear. I try not to make a habit of being strange in the kitchens of beautiful women," Benjin replied.

Catrin shook her head and asked Wonk to show her to her room. He led her to a small but private room. Despite being the first one in her bed, she was awake long after the others found slumber, and somewhere between sleep and wakefulness, she thought she heard the sound of birds taking flight.

* * *

Sitting before the dwindling fire, as the shifting glow cast wandering shadows over the faces around him, Strom tried to drive the chill from his bones, but still he shivered. "I don't know if I'll ever be warm again," he said.

81

"At least we made it here," Chase said, rubbing his hands together. "We could still be out in the Wastes. I'm just glad to have a full belly and a dry place to sleep tonight."

"I know I should be grateful we're here," Osbourne said, his eyes downcast, "but this place gives me the crawls. I feel like an outsider. You saw how that guard looked at us. I'm not sure we're welcome here."

Benjin had been quiet for some time, seemingly content to let the others express their concerns, and he had a distant look in his eyes, as if he were reliving the past. "It'll be all right," he said. "The Cathurans are a suspicious lot, and they tend to be aloof, but rarely are they cruel. Get some sleep, and things will look brighter by the light of day."

"I hope so," Strom said, but as he looked around, the anxiety of his companions was palpable.

"I'm going to bed," Chase said with a wide yawn. Despite his exhaustion, Strom knew he could not sleep--not yet. Too many fears dominated his thoughts, and he stayed in front of the fire until the coals no longer provided their welcoming warmth. With little to light his way, he stumbled to his room. As he crept along the dark upper hall, he wondered at the candlelight that washed from under one of the closed doors. A chill ran down his spine as he passed the room, and he tried desperately to convince himself that his fears were unwarranted.

Chapter 8

A single act of kindness can change the world.
--Byrber Dra, philanthropist

* * *

A jolly sort of noise brought Catrin drifting to wakefulness, but it was her nose that drew her from the comfortable bedding. She smelled bacon--bacon! The alluring aroma drew everyone from their rooms, and she soon found herself seated in the common room with her companions. A young girl served other customers, but Miss Chambril arrived at their table and served them herself.

The innkeeper didn't ask what they wanted; she simply brought plates laden with some of everything, and Catrin could not fail to notice the large cut of brisket she served Benjin. Reveling in the tastes of bacon, sausage, and cheese, no one at their table spoke a word.

One of the doors flew open and a tired-looking guard entered the common room. Catrin recognized him as the man who had searched them the night before. When he saw Benjin, he approached and went to one knee.

"A thousand apologies, sir. Mother Gwendolin wishes to see you immediately. I sincerely apologize for my insolence. I was out of line." He stayed on one knee, his eyes downcast.

Benjin laughed and patted him on the shoulder. "Come now, let us begin again. I'm Benjin Hawk."

The man seemed shocked that Benjin would not use his advantage, and he accepted Benjin's hand with thinly veiled uncertainty. "Burrel Longarm, captain of the guard, sir," he said, seeming more sure of himself after Benjin's firm handshake.

"Please join us and sit a moment, Captain Longarm. I assume your orders are to escort us to Mother Gwendolin?" Benjin asked and Captain Longarm nodded. "I cannot offend Miss Chambril by leaving these platters full, and we sure could use your help cleaning them if you'd be willing." Benjin winked and motioned for him to take a seat. Captain

83

Longarm was hesitant for a moment but then gave in to his hunger.

Benjin cut a large slice from his brisket and slid it onto the plate Catrin handed to Captain Longarm. Catrin spooned a bit of everything else onto his dish. He thanked them with his mouth full. Miss Chambril appeared impressed when she saw the empty plates, but then she noticed Captain Longarm.

"I suppose I'll need to bring a larger meal next time, I didn't realize you'd be feeding the guard as well," she said as she cleared the plates. Captain Longarm looked uncomfortable and seemed to be wondering if he had offended her, but Miss Chambril just laughed and brought him a basket of sweet rolls for the guards.

"Thank you, Miss Chambril. I'll make sure the men on duty get every one of these," he said, and she laughed, throwing another roll at him. He caught it deftly and smiled as he took a bite. "Many thanks, Miss Chambril. Many thanks," he said as he led Benjin and the others out of the First Inn. Within a few steps, he cast a sidelong glance at Benjin, who walked without limp or staff. "Your leg feeling better today?"

"Much," Benjin replied with a sly smile.

"I should get these to the men before they get cold," Captain Longarm said, a question in his voice.

"Yes, I agree. That gift would be wasted if delivered cold," Benjin replied.

Captain Longarm happily jogged toward the gates along the path that had been cleared through the knee-deep snow. He returned shortly after and led them on a different path, one that meandered toward a second set of massive gates. The gates opened as they approached, and no one questioned or searched them. The men manning the gates nodded in deference as they passed, and Catrin smiled in return. After passing through two smaller sets of gates, they reached an enormous temple. Built into the side of a mountain, the massive structure was covered with elaborate images of trees and animals meticulously carved into the rock face. So cleverly carved were some of the creatures that they seemed to move.

Craning her neck, Catrin tried to soak in the myriad of details while she walked. She nearly tripped a few times, but she got to see distant waterfalls, hanging gardens, and even small ponds filled with orange fish. If the monks Catrin saw noticed her and her party, they gave little indication. Some sat in quiet meditation; others read. Some had their heads and even their eyebrows completely shaved, and Catrin reflexively reached for her hair. It had grown long in the months since she had left her home. Even after it was singed, it grew back quickly, and she had come to like the feel of it on her neck; it made her feel womanly.

Engrossed in her thoughts, she didn't notice that the others had stopped, and she walked into Strom's back. He made no comment, but somehow he came to be standing on her toes. She pinched him, and he laughed as he stepped away. Before the entrance of the temple, Captain Longarm remained silent. One of the men standing guard simply nodded and disappeared into the temple. The other guard motioned them to follow him inside, and he led them to a small side chamber.

The entryway floor was of polished stone, and the walls were lined with shoes and boots. No one needed to tell them they should take off their boots, and the guard simply nodded when they started unlacing. Conscious of her pale and pickled-looking feet and her crooked toes, which had all been broken at least once, mostly under Salty's hooves, Catrin suddenly wished she did not have to go barefoot. The guard pointed to some washbasins, indicating they should wash their feet before entering the temple, and they respectfully complied.

As Catrin rinsed her feet, she caught movement from the corner of her eye. A petite woman walked gracefully toward them, her robes gliding evenly across the floor, as if she moved without walking. Distracted, Catrin lost her balance as she removed her foot from the basin. She hopped on one foot for a moment, took a bad hop, and slipped on the wet floor. Her feet were above her head when she struck the stone floor, and the air rushed from her lungs. With an angry bump forming on the back of her head, she could not have been more embarrassed and was grateful when

85

someone helped her rise from the floor. When her vision focused, she found it was the dainty woman who assisted her. "Greetings, child. I'm Mother Gwendolin. Are you hurt?"

"Um, no, Mother. I'll be fine in a moment--just a bump on the head," Catrin replied. She did not resist as Mother Gwendolin guided her into another, smaller room with thick carpets and comfortable-looking cushions strewn about on the floor. Mother Gwendolin led her to a large cushion and helped ease her down to it. Catrin slumped onto the cushion and ran her fingers along the back of her skull. She felt no blood, but the lump was tender to the touch.

"Greetings, Mother Gwendolin," Benjin said. "The years have been kind to you."

"It's good to see you again, Benjin. It seems like only yesterday we searched for herbs and roots together," she replied, and Catrin looked up to see Benjin give her a brief hug. The others seated themselves, and Benjin began by making the introductions. He worked his way around the room until he came to Catrin, and she suddenly realized she had not given Mother Gwendolin her name.

"This is Catrin Volker, daughter of Wendel and Elsa Volker," Benjin said quietly enough to remain discreet.

"I'm sorry I didn't introduce myself, Mother," Catrin blurted involuntarily.

Mother Gwendolin just smiled. "You need not fret. I'm not easily offended, and you did suffer quite a fall. My position often seems to impose courtesies that my ego does not require and that I would much sooner forgo. There are those who feel I must maintain my aloofness as a requisite, but I find it tiresome. It creates a barrier between me and just about everyone else. Ah, but I did not come here to tell you my troubles. Please, tell me the tale of your journey," she said, but she noticed Benjin make an exaggerated glance toward the open doorway. "Perhaps this is a tale best told in a more accommodating location. If you'll follow me, I'll find us a more comfortable place to talk," she said, and Benjin nodded in agreement.

She led them through the large hall and down a wide, rounded flight of stairs that opened into another equally large hall. Fewer people were gathered in this part of the temple, and many of the doors that lined the hall were closed. Catrin saw people in rooms where doors were open or ajar, but they made very little noise; most appeared to be in various states of meditation.

Another flight of stairs took them into a smaller hall with fewer doors on either side. Mother Gwendolin selected a room that had empty rooms on either side, and when they were all inside, she closed the heavy door behind them.

"I apologize, Mother, but our tale must be kept in confidence. I fear anyone who learns of it will be in danger. I'm hesitant to place such a burden on you, and I'm prepared to tell you pleasant lies if you decide that is best. I would ask your preference," Benjin said.

Mother Gwendolin smiled, nodding in acknowledgment of his warning. "First, I must ask you to address me as Gwendolin while we're in a private setting. It will lighten my heart to enjoy your company as equals. Second, I wish to hear your tale, no matter how dangerous the information may be. I sense this is no minor matter, and I'll do what I can to assist you."

Everyone in the room seemed to relax once those things were understood, and Catrin let Benjin's voice pull her along as he told their tale. He left out no details, shocking everyone with the extent of his disclosure. He spoke of Catrin as the one who had been declared the Herald of Istra, and Mother Gwendolin gave her more than a few glances during the telling of her deeds. Catrin immersed herself in Benjin's telling, and she let herself experience the tale from his perspective.

He wove the story with skill, and his details painted vivid impressions in her mind. She liked the texture of his rendition and stored his memories alongside hers. Mother Gwendolin made not a single sound. She listened intently until Benjin reached the last part of his tale. When he described their journey with Milo and Gustad, she dropped her face into her hands and sighed; then she laughed. Benjin fell silent and Mother Gwendolin looked at each of them anew.

"You've endured many trials along your journey, and you've more challenges ahead. Benjin's words tell me you have acted wisely and bravely, and I honor your courageous deeds. He also alluded to Catrin's desire to learn from us. I would ask what it is you seek."

"I . . . uh . . . I came here hoping to learn about my magic," Catrin answered, caught off her guard.

"Pah! Magic? What do you need with magic? Do you wish to perform tricks at country fairs?" Mother Gwendolin asked, incredulous, and Catrin gaped. "What you possess is not magic, child. You have *power*. Not the perception of power like that which politicians wield, but real, tangible *power*. It would seem you were right to seek us out, for you have much to learn, but we will remedy that, shall we not?"

"Thank you," Catrin responded. "I don't want to be a burden, but any help and information you can offer will be greatly appreciated."

"You couldn't just come to visit, could you, Benjin?" Mother Gwendolin asked with a wink.

"I suppose not."

"I think Catrin and I should spend some time together," Mother Gwendolin said. "Perhaps she could rejoin you this evening at the First Inn?"

"Certainly. We can find our way out," Benjin said.

"You should pay a visit to Milo and Gustad. I'm sure they'd be glad to show you their experiments," she replied with a wave, and Benjin closed the door behind himself.

Nervous and self-conscious when left alone with Mother Gwendolin, Catrin quailed. The woman's grace and eloquence made her feel crude and ignorant, and she was somewhat cowed by Mother Gwendolin's reaction to the word *magic*.

"Well now, where shall we begin, hmm?" Mother Gwendolin said. "Perhaps you could describe your experiences with power. That would help me understand what you know."

Catrin sighed, took a deep breath, and prepared to verbalize the indescribable. She began by detailing the events surrounding the attack on Osbourne and how she had thought she would die. Then she tried unsuccessfully to relate the feeling of the world flying away from her.

"Hmm, yes, that explains a great deal," Mother Gwendolin said. "It is my belief that the human brain is capable of much more than most people realize. There are doorways in our minds, like portals to ancient knowledge, most of which are closed. Some doors can be opened gradually over generations. I believe those opened by a parent before the time of a child's conception are made easier for the child to open, and I have hypothesized that these doors can be blown apart by traumatic experiences. It is my unproven theory that the unconscious mind can sometimes override the conscious mind for the sake of self-preservation, but I digress.

"It would seem a major doorway fell before the threat on your life, and you instinctively triggered a chain reaction, unleashing a blast of energy. It is my belief that one cannot create energy. One can store energy, harness it, release it, but not create it. Again, I digress, please continue," she said.

Catrin went on with a bit of excitement. She hadn't known what to expect, but at least Mother Gwendolin had some answers for her, even if they were vague and unproven. She managed to tell the tale of the destruction of the greatoaks without crying, but Mother Gwendolin's astonished reaction made it difficult.

"By the land. The Grove of the Elders and the Heartstone destroyed."

"You know of the place?" Catrin choked.

"Only from legends and scripture, but you described it perfectly. It was a very sacred place where the land's energy was said to be almost palpable."

"It was. I felt it." Catrin sobbed, once again suffering the guilt of destroying the once beautiful place.

"You could not have known, dear. Now, now, don't cry," Mother Gwendolin said softly.

Catrin then told of her experiences on the plateau and how the water seemed to repel her. She described the emotions she had been experiencing when she slammed the ground, and Mother Gwendolin looked thoughtful but remained silent. She went on to tell about her trials among the Arghast, and about the striking of the well.

"Clever," Mother Gwendolin said.

Finally, Catrin described her attack on the Zjhon fleet. She tried to express in words her energy vortex spinning in a similar manner to the rotation of the storm, and how exhausted she had grown trying to maintain it. Only when she reached that part of her tale did she remember the fish carving, and she quickly filled Mother Gwendolin in on the overlooked details. Mother Gwendolin's eyes flew as wide as saucers, and Catrin grew quiet.

"Wait one moment before you say anything more," Mother Gwendolin said. She went to the door and summoned a nearby guard. After she whispered something in his ear, he left at a run. Catrin wanted desperately to ask what was going on, but she sensed Mother Gwendolin had good reason for her silence, and she also sensed an aura of excitement.

A sudden knock at the door startled them both, and Mother Gwendolin rose to meet the guard. The man was winded and said nothing as he handed her a leather-bound book. Mother Gwendolin turned back to Catrin and quickly flipped the pages, clearly not wishing to prolong Catrin's torment; then she held the open book out.

"Does it look like that?" she asked, no longer able to contain her excitement. Catrin's heart slammed into her throat, and she knew before she looked at the pages that she had found and destroyed some ancient relic. One glance at the page confirmed her fears, and she nodded with tears in her eyes. She didn't miss the caption written in bold letters above the drawing; it read, *Imeteri's Fish*. Mother Gwendolin looked at her with a mixture of horror and foolish hope. "Please tell me you lost it," she pleaded then sat down hard as Catrin shook her head.

"I didn't know," Catrin said through her grief. "No one told me. I swear I didn't know. I needed the strength to stay alive. I didn't know." She sobbed and curled into a ball, and Mother Gwendolin held her.

"I'm so sorry, dear Catrin. I'm a foolish old lady. I didn't realize the extent of your pain, and I've only served to make it worse. You are a remarkable young woman, and I'm proud to be known by you. I'll be more careful from now on. I promise," she said while Catrin cried on her shoulder.

"I destroyed Imeteri's Fish."

* * *

The aroma that came from Miss Chambril's kitchen was enough to drive away most of the group's fears, but Chase had no appetite. Since their arrival at Ohmahold, a nagging intuition kept him from ever truly relaxing, and he paced the common room, waiting for Catrin to return.

"She'll be fine," Benjin said as if reading his thoughts, and Vertook nodded firmly in agreement, but even their reassurances sounded thin and weak to Chase's ears, and he continued to fret.

"What do you think will happen next?" Osbourne asked, his voice quivering, betraying his own fears.

"The snows have begun," Benjin said. "The passes will soon be impassable, and I doubt anyone will arrive at Ohmahold or leave before the spring melt. We have little choice now but to settle in for the winter and make the best of the time we have."

"What will we do?" Strom asked.

"Perhaps a visit to Gustad and Milo, as Mother Gwendolin suggested, would be a good place to start. Learn all that you can, for you can never say what knowledge will mean the difference between life and death. Keep me apprised of all that you hear, and somehow we will piece together a plan."

"You go," Chase said to Strom and Osbourne as they stood to leave. "I'll wait here for Cat." Strom looked him in the eye, and they exchanged a silent vow: Somehow they would keep her safe--somehow. Icy wind tore through the common room as Strom and Osbourne pushed opened the doors and leaned into the wind.

When the doors slammed shut, Chase kicked a nearby chair, venting his frustration. Catrin needed him, and he had no idea what he was supposed to do. Anxious and frightened, his thoughts ran in circles, and still no path became clear. He could only hope that something would show him the way. Until then, he would pace.

Chapter 9

The world is but a pyre of timber waiting for the tiniest spark to
unleash an inferno.
--Ain Giest, Sleepless One

* * *

Deep in the night, Catrin woke to find herself curled up
on a cushion. Nearby, Mother Gwendolin snored softly.
Catrin felt strange and scared in the silent darkness. Curling
into a ball, she concentrated on positive thoughts and sought
her center. As she drifted between sleep and wakefulness,
she began to feel deep vibrations of power from within the
stones of the temple. It was a comforting sort of energy, and
it lulled her back to sleep.

When she woke again, she was alone; a tray of fruits
waited in a corner. Rubbing the sleep from her eyes, she
plopped down next to the tray and helped herself to some
apple slices and a few grapes. The sweet taste refreshed her
and helped chase away her morning lethargy. Suddenly
remembering that Benjin and the others had expected her
back and knowing they were probably worried about her, she
scrambled to her feet and charged toward the door just as it
opened inward.

"Good morning, Catrin. How are you feeling today?"
Mother Gwendolin asked as she glided into the room.

"Much better, thank you. I'm sorry I was such a bother
last night. I didn't mean to keep you from your bed. I must
let Benjin know--" Catrin began, and she would have
continued if Mother Gwendolin had not placed a finger on
her lips.

"I sent word to Benjin last night, and you have nothing
to worry about. Now that the snows have fallen and
continue to fall, those within Ohmahold shall stay, and no
more will arrive before the spring melt. For now, you may
enjoy some respite," Mother Gwendolin said with a smile.
"I've asked Benjin and the rest of your party to dine with us
this evening, but there is something I wish to discuss with

you before then. Would you like a little more time to greet the day?"

"Now is fine," Catrin said, barely able to stifle a yawn, and Mother Gwendolin shook her head in a good-natured way.

"It seems you have a great many questions, but few of them are clear in your mind. Perhaps it would help if you were able to achieve a clearer state of consciousness," Mother Gwendolin began, and Catrin gave her a perplexed look. "A common belief among the Cathurans is that every bit of food and drink you consume affects the functions of your body and mind. Every substance you ingest alters your mental and physical state in some way. The only exception is clean water, the substance of life itself, which carries toxins from the body. I'm suggesting that you not only fast, but also undergo the purification ritual."

"What's that?"

"The ritual consists of a series of traditional ceremonies that help rid the body of stress and toxins. The ritual is also required of anyone who wishes to enter the Inner Sanctuary, which is where you may find some of your answers, though I make no promises. The ritual is not trivial. It lasts thirty days, during which time you will be unable to visit with anyone."

Catrin's anxiety must have been easy to see.

"Do not fear. I've undergone the ritual many times, and I find it helpful when I am undecided about something. I don't want to pressure you. The choice is yours. Would you like to walk in the gardens? Let us take in some beauty while we contemplate."

The thought of a relaxing walk appealed to Catrin, and the warm coat Mother Gwendolin provided would make it more comfortable. All the walkways had been completely cleared of the previous night's snowfall. The sun shone brightly but brought little warmth along with its light, and Catrin was thankful for the coat.

The gardens were breathtaking. Many plants still carried their fall shades of red and yellow, standing out in contrast to the pristine snow that partially covered them. Some of the colorful leaves were completely encased in sparkling ice. Droplets of water formed as the ice slowly melted, and

94

rainbows danced across the gardens. A lone monk, his long gray hair flowing behind him, stood silently. He held what looked like two small bowls, one on top of the other. The top bowl appeared to be ringed with small holes that had flowers painted around them.

Unsure what the man could possibly be doing, Catrin was shocked to see a rather large hummingbird land on the rim of the bowl, chirrup happily, and drink. Its extended visit gave her ample time to observe its markings: deep purple, with a bluish belly and a bright red throat. When she commented on the exotic bird, Mother Gwendolin seemed surprised that she didn't recognize the species.

"My father taught me to identify most of the birds that live on the Godfist, including several types of hummingbird, but I've never seen one like that before," Catrin said.

When the avian wonder sprang into the air, it zoomed backward then buzzed past Catrin's ear, causing her to duck involuntarily.

The monk lowered the dish and turned to his audience with a smile. "I'm glad I got to see him before he made his winter journey. He'll need the energy from that sugar water to get to the Godfist. It gladdens me to help the gorgeous creatures," he said in warm greeting.

"Catrin, this is Brother Vaughn. He tends to our aviary and has a love affair with anything that soars on the wind. Brother Vaughn, this is Catrin Volker. She'll be visiting with us for the winter."

"Splendid," Brother Vaughn responded. "It'll be nice to have a new face around the halls."

Catrin knew Brother Vaughn would appreciate knowing the hummingbird was most likely not flying to the Godfist, but she was unsure how much information to reveal. Mother Gwendolin looked at her briefly and skillfully used her body language and facial expression to communicate her opinion. Catrin got the distinct impression that Mother Gwendolin trusted this man, but it was up to her to decide what she would reveal, and she decided to trust him as well.

"I've studied the birds of the Godfist, and I have no recollection of ever seeing a hummingbird that large or with that coloring," she said, and his eyes lit up.

95

"You've seen the birds of the Godfist, for yourself, in their natural habitat?" he asked, and Catrin nodded. "What a treasure you've brought for me, Mother! I hope you'll allow me some time with Catrin. I have so many questions she may be able to answer," he said, his excitement clearly gaining momentum. He began talking softly to himself, listing the many things he would ask, and he excused himself so he could write down his list. "I don't want to forget to ask something important," he said with a smile.

Catrin decided it was good that she would have time on her hands. Brother Vaughn could probably keep her busy answering questions for days. For this day, though, she decided to simply enjoy the peaceful surroundings and majestic views. She and Mother Gwendolin spent the rest of the day touring the Outer Sanctuary, specifically avoiding discussions of any real consequence. Catrin enjoyed the amiable companionship, and she appreciated Mother Gwendolin's not pushing her into any intense conversations.

As the sun began to fall, they walked to a private dining room. A small fire chased away the chill and provided a rosy glow. Catrin sat near the hearth, warming her hands. She heard Benjin and the others as they approached, and they soon joined her around the rectangular table, where the long benches made for cozy seating.

The monks serving their meal must have been watching for the honored guests to arrive because they entered almost immediately with bowls of steaming broth and vegetables. Catrin and the others laughed as they all blew on their soup, and made slurping noises as they tried not to burn their lips or tongues. Other monks served platters of cheese and fruit, and they carried the empty bowls away. Mother Gwendolin ate in relative silence, letting them exchange news.

"We visited Milo and Gustad at the forge," Strom said. "They used the sand and ash to make perfectly clear glass. You should see it, Cat."

Osbourne beamed. "It's fascinating. You should come see the forge and the lenses they are working on. Milo said he would teach me to work glass."

Catrin smiled at their obvious enthusiasm. She looked down the table at Vertook and asked him what he did with his day.

"I talked to Brunson, the man with mule. He is a good man. Just don't lose his animals," he said. "I will teach him to raise a horse in Arghast way. He will ride without silly bridles by spring."

Catrin mentally wished Brunson luck; she could not imagine riding without reins in her hands.

It seemed all but Benjin and Chase had found ways to pass their days. She sensed grim determination from each of them, and though it pained her, it made her feel safe. They could spend the whole winter drinking and playing pickup, but she doubted they would.

Considering all the ways she could spend the long winter, she asked herself if she were doing everything she could to prepare for what lay ahead. She was not. It was an unpleasant realization, but she accepted the truth of it. She needed knowledge, understanding--comprehension; without those, she would wander in the dark. Mother Gwendolin had implied that the Inner Sanctuary was the place to seek such clarity, but Catrin had an unexplainable fear of the purification ritual; it just seemed too bizarre.

Catrin knew that others underwent the process, but thinking about it gave her a cold feeling in her stomach. In some ways, she was afraid of what she might find once she achieved clarity, but much of her anxiety was centered on the ritual itself. The thought of fasting did not appeal to her. She could not imagine dealing with the hunger pangs. She tended to get cranky when she was hungry, and she wasn't certain she would be able to control herself.

Still, the possibility of learning something important was almost irresistible. Mother Gwendolin sat in silence, and Catrin met her eyes briefly. No words were exchanged, but Catrin clearly understood that the decision was hers alone.

"Mother Gwendolin says there is a purification ritual that I must perform in order to enter the Inner Sanctuary, but it takes thirty days and I'm afraid. I don't want to be away from all of you for so long."

"What kind of ritual takes thirty days?" Chase asked. "I'm not sure I like the sound of that."

"I cannot tell you much," Mother Gwendolin said, "except that many have undergone the ritual before Catrin, and none have come to harm."

"Still don't like it," Chase said.

"I'm certain Mother Gwendolin would not invite Catrin do something that was not in her best interest," Benjin said. "But I'll not push Catrin into doing it either. You must make that choice for yourself, li'l miss."

"If you're not back in thirty days," Strom said, "we'll come in after ya."

"Thanks, Strom, Benjin. I appreciate your words. I heard what Chase said as well, but I cannot let fear stop me from doing what I must. I came here in search of knowledge and understanding, and I must pursue those above all else. I want to undergo the purification ritual, so I can enter the Inner Sanctuary," she said before her commitment wavered, and a small smile played across Mother Gwendolin's face. Benjin also seemed to agree with her decision. Strom and Osbourne said they would miss her, but she had their full support, and she drew strength from their encouragement.

"I don't like it," Chase insisted.

"I'm sorry, Chase. I have to do this."

"Be safe," he said. Then he grew very quiet.

When the meal was finished, Mother Gwendolin led her from the dining room. Catrin took one last look over her shoulder at her friends sitting at the table. They all smiled encouragingly at her. They would be only a short distance away, yet she would not see them for weeks. She would miss them, but it was comforting to know they would be nearby.

Catrin and Mother Gwendolin moved deeper into the Outer Sanctuary. They reached a hallway with plain wooden doors lining each side. One door was open, and Mother Gwendolin stepped inside. Catrin followed her into the sparsely furnished room. It contained a sleeping pallet, a small wooden chest, and a lamp hung on the wall, but it was otherwise bare.

"I must leave you for now," Mother Gwendolin said. "I've some things I must attend to."

Though the room offered little in the way of amenities, it was comfortable to Catrin. To her, it symbolized the beginning of a new journey, and she was determined to get everything she could from this adventure. Uncertainties that had nagged her became gleaming possibilities. No longer concentrating on what might be embarrassing or uncomfortable, she chose instead to focus on the good that could come from the experience.

Benjin had attributed his knowledge of meditation to the Cathurans, and Catrin hoped she, too, would leave with lessons that would last the rest of her life. Settling herself into serenity, she practiced some meditation techniques. It made her feel closer to her friends, despite the walls and distance separating them.

* * *

When morning came, Catrin had no recollection of falling asleep and woke feeling refreshed and ready to start her new journey; at least she thought she was ready. A gentle knock on the door made her jump. She got another shock when she opened the door: a robed and hooded figure stood in the hallway, hidden within the shadows of the cloak. A strange feeling came over her, and she suddenly wondered how trusting she could be within the Outer Sanctuary. Perhaps the anonymity of her escort was a test of some sort to see if she were ready for the ritual.

The hooded figure did not move or speak, but Catrin sensed impatience, and she mumbled a muted apology as she stepped into the hall. The figure made no response and glided deeper into the Outer Sanctuary. Catrin followed in silence, taking in the strange and wondrous sights. Indoor fountains and rock gardens drew her eyes, and they passed through massive arches that were elaborately carved with scenes of forests and animals. Paintings hung on some walls, and mosaics decorated the floors. None of the artwork she'd seen within the sanctuary depicted people; all seemed to focus on the glory of nature.

Catrin followed and marveled at the gracefulness of her guide. The fluidity of movement and the way the robes flowed along the floor gave the impression that her guide was floating rather than walking. The illusion was temporarily broken when they reached a spiral staircase that descended into the heart of the mountain. The gliding movements shifted to rhythmic, and Catrin watched the body of her guide bob up and down in front of her as they descended. The graceful and measured movements now gave the impression that her guide was made of soft springs, but she forced herself to concentrate on not falling.

They climbed down for what seemed a long time, passing many landings and archways but no other people. The bottom of the stairwell was lost in the darkness, and the dim light provided by occasional lamps stopped several turns below where they currently stood. When they reached the last illuminated floor, her guide turned and floated through one of the four archways that opened onto the landing, taking one of the lamps from its sconce.

Catrin tried very hard to shake the illusions surrounding her guide, and she concentrated on sensing the being beneath the robe. She explored the energy and tried to envision the shape based upon the aura she sensed. Only a fuzzy impression was revealed to her. Concentrating harder, she nearly stumbled when she sensed a male aspect of his energy; the sudden rush of it was bizarre yet wonderful. Her heart leaped to her throat, though, when he stopped gliding and turned to face her. Mortified that he had somehow sensed her intrusion, she froze, and despite his face being hidden in darkness, the reprimand was palpable.

When he began walking again, the illusions surrounding him seemed to have been shattered. His grace was still obvious, but he no longer appeared to float. Vindicated by the victory over her senses, she took note of her surroundings again. The hallway ended a short distance ahead. The walls of the corridor were unadorned, and the floor was smooth but unpolished. Cold emanated from the stone; it seeped into Catrin's bones, and she shivered as she walked.

As they approached the end of the hall, they came upon an opening in the left wall, and her guide walked into it. In this hall, the walls were carved with intricate patterns, and the floor was covered with many colored tiles. Unlike the mosaics she had seen, these tiles formed only varying patterns that seemed to follow no logic or reason. Her guide turned left where several corridors intersected; then he made an immediate right, his movements confident and sure. After a number of junctions and turns, Catrin could no longer recall the way back, and she guessed they were within a massive labyrinth.

The longer they walked, the more she came to think her guide was utterly lost. Watching the patterns on the floors, she was nearly certain they had passed the same spot several times, only to take a different passageway each time. She considered leaving some sort of marking on the floor or walls, but she didn't want to offend her guide again.

Her faith was tested again when they turned a corner and emerged into a small room. The center of the room was dominated by a massive stone table, and on either side of the slab stood a robed and hooded figure. The slab's resemblance to a sacrificial alter was disconcerting, and the effect was amplified by the gleaming knives held before the monks. Hesitating in the doorway, Catrin tried to convince herself it was safe. Instincts urged her to flee, but she knew she would only get lost within the maze.

If these people wanted to harm her, this was a perfect opportunity, yet no one rushed her or pressured her to move ahead. With renewed determination, Catrin stepped into the room and felt as if she had finally taken the first true step on her journey.

The man who guided her turned and walked gracefully from the room without a sound. Those who remained issued a wordless command for her to lie on the stone slab, and she did so with trepidation, wondering what she had gotten herself into. Lying on her back, she saw a large spiral, painted in purple, on the ceiling. As she stared, it began to spin and looked as if it would suck her in. Still on her guard, she closed her eyes before it put her in a trance.

Concentrating on the robed figures, she attempted to sense their gender. The hands holding the knives had looked decidedly female, but she ran her senses over them for confirmation. Now, knowing what to look for, she quickly confirmed her suspicion: both were female.

The confirmation brought her some comfort. She felt more at ease with her fate in the hands of women. Still, it startled her when the women moved to her sides and the tips of their blades descended toward her. It took every bit of restraint she possessed to remain on the table. As the blades hovered a mere finger's width above her eyes, she hoped and prayed that she had not been duped.

* * *

Rolling into a defensive posture, Chase squared off, planting his feet and flexing his knees. Quicker than he'd expected, Benjin charged in again and lunged, overextending himself. Seeing the opportunity to finally score a hit, Chase raised his sword for a mighty blow. Anticipating his move, Benjin spun in the air, landing his practice sword squarely on Chase's knuckles.

"Too slow," Benjin said as Chase writhed on the grass, holding his knuckles and cursing. "You had plenty of time to strike me, but you had to draw yourself up like a hero in a fireside tale. Trust me, real battles are nothing like that. If I leave you an opening, take it, but don't leave yourself exposed in doing so. Understand?"

In answer, Chase swung himself and kicked Benjin in the back of the knees. Benjin collapsed to the ground, and Chase approached with caution, ready for a surprise attack. Benjin groaned and held his knee.

"I suppose I deserved that, but try to take it easy on an old man's knees, will ya?"

Chase nodded, ashamed of himself for taking advantage of Benjin that way, and he offered his hand. Benjin clasped it and pulled Chase forward, planting his feet on Chase's chest and thrusting. Chase hurtled through the air and did a complete flip before landing in a not-so-forgiving bush. Two girls, not much older than Chase, watched from nearby, and they giggled as he climbed from the bush.

"Perhaps you should try walking," one of them said with a smirk. "You fly like a stone."

His face flushed, Chase returned to where Benjin waited.

"Don't let down your defenses," Benjin said.

Captain Longarm approached. "Takes time to learn such things, but you'll get it eventually. Those practice swords working well for you?"

"That they are," Benjin said. "It'd be better if we didn't need them, but these are dangerous times. Thanks again for your generosity."

"We do what we can," Captain Longarm said. "I fear you're right. I've got a bad feeling in my gut." His statement left tension in the air, and he coached Chase as Benjin squared off. Together they trained into the night.

* * *

"Too much you look at bone and muscle," Vertook said as Brunson stood from his examination of the weanling. "Look at eyes. Look at heart. Look at soul. There you see true measure of horse."

Trying not to offend Vertook, Brunson did as he said and was surprised by what he saw. Staring into the eyes of one weanling, he saw fear. In another, rebellion and pride. Off in a corner, though, was a weak-looking filly with short legs. Until then, Brunson had ignored the filly, figuring she was unsuitable for someone his size, but when he looked in her eyes, he saw love and loyalty and a yearning for someone to return those feelings. As he approached her, she trembled not with fear, but with what seemed like anticipation. Running his hands gently over her coat, she leaned into him.

"Now you see, yes?" Vertook asked.

"I think I do," Brunson said, surprised by his own heart's reaction to the filly. When Vertook had come to him, boasting of the Arghast way, Brunson had been skeptical, believing that his ways were the only ways to properly raise animals. Now he began to wonder if he'd been blind, for much of what Vertook said seemed to be true. Swallowing his pride, Brunson vowed to learn what he could from this stranger, and he felt a new journey was about to begin.

He watched with anticipation as Vertook approached each weanling, looking at their eyes only. When he settled on the colt that had seemed prideful and rebellious, Brunson failed to hide his surprise.

"Like me, this one is: stubborn but strong, willful and defiant. Farhallian is his name. What is filly's name?"

"I hadn't thought of a name yet. I suppose I'll have to think of something suitable."

"Think? No. She tell you her name. Look in eyes and ask; then you know."

Not certain Vertook was serious, Brunson knelt down before the filly, wondering if he were being made to look a fool. When he met her eyes and asked her name, though, he was shocked to have something immediately pop into his mind, and he knew it was right. It was not simply a name for the filly, it was *her* name: Shasheenia.

Vertook nodded and smiled when Brunson spoke the name. His voice an awe-filled whisper, he repeated it over and over, feeling its rightness.

Shasheenia.

Chapter 10

The stench of fear can be cleansed only by eliminating its source.
--Datmar Kahn, assassin

* * *

The feel of cold metal against her skin was the most frightening thing Catrin had ever experienced, but she was not cut or stabbed, and none of her blood was shed. She kept her eyes closed and her breaths shallow as the blades glided across her taught flesh. Starting with her eyebrows, they carefully and skillfully shaved her. Cool air brushed the newly exposed skin left in their wake. Bits of loose hair tickled her face, but she was afraid to flinch as her mind filled with visions of sharp knives biting deep.

Her hair fell away silently, without pain or struggle, but Catrin felt as if she were being assaulted. The robed women continued their ministrations until her head was completely shaved.

Upon completing their task, they helped Catrin stand. After helping her undress, they wrapped her in a warm, soft robe. When not bearing knives, the women seemed much less threatening. She sensed empathy and caring from them, and when they led her through a door in the opposite wall, she followed with a mixture of anticipation and wonder.

They emerged into a long corridor lined with doors on both sides, all of which were closed. Darkness shrouded the far end of the hall, hiding what lay beyond. The women approached the first door on her left, and it opened silently with the slightest push. The hallway beyond was dimly lit by the reddish glow of a small fire. Around a bend was what looked like a natural rock formation, though many of its features appeared to have been shaped by skillful hands.

Pools of clear water filled the room, a haze of steam shifting above them. Near the edge of the largest pool stood another stone table, but this one was topped with a soft pad. The women silently instructed her to disrobe and climb atop the table, and Catrin did so with less inhibition than she would have expected. Her embarrassment dissipated, and she found it liberating.

As she lay on the table, though, a chill tightened her flesh, and she wished for a blanket or something to cover her. Looking about, she saw the women use wooden tongs to remove a variety of smooth stones from the steaming water. They lined the stones along the pool's edge and, using their slender fingers, appeared to test the temperature of each. When they were satisfied with each stone, they placed them under and around her with care. Catrin reveled in the heat emanating from the stones, which were now in her palms, under her feet, and behind her neck, and still more were coming.

Soon Catrin wished she were wearing some sort of clothing just so she could take something off. The heat permeated her skin and soaked into her body. Sweat poured from her, and she wondered if she would shrivel into a dried husk, but she continued to shed water, beads of sweat sliding down her face and the length of her body. As the stones cooled, the women replaced them with hot ones. The purge was intense, and Catrin licked her parched lips.

After they removed the stones and returned them to the hot pool, the women brought basins of water that had been soaking in the hot pools. They dipped soft cloths in the water and cleansed the sweat from Catrin's body. As they helped her up, she grew dizzy, but the spell soon passed. She donned her soft robe again and gratefully accepted a large mug of water. It was cool and sweet and tasted delicious.

One of the women guided her back to the hall then walked straight to the opposite door. It led to a small room that contained only a sleeping pallet and chamber pot. The other woman arrived a moment later with a pitcher of water and a mug. Then they left, closing the door behind themselves. Left alone with her thoughts, Catrin spent the rest of the day in quiet reflection, trying to ignore pangs of hunger.

* * *

In the oppressive heat of the forge building, the cold and snow seemed a distant dream. Sweat rolled into Strom's eyes as they waited for the molten blob within the crucible to reach what Gustad considered the optimal consistency.

"Do you really think we can do this?" Osbourne asked.

"Don't know," Strom said. "Milo said we just need steady hands, and I suppose we have that."

"So much work has gone into making the glass; I don't want to ruin it."

"No worries, my boy," Milo said from across the room. "You boys are just what we need to achieve the perfect pour. Practice it may take, but you will succeed, of that I am confident."

"See," Strom said. "Milo believes in us."

"Yeah," Osbourne said, his voice barely above a whisper, "but that's coming from someone who sets himself on fire at least once a day."

"He hasn't gone up in flames today," Strom countered.

"The day is young yet."

Gustad bent down to peer into the small opening in the furnace, admiring the molten glass in the crucible. "I believe we are ready to pour," he said. "Remember, the key is slow and steady, and you must increase the rate of your pour as you reach the bottom of the crucible. Understand?" Strom and Osbourne nodded, though Strom wondered if his confidence were misplaced. He certainly had no reason to believe he and Osbourne were capable of a task that required such precision, but he was determined to try. "Steady now," Gustad said as they slowly eased the crucible out of the furnace, their arms hidden within long, thick, leather gloves.

Despite their efforts, hot coals clung to the crucible and fell to the floor. "Don't let any coals drop into the mold," Milo said, his eyes wide with excitement.

"Hurry now," Gustad said. "We must not let the glass cool. Begin the pour. Slow and steady, boys. Slow and steady."

Strom tried to keep his hands from trembling, but the pressure was on him. Osbourne's task was simply to balance the long pouring rod while Strom regulated the rate of the pour. Slowly he began to tip the crucible. Like heated tree sap, the molten glass oozed from the crucible, and Strom tried to ignore the sweat that was seeping into his eyes.

"Easy, now. Nice and slow," Milo said, moving closer to inspect the pour, his long robes gliding across the floor.

"Increase the flow," Gustad said after most of the glass had left the crucible; only a small amount remained. "Steady now. Steady."

Squinting, Strom tried his best, but his eyes burned, and the crucible wobbled slightly.

"Blast!" Gustad said. "So very close. You nearly had it. Put the pouring rod and crucible on the rack."

After replacing the rod, Strom turned and shook his head. "Milo," he said.

Milo ignored him as he examined the glass cooling in the mold. "Not bad," he said. "Almost as good as what we've accomplished on our own--only a few bubbles. If only my hands did not shake with age, we could have had this done a dozen times."

"Milo," Strom said more forcefully while trying to catch up with the monk who now paced the floor.

"I wonder if we should change the shape of the crucible so we don't have to increase the rate of pour so dramatically--"

"Milo!"

"What is it, m'boy?" Milo asked, suddenly sniffing the air.

"You're on fire again."

* * *

The next morning brought two more robed figures, and Catrin sensed these were not the same women from the day before, but women they were. Acquainting herself with the aura of each robed figure, Catrin became more adept at the process. Using only her senses, she examined the robed figures with no apparent reaction from her subjects, but she kept her investigations brief and cursory, not wanting her exploration to be discovered again.

They led her down the hall, past several doors, and picked a door seemingly at random. It led to a man-made chamber that housed another large stone slab, but this slab differed from the others in that it had a large cavity hollowed out of its base, which was filled with glowing red embers. The women helped Catrin from her robe and motioned for her to climb atop the table. Catrin ran her hand across the slab. It was quite warm. She seated herself on the end of the table and lay back slowly.

The stone seemed too hot on her skin at first, but as she eased herself down, the intensity seemed to lessen. Both women sorted through a tray of small vials; then they anointed her with hot oils. Each drop brought its own unique sensation, and a variety of pungent smells assaulted her senses. The mixture was heady, and it nearly gave Catrin a headache, but as she relaxed, the pain subsided. As the women massaged the oils into her skin, she relaxed further. Kinks in her stiff muscles seemed to melt, and she was amazed by how many places were sore. She'd felt fine before she lay down, but the women worked knotted and sore muscles she had been completely unaware of.

They brought her water and gave her time to drink. When Catrin had had her fill, they motioned for her to lie back down, and she complied without complaint. The massage treatment had been wonderful, leaving her feeling limber and relaxed.

She wasn't certain what to expect when they returned to her side, each holding some sort of narrow cone that was as long as her arm and appeared to be made of waxed cloth. After inserting the small ends of the cones into Catrin's ears, they placed her hands around them, making it clear she was to hold them in place. Catrin had begun to expect unusual things during the ritual, but she could not imagine what would come next.

They returned, each holding a long piece of dried reed. They knelt down, and when they stood, the ends of the reeds were afire. Catrin nearly shrieked when the women lowered the flaming reeds toward the wax cones. Instinctively, she thought of her hair then realized she no longer had any. Tilting the cones forward, she saw flames dancing on the ends of the cones from the corner of her vision, but the waxed cloth burned slowly. A strange but not unpleasant sensation filled her ears, and she laughed. The hooded women just stood and watched the wax cones burn, but Catrin sensed their mirth.

"I know you're smiling under those hoods," she said, and she stuck her tongue out at them. While they showed no visible reaction, she could almost feel their mental laughter, which made her smile. She tried to relax and trust the women not to set her head on fire, but it was difficult, and she was glad when they removed the burning cones from her ears.

* * *

Within the halls of Adderhold he stood, the boy with no tongue. He watched as liveried servants prepared a banquet, but he knew it for what it was: a trap. Soon the nobles would arrive, dressed in finery and expecting to be treated as honored guests, and so some would be, but for others, there awaited a surprise.

Keeping to the shadows, the nameless boy watched and waited, knowing there was nothing he could do to stop it; there was nothing he could do to gain his freedom or to preserve the freedom of others. He was powerless, a slave, capable of little more than serving his master, and to this fate he resigned himself. There was no one who cared for him; no one would come to rescue him from this prison of flesh and bone. He was alone--now and for the rest of his days.

With a sigh, he moved through the dark corridors known to only a few and made his way to the banquet hall. Standing behind scarlet curtains with gilded trim, he hid, hoping no one would remember he existed. Once he had been brash and proud, but now all he wanted was to be left alone, to be forgotten.

As the guests began to arrive, he watched, waiting to see who would show the signs. His heart beating faster with every arriving noble, he almost dared to hope, almost convinced himself that none would have real power. When the nobles began to take their seats and servants served the first dishes, it seemed his wishes had been granted, but he knew better. Nothing he had ever wished for had really come true, and he had no reason to believe things would change now.

When servants rushed to escort a late arrival to the hall, he was not surprised to see a nimbus of power around the man they led. Dressed in lavish colors and bejeweled raiment, the man stood tall and proud. This was a man accustomed to power, both physical and political, but it was obvious he knew nothing of his real power, the very thing that made him, in this case, most vulnerable.

With a shuddering sigh, the nameless boy retreated, not needing to see any more. He knew what was to come, and he could only lament. He was powerless--a slave.

* * *

That night Catrin was led to a large room, most of which was taken up by a huge stone basin filled near to capacity with a colorful array of rounded and polished stones. Two pitchers of water and a jar for drinking were also present in the room, along with a few other amenities. On the edge of the rock basin was a single red rose. Her guides gave her no indication why it was there. Instead, as they left, they wordlessly instructed her to sleep in the stone basin.

Her thirst unquenchable, Catrin drained one of the jars before approaching the basin. The rose drew her closer, and she inhaled its fragrance, felt the texture of the petals with her lips, and marveled over the bead of moisture hidden within its folds. It was surprising how enamored she could become with a rose, something she had walked by a hundred times without really noticing, but here, in her isolation, taken out of its context, the rose was a magnificent work of art. Soft, red petals stood out in contrast to the emerald stem with its brownish thorns; it seemed a magical thing.

As she climbed into the strange basin, the stones were cool against her skin. The more she moved, the deeper she became submerged in the rainbow of spheres. She saw topaz, turquoise, black onyx, and a host of others she could not identify. The energy of the stones surrounded her, and she basked in it. Each type had its own unique energy, much

111

in the same way that each type of living creature had its own signature.

Turning the basin into a game of sorts, Catrin wiggled her feet through the stones, grabbing at random with her toes. Then, using only her impression of the stone and her physical contact with it, she tried to identify what kind it was. For those types whose names she did not know, she made up names such as "Pretty Red" and "Purple Swirly." Within a short time, she could correctly identify four out of five stones without looking at them. As enjoyable as she found her little game, she paused and took time to simply bask in their energy. Within moments of quieting her mind, she slept.

* * *

"Please, Lord Jaharadin, do come in and sit with me," Archmaster Belegra said.

"Thank you, Archmaster. You honor me," Icari Jaharadin replied as he eased himself into one of the chairs near the fire. The upholstery was far too gaudy for his taste, but the deep cushions were softer than they appeared, and the chair seemed to suck him in, as if it were consuming him alive. It was a feeling that left him on edge.

While an audience with the archmaster was indeed an honor, Icari couldn't shake the feeling that he was in grave danger. Still, he could not resist the opportunity to bring greater standing and wealth to his family, not that declining was an option; to do so would be too great an insult. He had seen what happened to families that displeased the archmaster, and he had no wish to find himself working in the fields or rotting in a dungeon. "My mother sends her respects and asked that I extend an invitation to our humble--"

"Yes, of course she did," Archmaster Belegra said, his eyes narrowing and a feral grin crossing his face. "Your mother is a weathered hag, and I'd sooner wallow with the pigs than dine in your hall. You are here for a reason, Icari, and that reason is not to flatter me."

Icari could not have been more shocked, though he did what he could to conceal his reaction.

Still, Archmaster Belegra chuckled and leveled a finger at him. "What would you do for me, Icari? Tell me. What would you do?"

Squirming in the chair that now seemed a prison, Icari wanted to flee, but his limbs would not respond. Trying desperately to find words, he found his mouth worked of its own accord. "I would die for you," he said involuntarily.

Tilting his head back, Archmaster Belegra erupted in laughter that held no joy. "Of course you would, my servant. Of course you would."

* * *

It was an unusual awakening as stones fell from Catrin's face and cheeks when she raised her head. Some defied gravity for a moment, clinging to her skin, as if they had become embedded in her flesh. Standing slowly, she brushed off the few tenacious stones that still adhered to her and laughed at the strange patterns left on her skin by the stones. She looked almost reptilian, as if she had scales. The effect did not last long, though, and her skin returned to its normal state.

Wondering how soon the monks would arrive, she climbed free of the basin. When she went for a mug of water, she noticed that the pitchers had been refilled, and she wondered if this were a subtle hint. It became obvious later that the monks would not return for her that day, and she decided to spend her day napping and amusing herself. One of her naps ran into the next morning.

* * *

Oily, black smoke rolled from the lamps that lit the Watering Hole, and Miss Mariss wiped the tears from her eyes. The smoke from the makeshift lamp oil was only part of the reason she cried; what had once been a joyful existence had turned into constant struggle. Everything was in short supply these days, especially good humor. Without decent food and drink, business was slow, and she spent much of her time simply trying to survive. Scrubbing the soot from the walls, she did what she could to keep her inn clean, but it was a battle she always lost, and she began, once again, to despair.

Many of the people she held dear were in the Chinawpa Valley, beyond the atrocity known as Edling's Wall. Construction of the wall sapped the Pinook of resources when they were needed most. Miss Mariss could not understand how people could spend their time building a barrier between themselves and their countrymen when there was not enough food to go around. Fools they were, the lot of them, she thought.

Looking around, she wondered why she stayed, why she didn't just join those in the Chinawpa Valley, those with good sense. But just like every other time the thought had occurred to her, she realized she could not leave behind her inn--the place that had been her mother's life and her grandmother's before that. No. She would stay and try to make the Masters see that they were wrong to divide the Godfist. Knowing they would never change their minds or their greedy ways, she returned to scrubbing, her tears running anew.

* * *

The first sight Catrin saw when she woke was a hooded figure leaning over her, and she squeaked in surprise. The figure backed off quickly and waved a silent apology while Catrin tried to figure out where she was. Her mind muddled, the stone bath confused her, but somewhere between sleep and wakefulness, it all rushed back. She shook her head to clear the last of the drowsiness then climbed from the basin.

As she stood too quickly, the blood seemed to rush from her head. Dizziness overwhelmed her, and the monk lent support while she regained her balance. Catrin thanked the woman and drank three mugs of water while she waited for the spell to pass. Slowly she began to feel better. Supporting herself again, Catrin gave a nod, and the monk led her back to the hall and opened the third door in. Catrin

114

followed, whimsically wondering how they could top the previous days, and she tried to prepare herself for the unexpected.

Inside stood another stone table next to a bubbling pool of murky brown mud that shifted and moved. Tiny specks of something shiny caught the light as they shifted, giving the pool an even more mystical appearance. Another female monk waited inside, and Catrin marveled at how adept she had become at gender identification; it had become almost effortless.

Once Catrin was supine on the table, the women coated her with a thick layer of the sparkling mud that almost immediately began to dry. When she was thoroughly coated, they left her to dry in silence. The drying mud pulled at her skin as it shriveled and cracked, and in some places it itched terribly, but she endured, not wanting to move. It was not long, though, before the women returned. They peeled the husk from Catrin, and the feeling of cool air on the newly exposed skin was intense. They wiped away the rest of the mud with a damp cloth, and the entire process was repeated, consuming the rest of the day.

* * *

Fierce winds drove the sleet, turning it into stinging projectiles that immediately froze on whatever it struck. Borga Jahn walked with his head down, each step a trial as he had to stomp through the thick layer of ice that coated the snow; to walk on top of the ice was impossible.

"We should turn back," Enit said. "We'll die long before we ever reach Ohmahold."

"You knew what you were getting into when you accepted this assignment. Keep walking." Both knew this was a mission from which they would not return; they also knew they had to succeed. General Dempsy would keep his word, which meant there was no turning back. He did not know what deal Enit struck, and he did not care to know. For Borga, success was the only option. To fail was to send his daughter, Bella, to her death, and that he could not even think about.

115

Bella was a good girl; too kind and sweet to be in an army. Borga could not blame her for deserting, and with his final act, he was determined to set her free. This task would be completed even if he had to do it alone, and given Enit's whining, that was beginning to seem increasingly likely.

Borga looked around and said, "We need to make shelter for the night, or we'll freeze to death."

"Make a shelter out of what? Snow and ice?"

"Precisely. Now dig. We need to form a pocket of air beneath the snow; that'll keep us warm."

"Warm?"

"Warmer than we would be exposed to this wind. Shut up and dig," Borga said, tempted to just kill Enit now and go on by himself, but he knew that together they had a better chance of succeeding. He would tolerate Enit for Bella's sake.

When they had a shelter large enough to hold them both, they settled in for what would be a long night.

"I thought you said it would be warmer in here."

"Shut up, Enit."

* * *

Catrin woke in a strange room that was moderately furnished, but she did not recall how she had come to be there. It was an uneasy way to start her day, but she still looked forward to whatever adventure it would bring. When the monks arrived, she discerned one male and one female. The male was obvious due to his height and girth, but she confirmed her visual assessment with her other senses.

When the monks selected a door, Catrin was almost certain she had been through that one before, but the room beyond was nearly empty. Lamps hung on the walls, and a thin layer of cloth lined the floor. The cloth was tightly woven and appeared to have been treated with some sort of sealant. When Catrin stepped into the room, the cloth gave way, cushioning her foot. She followed the trail of footprints left by the monks and amused herself by walking in the man's large footprints. By the feel, she guessed that the floor had been covered in a layer of sand before the cloth had

116

been laid. Intrigued, she wondered what its purpose could be.

The male monk approached her and nodded a bow that Catrin respectfully returned. She steeled herself as he moved behind her. Using his hands, he began to manipulate her, stretching her stiff muscles, and she felt like a clay doll in his powerful grip. Some of the stretches and contortions were painful, but others felt wonderful as they released pent-up tension.

Bones occasionally popped and shifted as she stretched, and it felt glorious. She was surprised, though, when the man contorted her body, seemingly for the sole purpose of producing loud pops. The positions were not all that uncomfortable, and the releases felt good, but she couldn't shake the impression she was being attacked by a bear. When he grabbed her head, swiveling it back and forth, she prayed he did not underestimate his strength and twist it right off her neck.

A sudden jerk of his hands was accompanied by an alarmingly loud series of crunches, and for an instant she feared he had snapped her neck. When he removed his hands from her head, she moved her neck tentatively and not only found it still attached, but discovered the knot in her neck was gone, and she hadn't even realized her neck was sore until after the relief of tension.

He gestured for her to lie on the floor, and Catrin wondered what he would do to her next. He rolled her to one side, manipulating her low back in ways she would have never imagined. The pops and cracks were not as loud or as plentiful, but those that occurred felt massive. Rolling her onto her stomach, he placed his hands on her head for a moment then departed.

The female monk approached, and Catrin was a bit shocked when the woman stepped on her, and she was even more surprised when the second foot followed. More loud pops and cracks accompanied the woman's footsteps as she worked Catrin's flesh with her toes. Catrin was glad the female monk was performing this part of the ritual; the man would have crushed her.

117

When the treatment was completed, she was led back to the room with the stone-filled basin. The energy of the stones beckoned to her, and she rushed to finish drinking her water, anxious to immerse herself in the rainbow of energy textures.

* * *

"Do you think Catrin is purified yet?" Osbourne asked over the evening meal.

"With as much manure as she shoveled over the years, they've got a lot of purifying to do," Strom said, laughing.

"Do you really think they'll make Cat cut her hair?" Chase asked.

"There's a good chance," Benjin said. "I only told you it was a possibility so you would not be surprised. She may not be very happy about it."

"I can't imagine Cat without any hair."

"It'll grow back," Benjin said softly, and he looked around the common room. Tables were beginning to fill up. They had agreed to keep Catrin's activities to themselves, and he did not wish to be overheard. The murmur of many voices filled the air, but still he kept his voice low. "Just keep doing what you are doing, and everything will be fine."

"I know," Osbourne said. "I'm sorry. I just keep thinking about what they might be doing to Cat, and it gives me the crawls."

"This whole place gives me the crawls," Strom added.

"Things here may seem strange," Benjin said, "but if these people journeyed to the Godfist, they would find our ways just as strange. You'll get used to it."

"I just want to see Catrin do whatever it is she's supposed to do, so we can all go home," Chase said.

Benjin looked at the faces around him, knowing none of them would be going home soon, knowing their homes may no longer even exist, but he said nothing. The rest of the meal was eaten in silence.

The days and nights that followed were variations of the first few days, and Catrin enjoyed herself thoroughly, although she was not overly fond of shaving. Despite the lack of food, she seldom felt pangs of hunger. It was more the desire for taste and spice that gave her cravings than it was the desire for solid food. She lost count of the days and lost track of which doors in the hall led to which rooms. As she approached what she thought to be the final days of the cleansing, she was immensely proud of herself for having gone through with the process. It had been a scary thing to take on alone, and she felt strengthened by the experience.

When four monks, three female and one male, arrived for her one morning, Catrin anticipated the conclusion of the ritual. She followed the figures in respectful silence and did her best to perform her part. Although she had laughed and teased the monks during part of her time with them, she could feel the seriousness in the air. This was a sacred affair, and she was determined to show proper humility and respect. They took her to a narrow room with oddly shaped openings in the walls.

Without instruction, she climbed atop the table. Trying to center herself, she closed her eyes, took slow, deep breaths on the count of seven, and calmly addressed her thoughts. No one touched her, but she could feel the presence of hands above her head, feet, hands, and naval. She felt no pressure, but a warm tingling sensation infused her flesh as the energy shifted and moved.

Her meditation evolved into a deep trance, her body feeling as if it were waving back and forth without moving, and at first, she didn't notice the sound. Rhythmic music created by many voices chanting in harmony started low and soft, but it gradually grew in volume and intensity. There seemed to be no distinct words or meaning, and Catrin immersed herself in the deep bass vibrations. Two distinct chants merged around her: one came from the left, the other from the right. As one intensified, the other would subside, and gradually they reversed, creating a deep, pulsating sensation.

The joy of floating along the energy now swirling around her was magnificent, but it felt self-indulgent; she was here to be cleansed, not pampered. Beginning her meditation again, she concentrated on each thought as it came to her. Some were dark and challenging; others, light and amusing. Each one she processed and accepted before casting it away. Having become more adept at the process, and in the midst of the energy, she found it possible to admit and accept some very difficult things--things that would normally have driven her to tears.

Envisioning a fountain of energy flowing from her forehead to the sky, she poured all the hurt and pain from her soul into the wellspring. She allowed it to be as it would be and embraced the things that made her who she was. It seemed, at first, as if her fountain of anguish would flow forever, but it finally began to abate. As it dwindled, a pure flow of energy took its place. More and more, love and joyfulness washed away the pain. As the flow became pure joy, she cast it out in all directions, to be shared with everyone and everything. The energy poured through her and from her, and it felt as if a worn, dead shell were blasted away before the onslaught.

The next breath was like Catrin's first. Inhaling deeply, she savored every scent in the air, each one a marvel. The air around her body vibrated as if alive, and she kept her eyes closed, afraid to break the spell. As her mind settled, she found the center of her focus. It was a small dot in her consciousness that seemed far away at first, but she applied her will and flowed closer. It grew no larger as she approached; it just felt nearer.

When she could finally touch her center, it was sharp, like the tip of a pine needle. Catrin figured something so important should be larger; then maybe it would not get lost so often. As the energy surrounding her reached a crescendo, she applied it and her will in an attempt to enlarge her center of focus. It grew slowly at first, resisting the change, but the rate of growth became exponential, and on every breath it seemed to double in size.

Letting the energy flow, she experienced the life essence around her. As her energy field grew, it enveloped the monks. Using it, she expressed respect and love to them, and she thought she sensed reciprocation. Her consciousness expanded into the stone and began to encompass the rooms in the hall. She felt the mud baths, the rock basin, and still she flew outward. Feeling the life within the temple, she embraced it.

A nagging absence of life in one part of her awareness tugged at her, but she could not focus on it. As she tried to narrow her perceptions down to that feeling, she sensed ancient life in another part of her consciousness. The chanting began to grow softer, slowly and gracefully dissipating, denying Catrin the opportunity to investigate the strange sensations. She gradually drew her consciousness back in as she lost the ability to maintain her far-reaching center.

When her center shrank to the size of a melon, she grabbed on to it with her mind and solidified it. She imagined it as a large version of the polished onyx from the stone basin. It had weight and texture; it was solid and real. With a deliberate mental effort, she stored it in a very special location: floating atop the night-black stone at the center of the Grove of the Elders, which still existed in Catrin's memory.

Utter silence filled the room in the absence of chanting, and Catrin could no longer feel the monks contributing to her energy flow. Her body tingled and still seemed to vibrate long after the monks departed. Left to revel in the feeling of having been cleansed and remade, her body and consciousness sang. Gradually, the effects wore off, and exhilaration was replaced by weariness. Somewhere in between, she drifted into a deep and dreamless sleep.

Chapter 11

True success is nearly impossible to realize alone. Seek out those who are skilled where you are weak, and together you will prevail.
--Archer Dickens, scientist

* * *

"The boy has some good ideas here," Gustad said as he looked at Strom's rough sketch.

"You replaced me with a stick?" Osbourne asked.

"A very special stick," Gustad said. "We'll need to grind the notch smooth so it won't bind."

"The real magic is in the strap," Strom said. "We confine it to a narrow channel as it gets wound around the shaft. Every turn, the shaft becomes larger and increases the speed of the pour."

"That just might work," Milo said, a gleam in his eye. "How soon can you have it done?"

The question was like a kick in the stomach, and Strom had no idea what to say. He'd been so excited about his idea, yet he really knew nothing of how to actually make it. Gustad stood mumbling over the drawing then began making his own markings.

"Forty days," he said.

Strom smiled, allowing himself to hope. Maybe he, too, was meant to do something special. He looked back at his friend and the monk who remained in the room before he followed Gustad to the forge.

Osbourne watched as Milo pored over Strom's sketch and Gustad's markings. Seemingly without thinking, he moved the candle away from Milo's robes.

* * *

A gentle nudge brought Catrin from her slumber. A female monk helped her dress in a warm robe and soft, fur-lined boots then led her from the room. Unsure if she would be led to yet another room, she was hesitant to set her expectations differently, not wanting to be disappointed. She was thus pleasantly surprised when they went beyond the last door and into the dark hall beyond.

The hall was unlit through a series gentle bends, and Catrin used her senses as guides. Then a faint light illuminated the base of a spiral stair hewn from the walls of a towering cylindrical shaft. When they reached it, Catrin stopped to look up. The stairs seem to rise for an impossible distance. High above, sunlight streamed through an archway, illuminating parts of the stair and leaving other parts in shadows and lamplight. The climb was arduous, and Catrin was short of breath when they finally reached the landing.

Beyond the archway waited a stunning view. A valley lay cradled between three mountain ranges. At the center stood an ancient tree, massive in size. Not tall like a greatoak, it sprawled. Its branches thicker than the trunks of most trees, it shaded most of the valley. Covered in deep green moss, the bark had a life of its own, and hanging bunches of silvery threadmoss clung to the mighty leviathan.

At the far end of the valley, Catrin could just barely see a shaded entranceway, and the wonders that lay within beckoned to her. The monk led her onto the snow-covered grass and along a path that led to the tree's trunk. Beneath its bows, snow covered only small patches of ground, and lush grasses emerged in tufts. Gold-colored seedpods dotted the grounds, and Catrin was amazed that something so large could grow from something so small.

Near the massive trunk, several monks sat in a circle, all their heads completely shaved. Catrin recognized Mother Gwendolin and Brother Vaughn, though they both looked much different without hair. Honored by their sacrifice, Catrin felt her eyes well with tears. The others were unfamiliar, but they turned to watch her approach. Though she tried to mimic the graceful stride of the monks, Catrin fell short of creating the gliding effect.

Mother Gwendolin waved with a smile, and Catrin was thrilled that someone might actually speak to her. She had not realized how much she depended on interaction with others until she had been in relative seclusion.

"Greetings, Catrin. I hope the day finds you well," Mother Gwendolin said.

"Thank you, Mother. I feel wonderful."

"Please sit with us," Mother Gwendolin said. "I've asked a few others to join us. You've already met Brother Vaughn, who not only cares for the aviary, but also has great knowledge of the Greatland's geography. To my left is Sister Hanna, who is an accomplished historian and scholar specializing in the time of the Purge. To her left is Brother Jamison, who is responsible for analyzing the political climate and nuances here and abroad. And to my right is Sister Velona, who is somewhat of a historical detective and mystic. For decades she has been studying every available piece of material related to Istran phases."

Catrin greeted each of them warmly and thanked them for taking time to talk with her. Those who had not already met her seemed taken aback by her humility.

Intimidated by the vast amount of knowledge attributed to these people, Catrin hoped she did not appear to be a complete fool. At the same time, she was ecstatic to finally have access to people who might have some real answers.

"You have completed the purification ritual, and you are to be congratulated on your accomplishment," Mother Gwendolin continued. "Many do not complete the ritual on their first attempt. Some elements are simply beyond their level of acceptance, but you persevered. From what I've heard, though, those who administered your ritual shall never forget it. I'm told you were a very unique subject to observe . . . and to be observed by," Mother Gwendolin said with a raised eyebrow, and Catrin blushed, remembering the man who had sensed her probing.

"Completion of the ritual grants you access to the Inner Sanctuary, and from now on you need only go through a brief cleansing to regain entry. Those within this circle agreed that clarity would be crucial during this time and chose to undergo the ritual as well. Many elements of the ritual need not be performed in specific order, and we have done simultaneous purifications in the past, but never have we done this many at one time. It required the efforts of every trained monk in Ohmahold to make it happen, and I'm proud they rose to the challenge."

124

Catrin's awe at their dedication to what was essentially *her* cause was extreme and left her with a feeling of gratitude toward these people she had just met. "Thank you all for what you've done."

"Everything we discuss will be held in the strictest confidence, but we understand some things should remain clandestine. You will need to decide what must be disclosed, and to whom you trust that knowledge. We realize that you will need to discuss some things with Benjin and perhaps others, and we will not ask you to swear a vow of secrecy, but understand that under any other circumstances, we would."

Catrin nodded her understanding.

Mother Gwendolin continued. "There are many things we wish to discuss, but I know you have come to us in search of answers, and I will let you ask some of your questions first."

After considering carefully for a moment, Catrin decided to reword her reason for seeking out the monks. "I've come seeking knowledge and understanding regarding the power I wield. I don't understand it, and while I have done some amazing things, I have no real control over my power. I don't understand why I was chosen to be the Herald of Istra. What am I supposed to do?"

Mother Gwendolin rocked back on her heels with a whistle. "Not one for simple questions, are you? I must tell you first that we will not be able to tell you what you are supposed to do. None of us know. In order to give what answers we can, you must understand some things. The Cathuran order is devoted to knowledge and understanding of the world around us and the creatures that inhabit it, including ourselves. We have all taken an oath of neutrality, which forbids us to interfere in the affairs of the world under most circumstances.

"We will give you our open and honest opinions as we are able, but you must understand that each of us has our own personal views, and we will only be expressing our individual perceptions of the world. It is our belief that life is the greatest mystery ever conceived and that no one will ever know the true meaning until after they depart this world, perhaps not even then. Do not take our words for absolute truth. Instead, use them to formulate your own perception of truth. Do you understand?" she asked.

Catrin nodded her understanding again, though she was beginning to wonder if she would ever get a straight answer.

"Do you believe in predestination?" Mother Gwendolin asked. Catrin wasn't certain she understood, which must have shown on her face. "In other words, do you believe the course of future events has already been determined?"

"I don't know," Catrin answered hesitantly. "I don't think so."

"Interesting," Mother Gwendolin replied. "It would seem to me that one must believe in predestination in order to believe that prophecies can be real. If the course of events has not been predetermined, then true prophecy could not exist. Prophecies, you see, are paradoxical in nature and can only be proven authentic if they are unknown during the events they portend. Otherwise, knowledge of the prophecies can affect the course of events. Thus, a prophecy can be instrumental in its own fulfillment. Would you have attacked the Zjhon if they had not invaded the Godfist?"

"No. I wouldn't have attacked anyone. I had no reason to destroy the Zjhon. I wasn't even certain they existed, and I still have no desire to destroy anyone. I want only peace," Catrin replied.

"Then I think we must regard the prophecies of the Herald of Istra to be nothing more than self-fulfilling prophecies and glorified predictions. The writer knew Istra's return would surely result in some individuals displaying unusual powers, just as they did during the last Istran phase."

"But why am I the only one to have these mysterious powers?"

"You are not," Mother Gwendolin responded. "Others across the Greatland, and I presume on the Godfist, have experienced changes as well, but most have been subtle. The trauma of your near-death experience shattered barriers within your mind, whereas others have only caught a glimpse of what lies beyond. Healers have seen their treatments become more effective, animal trainers have found their innate ability to communicate with animals strengthened, along with a host of other subtle occurrences.

"One extreme case was reported in the Southland. Witnesses say a young man caused a huge explosion when bandits attacked him. The explosion killed the bandits. Unfortunately, the resulting rockslide killed the young man as well. All these occurrences, in and of themselves, are not that remarkable and can be easily dismissed as exaggerations. You, on the other hand, lived on the Godfist and wielded considerable power. You were not chosen by Istra to be her Herald; you were chosen by the Zjhon. The prophecies created the image of a great destroyer, and you fit the painting."

Catrin swayed as she digested Mother Gwendolin's explanation. Could it be that simple? Could it be a huge coincidence or, as Mother Gwendolin put it, the self-fulfillment of a prophecy that was based on probable predictions? It seemed a cruel and cold explanation, and one that provided no real indication as to how she should handle it. If she was only the Herald because of what the Zjhon believed, then how could she possibly remedy the situation? How could she make the Zjhon believe she was not born to destroy them? She did not voice the questions, fearing she already knew what the answers would be.

"Your survival may be all you can hope to achieve," Mother Gwendolin said, as if reading her thoughts. "The Zjhon are devout in their beliefs, and they will not easily give up their search for you. Perhaps you will be able to create peace among the nations, but it is impossible to say. In my reality, the future is undetermined; therefore, endless possibilities exist. In such a reality, one can achieve incredible things with effort and determination, or they can lose everything by making bad decisions. It is a magical and tenuous existence. It is up to you to decide what is in *your* reality."

Catrin was not sure if she should be encouraged or depressed, and she tried to find her center. The revelations of the day befuddled her, despite the clarity she felt as a result of the purification, and she struggled to focus. She traveled in her mind to the Grove of the Elders and located her visual representation of her center. It was smaller than when she left it, and she took a moment to expand it. This simple exercise in self-control helped her tremendously, and she found her confidence along with her center. "I accept your counsel on the matter of prophecies, and I thank you for the imparted wisdom. I've adjusted my perception of reality and will continue to do so. Can you teach me to control my powers?" she asked.

Mother Gwendolin exchanged a glance with the other monks.

"She's definitely not one for asking easy questions, Mother," Sister Velona said. "I've searched for many years, but I'm afraid I can tell you very little of how to control your powers, as it seems to be different for each individual. I can, however, tell you some things you should avoid at all cost. Are you familiar with the stories of Enoch Giest and the Sleepless Ones?"

"I've heard stories, but I don't remember all the details."

"During the wars between the Zjhon and the Varics, there were many gruesome battles, and both nations lost many men and women. Enoch Giest was a captain in the Varic army, and he was determined to defeat the Zjhon. During a relatively minor skirmish, he was wounded and lay dying on the battlefield. He'd always thought himself gifted but had never been able to use Istra's power," Sister Velona said.

"As his lifeblood flowed from his body, he knew he was dying. He hoped and prayed he would somehow survive, and then, as the result of some epiphany, he tried to heal himself with Istra's power. He'd never succeeded at anything else with the power, and he had no reason to believe it would work, but given no other options, he applied his will to the task. Somehow, he broke down the barrier between his conscious mind and his subconscious mind.

"It's the subconscious mind that controls the beating of our hearts, our breathing, growth, healing, aging, and more. Under normal circumstances, our conscious minds have very limited control over these functions. For example, you can affect your rate of breathing and even hold your breath, but you cannot kill yourself by deciding to stop breathing. If you hold your breath long enough, you will only pass out, as your subconscious mind takes over.

"We're not certain how, but Enoch took control of his bodily functions. He stopped the bleeding and, afterward, found it easier to continue healing himself. He communicated directly with his formerly subconscious mind, which then became his alter-consciousness. He learned exactly what his body needed to repair itself, and working in concert with his alter-consciousness, he made himself anew," she continued.

"Enoch was so excited about his discovery that he explored ways to pass along his ability to his countrymen. Most could not duplicate the feat; only two others managed to break down their barriers with his guidance and assistance. Discouraged by his failures, he roamed the battlefields, searching for those mortally wounded, and his success rate increased dramatically. Word of his exploits spread, and his appearance on the battlefield drove men to discard their fear. They fought with wild abandon, winning many victories, and Enoch passed his ability to many dying men. But he could not bring back the dead, and hundreds died despite his efforts.

"Within a decade, almost every Varic man still alive had gained the ability to heal themselves. The Varics were not far from conquering the Zjhon, and the Elsics believed they would be next, but that is another story. The Varic nation began to thrive again with the aid of Enoch's imparted healing powers. There were times, it was said, that every Varic woman alive was pregnant. But the next generation of Varics proved to have very little aptitude with the power of Istra, and almost none attained healing powers.

"The passing of traits from one generation to the next is a mysterious process, and it was not until the grandchildren of Enoch's generation were born that the unexpected aftereffects manifested. The second generation since the time of Enoch's discovery was decimated; most did not live past birth. Of those that survived birth, the majority died soon after. They would simply fall asleep and never wake. Enoch watched in horror as his nation's death knell rung, and it was far too late to effect any change.

129

"By this time, many of the first generation of healers had gone to their graves from either old age or deadly wounds they were unable to heal. Despite the ability to heal themselves, they were unable to heal others. If a self-healer took a wound that rendered them unconscious, they usually perished. Enoch saw the healers dwindling in number and waited in horror for his own grandchild to be born.

"Determined to save the life of his grandchild, even at the cost of his own, he assembled everyone adept with Istra's power and gathered them around his son's wife, Alia, to await the birth. Alia's labors produced a baby boy in apparent good health, but Enoch knew his grandchild would most likely die if he ever fell asleep. He used every conceivable technique to keep the infant from sleep, but it soon became apparent the child would eventually succumb to exhaustion.

"Driven by desperation, he used his powers to reach into the infant's mind and establish a mental link. He smashed the feeble barriers of the impressionable mind and used his alter-consciousness to supplant that of the child. In this way, Enoch was able to control the child's breathing and other body functions, keeping him alive. He hoped to break the link once the child grew stronger, but it was not to be. The boy, Ain, was wholly dependent on Enoch for the maintenance of his bodily functions. The two had to remain together always and could not even go into separate rooms without both becoming violently ill.

"Legends say other Sleepless Ones survived, but those instances were rare. The stories of Enoch and Ain say that, together, they were able to stall the aging process and gain longevity. It was said they committed themselves to preventing the same thing from happening during the next Istran phase, but then the madness set in. Both Enoch and Ain were faced with situations no other mortal would encounter, and their beliefs crumbled around them. The ancient writings say they went mad, but I often wonder if they actually entered a new reality. Either way, they disappeared from the writings of men. I've told this tale so you will clearly understand the gravity of the situation and the seriousness of my warning. Do not try to heal yourself," Sister Velona concluded.

Catrin needed a moment to absorb and store all the details; then she nodded and thanked Sister Velona. "If the Herald prophecy is false, then perhaps I should just go home. I don't need magic or power in my life, and I can just go back to being normal."

"I'm sorry, dear. This has gone too far for you to disappear now. Too many people are focused on finding you and destroying you. Your only choice in this matter is to fight or die. There will be no going back to normal."

Despair was starting to settle on Catrin when Mother Gwendolin interrupted her thoughts. "Perhaps this would be a good time for you to tell us a bit more of your story. It may answer some of our questions and raise new ones in your mind. I know it may be painful, but would you tell us of your mother and the circumstances of her death?"

Catrin did not object to telling what she knew; the pain was old and did not cut as deeply as it once had. She told them of the days preceding her mother's death, or at least what she knew of them. She did not remember much of the events herself, but she remembered very clearly the things she had overheard when she was older--things not intended for her ears. She told of her mother and aunt going to market to get the ingredients for a special meal. Catrin did not know what they had been celebrating. Whatever it was, it no longer mattered.

She told of the glorious meal, some of which she remembered for herself. She recalled how excited her mother had been to let her try a sweet bun, but Catrin had not liked the taste and spat out the only bite she took. She remembered everyone else laughing while they enjoyed their buns; it was a memory that still stung, which surprised Catrin.

When she began to describe the symptoms her aunt and mother developed, Mother Gwendolin went pale and sat with her hand over her mouth, but she let Catrin finish her description. By the time Catrin finished telling the details she had overheard from her father and Benjin over the years, Mother Gwendolin had tears in her eyes and she looked as if she would be ill. The usually serene woman appeared absolutely stricken, and she let out an awful wail. Catrin watched in confusion as she writhed in anguish.

"Oh, Catrin," she sobbed, pounding the soil with her fists. "I'm sorry. I'm so very sorry. I could have saved them; I should have. How could I have been so selfish and blind?"

Chapter 12

In the days beyond her coming, echoes of the past shall peal like thunder.
--Prophet Herodamus as translated by Brother Jamison, Cathuran monk

* * *

"This challenge will be extra difficult," Benjin said. "I told the merchants you would be coming, and I purchased the goods you are going to steal. The purpose is to test your ability to move with stealth. If any of the merchants see you take anything, then I will lose my wager with them. You don't want me to lose my wager, do you?"

"I wouldn't bet on it," Chase said, looking over the list: One red pepper, one loaf of apple bread, and three balls of netted cheese. "No problem. I'll be back soon."

"Good luck," Benjin said.

Though he didn't need stealth to approach the market, Chase kept himself hidden and watched what everyone around was doing. When he saw the vegetable vendor, he settled in for a good look. The vendor was a young man who seemed to be looking everywhere at once. He stood right behind the display of red peppers, ready to fend off a would-be thief.

For a while, Chase just watched. Then he saw an opportunity. Two beautiful girls were walking toward the shop. When the vendor's head was turned, Chase darted across the narrow street and approached from the opposite direction as the girls.

"Good day, ladies," the man said, and that was all the time Chase needed. Quickly and quietly, he reached out and grabbed a single red pepper. When the vendor looked back, Chase was already seeking the next item on his list.

While hiding in a darkened alley, he spotted a young boy playing with a ball and stick. "Ho there, young man," Chase said. "I'll give you a copper to ask the baker a bunch of questions."

"I can do that."

Chase smiled, handed the boy a copper, and slid into the shadows, one step closer to his loaf of apple bread.

* * *

Confused, Catrin moved to Mother Gwendolin's side and tried to console her. From the looks the other monks were exchanging, they were as confused as she was. Mother Gwendolin took several deep breaths and gradually regained her composure. A young monk approached with jars of water, and Mother Gwendolin drank deeply when Catrin offered one to her. Catrin could barely stand the suspense, but she respected Mother Gwendolin and gave her time to calm herself.

"I'm sorry, Catrin," Mother Gwendolin said after another deep breath. "Your mother and aunt were poisoned. They were given a deadly overdose of mother's root, and I believe you were also a target, for mother's root only affects females."

Catrin was stunned. Her father and Benjin had always believed there had been some sort of foul deed involved with her mother's and aunt's deaths, but it had never felt real to Catrin. Now that Mother Gwendolin confirmed their suspicions, Catrin felt a deep, burning anger rise from the depths of her being. She had suppressed it for so long, uncertain it was warranted, but now the justification existed. She balled her hands into fists and wished she had something to punch, wanting very much to vent the searing fury before it consumed her.

"I wasn't certain at first," Mother Gwendolin said, breaking the heavy silence, "but you described every symptom of a mother's root overdose, and the sweet buns would have made a perfect vessel. Mother's root has a sickeningly sweet taste that could be masked with honey or sugar and become almost undetectable. Had you eaten your sweet bun, you would most likely be dead. And were it not for my envy, your mother and aunt would most likely be alive." Catrin was taken aback by the admission and waited silently for an explanation.

"When I met Benjin, he was trying to make his way back to Endland after parting company with your mother and father. He was so handsome, honorable, and in so much pain. I was drawn to him, and I admit I fell in love with him," she continued, looking embarrassed. "Benjin was smitten with your mother, and his heart was broken, but I didn't see it--didn't want to see it. I convinced myself he would fall in love with me and we would be happy together. We both had a love for herb lore, and we spent days discussing various rare plants and roots, but he did not fall in love with me. He didn't even seem to see me as a woman. I was jealous and hurt, which made me most uncharitable.

"During our last days together, Benjin asked me to help him transcribe my notes on several rare herbs of which he had no previous knowledge. I remember it clearly, though I wish I didn't. I was angry and didn't want to help him. I copied the section on mother's root, and I remember omitting the information on the effects of an overdose simply because I didn't feel like doing it. I included the information that warned against overdoses and left it at that. Now I see how high the price of my envy was. I would change it all if I could. I'm so sorry."

Catrin tried to find words to absolve Mother Gwendolin of guilt, but she found none. Instead, she gave her a hug, and they cried together for a while. Mother Gwendolin regained her composure and seemed to realize it was pointless to torture herself.

"I will send Benjin an invitation to meet with us this evening. There is nothing we can do about it now, but he deserves to know the truth," she said.

At that same moment, another young monk approached. "Many pardons, Mother, but Brother Vaughn asked me to come right away if any birds returned. These just came in from Drascha Stone," he said, bowing, and he presented several small, rolled pieces of parchment. She received them with a sad smile, her cheeks still shining with tears.

While Mother Gwendolin read, Brother Vaughn proudly explained their system of using pigeons to send messages between holds. He said several monks from each hold would travel to the other holds during the warm months, and they would carry many birds with them. The birds could then be released at any time to carry messages quickly back to their home hold. It was not a perfect system, he said, and messages were often lost. Important messages were sent with multiple birds, and any urgent messages received by one hold were forwarded to every other hold upon receipt. This, he said, helped to ensure that no Cathuran stronghold would ever be completely isolated from the others.

Mother Gwendolin looked up from the messages and handed one to Brother Vaughn. "I think this will be of most interest to you. It would appear a landslide in southern Faulk has uncovered the skeletal remains of a giant winged beast. The message indicates the beast would have been larger than a warship--incredible," she said. "There is also word of Zjhon troop movements. Several large detachments are converging near the northern tip of the Inland Sea in Lankland. I suspect they will be bound for Ohmahold by the spring melt. It would appear the Zjhon have reason to believe Catrin is here."

The news gave Catrin a cold feeling in her stomach. Now Ohmahold would be subjected to a siege simply because she was there, much as the Godfist suffered because of her. She tried not to castigate herself, knowing, deep in her heart, it was not her fault, but that failed to lessen her anguish. It was difficult to sit near Brother Vaughn, who could barely contain his excitement. The discovery of the winged beast clearly had his imagination running wild, and she tried to draw from his enthusiasm rather than dampen it with her melodrama.

"Do not be overly concerned," Mother Gwendolin said, sensing her thoughts. "Ohmahold is well defended and well provisioned. We can be completely self-sufficient in the event of a siege, and the Zjhon will have to battle the Wastes. When they launched their attack on the Godfist, they sent nearly two-thirds of their strength, and now they are left with insufficient troops to hold lands only recently conquered. I'm told the armies are now conscripting young women into service. These nations have already lost most of their working-age men, and now the Zjhon are sapping them of young women as well. The rural farmers have been the hardest hit. The Zjhon come unexpectedly, and the farmers have been ill prepared to defend themselves. The Zjhon take their young folk and livestock, and they make notes of any small children, so they can return for them later.

"In the meantime, the elderly and the very young are left with all of the work of growing food and caring for what remains of their livestock. The Greatland is on the cusp of famine and a full-scale revolution. I fear there are dark days ahead of us, and there is little we can do to stop it."

"I must accept the things I cannot change and focus on what I can do, I suppose," Catrin said, trying to find some escape from the futility. She glanced at Sister Hanna, who had not said a word since their introduction. "Sister Hanna, perhaps there is something you can help me with. I've been trying to translate a phrase from High Script. Do you know what Om'Sa means?" she asked.

Sister Hanna appeared impressed that Catrin would attempt to translate High Script. "I've seen that phrase only once in all my studies, and that was in one of the oldest texts we have. High Script evolved over the centuries, and the earliest versions are the most difficult to translate. From the context in which I saw the phrase, I interpreted it to mean *departure* or *exodus of the first men.* I cannot be certain my translation is correct, for phrases in early High Script can have many meanings, depending on the order of the words and their context, which makes the translation more art than science. In what context, may I ask, did you see this phrase?"

"Om'Sa is the name of a book that was given to me. It's very old, and I could not translate much of it. It's in my room at the First Inn, perhaps we could ask Benjin to bring it with him this evening," Catrin said, and Sister Hanna seemed genuinely excited about the prospect.

Mother Gwendolin added the request to her missive and sent the young monk to deliver the message.

"I know this has been a trying day for you, Catrin, and for me as well, but I sense events are beginning to accelerate. I'm sorry to bring this up, but I think it will be important for you to understand the nature and properties of noonstone,"

Mother Gwendolin said, and Catrin wondered what noonstone was.

"From what we know, the fish figurine you found, Imeteri's Fish, was carved from noonstone. Noonstone is very rare, and as you found, it can be used to store a finite amount of Istra's energy. In truth, noonstones are actually crystals that only form under the most rare circumstances. The old texts say they only form during the Istran noon, when thousands of comets can be seen in the skies at any given time. Even then, it is written that they only form under deep salt water and only when the wind is blowing east."

Catrin found it hard to imagine anything could be so rare, and again she felt the sting of having destroyed Imeteri's Fish. "How did the ancients find and retrieve the crystals if they were under deep water?"

"We don't know," Mother Gwendolin admitted. "While that remains a mystery, there are some things I do know. Noonstone is clear and shiny when it is fully charged, and it becomes chalky and porous when its store of energy has been depleted. When energy is drawn from the stone, it grows warm to the touch, and if you draw too much energy too fast, then it will get hot. If you continue to draw upon a depleted stone, it will eventually disintegrate, and the crumbled remains will no longer be viable. The stone will be destroyed."

Catrin nodded in acceptance. Much of what Mother Gwendolin said confirmed what she had deduced on her own--only too late. It was good to have the information confirmed, but Catrin doubted she would ever find another noonstone, which made the discussion seem pointless.

"What is Istra? Is she a goddess or a bunch of rocks in the sky?" Catrin asked, partially in an attempt to change the subject.

Mother Gwendolin laughed and shook her head. "You've a talent for asking questions that are nearly impossible to answer," she said. "Again, understand that this is my opinion. I believe the ancient peoples had no way to explain heavenly bodies, so they made up stories of gods and goddesses to define the unknown. Istra was their personification of the comet storm that lasted for over a hundred and fifty years. And comets are not big rocks in the sky; those are called *asteroids*. We believe comets are made of ice and they radiate their own energy. It is this energy you feel, much like you feel the warmth of the sun.

"If you explore ancient legends and stories of the gods and goddesses, you will find all the major heavenly bodies represented in some way or another. The sun is known as Vestra, the periodic comet storm is known as Istra, and the moon is known as the Dead God, father of the gods and goddesses, who was said to have been killed by his children. Groups of stars were given names and attributed grand deeds. It was even believed that great kings and heroes would become chains of stars upon their deaths. I believe the comet storm is a very natural occurrence, and some of our order have even hypothesized that comets may have been the very source of life itself. If comets are truly made of ice, then it could have been a comet that collided with Godsland and provided her oceans."

Catrin watched as her simple world of gods and goddesses dissolved into a highly complex universe of endless possibilities. If the gods did not really exist, at least in the form of omniscient super-beings, then who decided fate? Could life possibly be nothing more than a series of random occurrences? The evidence pointed toward something even grander than predestination and far more logical than random chaos. Life seemed to consist of many patterns and appeared to follow certain rules. The rules allow for a certain amount of predictability, whereas the complexity of the interacting forces provide entropy, resulting in a constantly changing universe based on orderly precepts--order within chaos.

The thoughts were as confusing to Catrin as they were revealing, and she had a difficult time coming to terms with the multitude of possibilities. She sat quietly for a time, simply allowing her thoughts to flow.

Mother Gwendolin must have sensed that she was overwhelmed because she adjourned their meeting for the day. In addition, the afternoon shadows had grown long, and they needed to get back to the Outer Sanctuary to meet with Benjin. The other monks bade Catrin and Mother

139

Gwendolin a good evening and returned to their own tasks, and Catrin followed Mother Gwendolin back to the Outer Sanctuary.

When they arrived at one of the private dining rooms, they found Benjin already seated and in the middle of a glass of wine. Catrin's waxed leather bookcase sat on the table. Mother Gwendolin left Benjin and Catrin in privacy for a while.

"How are the others faring?" Catrin asked and was relieved to see him smile.

"Better than I would have anticipated, which is a blessing; it could have been a very long winter. Instead, Osbourne has taken up glassmaking and has really shown some promise. Milo seems truly thrilled to have an apprentice. Gustad has taken Strom under his wing, and I think he might be the father figure the boy needed. Strom has already proven himself a capable smith under Gustad's instruction, and I foresee a new future ahead of him. Vertook is in his absolute glory. He's managed to get Brunson to attempt the Arghast method of horse training. Brunson allowed Vertook to select any foal he desired, and then he selected one for himself. Now the two of them are spending every waking moment bonding with the foals. They even sleep in the fields with the animals.

"I've been working with Chase on his swordsmanship. He's quickly becoming a capable fighter, and the exercise is helping his arm heal. We spend a good deal of time discussing strategies and gambits. He's made it quite clear that he's committed to protecting you. He doesn't begrudge the others their pursuits, but he'll have none of it. All his efforts are dedicated to preparation for what may lie ahead." He paused when Mother Gwendolin returned, her face an impassive mask, and Benjin was clearly taken aback by her stark visage. Catrin sat in quiet suspense, trying to decide if she should leave the two in privacy, but she could not make herself move.

"Benjin, I have wronged you, and I am very sorry," Mother Gwendolin began. "I'll put this as kindly as I can, but there is no easy way to tell you. When we first met, I fell in love with you, and I was envious of your feelings for Elsa.

140

You pined after her when I was right there for the taking."
She stopped a moment when she saw the look of shock on
Benjin's face, which slowly turned to one of comprehension
and shame.

"How could I have been so blind?" he said softly, but
Mother Gwendolin gave him no time to feel guilty.

"Do you remember when you asked me to help you
transcribe my notes?" she asked, and he nodded mutely. "I
was angry and my feelings were hurt, and I did a poor job on
the pages I transcribed. I copied what I considered the most
important things and left out some of the cursory details. My
omission cost you dearly, and again, I'm very sorry. I would
change it if I could," she said, and she handed him a page
from her notes--the page describing mother's root.

He looked baffled at first as he read over the
information he had memorized years ago, but then he came
to the part Mother Gwendolin had not transcribed, the part
that described the symptoms and treatment of an overdose.
His face lost all color, and every muscle in his body seemed
to tense as he read the words that could have saved Elsa and
Willa. Veins stood out on his neck and forehead, and Catrin
thought he might explode. Tears streamed down Mother
Gwendolin's cheeks, and her lip quivered.

Benjin set the parchment down slowly then stood.
Catrin thought he might leave without another word, but
instead he paced slowly around the room, looking like an
angry cat about to seek revenge, his lithe movements
promising a quick death. After some time, his shoulders
hunched as his anger seemed to turn to sadness.

"You must not blame yourself for this, Mother, nor
should I be allowed to blame myself," he said in a voice thick
with emotion. "We are not responsible for their deaths. We
did not murder them. If circumstances had been different,
perhaps I would have been able to save them, perhaps not.
We would have saved them if we could, but we could not."

Mother Gwendolin nodded and wiped the tears from
her cheeks. Then she rushed to hug him. "I'm so sorry," she
whispered through fresh tears.

"I'm sorry as well, Gwen. I never meant to hurt you. I just didn't realize," he replied, but Mother Gwendolin silenced him with a finger on his lips.

"You need not explain. You are already forgiven. Now that we better understand the past, let us deal with the present," she said.

Benjin began pacing again, his hostility returning full force.

"When I find Baker Hollis, there will be justice."

Chapter 13

In the absence of drive and purpose, talent can remain forever undiscovered.
--Vitrius Oliver, sculptor

* * *

The reality of her mother's murder settled in slowly, inexorably, like the measured beat of a chisel being driven into her soul. How could anyone be so wicked? What had her mother and aunt done to deserve such hatred? Deep down, though, other questions haunted her. Was it because of her, because of something she did? Was she to blame for their deaths? Perhaps if she had done something differently, her mother and aunt would still be alive.

Nothing could bring them back; she knew that, but the pain was now fresh, as if the loss had been only yesterday. She wept for the hole in her world, the place they should have filled. Then she felt a feeling of peace wash over her, as if they were safe and happy--and with her. She wondered if it was her imagination that conjured the smell of roses, but then she decided it didn't matter; it brought her joy and absolution.

* * *

Covered in sweat and grime, Strom ran the file along the last tooth of the final gear. Finally, they were ready to assemble his machine, and all he could do was hope it would work. Nagging fears of failure made his stomach ache. Hard work helped keep his mind from worry, and he poured himself into the task. If his boiling machine did not pour glass, then it would not be due to a lack of effort.

Milo hovered nearby, always silent but always watching. He knew they were nearing completion, and Strom thought he might not be able to stand the anticipation any longer.

"I think it's ready to go on the shaft," Gustad said. "You've done an excellent job. Now it's time to put your idea to the test. Are you ready?"

"I'm ready," Strom replied after he secured the final gear in place. With dread, he grabbed the handle and started to crank. Slowly the crucible began to turn. After cranking the crucible back to the upright position, Strom filled it with sand and placed a bowl beneath it. Trying to be as smooth as he could, he cranked the handle and simulated the pour.

"Just a little too fast," Milo said. "It accelerates the pour too soon."

"I can't believe it works at all," Osbourne said.

Strom ignored Osbourne's comment, determined to find a way to slow the initial part of the pour. "What if we cut off the first part of the strap and stitch on something thinner; then it won't accelerate much until it reaches the thick strap," he said.

Milo produced a sack made of strong but thin material, and he cut a length from it. After a few more tests pouring sand, Milo calculated the length of strap to be replaced. Stitching the light material and leather proved to be difficult, but Gustad showed Strom how to use an awl to make holes in the leather.

After a few more test pours, Milo declared the pouring machine ready for a test with real glass. They were running out of sand, and Strom felt the pressure.

When Osbourne pulled the crucible from the furnace, he performed his practiced movements and placed the rod on Strom's machine. When he went to secure the strap, though, the heat was too much, despite his thick, leather gloves. By the time the strap was attached, the glass had already cooled too much.

"Don't despair, young Strom. No one designs machines without flaws; the real challenge is to overcome those flaws. We'll just find a way to fix it and try again. Eventually we will succeed."

"How much sand do we have left?" Osbourne asked.

* * *

The modest room Catrin had been provided within the Inner Sanctuary offered little in the way of distraction. She

144

was glad when Mother Gwendolin arrived, if only for something new to think about.

"I hope the morning has greeted you kindly," Mother Gwendolin said as she led Catrin through a maze of corridors.

"I've had a great deal to consider, but I'm feeling a bit better about things. Thank you."

"I'm sorry to burden you further, but time rushes away from us, and there is much we must learn," Mother Gwendolin said, and Catrin nodded. "Much of the information we have regarding ancient times is isolated and without context, which makes it exceedingly difficult to give any of it credence. But there is something I've benefited from personally, and I would like to share it with you. I think, perhaps, it will help you to see more clearly."

"Please, go on," Catrin said, eager for anything that might give her direction. She felt lost in a sea of critical decisions she wasn't prepared to make.

"It's called a viewing ceremony, and I find it helps me focus when I'm unable to resolve a debate or conflict. Would you like to try?"

"What does it involve--I mean, it's not painful, is it?" Catrin asked, feeling silly, and Mother Gwendolin laughed. Her laugh was like the tinkling of fine chimes, and it set Catrin's heart at ease.

"No, child, it's not painful. The viewing chamber is a very special room with two adjoining chambers. A group of specially trained monks will gather in each of the chambers, and they will perform an ancient melody. It's actually quite enchanting."

"Yes, I think I would like that. Thank you," Catrin said, and she wondered what she was getting herself into. The opportunity was certainly too good to pass up, but the Cathurans had already proven full of surprises, and she wondered what the viewing ceremony would reveal.

When they arrived at their destination, a hallway with three elaborately painted doors, they were greeted by a large gathering of robed and hooded monks standing in silence. Catrin smiled, realizing Mother Gwendolin had assumed she would say yes. With a simple nod, Mother Gwendolin sent

145

the monks to their respective chambers. As they filed through the outer doors that bore images of colorful birds, Mother Gwendolin led Catrin through the center door. This door was painted to resemble the night sky, which Catrin noted contained no comets.

Within the chamber stood a large, thronelike chair that was made of a glossy, umber stone streaked with veins of silver and obsidian. Directly across from it, at eye level, was a round hole in the stone wall, beyond which lay open sky. On either side of the chair were twisted orifices that presumably led to the outer chambers where the monks awaited. Mother Gwendolin led her to the seat. Catrin climbed atop the cold, hard stone, doubting she would be able to get comfortable enough to meditate.

"Try to clear your mind of all things. The old writings say, 'Ride the vibrations and you will be free.' I don't think I've ever achieved the desired effect, but it has been helpful nonetheless. When you feel you are finished, just ring this bell," Mother Gwendolin said, and she produced a delicate pewter bell from her robes. It bore the figure of a fairy clinging to the bell, and its ring seemed impossibly loud and clear. Catrin placed the bell on the arm of the throne.

Icy wind gusted through the opening in the wall, and Catrin shivered, wishing she had worn something more substantial than her leather jacket over a homespun top and leggings. Removing the heavy shawl from her shoulders, Mother Gwendolin wrapped it around Catrin with a benevolent smile.

Pulling the shawl tighter, Catrin soaked in its warmth.

"I will leave you now. May you find that which you seek," Mother Gwendolin said, and she left the room, shutting the door behind herself.

The melody drifted to Catrin slowly as she sorted her thoughts and sought her center. A different cadence and tone came from each side, but they merged into seamless harmony--not the disjointed noise of two independent groups, but intentional and purposeful diversification. The two dissimilar parts formed a perfect whole. Drifting on the music, she let it carry her from her burdens.

146

As she let her spirit float, the drums began. Starting softly, they grew to a pounding crescendo, resonating in a way that seemed impossible, and Catrin could feel them more acutely than she could hear them. The thunder of them rattled the foundation of her being and seemed to shake loose the dust and clutter from her soul. It was as if she were shedding a dead skin, and she experienced herself as a wave of energy rather than her physical form. It was glorious and terrifying.

Despite the exultation of these new feelings, she grew frustrated. Surely some revelation should have come to her by now, some inkling of what path she should take. But the ecstasy was void of insight, and she felt as if she were missing something critical, something just out of reach. Concentrating, she squeezed her eyes shut but still struggled in vain. After numerous attempts, she relented, her will spent.

With a forlorn sigh, she resolved to ring the bell, but as she leaned back, too fast, the back of her head smacked against the unyielding stone with a hollow *thunk*. Her jaw dropped and her eyes flew open with the shock of pain. Her vision focused on the sky beyond the opening in the wall. It was beautiful and inviting, and in her next breath, she was soaring through it.

Her awareness flew among the clouds, and she reveled in the glory of existence for a time, but the strangeness made her wary. She wondered at her lack of form and realized a silvery thread of energy trailed her, like a strand of gossamer leading back to her physical vessel. The confining husk that usually held her awaited in the viewing chamber. She could feel the connection, and she clung to it. Though she enjoyed the invigorating freedom, she knew she would need to return to her prison of flesh; she would be lost without it.

Lost.

Like the sudden realization that one is falling, Catrin snapped to her senses and realized she had no idea where she was. Her consciousness soared across the heavens with alarming speed, the land sliding away beneath her. Pristine snow gave way to a brilliant display of late fall colors. The coastline of what Catrin guessed was the Inland Sea came

147

into view, and she soared closer, changing course by the sheer force of her will. The rocky coast was breathtaking from above. Sunlight danced off the sea, and the land rose in sharp contrast, a myriad of details and textures.

Though she was tempted to orient herself from what she remembered of the maps and where the Inland Sea was, she realized it was too risky; she needed some confirmation. With trepidation, she soared over the waves, hoping she would not get lost over endless seas. Lulled by the monotony of the homogenous waves, Catrin felt herself being drawn into a strange trancelike state, and she fought to keep her concentration.

When rocks jutted from the waters below her, Catrin felt a thrill of expectation, and when a smooth and sandy coastline materialized in the hazy distance, she soared with confidence. Now she was almost certain she was somewhere over Faulk, and she prepared to find her way back to Ohmahold, but a curious sight drew her attention. Like a trail of ants, a line of people snaked along the coast and through the plains, and it was difficult at first to determine which way they moved. South, Catrin decided.

Intrigued by the masses, her curiosity won out over her desire to return to her body, and she flew along, letting the trail of humanity guide her until she came upon a place crawling with activity. Devastation greeted the eye; it looked as if the side of a mountain had fallen onto the plains, and the mass of its rubble could obscure entire towns. Rich, brown soil, newly exposed to the sun, looked like a gaping wound on the land, and as Catrin looked closer, she saw a thin line of people climbing toward an area framed with fallen timber. The obviously man-made fortifications stood out in stark contrast to nature, even in its disorder.

Willing herself closer, she hovered above the odd structure. It was not tall; in fact, it seemed only to form a stable platform. At its center, though, lay the partially exposed skeletal remains of a giant creature. Catrin became excited when she realized this was the beast the monks had reported, and she tried to commit as many details as possible to memory for the sake of Brother Vaughn.

It seemed odd that there were no workers busy uncovering the rest of the beast, and she looked, once again, at the line of people. They continued past the man-made plateau, as if the ancient remains were of no interest. They wound around the mountain to the opposite face. The southern face was nearly whole, with one notable exception. Nearly halfway to its peak, a large section of rock had been torn asunder, leaving a gaping chasm. An eerie glow emanated from the chasm, and it was there the throng congregated, their faces reflecting the ominous light.

Fear and uncertainty crawled across Catrin's consciousness, and she could almost feel the hairs on her physical body rise. A faint urging called her back to her body, but she pulled away, needing to see the source of the bizarre light. She hovered closer to the chasm, past the enraptured faces, until she was directly above it. There, staring back at her was the face of a goddess, larger than a giant and throbbing with inner light. The sight shocked her, and for a few moments, she wondered what it could possibly be. When the realization came, it blotted out all thought and all other possibilities. It left no room for doubt or conjecture; it was as certain as the sunrise.

It was one of the Statues of Terhilian, the bane of humanity.

Cold realization after cold realization slammed into her consciousness, and she reeled in horror, suddenly wishing she had been more attentive during her lessons. Before her was the greatest threat to ever face her world, and it looked as if the Zjhon were determined to exhume it. If what she had been taught was true, the statue would charge in the light of Istra and Vestra; then it would detonate. She did not know what the scale of the explosion would be, but the vision her mind created made her quail. A deceitful weapon, left over from a war long past, once again threatened all life on Godsland.

A strange wrongness floated to Catrin along the thread of energy that led back to her body. It felt of worry, anxiety, and mostly fatigue. With a final glance at the face of Istra and the bones of the beast, she stored as many details as she could then started her retreat. Intent on returning with all due haste, she raced along her thread. It was taut and straight as the path of an arrow, and she let the tension of it guide her.

The resonance of the melody changed suddenly, and her thread of energy wavered and went slack. It was a frightening sensation, but it lasted only a moment before the harmony became strong once again--different, but strong. With renewed vigor, she pulled herself along, the land rushing away beneath her. Once she moved back to the east side of the Inland Sea, she soared north.

Giggle.

Catrin cast about her, trying to locate the source of the strange, disembodied voice when it sounded again.

Giggle.

This time Catrin sensed the direction the noise came from, and she scanned with her senses. A male energy, full of mischief and humor, soared alongside her. She could not see anything to indicate the presence, but she could feel it, taunting her, constantly flitting away from her scrutiny.

Consumed by her desire to return to Ohmahold, Catrin tried to ignore the entity and continued watching the horizon, but the land seemed to crawl past her now, as if she were flying through mud.

The impish presence followed her, and she felt a change come over it: shame, grief, regret, and anger all flowed freely. The feelings struck her, and she felt pity. No one should have to feel so much pain without consolation, and that was the prevailing undercurrent: *No one cares. No one will comfort me. No one loves me. I am no one.*

It was painful, even from the outside, and Catrin changed her approach. She poured love and understanding toward the wayward energy, and it responded to her with disbelief, but she continued to convey kindness and caring.

Confusion, helplessness, and a deep wave of regret slammed into Catrin. She felt as if the entity were resisting someone--not her, it was someone else. She could feel the presence by proxy, through the reactions of the anonymous energy. The reactions were childlike, and Catrin suddenly realized she was dealing with a young energy, one that was being coerced. She decided anonymity was a barrier that hampered communication, but when she asked for a name, she received shame and grief in return--no name.

Catrin tried to understand how it would feel to have no name, and she was overcome with compassion. Everyone deserved a name, and she was determined to name the energy, to give him something to hold on to, something around which he could build his own identity. A name was more than a label or moniker. It was the center of one's perception of one's self. It was indelible and, once given, could never be taken away. All of this, she conveyed while searching for the right name.

Prios. A name of power, of that Catrin was certain. She wasn't certain it had any true meaning, but to her, it meant strong of heart. She conveyed this as best she could, and the response she received was one of great honor, but it was short lived.

Pain. Fear. Regret.

Confusion washed over Catrin, but now it was her own. The world seemed to twist and veer beneath her, and the link to her body went slack. In an instant, it became tangled and knotted, and she tumbled out of control. Panic clutched her, and she could feel the wrongness in her tangled lifeline. Prios battered her with energy, and whenever she seemed to have righted herself, he sent her spinning again. Light and dark fluctuated around her, as if the sun and moon had suddenly sped up, and she was helpless to stop it.

In a desperate attempt to dissuade him, she sent forth the mental image of her mother and, more generally, the feeling of unconditional love--the feeling she got when she delved into her earliest memories: mother, safety, warmth, caring, all wrapped up in single-minded intent.

Searing pain. Loss. Regret.

The feelings pummeled her until she relented, and she realized that Prios had relented as well. He was gone, no trace of his energy remained, but the damage was done. Catrin had no idea where she was or how to find her way back. To make matters worse, she sensed pain from her physical body and suddenly knew she was near death. If she did not get back soon, she would never be able to return. It was not just a feeling she had; she could almost hear someone shouting the words at her, repeatedly, like a mantra.

Scanning the landscape below, she saw no snow, only brownish farmland, and she guessed she was still in the south. A glimpse of the sun gave her a bearing on direction as it set at its normal, inexorable pace. She moved north with all the speed she could muster, but the tangle of energy still connected to her body slowed her even as it grew weaker. Snow appeared on the ground below, and her hope was renewed.

When the northern coast of the Greatland loomed on the horizon, she urgently turned east. Mountains pierced the clouds ahead, and she could almost feel the closeness of her body as it called to her in its final throes of life. She felt herself begin to waver and focused all the energy that remained in her. The vibrations took on new intensity, as if the monks knew she was preparing one final attempt to return.

Soaring toward the mountains, she moved faster, now guided by the pain and tingling of her physical form. She was close, and the closer she drew, the more intensely she felt the discomfort. It was strange to seek out pain when her instinct was to avoid it, but it was preferable to the encroaching numbness. In this case, pain meant life, and she hurtled toward it. Cold stone stood before her, an impenetrable barrier, but she passed through it without the slightest lessening of speed. It granted her passage without complaint.

Solid rock gave way to a labyrinth of corridors and rooms, both natural and man-made. Catrin paid them little mind as she struggled to close the distance separating herself from her dying body. Only when she entered a vacuous hall, filled with relics and tomes from a time long past, did she even notice her surroundings, and the myriad of curious items within the hall impressed themselves upon her mind.

The next instant brought relief as she pierced the walls of the viewing chamber. Her body sat in ashen stillness upon the stone seat, and even as she drew close, it took on a bluish hue. Her consciousness slammed into her physical form with jarring impact, and she struggled to orient herself, questing for the remembrance of her form. Her body no longer seemed to fit, as if it could not contain her, but she forced herself into its confines.

She had expected great amounts of pain, but her limbs were leaden, and she was unable to move. Numbness nearly claimed her, and she made herself draw a deep breath; it became more of a choke, but she did begin to breathe again. Her vision was clouded and dark, and though she noticed shadowy forms moving around her, she could identify no one. Sounds collided with her senses, but she could make sense of none of it. The only thing that mattered in the world, at that moment, was breathing. With each breath, the tingling in her flesh grew, and the pain charged in behind it.

Catrin welcomed the pain; she embraced it. Cramps, burning agony, and sharp pangs were all wonderful and delicious. She felt them acutely and relished them. As her breathing grew to a steady rhythm, her senses returned, her eyes focused, and she was stunned to see Benjin, his head completely shaved. He knelt before her with tears in his eyes. He must have sensed her return to cognizance because he rushed forward to hug her.

"Thank the gods you've come back," he whispered, and Catrin returned his hug with her unwieldy arms. She tried to speak, but her throat was so parched that she feared it would crack apart. Mother Gwendolin appeared with a mug of water. She looked horrible, as if she were afflicted with some ghastly illness. Her eyes were sunken; her skin was nearly as ashen as Catrin's, but a weary smile crossed her face. She handed Catrin the mug and waited for her to drink.

Catrin's hands shook as she tipped the mug, and sweet water dribbled over her lips. There was only a small amount in the mug, but it was like a cup of pure life, and it rejuvenated her as it moistened her dehydrated throat. She handed the drained mug to Mother Gwendolin and wordlessly begged for more. Another mug was handed to her, and it contained little more than the first, but Catrin was glad to have it.

"You must rest now," Mother Gwendolin said, but her voice cracked and sounded raw.

Catrin realized for the first time that she was wrapped in warm blankets. Benjin scooped her up, blankets and all, as if she were little more than a fallen leaf. Mother Gwendolin guided him to a sleeping room, and he gently laid her down on the bedding. Once he was certain she was comfortable, he retrieved another mug of water from Mother Gwendolin, into which he stirred a pinch of brown powder.

"Drink this. It'll help you rest."

"Not yet. I have dire news," Catrin croaked as she sat up, but Benjin forced her back down with only a slight push of his finger. He placed the mug in her hands and crossed his arms over his chest. "Whatever it is, it can wait until morning."

Too weak to argue, Catrin drained the mug for the sake of her thirst as much as anything else. Within moments, she fell into a deep sleep, haunted by visions of a glowing face.

Chapter 14

Fanaticism is a plague. It threatens the fabric of our world and must be stopped regardless of the cost.
--Von of the Elsics

* * *

"You gave us quite a scare, young lady," Mother Gwendolin croaked, wagging her finger at Catrin in a good-natured way. "Please, tell me of your experience. The unknown is driving me to distraction."

"How long was I gone?" Catrin asked, her own voice still rough and grating.

"Fourteen days."

Fourteen days! Catrin was stunned. Her journey had felt like little more than an afternoon jaunt, but then she recalled the cycles of light and dark during Prios's attack, and she surmised that he had somehow affected her perception of time. She didn't hate him for it, convinced he had been coerced, but she also realized she was lucky to have survived. After weeks of fasting, her body had been in no condition to sustain her.

"We had to train every monk available to keep up the ritual chanting, and there's not a clear voice left in the hold. Benjin insisted upon being at your side, and he underwent a condensed version of the purification ritual. He never slept; he just sat with you and held your hand. We were worried beyond reason, and I fear he blames me for endangering you. He sleeps now, though he'll be wroth with me when he wakes. I slipped a bit of sedative into his tea."

Guilt stabbed at Catrin, and she resolved herself to set Benjin straight about a few things when she saw him next, but she was so weary. Her journey had taken its toll, and she wasn't certain she would ever be whole again; she felt disconnected and isolated. She seemed more of a spectator than a participant in life, tucked away in her bed, and she yearned to move about, but her body resisted her attempts.

"The journey was dangerous," Catrin said after a moment's consideration. "But it was made disastrous by means of outside interference. Someone was coerced into interfering with my journey. I know it; I could feel it. You did not place me in danger. My enemies did that. Regardless, I bear momentous news. One of the Statues of Terhilian has been found and is being excavated."

Her words seemed to ring Mother Gwendolin's reality like a bell. She sat in stunned silence, unable to formulate a response.

"I followed a trail of pilgrims to their destination, and there I found the bones of the great beast, but it was the exposed face of Istra, on the opposite side of the mountain, that drew the throng. I looked upon her, and she shone back at me. I cannot say for certain what others saw, only my perception of it."

Tears slid down Mother Gwendolin's tired face, and her breath shuddered when she made to speak. "This is the worst possible news, and it comes on the heels of other ill tidings. General Dempsy has returned from the Godfist with only three of his ships. He's spreading a wild tale of destruction that lays total blame at your feet. He claims you destroyed his armies in cold blood, single-handedly, leaving a trail of gore wherever you trod. He has joined with the forces gathering to assault Ohmahold, and we have word they are constructing monstrous siege engines."

General Dempsy was the man who led the siege on the Godfist. Now she had a name, which granted her power, and Catrin stored the information away.

"The Greatland is on the verge of widespread famine and starvation," Mother Gwendolin continued. "Drought and the lack of capable hands threaten to leave thousands without food. The armies have conscripted the majority of able-bodied persons along with the majority of the livestock, and the seeds of war are all that have been sown. Our civilization is on a path to destruction, and events are moving faster than anyone could have foreseen. And now a Statue of Terhilian enters the fray. It is hard to believe, but I do believe you. If you say you have seen the face of Istra, I believe you. I just have no idea what to do about it."

Catrin could empathize. The news was all very overwhelming, and she could find no suitable course of action to take. Depression settled on her, and she shook herself physically to dislodge it. "I need to get out of this bed."

"I suppose we could walk a bit if you are feeling well enough, but we should not go too far."

Sudden flashes of memory returned, images of tomes and artifacts obfuscated by a thick layer of dust. Catrin recalled her frantic return and the wondrous sight that had caught her attention. "I don't mean to pry, but are you aware of a large hall, within Ohmahold, that is filled with books, swords, and a variety of oddities covered in dust?" she asked.

"I'm not aware of any such hall. How did you come to know of it? There is no place in this hold that is allowed to accumulate so much dust."

"When I was returning from the south, the strange presence confused me and I was lost. I came back into Ohmahold through the stone, and during my journey, I passed through the hall. I think I could find it."

Curiosity seemed to overcome Mother Gwendolin's reluctance to tax Catrin's strength, but not without due consideration. "Are you certain you feel strong enough? Is it far?"

"I want to try. I'm not certain how far it is, but I'll let you know if I get too tired." In truth, she was already weary, but her own curiosity drove her onward. She could sleep when she knew what the mysterious room actually contained. Perhaps some lost volume held the answers to her questions. She let her instincts and her memories guide her to the area she had passed through. The trail led them to the maze that secured the entrance of the Inner Sanctuary. "It's in there."

"Are you certain? We've mapped the entire labyrinth, and only the halls that bear the death symbols remain unexplored. You see, the ancients left us a code that we use to identify the safe passages within the labyrinth, and the defensive halls are marked with specific patterns of symbols."

"It's this way," Catrin said as she grabbed a lantern and led the way into the maze. She followed her instincts, and Mother Gwendolin confirmed the safety of every corridor before they entered it. Letting Mother Gwendolin concentrate on remembering where they were, Catrin concentrated on where they were going.

"I've never walked this part of the maze before. This passage is almost never used to my knowledge, for it leads nowhere. There are only death passages leading from it," Mother Gwendolin said, but Catrin walked in anyway. This was the passage, every bit of instinct and guidance she had pointed just beyond it. When they reached a four-way junction, Catrin stopped, and Mother Gwendolin carefully inspected the markings. Catrin was not certain which of the decorations were significant and which were frivolous.

"All these corridors are death chambers. We can go no farther this way."

Catrin used her senses to peer ahead. The corridor that stood directly across from her was the one; she knew it. "What exactly are the death chambers?" she asked.

"We don't know every variation, but they are filled with traps, many triggered by pressure plates. Some will crush you under a pile of rock, while others impale their victims on sharpened stakes. None has been triggered in my lifetime, and I'm uncertain what exactly lies down that corridor." Driven by an impulse, Catrin strode into the hall, and Mother Gwendolin drew a sharp intake of breath.

Nothing happened.

Catrin's steps did not falter, and she did not hesitate. She let her confidence carry her farther along the hall, and still nothing happened.

Mother Gwendolin conquered her own fears and joined her. She took Catrin's hand and held it in her own. "You are very brave. Are you certain you wish to go deeper? We could both die."

"I'm willing to risk my life. I believe I'm right, but I'll not ask you to risk yours, nor can I ask another to go in my stead. This is mine to do."

"And I have faith in you. I believe in you, and I'll walk beside you in this," Mother Gwendolin said, tightening her grip on Catrin's hand. With a squeeze in return, Catrin strode ahead. A small part of her mind warned against arrogance, but she knew she was safe; this was the way. The two walked, hand in hand, in the lamplight, and when they reached a corner, they each began to breathe again. Resting for a moment, they prepared themselves for what lay ahead. Then they turned the corner together.

Awaiting them was a sight beyond even Catrin's expectations, her memories accounting for only a small fraction of what she saw before her. Row upon row of shelves stood in ranks, lined with hide-bound tomes. Racks of weapons lined the walls, and enormous tapestries hung high above. Fantastically complex devices filled a large corner of the hall, and the sight of them sparked the imagination: Who knew what wondrous purpose they could serve? So much of what she saw was foreign and unidentifiable that it was overwhelming. Mother Gwendolin stood at her side, bereft of words. Her hands were plastered to the sides of her face, and she simply stared in wonder.

The rush of the excitement faded immediately, though, as shouts echoed loudly through the halls and the sound of many booted feet shattered the silence. It was muffled and distorted in the great hall, but its portent was clear: something was very wrong. Mother Gwendolin immediately bolted from the hall and rushed back to the maze. Catrin was close on her heels, her exhaustion banished by fear. When they gained the mighty stair, Mother Gwendolin shouted to those above.

"What is it?"

"Men down in the pastures," someone called back. "Enemy in the hold!"

A chill ran up Catrin's spine, and the words drove her feet. She and Mother Gwendolin pounded up the stair, following a stream of armed men and women. Benjin charged among them, some three turns above her, and still Catrin wondered at his appearance without his hair. He had let it grow for so long, and she felt guilty for getting herself into trouble. Otherwise, she was certain he would not have allowed his head to be shaved.

The effort of the climb and the close quarters, jostling as they climbed, started to wear on Catrin, and she felt light-headed. When they finally reached the upper level, the throng poured onto the plateau and surrounded the highest pasture. In the center of the pasture lay two still forms flanked by two foals that wailed in their mourning.

"Vertook! Brunson!" Catrin shrieked as she ran headlong toward the bodies, her heart pounding. No enemy showed themselves. There was nothing but serenity surrounding the two dead men. When she drew close enough to make out the details, she saw the shafts of arrows protruding from their backs. Bright red fletching caught the light and shone like a beacon of death. The pain in her chest made her wonder if she would die of a broken heart.

The burst of energy she used to get there wore thin, and emotions overwhelmed her. Grief and anger flared high. Deep-seated fears and regrets were merciless in their assault. Leaning to one side, her knees buckled. Mother Gwendolin stepped in front of her and reached out to catch her. Catrin hit the ground hard, and she wondered a moment that Mother Gwendolin had failed to catch her.

Mother Gwendolin stood, frozen, her face locked in a look of extreme shock. The color drained from her face, and a crimson rose bloomed on her smock. She crumbled to the ground in the next instant, and Catrin cried out in horror. A shaft protruded from Mother Gwendolin's back, and the plateau exploded with activity. Two archers had been hidden among high rock formations, but they had revealed themselves to take the shot.

Guards climbed toward them, but one assassin turned and leaped off the cliffs to his death. The other nocked an arrow and drew. Three arrows struck him before he could release, and his shot flew high over Catrin's head. With a scream of agony and frustration, the second assassin fell from the cliff.

Catrin was mired in confusion--everything had happened so fast. Unwilling to believe this was real, she prayed it was all a dream and waited for something to wake her, but nothing did. Rough hands grabbed her and pulled her from the plateau, back into shelter. When her eyes met those of Captain Longarm, tears blurred her vision, and she barely recognized him. He gave her a sad smile.

"I'm sorry for your losses, Lady Catrin, and we'll all grieve Mother Gwendolin, but I must get you to safety. We don't know if there are more men laying in wait, and I'll not take any chances with your life," he said as he guided her to a hall filled with the largest table she'd ever seen. With a highly polished surface, the table looked as if it had been carved in place. Hooded monks already occupied many of the chairs surrounding it, but no one acknowledged Catrin when she arrived.

The mood in the air was appropriately somber, but Catrin found it oppressive. She could not seem to comprehend the day's events. Everything seemed to be happening around her, but she did not feel a part of it. She had no influence on the course of events.

"What was she doing on the plateau?" Sister Velona raged as she entered the hall, her face revealed by her erratic movements, and her tirade broken only by random bouts of sobbing. "How could anyone have been so foolish as to allow her safety to be jeopardized in such a way? Your incompetence has been fatal this time. Boil you all!" News traveled fast around Ohmahold, and those of station soon packed the hall. The gamut of emotions was expressed, shouted, cried, and rehashed.

"To the harpies with the Zjhon and their evil ways! They must be stopped," one man shouted as he pounded his fists on the table.

"Hang those who allowed her to go into harm's way," another demanded, but cooler heads prevailed, and such overreactions were quickly quelled.

Catrin shrank in on herself. The deaths were all because of her. This was all her fault. Ultimately, she could be blamed for much of the problems facing the world--it was a difficult thing to accept. When Benjin arrived, her composure completely fled, and she ran to him. Sobbing into his robes, she let him lead her back to a seat.

When her tears had run their course, she looked up at him; his face was a mask of grim determination. Only the tears that slid down his cheeks gave evidence of his pain and mourning. The meeting came to a sense of order as Brother Vaughn pounded a gavel against the table, and the noise cut off all conversation.

"It is a dark day for us, brethren, but we must maintain our resolve. Two men scaled the cliffs to gain access to Ohmahold. They took the lives of two good men and our beloved Mother. This cannot be changed, and only those who committed the heinous deeds can be held responsible. They stole from us the chance to exact our preferred manner of justice, but in taking their own lives, they did justice. They admitted their guilt and removed themselves from our world."

His words were not joyful, but they kindled reason among those gathered, and some who had been so vocal at first were now abashed and subdued. Catrin leaned on Benjin's shoulder and took whatever comfort he could offer. The pain in her chest had not abated, and the throbbing was impossible to ignore, but she endured as best she could.

"In the event of her passing, Mother Gwendolin requested Sister Velona succeed her. I make the motion to enact the late Mother's wishes. What say you?" Brother Vaughn asked. The response was muted but in unanimous agreement. Sister Velona appeared stunned, as if she had been unaware of Mother Gwendolin's desires, and she was removed from the room to prepare for her ascension. In her absence, Brother Vaughn continued to moderate.

"The Cathuran order has always advocated neutrality in the affairs of the nations, but under these circumstances, we cannot remain indifferent. War is upon us. Lady Catrin's cause is to defeat the Zjhon, and I make the motion that we support her in her quest. What say you?"

Heated debates raged around the table, and Brother Vaughn let the collective sort their opinions and establish their stances before he called them to order.

"What say you?" he asked again, and the motion was approved but with little enthusiasm. Catrin could not blame them. They had suffered a tremendous loss, and none of them had known her for very long. "We all have our own preparations to make for the interment, but I suggest we form committees to handle the basic governing of Ohmahold until after Sister Velona's ascension. What say you?" This was met with almost unanimous agreement, and they proceeded to assign committees and their chairs. Catrin turned to Benjin with uncertainty in her eyes, but he was still unaware of her dire news, and she decided on her own to stand and speak out.

"Brother Vaughn and those of the Cathuran order, I request permission to address the assembly," she said, trying to honor the formalities. She flushed as every eye turned to her; the fact that hoods obscured the eyes and faces made the experience increasingly disconcerting.

"I make the motion to grant Lady Catrin the floor. What say you?" Brother Vaughn intoned, and Catrin was surprised to receive unanimous approval.

"I, too, mourn the loss of Mother Gwendolin. She was kind, and I will always cherish her memory. But I also bear distressing news that I had only just reported before . . ." She trailed off, not wishing to say the words, and she sensed approval. "During my time in the viewing chamber, I found its true purpose. I left my physical body and soared through the heavens." She paused as reactions rippled through the room: disbelief, wonder, distrust, and excitement all within the mixture.

"My journey took me south, where I spotted a line of pilgrims that stretched across the land. When I located their destination, I saw a great landslide and the bones of a mighty beast being excavated. It was not the bones, though, that drew the pilgrims. On the other side of the rockfall, I found a chasm, where the land had been torn apart, and within, I saw the glowing face of Istra. They are exhuming a Statue of Terhilian." Shock and horror radiated through the room, and not a sound was made for some time.

"Von of the Elsics created the statues to trick the Zjhon and the Varics into destroying themselves, and it nearly worked," one hooded figure said, and Catrin thought she recognized the voice of Sister Hanna. "Both nations gathered around what had been described as tokens of peace from the gods. Even after the destruction caused when the statues exploded, the Zjhon continued to believe the statues were truly divine--gifts from the gods themselves. They were convinced the statues weren't responsible for the devastation, rather they blamed it on nonbelievers. They'll parade the most deadly artifact ever created as if it were a

163

trophy, a true sign of their superiority. It seems we find ourselves faced with the same debate that raged nearly three thousand years ago. Are the Statues of Terhilian divine gifts that must be honored and worshipped in order to please god and goddess, or are they gruesome weapons that will release cataclysmic forces once charged?"

Sister Hanna turned to Catrin directly. "You are certain you saw this, are you not? This is not a matter to be taken lightly. You did say the face glowed, did you not?"

Her questions hammered at Catrin's resolve, but she did the best she could to maintain grace in the face of such scrutiny. "I am certain," she said without a trace of doubt. Debate raged in the hall, and Catrin returned to her seat. Benjin cast her a questioning gaze, and she related the tale of her vision journey. He listened intently, and Catrin had to raise her voice above the din.

"Our world has become a very dangerous place indeed," Benjin said when she finished her tale.

"Agreed," Brother Vaughn said as he approached them from behind. "I apologize. I did not mean to impose upon your conversation, but I feel we should meet in private when this meeting has adjourned, which should be shortly. Please remain behind when the others depart." Catrin and Benjin nodded their assent, and Brother Vaughn returned to address the assembly. At the same time, Catrin remembered the hall.

"Brother Vaughn," she said, and he returned to her side. "I nearly forgot in the insanity of this day. I have good news as well."

"Good news would be most welcome on this otherwise lightless day," he said, and Catrin could see how drained he was. She could feel his fatigue and anguish as if it were her own. In many ways, it was. When she told him about a lost hall filled with ancient treasure, a flicker of hope crossed his visage, and he thanked her.

"Brothers and Sisters, a light shines in the darkness; we have been blessed with new hope to face the despair. I've just been informed that Lady Catrin has located a cache of ancient knowledge within Ohmahold. I make the motion that we send a committee to investigate and convene this meeting until the evening meal. What say you?"

Excitement washed over the room but was quickly subdued in the memory of their loss. Nonetheless, it was at least one good omen, and some clung to it. A committee was assigned, and Catrin found herself whisked from the hall. Brother Vaughn led the group, and she spoke to him as they walked, filling him in on the details.

"You walked into a death chamber?" he asked, incredulous.

"It seemed like the right thing to do at the moment," she said under Benjin's accusing glare, but when they reached the hall, she did not hesitate. She marched ahead of the group, despite the many protests. Brother Vaughn and Benjin matched her stride, and she was honored by their display of trust. Only when Brother Vaughn exclaimed, "By the heavens! So much knowledge that has been just beyond our reach," did the rest of the group edge along the hall.

Brother Vaughn visibly resisted the urge to explore and left another monk in charge of the investigation. "Come, let us slip off while the rest are occupied," he said, and Catrin followed him with Benjin on her heels.

Chapter 15

Nothing could be more terrifying than horrors wrought by one's own hand.
--Imeteri, slave

* * *

Brother Vaughn led them to a warm and cozy section of the hold. Thick carpets covered the floors, and lanterns bathed the halls in an inviting glow. Elaborately carved doors were staggered along the halls, and he stopped at one that bore a scene of eagles soaring over a magnificent waterfall. He paid it little mind as he admitted them to his personal apartments, which was an honor, and Catrin recognized it as such.

The walls of his home were covered in paintings and sketches of birds, which were fantastic in their variety and beauty. A partially completed sketch of the violet hummingbird rested on an easel, and Brother Vaughn's talents were obvious; the detail and accuracy was without equal. Shelves and tables were covered in scrolls and sheets of parchment with scribbled notes. Only one of the four chairs around the table was free of scrolls and bound tomes, and Catrin decided to stand rather than disturb the organized clutter. Benjin paced the floor, a fury of emotions plain in his visage. Brother Vaughn seemed to have forgotten they were with him as he searched under various piles of parchment.

"I know they're here somewhere," he said as if he speaking to himself. "Ah, yes, here they are." He held a wooden box that barely filled his palm. It was made of dark, rich wood and had a lustrous finish; gold filigree covered the corners, and the clasp formed the head of a fearsome serpent.

"There are those within our order who spend their entire lives seeking artifacts from antiquity. You have Brother Ramirez to thank for finding, identifying, and preserving these. Though he went to his grave many years ago, I'm sure he would be thrilled to see you have them. Mother Gwendolin planned to give them to you, and she

166

asked me to retrieve them. I deliver them to you now as the fulfillment of one of her final wishes," he said and raised the lid. Light reflected merrily off two fully charged noonstones that lay within. They were much smaller than Imeteri's Fish had been, but now that Catrin knew their value, they seemed large--a treasure.

Catrin accepted the box with trepidation. She did not feel comfortable accepting such a valuable gift, but she did not want to dishonor the wishes of Mother Gwendolin, and she chose to receive the endowment with grace. She would bear the gift along with the memory of Mother Gwendolin, a tribute to her kindness and wisdom.

"It is a precious gift, indeed. I vow to use these only toward the good of the world, and when I have finished my work, I will return them to you. You have my word," Catrin said, and she bound herself to the commitment. Brother Vaughn gave her a smile and a small bow as she tucked the gilded box into her pocket. Just having the stones near her brought comfort and solace, and she would treasure them for as long as she possessed them.

"I'm afraid we must move on to less pleasant subjects," Brother Vaughn said. "I have enough support within our order to help you on your way, but you'll not be allowed to remain at Ohmahold. Please take no insult from this. We Cathurans are not without our own politics, and with our long history, there are long-standing issues at hand. The ascension of Sister Velona will not be a smooth one, and while I fear no attacks from within our order, I don't think you should be here come spring. The armies will be at our doorstep, and there will be no telling what will happen." It was obvious his heart was heavy with sadness and regret.

Catrin reeled. Where would she and her companions go? No refuge awaited them. Nowhere was safe. She couldn't think of any place that would accept her, and a sharp pain pierced her heart. Nowhere was she welcome. Benjin gave her arm a squeeze, and she appreciated his support and calm.

"It would be terribly difficult to remain inconspicuous while traveling with young men," Brother Vaughn continued. "It'll be hard enough to explain why you aren't with the armies. Benjin is old enough that he should be able to appear lame. We do not object, in any way, to Osbourne, Chase, and Strom staying with us. We have no grievances with any of you, and it may be the safest place for them to be," he said.

Catrin was torn and confused. She couldn't imagine them sending her and Benjin out into the snow; it would be as good as sending them to their graves.

"Before you come to any conclusions, there is more," Brother Vaughn said in response to her consternation. "I am violating protocol, but I will do what I feel is right. There are mines that run throughout these mountains, and we recently discovered an ancient complex that stretches for hundreds of miles. It is a perilous journey, but there is one way out that I am familiar with. It's far from pleasant, but I can get you to a place within the virgin forests of Astor. From there, I can try to summon Barabas and hope he sees my signal. It may take some time for him to arrive, but he will guide you through the wilderness."

"Who is Barabas?"

"He's a trusted friend. Otherwise, I find him indescribable. You'll simply have to meet him for yourselves."

"I'll need to speak with my Guardians about this," Catrin said, unsure of what to do, though it seemed she had little choice, having worn out her welcome.

"Yes, of course, I understand. But I'm afraid we have little time. If I am to guide you, we must leave this day. Soon I'll be entrenched in ceremony and ritual. I have but ten days before the rites of ascension begin, and I'll be hard pressed to make it back in time. Please do not delay."

"Thank you. Your kindness and support are greatly appreciated. I'll seek out my Guardians this instant and will return to you as soon as possible."

"I would do more if I could, but I am bound by my duties," he said as Catrin and Benjin departed for the First Inn. Before they closed the door behind themselves, though, he called after them. "Have you any weapons at the guardhouse?"

"Yes. Thank you for reminding me," Catrin replied.

"I'll write you a weapons pass so that you may arm yourselves," he said as he scribbled on a piece of parchment, closing it with his wax seal. "Just give this to the guard, and he will return your weapons. Keep it with you in case any of the guards stop you on your way back."

Catrin and Benjin spoke little during the long walk, but his presence alone was comforting. The uncertainty of her future consumed Catrin's thoughts. She considered Brother Vaughn's words regarding the boys, but she hated the thought of leaving them behind; they had all come so far together. But even if they stayed, at least she would not have to go alone.

Word of the attack preceded them. The streets were empty, and a somber pall hung over the common room at the First Inn. Chase, Strom, and Osbourne sat at a corner table. When Catrin and Benjin entered, they leaped from their chairs and rushed to greet them. Tears flowed freely as they shared their grief along with the joy of seeing one another. Benjin urged them back to the table. They huddled together, and Catrin rattled off the news in a whisper.

"No," Chase said. "I'll not be left behind to hide while you two go off into danger. I'll not hear of it."

"Now, Chase . . ." Benjin said.

"Absolutely not."

Catrin was torn. She didn't want to hurt Chase, but his presence would be a danger to her. A plan began to form in her mind, one that would never work, but at least it was a plan. She left the others to argue while she plotted the path in her mind, and she heard not a word they said. When her mind was set, she interrupted their debate.

"Benjin and I will depart this day. Brother Vaughn will guide us, and we'll make for Faulk. We should be able to blend in with the pilgrims until we reach the statue. I'll destroy the statue, and then we'll continue south to the coast." Chase tried to interrupt her, but she plowed over his efforts. "Chase, your task is most important. You will depart following the ascension ceremonies, when Brother Vaughn is available once again. You will locate us a ship and arrange for it to pick us up on the southern coast of Faulk. Strom and Osbourne will stay here and assist the Cathurans in their ventures until I send word. Agreed?"

"That's the craziest plan I've ever heard," Chase said, and Benjin chastised him with a look. "How are you going to destroy the statue? And once you do, how are you going to escape? And even if you manage to escape, which seems highly unlikely to me, how will you locate the ship along such a large coast?"

"We'll meet you at the most southern and western tip of Faulk, then. The rest I haven't figured out yet, but it is the best plan I have come up with so far."

"You've lost your senses," Chase muttered.

"Actually, I think much of her plan has merit," Benjin countered. "I agree there would be no good way to explain your presence travelling with us. Everyone on the Greatland of your age has already been conscripted. If you walk free, that marks you as either a traitor or deserter. It would seem the task Catrin assigned to you is the most dangerous of them all, but you've trained well for it, and I've faith in you. Catrin and I can travel in disguise. I'll be a lame old man and Catrin my youngest daughter. We can simply tell folks her brothers and sisters were conscripted, and she was left to care for me."

"I still don't like it," Chase said, but he seemed to realize the necessity of their separation.

"Neither do I," Catrin said. "If I had my choice, things would be much different, but they are what they are, and we must do the best we can given the circumstances."

Chase nodded in morose silence. Strom and Osbourne did not object to her forceful requests, and she truly believed they could help the Cathurans in some way. She worried about their safety, but security seemed to have vacated their world, leaving only fear and despair to fill the void.

"It's all so sad," Strom said. "I wish things could go back to the way they were. I don't want you to leave, but I understand. I just hope we really do get word from you someday soon. You do promise to come back for us, don't you?"

"I give you my word. If I'm able, I'll come back for you."

170

"And I give my word as well," Benjin added.

"You take good care of her," Chase said, his voice heavy with emotion as tears rimmed his eyes. He gave Benjin a tight hug and faced Catrin.

"It's a tough world out there, Cat, and I won't be there to grant your kills a quick death. Be strong, take care, and meet me on the shores of Faulk. I'll await you there." He managed to say it all without his voice cracking.

Catrin embraced him. She kissed him on the forehead and promised she would be there; nothing could keep her away.

After she retrieved her staff and her personal items from her room at the inn, she and Benjin left, waving farewell. It was surreal, walking away from the First Inn, intent upon leaving her companions, her Guardians, her friends. It was a painful parting, and despite her promises, she knew she would probably never see any of them again. Chase had been right; her plan was insane, and she didn't expect it to work, but at least she would leave this world doing the best she could. If there were some way she could avert the disastrous threat the Statue of Terhilian posed, then she would have done a great deal for the world. It was a worthy cause and, she supposed, one worth dying for.

"You mean to go through with your plan?" Benjin asked as they huddled against the icy winds.

"I don't know. I have to at least try to destroy the statue before it detonates, which is most likely suicide, but what other course of action could I take and keep a clear conscience?"

"We will just have to deal with the details along the way. We'll find some way to overcome the obstacles, you and I. We always do." His words offered Catrin a small amount of comfort, and she leaned on him as they walked. So many times he had been there for her; she did not know what she would do without him.

Captain Longarm was not in the guardhouse when they arrived, but another guard retrieved their weapons and returned the parchment to them. Benjin handed Catrin her knives and grabbed his own knife and sword. The rest he asked the guard to return to storage, and with that, they departed for the Inner Sanctuary.

Brother Vaughn looked nothing like himself when they returned. He was dressed in leathers with picks and hammers dangling from his belt. He wore a sturdy leather cap and gloves, and he slung a pack over his shoulder as they entered. Two more packs, near to overflowing, sat in a corner. Catrin and Benjin needed no prompting, and they shouldered the packs. Catrin stood with her staff in hand, trying to be confident, but her knees shook. This was perhaps the most dangerous parting yet.

"There is no time to waste. We must leave at once," Brother Vaughn said, but he stopped to flip through a book that contained charts and drawings of the moon.

"I must beg a favor of you," Catrin said. "I have a mission for Chase that requires him to depart after the ascension. Will you guide him?"

"It won't be easy. The rites of ascension are long and will require much of my time. I cannot abandon my responsibilities at such a crucial time, but I will find a way to accomplish it."

Catrin nodded her thanks, aware she was asking a great deal of him, and also knowing he would keep his word regardless of the cost. She was glad he did not downplay the inconvenience; she valued his honesty, even if it did make her feel guilty. It was preferable to pretty lies.

Brother Vaughn led them to the main stairwell, and they descended to its base, where the air was icy and dank. Lanterns had been left for them, and only the light they shed kept the darkness at bay. From his pocket, Brother Vaughn retrieved a small sand clock, which he turned over and put back in his pocket.

The rough-hewn tunnels beneath Ohmahold often intersected with other tunnels and passages. After only a few turns, Catrin was completely lost. Several times, they passed monks working in the mines, using mules to pull cartloads of salt and ore.

"Much of our livestock is born and bred within the mines," Brother Vaughn said. "It saves us the need to hoist the animals, and it also provides a secure food source in the event of a siege. We've water, salt, ore, and, in some cases, light, all within the mining complexes. But until recently, there has only been one way in or out of the mines for the sake of security. Only when the salt miners tunneled into an existing mine did we realize the ancient complex even existed."

"What about the place where we will exit the mines. Is it well hidden?" Benjin asked.

"Extremely," Brother Vaughn replied as he checked his sand clock. "We need to move faster," he said as he strode ahead of them.

Most of the tunnels looked exactly alike, rough-hewn rock supported by wooden buttresses and joists. The wood was treated with creosote and kept in good condition, but Catrin still felt like the mountain might crush her under its weight.

After what seemed like a day of walking, they reached a rough section of tunnel that ended in an oblong breach.

"This shaft leads to the ancient mines, but it is quite a drop to the floor below. Take care when you enter," Brother Vaughn said as he climbed through the opening. Benjin followed, and Catrin heard his low whistle when he reached the floor. She handed her staff down to him, and she dropped through the orifice. The fall was farther than she anticipated, and she landed hard, knocking the breath from her.

The floor on which she lay was cut into geometric patterns, and though covered with grime, they were still a marvel. The tunnel dwarfed those recently mined. The walls were cut smooth and straight, and the ceiling was lost in the darkness. Evenly spaced arches supported the tunnel, and they were carved with images of trees and flowers. Some bore images of wildlife, but no human forms were present. Catrin dusted herself off and turned in a full circle, taking in the majesty of the place.

Brother Vaughn did not give her long to enjoy the sights, though, as he set off at a brisk pace after once again checking his sand clock. The floors were level and the tunnels free of debris, which made for easy traveling. Intersections came and went, but Brother Vaughn gave them scarcely a glance as he passed them. The only indication that he noticed them at all was his mumbled count incremented at each one. When he reached what Catrin thought was the twelfth nearly identical intersection, he turned right.

The turn made Catrin feel they had made progress, and she fooled herself into thinking the journey was near complete. It seemed impossible that the mines could go on much farther, and the monotony of it played tricks with her mind. When Brother Vaughn called for a rest, Catrin had no idea how long they had been walking. Time seemed to lose meaning beneath the land, and Brother Vaughn's desire to keep track of the hours was starting to seem more reasonable.

They ate in silence, each consumed with his or her own thoughts. The salted beef satiated Catrin's hunger, but her spirit was restless. She missed the sun and stars, and though they had been in the mines only a short time, she felt separated from Istra's energy. The lack of power made her feel vulnerable, and she pulled the noonstones from the gilded box. They felt wonderful in her hands. She rolled them in her palm and let them soothe her, not drawing any of the energy they held in reserve; instead, she just basked in their existence and the security they gave her.

An enormous arch loomed in the distance. Like the gates to a dark dimension, it was guarded by a multiheaded serpent whose fangs dripped with venom. Though carved from stone, it was a fearsome sight, and Catrin was loath to enter such a mystical portal. Brother Vaughn paid it no mind, and the serpent did not strike him as he passed through, but Catrin felt the reptilian stare intensely, and she had a vision of the beast coming to life. It was almost as if the carvings spoke to her: "Your descendents will pay dearly for your trespass," said the vision. Catrin shivered as if it were a premonition rather than the conjuring of her frightened mind. Benjin seemed troubled as well, and he looked over his shoulder frequently, which drove Catrin to do the same. She felt as if she were an intruder, and she half expected an army of ancients to descend upon them.

Beyond the intimidating arch lay a domed room that seemed impossibly large. Every part of the walls, with the exception of periodic archways, was carved to resemble a forest, and the detail boggled the mind. It was as if she stood in the center of a grove of stone, where each leaf, branch, and trunk was a masterpiece. Birds soared through the skies, and butterflies rested on rose petals. Even without motion, the enormous waterfall seemed alive, so clever was the craftsmanship.

"I would speculate these mines were in use for at least a thousand years," Brother Vaughn said, seeing the looks of awe on their faces. "I do not see how such mastery could have been achieved in any shorter span of time."

Catrin felt oddly at home among the still trees, and she almost didn't want to leave the hall, but Brother Vaughn moved steadily toward the fourth archway on their right. She ran her fingers along the magnificent carvings and marveled at smooth lines and lifelike curves. Some of the leaves were so thin, she imagined she could see through them, and she wondered how they could have been created. To see such delicate forms made from rock seemed impossible, yet it stood before her in all its glory.

As they exited the cavernous dome, Catrin glanced back at the archway and saw that it, too, was guarded by a mighty serpent. She could feel its eyes on her back, and she looked over her shoulder twice as often as Benjin. When a loud sound echoed through the halls, they froze. Straining their ears, they tried to figure out where the noise had come from, but the acoustics of the mine made it nearly impossible to pinpoint, and Brother Vaughn grew nervous. He looked over his shoulder as often as Catrin and Benjin, which did not make either of them feel any better, but they left their concerns unspoken.

The halls once again became a monotonous blur, and the dull cadence of their steps, a lullaby. Exhaustion dogged Catrin, and every step was a struggle. She leaned on Benjin, and they shuffled along together. Her vision blurred as she walked in a stupor, kept upright by only Benjin and her staff. Not wanting to complain, she did her best to deal with the fatigue, but it was overpowering. Her eyelids were leaden, her eyes burned, and she let Benjin guide her.

"We have to stop," Benjin said.

Brother Vaughn suddenly became aware of Catrin's condition. "Yes, yes, of course. Please forgive me. I should have realized."

Catrin slid to the floor and curled into a ball as soon as Benjin stopped. The throbbing in her head made it difficult to formulate any coherent thoughts, and she cradled her head in her hands. Benjin offered her food, but she refused. Her appetite had fled, and only pain and misery filled its place. As much as she would have liked to sleep, though, she remained awake and restless. Obscure fears and anxieties nagged at her, and she was helpless against them.

Would the Zjhon capture them? Would Chase survive his quest for a ship? Did Ohmahold stand any chance against the encroaching siege? The uncertainty gnawed at her, and she felt responsible for too many lives--too many futures. Her confidence waned, and she wondered how she could have been so foolish as to act on her ridiculous plan. There was little chance of success and an even smaller chance of survival. Her mind tormented her with all the possible ways she could die. Fires scorched her skin, axes cleaved her, swords severed limbs, and arrows pierced her flesh.

Unable to contain her pain, she wept, and Benjin pulled her close. With his powerful arms around her, she felt almost safe; he would keep the horrors at bay. Still, it took her far too long to find sleep, which she knew she would regret on the morrow.

* * *

Rolling into a tucked position, Chase hesitated only a moment before he sprang. He took three steps then launched himself into the air, tumbling and swinging at the same time. The crack of the impact echoed off the mountains, and Captain Longarm dropped to one knee, clutching his thigh.

"I'm going to feel that in the morning," he said.

"Sorry," Chase said.

"You've gotten better, but I'm getting too old to take that kind of beating, maybe one of your friends will spar with you," Captain Longarm said, pointing to where Strom and Osbourne stood talking to a pair of girls who'd come to watch the spectacle.

"Oh no. Not me. No, sir," Strom said as they approached. "You'll have to find someone else to beat on. My hands are my trade."

"Your trade, huh? I thought you were going to be a stable hand the rest of your life," Chase said.

"You heard me. I'm to be a great smith. Perhaps, if you're nice to me, I'll make you a *real* sword."

"Don't look at me," Osbourne said as Captain Longarm turned a questioning gaze to him. "I'm still sore from last time."

"I suppose you're just going to have to find a real enemy to take your frustrations out on, young man," Captain Longarm said, and he turned to leave.

"Thanks for everything, Burrel. Sorry about the bruises," Chase said, but Captain Longarm just waved his apology off. Still breathing hard, Chase sat on a nearby stump and regained his breath. There was no excuse for his hitting Burrel as hard as he had, but he could not stand waiting any longer. As foolish as he thought Catrin's plans were, he was still determined to do his part, and soon he would leave the shelter of Ohmahold; he needed to be ready. For today, though, all he could do was wait.

"I see you no longer fly like a stone," said a familiar voice from behind him. "Perhaps you could show me how to defend myself against unwanted advances."

"Certainly, Winnette," he said. "First let me show you a proper defensive stance."

Perhaps waiting wouldn't be so terrible after all.

Chapter 16

Beneath the soil lies the heart of the world, and her veins run gold and silver.
--Tobrin Ironspike, miner

* * *

Catrin grew weary of the mines and the walking. They passed various chambers of different sizes along the way, but they stayed within the halls and plodded along in the gloom. Faint echoes teased them, and at times, Catrin thought she heard the slow drip of water.

After what seemed like a month, they reached an intersection, and Brother Vaughn turned. The new hall seemed like all the rest at first, but then Catrin noticed a change: They were ascending. The incline was slight and barely discernable, but Catrin felt it in the backs of her legs. Longing to see the sky, she hoped they were nearing the exit.

The incline continued, and from the shadows, a curve in the hall appeared. It was the first time the tunnels had been anything but straight, and Catrin grew anxious. Beyond the gentle curve, a narrow cavern emerged, and nestled within it was a pond of dark and foreboding water that lay under a haze of steam. Brother Vaughn extinguished his lantern and asked Benjin to douse his as well.

Total darkness crowded around them, and Catrin could see nothing in the pitch, but after a moment, Brother Vaughn rekindled his lantern. The sudden brightness hurt Catrin's eyes, but it was better than the impenetrable darkness.

"I believe it's safe to exit, but if I do not return, wait for half a day before following. There is an opening in the far wall, just below the surface. You must swim under the rock, and when you clear it, you will be outside. Use the wax in your packs to seal them as best as you can. I'll see you on the other side." After one final look at his sand clock, Brother Vaughn handed it to Benjin. Looking doubtful and concerned, he swam to the far end of the pond and disappeared below the surface.

Catrin held her breath. She didn't know what possible dangers could prevent Brother Vaughn from coming back, but icy fear clutched her bowels. She'd lost too many friends already, and she desperately wanted Brother Vaughn to return safely. Bubbles appeared in the water near the far wall, and Catrin jumped when Brother Vaughn's head popped up not far from where she stood.

Benjin assisted her with the sealing of her pack, and they joined Brother Vaughn in the water. It was not a complete surprise to find the water unusually warm--the steam had been a clue--but it still seemed a bizarre phenomenon. Brother Vaughn wasted no time, and he dived below the surface again. Benjin waited a moment then ushered Catrin through next.

With a deep breath, she ducked under the water and pushed off with her feet. It was difficult to swim with her staff in hand, and she hoped she did not have far to go. A flurry of small forms bumped into her along the way, which was uncomfortable and disconcerting, and she struggled to remain oriented. She used the staff to feel for the end of the stone, and as soon as it gave way, she thrust herself to the surface. Icy night air greeted her, and she gasped for breath.

"Stay in the water for now," Brother Vaughn said as he gained the rocky shore. A full moon shed plenty of light to see by, and Catrin watched as Brother Vaughn gathered wood for a fire. She could see the mist of his breath before him, and she knew he must be freezing. With wet and shaking hands, he attempted to kindle a fire, but it refused to catch. Catrin and Benjin wanted to climb free of the water, but they were already soaked to the bone, and the cold air would assault them, just as it sent shudders through Brother Vaughn's form. For the moment, they held their packs high and waited.

A small orange glow gave them hope, and Brother Vaughn blew gently. A wisp of smoke rose into the air, and the crackle of burning pine needles carried across the water. At the first sign of flames, Catrin pulled herself from the water, but she soon regretted it. They would need a sizable bonfire to keep the frigid winds at bay, and she paced around the meager fire, rubbing her hands along her raised

179

flesh, hoping to generate warmth and stave off the numbness.

As she paced along the shore, she tripped on an unexpected obstruction. The fire suddenly leaped higher as Benjin tossed more pine needles on, and Catrin could see the obstacle: it was the skeletal remains of a large animal. Perhaps a horse or bear, she was not certain. In the light of the growing fire, she saw other skeletons of various sizes.

"What danger did you fear when you swam through?" Catrin asked.

"Daggerfish," Brother Vaughn replied, and Catrin was shocked by his words. She had learned of daggerfish many years ago. They were said be capable of removing the flesh from a horse in a matter of moments, which was further evidenced by the bleached remains strewn along the shore. Though small, daggerfish possessed razor-sharp teeth and voracious appetites. They were said to travel in schools, and their attack was likened to a cloud of death.

"You suspected there were daggerfish in these waters?" Catrin asked, incredulous.

"Suspected? No. I knew for a fact these waters are infested with them. I was just uncertain what time of day it was. Had I been wrong, we would not be speaking now," he said with a shrug.

Catrin was too stunned to speak, and she just stared at him in horror.

"It is a little-known fact, you see, that daggerfish will not feed under a full moon. Most folks are warded off by the evidence of their presence, and few are willing to risk their lives to find out such a thing."

Chills ran along Catrin's spine as she realized it was the daggerfish she had bumped into during her swim, and she shivered. She could not imagine what it would be like to be torn apart by razor-sharp teeth, but macabre visions filled her mind.

"I'm truly sorry for not telling you, but many would have balked no matter what I said; thus, I left you in ignorance. Please accept my apologies," Brother Vaughn said, looking sheepish.

"Well. We're still alive, thanks to you," Catrin said, "and I'm grateful for that, but please, if ever we are in a similar situation, apprise me of the danger. I would rather know what death I face," Catrin said, and Brother Vaughn nodded his assent, however unlikely it was they would ever be in similar circumstances.

The heat of the fire seeped into Catrin's clothes, and steam rose from them as they dried. The surrounding land soared at steep angles, with the exception of the north, where it opened into a rolling forest. The trees were not as large as greatoaks, but they were some of the largest oaks, elms, and sycamores in the world.

"Our fire should only be visible in the forest to the north, which is, for the most part, uninhabited. It should signal Barabas of our need, and I hope he'll arrive before long. I don't want to leave before you have become acquainted, but if he does not arrive soon, I will have to leave you," Brother Vaughn said, and they settled around the fire to wait.

Catrin turned her back to the fire so it would dry the rest of her clothes. The chill had mostly left her, but still she shivered.

Benjin wandered nearby as he gathered bits of wood for the fire.

Brother Vaughn rested. "Will you wake me after two turns of the sand clock?"

"Yes," Benjin said, accepting the sand clock. "I'll keep watch until then."

Catrin's thoughts wandered to Vertook. In all the chaos, she hadn't had time to properly grieve his loss. He'd been a good friend to her, and his death was as unfair as anything Catrin had ever experienced. The pointless waste of life filled her with rage, and she longed to lash out at someone-- anyone. Benjin seemed to sense her unrest, and he placed his arm around her shoulders. She shared his warmth but found no solace.

Too much had been taken from her in such a short time, and she began to harden to the cares of the world. Why should she even attempt to save the Zjhon from the Statue of Terhilian when they would kill everyone around her to prevent that very thing? Perhaps she should simply let them suffer the consequences of their folly, but the thought rang discordant, and she knew she could never be so callous; it was simply not her nature. She cared deeply about every living thing, and no amount of hardship could change that, she hoped.

Her thoughts turned to the gods and the origins of her world. She'd heard fanciful stories about gods gambling on the outcome of seemingly random events and cheating each other with their subtle influences on the lives of men. Those tales had never rung true for Catrin; it seemed too petty a pastime for beings capable of creating such a beautiful and amazing place.

Considering what she'd heard about ancient peoples making up stories of gods in order to explain the unknown, she wondered if people in the future would look back on her generation and laugh at their misconceptions. Perhaps they will laugh away many of society's current superstitions and beliefs, and yet they will still probably have their own delusions.

She wondered where the religious pomp and ceremony had come from and who had written the sacred writings. As far as she knew, no one in at least a thousand years had written anything considered sacred, and she wondered why the old writings were sanctified. She began to think the sacred texts had been written by ordinary men and were littered with the opinions of those men, who claimed to have been influenced by the gods.

Catrin had seen what society did to those who claimed anything close to divine inspirations. She had seen Nat Dersinger ostracized for that very reason, and she had been a party to it. She'd held tightly to the beliefs taught by ancient prophets and had cast insults at a living prophet. How could one believe prophets existed in ancient times but somehow could not exist now? The realization shamed her, even if it conflicted with Mother Gwendolin's teachings.

It took time to reconcile herself to many of her feelings, and she had more questions than answers. She imagined what life would be like if she had all of the answers, and she decided it would be much easier but excessively boring. If

182

she always knew what was about to happen, then there would never be any excitement or surprises in life, and though she was weary of surprises and excitement, she could not picture life without them.

Brother Vaughn's snores broke the silence, and Catrin steeled herself from sleep. Someone needed to stay alert, and she was unwilling to ask it of Benjin alone. She stood and walked circles around the fire in an effort to keep her blood moving and the lethargy at bay. Benjin saw the wisdom in her actions and joined her. He walked in the opposite direction, and they smiled at each other every time they passed.

Catrin nearly leaped from her skin when a voice like grating stone bellowed from the trees: "Greetings, landfriends."

A great bear of a man strode from the forest. He stood taller than anyone Catrin had ever seen, and his chest was as big around as a barrel. The furs and skins that adorned him accentuated his fearsome appearance. His hair was dark and coarse, like that of a horse's tail, and the curls of his beard covered much of his face. Still, a wide grin was visible beneath it.

"Barabas, my friend," Brother Vaughn said through a stifled yawn. "It's good to see you well. I'm sorry to call on you, but the need is great."

"Have no fear, landfriend. I come freely and will assist you if I can. Strange powers are afoot. I feel danger encroaching, but we'll face this new challenge together. Yes?"

"I'm sorry, old friend, I cannot join this quest, for I must return to Ohmahold. Our dear Mother Gwendolin was laid down by the Zjhon, and I must attend the ascension of her successor," Brother Vaughn said. A frown crossed Barabas's face, carving deep furrows on his brow.

"This is Catrin Volker of the Godfist," Brother Vaughn said, but Barabas interrupted him.

"She's more than that," he said, his eyes full of Catrin, as if she were a treasure. "Greetings, heart of the land. I've awaited you. And your shield, I see. You are her protector. Yes?" Barabas asked, his eyes on Benjin.

"You are correct. I am Benjin Hawk. It is a pleasure to make your acquaintance, Barabas." He stepped forward and offered his hand to the large man, but Barabas surprised them all by lifting Benjin from the ground in a mighty hug.

"You've done well to get her here alive, Guardian Benjin," he said as he lowered Benjin to the ground. "And you, heart of the land, you've done well to survive the perils of your journey. It pleases me to see you both."

"And it pleases us to see you," Catrin said in an attempt to return the compliment. His words were strange, and she wondered what he meant by her being a heart of the land.

Brother Vaughn stood and spoke quietly with Barabas a moment; then he turned to Catrin. "I must leave you now, while it is still dark, but I wish you a safe and blessed journey. May fate be kinder to you than it has been in the past, and may we meet again under brighter skies."

"You have my most sincere thanks, Brother Vaughn," Catrin said. "I'll never forget what you've done for me, and I'll keep my word. We will meet again, and I'll return what you've left in my keeping. Until then . . ." She stepped forward to embrace him, and he hugged her warmly.

Benjin stepped toward the monk, his hand outstretched. "I cannot thank you enough, and I know we've asked more from you yet. I hope our requests don't inconvenience you terribly."

Brother Vaughn took the offered hand. "Do not fret. My journey will be a pleasure compared to what you face. Blessings to you all," Brother Vaughn said as he entered the steaming water, and soon he was lost in the depths.

Catrin was sorry to see him go. He was one of the few pillars of strength left in her world, and she cherished him for that, but she knew he had left her in capable hands. The energy that radiated from Barabas was filled with rightness, as if he lived more like a tree than a man.

After removing a tanned skin from his raiment, Barabas used it to carry water to the fire and extinguish it.

"Come, landfriends, we've dallied too long in the light of your fire. We should be gone from here before others respond to the beacon," he said, and he led them into the night. He bore no torch or lantern, and in the shadows of

184

the mighty trees, they followed him by sound more than sight.

Moonlight streamed through bare branches, and what Catrin did see was a wonder. The life within this forest was as pure as any she had ever encountered. It was mostly untouched by man and lived by its own rules. It was pure and just felt right.

When she reached out with her senses, the land responded. It greeted her and made her feel at home, as if it had been awaiting her return. It was a strange thing to think, given the fact that she had never been there before, but something about it was familiar; it was home. Oddly, she felt even her staff respond to the land, as if it were reaching out to greet its brethren.

Barabas smiled as he watched her, as if he could sense her questing as well as the response. "The land greets you well, does it not, heart of the land?"

"It does, Barabas. But may I ask why you call me that?"

"You truly do not know?" he asked, clearly astonished by her question.

"I fear I do not," Catrin said. "There are many things I do not know."

Barabas laughed from his belly. His laughter was pure and joyous, its deep chorus akin to the sound of stones being poured into a bucket. "So you've chosen forgetfulness in this life. Your spirit knows all there is to know about this world, but the mystery can be fun. Yes?" Barabas said, confusing Catrin even further. "Even if you've chosen to forget, I suppose there is no harm in telling a bit. Your spirit has been here before, and it shall come again. You are a heart of the land because you have lived as every form of life on this blessed planet. You've basked in the sun as a blade of grass, soared in flight as a swallow, and swum the seas. You know the pain of childbirth and death, and you know the joys of rebirth. You and I, we've traveled far and wide together, and I must admit, I'm surprised you do not at least recognize me. I take no offense, mind you. I'm just surprised. There are others like you, but normally only a few are here, in this world, at one time. My kind have been called the souls of the land, and your kind have been called the hearts of the land."

"I don't have the images of those memories," Catrin said," but I feel a kinship to you and this land. It speaks to me. I've touched the land in other places, and I've felt its life, but never has it greeted me as such."

"Ah, then at least you've not left all memory behind. Perhaps our time together will awaken that which lies hidden, hmm?"

"You may be right. It seems your words have already changed me."

"Hmm," he said, his eyes far away. He led them deeper into the forest. "Where are you bound, Catrin?" Her name sounded strange on his lips, and he looked as if he were not sure it was befitting of her.

"We're bound for southern Faulk. The Zjhon have unearthed a Statue of Terhilian," she said, but she stopped when he slowly turned to face her.

His face was crimson, and the veins stood out on his forehead. The cords of his neck strained against his anger, and his clenched fists quivered at his sides. "To the deepest abyss with Von of the Elsics. The land has not yet cleansed itself from the last time his aberrations were unleashed. We should've destroyed them when we had the chance, but the time was too short, and once Istra's power was gone from the world, we were without the means. The land must not be made to pay the price for the madness of men--not again," he said.

Catrin was relieved she was not the target of his rage. He was a fearsome man when he was calm, but in his anger, he was terrifying. "Be not afraid, heart of the land. I've no quarrel with you, but the news you bring darkens my soul. The Statues of Terhilian use the faith of the devoted as a weapon against them. It is death brought about by deceit, and such a thing should never be done. We've still to pay for mistakes made by Von of the Elsics."

"I wish it wasn't true," Catrin said, and Barabas nodded. His steps were firm as he stormed ahead with purpose, and keeping up with him became a challenge. He said no more as he walked, and Catrin suspected he was too angry to be civil. He so closely resembled a charging bear that it almost frightened her, but she could not blame him. If what she had been taught about the statues were true, then the Zjhon were essentially condemning themselves.

"Do you think there is any way to convince the Zjhon the statue is deadly?" Catrin asked.

"Hmm. There is always the possibility, but I think it highly unlikely one could accomplish it in time. The energy shed by Istra does not pass through rock and soil freely, but some does penetrate, and it's possible the statues will detonate during this pass even if they remain buried. Exposed, they are an immediate threat and could discharge at any moment."

Catrin could find no words to respond. She struggled to find some solution, anything that would prevent massive loss of life, but she doubted they would ever be able to get close to the statue . . . unless they were in shackles.

The rustling of leaves beneath their feet was the only sound. Some foliage still clung to the trees, but the forest floor was thick with them, and silent movement was nearly impossible. Ahead of them materialized a tree that was larger than most and bore a roughly triangular opening in its trunk. Over the opening hung several skins that had been stitched together, and Barabas pulled them aside.

"Welcome to my abode."

"Beautiful," Catrin said. "It's amazing you found such a tree."

"Amazing? Certainly not. I asked the forest for shelter, and it provided for me--just as it should be," Barabas replied, and her confused look seemed to surprise him. "When I need meat, I ask the herd, and a sacrifice presents itself. If I have need of fire, then the forest provides me wood. Whatever I need of nature, I have but to ask. Too many have forgotten this. They just take what they want from the land without any thought or respect, and they strip her of wealth that cannot be replaced. Surely you remember this at least."

"I'm sorry, Barabas. I've much to learn," she said, and he sighed heavily.

"Truly, heart of the land, you've chosen a trying time to embrace ignorance."

Chapter 17

Each of us is uniquely qualified for some task. We have but to find it.
--unknown philosopher

* * *

The interior of the tree was as remarkable as its outer appearance. The wood within was polished and richly grained, but most astonishing was the formation of shelves and a sleeping crevice large enough for Barabas. A ring of stones formed a small fire circle in the center of the chamber, and in the domed ceiling, a funneled opening bore a layer of soot. Catrin suspected the opening continued to open air and formed a natural chimney. Little else adorned the relatively small living space, and they stood elbow to elbow as Barabas tucked dried fruits and meats into his pack. He allowed Catrin no more time to contemplate his dwelling as he urged them back into the night.

"We've no time to dally. We can travel within the forest to the center of Astor, and from there, we will need to skirt between smaller areas of woodland. We are certainly not the most conspicuous of bands," he said with a chuckle and immediately set off at a pace that was difficult to match. Catrin's legs burned from the exertion, and she tired long before Barabas. He seemed to sense her fatigue, and not long before she would have had to ask for a rest, he simply stopped and lowered himself to recline against a towering elm. Catrin and Benjin joined him, and they ate in the stillness.

The forest was a riot of scarlet and umber, and the quiet murmur of the life within it was like the heartbeat of the world. Tranquility such as this could not be constructed; it could only grow naturally. All of man's attempts at beauty and grace paled in comparison to the architecture of life. Even creatures that were at times frightening and strange had their own unique elegance. A small lizard scurried through the leaves, and its rough, angular hide so closely resembled tree bark that it could become nearly invisible. Catrin admired the function of its form, and she recognized its beauty, even if the thought of touching it made her skin crawl.

When she considered Barabas, she was faced with an enigma, and she struggled to understand his place in her world. It was not that he seemed out of place. On the contrary, he could almost become a part of the scenery-- much like the lizard. Taken out of his element, he was remarkable and unusual, but within his world, he was simply a part of nature. Eventually, her curiosity won out over her fear of being uncouth.

"I mean no insult by this question, Barabas, but may I ask what manner of man you are?" she blurted, and the words did not sound at all like what she had intended. "That is . . . I mean . . . You're very different from everyone I've ever met, and I'd like to understand you better." Still, she felt clumsy and rude, but Barabas just let his infectious laugh roll from him, as if he had no such inhibitions or insecurities. She envied him.

"You tickle me, heart of the land. Truly you do. You are wise beyond your years, and yet you've not the knowledge most would require to become wise. It amazes me. Your very existence is a paradox," he said, shaking his head. "Do not fear you will offend me with your questions. I'll answer them as best I can. As to what manner of man I am, some would label me druid, others shaman, and still others see me as a madman. I see myself as a part of life, a piece of the whole. Like a thread in a tapestry, I am not important in and of myself, but without me and the rest of the threads--the tapestry--would cease to exist. Do you understand?"

"I think I do, but how did you come to be this way? Did your parents teach you these things?" she asked, and she was unsettled to see a flash of pain in his eyes.

"The land raised me and provided for me. I never met those who brought me into this world, but men and women have helped me, and they have taught me much. They influenced much of what I am, and I've always tried to take with me the best of all the beings I encounter, just as pieces of you will always go with me from now on. The memory of you is a part of me, and the memories of all my teachers, human and otherwise, are parts of me. The land and the

189

animals have taught me as much, if not more, than my human mentors."

Catrin was not sure she understood any more about Barabas than before she asked, and she hoped his words would make more sense in time.

* * *

"We should've brought this thing up in pieces," Strom said through gritted teeth. "We could've assembled it once we got it all up there." Milo and Gustad launched into their usual debate, and Strom was frightened by the fact that he was beginning to understand them. Sometimes he was even tempted to interject his own thoughts, but it just seemed like asking for trouble.

"I'm losing my grip," Osbourne said. "We need to put it down."

"Be careful of the lenses, boys," Gustad said.

"We know. We know," Strom said as they eased the looking glass to the stairs. All of their effort had gone into reconstructing this ancient relic, and though they could see little through the parabolic lenses when in the workshop, Milo remained convinced it would work. He said it had been found atop Limin's Spire, and there it could be used to see the stars. Looking up, Strom gave up trying to count how many more stairs they had left to climb.

"We must get the looking glass to the spire before nightfall," Milo said, as he had a number of times before.

Strom was tempted to go get some big, strong men to carry the looking glass, but he knew he could not. No one else knew how much work went into repairing this relic, and he could not trust anyone else to handle it. Thinking back to the feeling of success he'd had when they finally produced a workable lens, he smiled. Though they never achieved a perfect pour, Strom was proud to have gotten close. The imperfections in the first lens were few, and there was a perfectly clear area in the center. The second lens was even better, for which Strom was thankful; there was barely enough material left to make even one more pour. Milo was insistent that they not resort to remelting glass, and Strom often wondered what it was he feared.

"I'm ready," Osbourne said.

Grunting, they lifted the looking glass and, once again, began to climb.

"This thing better work."

* * *

After a few days in Barabas's company, Catrin came to see him as a guardian of the land, and that image pleased her. It seemed at times that he spoke to the trees and the soil itself, as if asking directions, and he would move off with confidence. Catrin had her own way of communing with the natural world, but she did not receive coherent thoughts. Instead, vague impressions brushed against her consciousness. She tried to listen in on his conversations with nature, but they were simply beyond her grasp, as if she were listening for something that could only be seen.

On the fifth day of their journey, though, vague impressions became an almost overwhelming expression of emotion. Tears streamed down her face as waves of joy mixed with sadness washed over her. It came from all around her yet felt as if it were her own. When she glanced at Barabas, she saw his eyes welling, and Benjin sniffed.

"You sense it, heart of the land?" he asked, and she nodded, mute. "What of you, Guardian? You sense it as well?"

"I feel joy and sadness all around us, and . . . I think . . . a melody," Benjin said.

"Hmm, indeed. The dryads are singing a farewell dirge, which does not bode well for our travels. I know not what danger they anticipate, but I've never heard the virgin forests sing of such an end. It's as if the trees expect to be wiped out almost completely."

"That's horrible! We must save them," Catrin cried, but Barabas laid a hand on her shoulder.

"It's not all sadness, heart of the land. You can sense the joy as well. In death, there is rebirth, the chance to begin anew. The forest prepares for a catharsis rather than extinction. I will miss the trees; they have been good to me, and I love them dearly. But I know they will return someday, and so will I, and then we will once again breathe the same air. Still, in this time of peril, I fear the implications this will have on our journey."

His words created an anxious mood, and they moved in wary silence, alert for any signs of danger to the trees and themselves. It was not until late that night that the first signs of trouble showed themselves. The air had become unseasonably warm--not balmy but well above freezing--and distant thunder told of storms. Occasionally they saw far-off flashes of lightning, but it was the growing orange glow on the northern horizon that alarmed them. Within a short time, the acrid smell of smoke assaulted them. The forest was afire, and Catrin knew they were but kindling before the fury of the inferno. Dried leaves would need little urging to ignite, and the glow became brighter as the night wore on.

"Should we flee the forest now? I don't want to be burned alive," Catrin said, reluctantly revealing her fears.

"The trees will guide us and will warn me if we are endangered. For now, I sense the danger is greater beyond the trees. If we go into the open now, I fear things will not go well."

"I trust you, Barabas, and I trust your instincts, but can you be sure the trees will know when we must leave?"

"Nothing is certain, but I trust them more than I trust myself," he said.

She tried to have faith, but fire struck her with a primal fear.

"The winds are from the west at the moment," Benjin said, "but if they turn to the south, we could be in trouble. Stay aware of the winds, and we will know when the fires will approach."

"Well said, Guardian."

Catrin tried to share their confidence but found it difficult to sleep with the smell of fire in her nostrils. When morning arrived, a haze hung over the land until the winds picked up and clouds of smoke rolled across them. The winds were still mostly out of the west, but they seemed to be taking a southerly turn. By midday, the fires came into view, and the devastation was appalling. Flames climbed high into the sky and became so intense that tornados of fire raced through the hills, leaving nothing but smoldering ash in their wake.

Large embers and bits of ash clogged the air, and the smoke threatened to choke them, but still Barabas kept to the trees. He skirted around the fires and always seemed to find some stretch of land that had not yet been burned until they reached a hillside that was nothing but cinder. Hot embers lay under a blanket of gray powder, and they picked their way through the remains of the fire. The soles of their boots were poor protection from the intense heat, and they moved as quickly as they could to reach an island of trees that lay beyond the hill.

The remaining trees stood as a bastion of hope. Some part of the virgin forest remained unmolested, and yet as they drew closer, the song of the dryads grew stronger. The land resonated with it, and it was clear the danger was not past. When they were nearly halfway across the field of ash, darkness washed over them. Banks of ominous clouds rolled eastward, and they blotted out the light. No lightning brightened the landscape, but a heavy rain began to fall.

Rain seemed like a boon at first, for it doused the embers and cooled their feet, but the steady fall intensified and became a downpour, and the distant trees disappeared in the haze. The group struggled through clinging mud, and Catrin often lost her footing. Unseen stumps and roots were concealed under a blanket of ash, waiting to snag the unwary, and the wet ash was deadly slick in places. As they moved with dreadful slowness, fears blossomed in Catrin's mind. The song of the dryads did nothing to assuage them.

At one point they stopped and huddled together. The winds shrieked and tore at them, and only the support of Benjin and Barabas kept Catrin on her feet. Later the rains abated, and they were left to slog through knee-deep mud. It was excruciatingly slow, and their goal was just beyond their reach. Unburned trees loomed ahead of them, and they drove themselves onward as if that stand of ancient trees would be their salvation.

The rumble began so low that they thought it was the rains, but it grew louder until it became an ear-shattering roar. The ground trembled, and through the mist came a wave of death. It came from high in the mountains where the storm had rapidly melted the snow, and the burned-out landscape offered nothing to slow it. Nothing stood between the flux and them, and the flood gained momentum as it roared across the land.

"To the trees!" Barabas shouted over the clamor, and they tried to run, but the mud clung to them and made their legs and boots heavier and heavier. Each step was a struggle, but fear drove them, and as the massive wave crested the hills above them, they reached the first of the remaining trees. Catrin was about to discard her staff and climb when Barabas grabbed her by the waist and tossed her high into the air, far higher than she would have thought possible. Branches rushed toward her at alarming speed, and she latched onto one as she reached the top of her arch.

Barabas gave Benjin a boost to begin his climb, and Benjin was barely above Barabas's head when the flood reached them. It happened so fast that it didn't seem real. A wave of brown and gray rolled across the land and wiped it clean. It overtook Barabas before he could climb to safety, and Catrin cried out as he was washed away.

"Worry not, heart of the land," she heard him yell as he was carried beyond her sight. The dryads continued to sing their farewell, and many of the trees succumbed to the deluge. The sight of the massive trees being washed away was awful, but the slow tilting of the tree they were in was terrifying. Catrin and Benjin climbed higher, but the mighty tree leaned farther, and the roiling flow grew ever closer. When the tree broke loose from the soil, it moved in a lumbering circle, slowly spinning in the current. Its top remained above water, though, and they huddled in the branches. Other trees and debris battered them, and Catrin used her staff to fend them off.

Cradled by the limbs, she sensed the dryad with her, protecting her in one last dying effort. Catrin sent her thanks into her physical bond with the tree, and she felt she could lend her strength to the dryad. Her energy poured into the

194

bark and into the flesh of the tree. She was not sure if it was due to the effort of the dryad or pure luck, but they dipped into the roiling waters on only two occasions, and each time they were thrust back into the air.

As the flow diminished, the tree became wedged against a tangle of downed trees and vegetation that was knotted between a pair of hillocks. Catrin and Benjin held on to one another and lent each other warmth and strength as they waited out the flood.

When the waters receded, the landscape was nightmarish. What had been lush forest was now a wasteland, and not a single tree remained standing within their sight. Mud and rock clogged the valleys, and large sections of land had been ripped from their moorings, leaving huge gashes in the countryside. Benjin helped Catrin climb from the twisted mass, and they fought to break free of the mud.

Night closed around them, and they shivered in the cold air. No dry wood could be found for a fire, and they kept moving just for the sake of the warmth the activity provided. Catrin feared if they stopped, they would never rise again, and despite her nagging exhaustion, she pushed on, determined to live. She couldn't allow those who had died for her cause to have died for naught. She did not add Barabas to her mental list, for she felt he was still alive. It was not merely a foolish hope; she could sense him. She could not tell the direction in which he lay, though she had some clues about that, but she just got a general sense that he lived, as if he sent reassurance to her across the distance between them.

She and Benjin listened for anyone who might be in need of help, but the night was eerily quiet; only the sound of draining water disturbed the stillness. When morning arrived, it brought bright sunshine that seemed inappropriate in the face of such carnage. It almost seemed the sky should mourn the losses on the land below, but it acted of its own accord and blinded them with its glare. By midday, they found a hill that still bore trees, and they climbed to its top. There they built a small fire and tried to get warm.

Though no longer completely sealed with wax, the packs had kept out most of the water and mud. They shared some dried beef strips from Benjin's supply. Despair washed over Catrin as they ate. Even though they were alive, she felt lost. If Barabas did still live, it was doubtful he would find them, and they were now faced with traveling on their own. Benjin's presence was all that kept her from spiraling into a deep, dark depression, but he seemed to be struggling with demons of his own, and neither of them spoke for the rest of the day. No words seemed suitable for such dire circumstances.

After a brief respite, they descended into the mud once again. Despite traveling along high ground whenever they could, much of their time was spent knee-deep in the quagmire. Near dusk, they reached a broad river that was swelled beyond its banks and clogged with debris. It was there that the flood had reached its end, and Catrin could only hope the banks would hold, for beyond lay perfect rectangles of farmland, though few crops grew in the fields, and not a single soul could be seen.

Following the mighty river south, they looked for a place to cross but found none before darkness surrounded them, and they spent another night huddled in each other's arms. Catrin did not remember falling asleep, but she woke to Benjin's deep snores, and she let him sleep. Leaning her head against him, she enjoyed a few moments of peace.

When Benjin woke, they moved farther south, and not long after, a stonework bridge appeared in the distance. As they drew closer, it became apparent that the bridge was an engineering marvel. The river was not much more narrow there than anywhere else they had passed, and huge supports disappeared into the muddy waters. Catrin could not imagine how such a bridge had been constructed, and she stared at in wonder. The water was only a few hand widths below the arched bridge in places, and she wondered if the swelled river would simply carry it away.

A crowd of people was gathered near the bridge, and when they saw Catrin and Benjin, they came to help. Fear clutched Catrin and she looked at Benjin, who seemed to be torn, but then he leaned close and took the staff from her hands.

"They've already seen us," he said. "If we flee, they'll most likely alert the local militia . . . that is, if any militia still remains. It's too great a risk, I think. Let me do the talking."

Catrin wanted to argue, every sense told her to flee, but the lure of warmth and food was too great, and her fatigue was too intense for flight. Thus, they moved slowly toward the approaching crowd. Upon closer inspection, she saw that the group was made up of the aged and the very young. Benjin leaned heavily on the staff as they walked, and his affected limp was quite convincing.

Covered in mud and ash, they must have been a remarkable sight. When they arrived, two men helped support Benjin as he walked. A girl of maybe four summers brought Catrin a flask of water that she accepted eagerly if not to quench her great thirst, then to wash the filth from her face.

"Yer lucky to've survived," an elderly man said as he approached. "From where d'ya come?" he asked, and Catrin immediately sensed his distrust. Her clean face made her age easy to guess, and that alone made her suspicious in their eyes. Catrin regretted washing her face, but there was nothing to be done about it now, and she held her tongue.

"We hail from northern Astor, but the fires drove us from our home, and the flood washed us here," Benjin replied in a trembling voice, his accent thick with northern, rural qualities.

"Pardon my insolence, stranger, but why's this one not been conscripted?" the man asked, pointing to Catrin.

"My five sons and two oldest daughters are in the Northern Wastes, and I fear I'll never see them again," Benjin said, his voice cracking and tears welling in his eyes. Catrin would have been impressed by his dramatics, but she knew he had an abundance of real pain to draw upon, and his tears need not be forced. The sight of his tears filled her own eyes, and her lip quivered as he continued. "This's my youngest daughter, and since my lady-wife passed to the grave, she's all I have. Even the armies could not part her from me." He said the words with conviction and stood with his chin high. He did not back down from the stares, and his fierce pride seemed to endear him to them.

"Many pardons, friend. I'm sorry fer yer losses, and yer welcome to join us, though we've little to offer. The armies have taken all we could give, and then they took more. We may be poor hosts, but we welcome you. I'm Rolph Tillerman," he said as he extended his hand to Benjin.

"Well met. I'm Cannergy Axewielder, and my daughter is named Elma," he said, and Catrin did her best not to appear surprised. She hadn't even thought about the danger of using their real names, and she chastised herself for her foolishness.

"Ah, a woodsmen, eh? That'd explain a great deal. Let us be gone from this place, the smell offends me, and ya look like ya could use a warm fire and some food."

Benjin allowed the men to aid him as he walked. The steady flow of water beneath the bridge was unnerving, and Catrin feared the bridge would collapse under their weight. The thought of falling into the frigid water nearly drove her to a run, but she restrained herself and matched the pace set by Benjin and his escorts.

Beyond the fields stood a cluster of homes and barns that seemed like the hub of a great wheel. It seemed odd to Catrin, who was accustomed to each farm existing as an island, whereas these huddled together, and their lands extended like spokes. Despite the strangeness of the configuration, there were many things that reminded her of home, which brought a sharp pain to her chest. The smell of a cook fire, a whiff of horse manure, and the hearty folks who surrounded her all invoked vivid memories, and she failed to hide her anguish.

"Don't cry, dear'n," an elderly lady said as she took Catrin's hand. "You're safe now."

Catrin wished she could believe it.

Chapter 18

Kindness, unlike most things, becomes greater when it is given away.
--Versus Macadilly, healer

* * *

Rolph led them to his home, which was painfully similar to the one Catrin had grown up in, and his wife, Collette, pulled her aside.

"Come with me, Elma. Let's get you cleaned up. Shall we?"

"Thank you, Lady Tillerman. You're very kind," Catrin replied, trying to match Benjin's accent and fearing it came out sounding contrived.

Collette laughed a light, tinkling sort of laugh. Lines spread from the corners of her eyes when she smiled, but the sparkle in her eyes spoke of inner youth. "I'm no lady, that's a'certain. Call me Collette," she said, and Catrin was struck by her kindness and by the similarity between these people and her own. These were good people. They were not filled with malice or spite. They led simple, wholesome lives, and she felt a kinship to them. The realizations made the entire conflict seem even more ludicrous. She had no quarrel with these good folk, and they harbored no ill toward her. Yet it was their blood that was being shed, that of their children. Catrin began to think of these people not as the Zjhon, but as the people of the Greatland. The Zjhon were the ones who desired war, and all others were simply their victims.

Collette led her to a private room that held a large iron tub.

"Take off those filthy clothes, and I'll bring you some bathwater," she said, but Catrin drew a sharp intake of breath when saw a pair of deep-brown eyes peering through a crack in the wall, and Collette turned. "Jessub, you scoundrel, shame on you! That's no way to treat a guest. Off with you! Straight to yer grandpa you go, and tell 'im what you've done. And don't think I won't check with him either," she said, and then she turned to Catrin. "Forgive him, m'dear. He's young and naturally curious, and you're a fetching lass."

Catrin flushed crimson. She certainly didn't consider herself fetching, and she eyed the crack in the wall with trepidation. Collette smiled kindly and covered the crack with a towel.

"He'll bother you n'more. I assure you of that," she said as she left Catrin to her privacy, and Catrin was certain she was correct, for Jessub's cries rang out loudly as he received his punishment. Catrin felt bad for him and wished they wouldn't spank him on her behalf; she'd always hated being punished as a child, and she felt Jessub's shame as if it were her own.

Only the luxury of the steaming tub could pull her thoughts away, and she eased into the water, which soon turned black with mud and soot. Despite her efforts, her skin would not come completely clean, and she settled for mostly clean. As the water began to grow cool, Catrin emerged from the tub, and she toweled off her raised flesh. Collette had left fresh clothes for her, and Catrin shook her head. She seemed to always find herself donning the clothes of others while a stranger washed her garments. She supposed she was growing accustomed to it, for it did not bother her as much as it had in the past. The loaned garments were overlarge and well worn, but they were clean, dry, and not uncomfortable.

An alluring aroma wafted into the room, causing her stomach to grumble, and Catrin was grateful when Collette handed her a bowl of broth. It was a light soup made of potato and onion, but it tasted delightful, and it warmed her soul as much as it did her belly.

"I wish we'd more t'share, m'dear, but times are hard," Collette said with a sad smile.

"It's wonderful, and I'm thankful for your generosity. I only hope I'll be able to repay you in some way."

"Nonsense. It's our duty t'help those in need, and you owe us nothing, but I appreciate the thought," she said as she brought Catrin a small loaf of bread. The crust was dark and hard, but the inside was light and airy, unlike the bread made on the Godfist. Catrin did not mention it for fear of revealing her ignorance. Perhaps this type of bread was common in the Greatland, and she did not want to raise any more suspicions.

Benjin and Rolph joined her in the common room, and Benjin looked much better after his bath. His clothes were strange, but they fit him well. Catrin rummaged through her pack and brought out some dried fruit and cheese that she shared with the rest.

"Good cheese," Rolph said with his mouth full, and Collette scolded him for his manners. A young boy came in meekly, refusing to meet Catrin's eyes. From his shamefaced look and the awkward walk of one with a sore bottom, Catrin guessed this was Jessub. When she offered him some dried fruit, he accepted it with tears in his eyes. Rolph gave him a steely glance, and Jessub raised his red eyes to hers.

"I'm sorry I peeked, Lady Elma," he said with a catch in his voice. He looked to be no more than seven summers, and Catrin could not be angry with him.

"It's a'right, Jessub, 'long as it doesn't happen again. Agreed?" she asked, the flush returning to her skin as all eyes rested on her.

"Yes, ma'am," he said, and he retreated from the stares. With a shove on the door, he was gone.

"Takes after you," Collette said with an accusing glance at Rolph.

"Don't glare at me, woman. I didn't peek. Though I can't say I blame the boy. Yer the prettiest thing to grace this house for some time," he said with a wink at Catrin, and she blushed anew. Benjin nearly choked on his bread, and mirth danced in his eyes, but he said nothing.

"Leave the poor girl alone, you wretched old man," Collette said, and she stood behind Catrin as if guarding her virtue.

"We can put you up in the barn fer a spell," Rolph said, ignoring his wife's glare. "It's not much, but it's dry and there's straw you can bed on. We've some blankets t'spare, so you won't freeze t'death."

"Elma can sleep in my room," came a high voice from outside, and Collette chased Jessub off with a broom.

"Off with you, you naughty child. You've caused enough trouble fer t'day."

"I thank you for your hospitality," Benjin said. "We should leave on the morrow and will not outstay our welcome. I've a brother in the south, and I hope to find work there, for my livelihood left with the fire and flood."

"Tough times fer all, these are. Come, I'll show you to the loft," Rolph said, and they followed him to the barn. All but two of the twenty stalls were empty, and those held swayback mares. At the far end of the barn, a ramp led to the loft, which was not a difficult climb, even for Benjin with his affected limp. Many of the bales were broken, and loose straw lay in mounds. Catrin tossed the blankets Rolph had given her over one mound, and she did what she could to form it into a comfortable bed. The crisp night air frosted their breath, but beneath the warm blankets, she and Benjin quickly dropped into sleep.

* * *

Looking out over the Falcon Isles and the seas beyond, Nat found himself in awe of creation. Blue skies harbored fluffy, white clouds, continually morphed by gentle breezes. Neenya stood at his side, tears streaming down her cheeks, seemingly overwhelmed by the beauty of nature. Slowly, Nat extended his hand until it brushed against her fingers. For a moment, he seemed frozen in time, waiting for her to respond. At first she seemed not to notice, but then a thrill ran through him as Neenya's fingers closed around his. In the next instant, her grip was all that kept him from tumbling over the ledge as his vision clouded and his knees would no longer support him.

Wrapped in a frilly dress, Catrin danced and spun. All around her, dangers lurked, like grisly thorns waiting to snag and entangle her. No reaction registered on her face, as if she were oblivious to the threats, and only sheer luck kept her safe. Slowly the vines encroached, surrounding her and constricting; still, Catrin danced.

Never before had the vision seized Nat so utterly and completely, and never before had the vision been so clear. "May the gods have mercy on her."

202

When the morning sun crept through gaps in the walls, Catrin rose to stretch her sore muscles. She and Benjin had slept later than they had in a long time and felt better for the rest. As they climbed down the ramp, Catrin saw a group of men, Rolph included, leaning against the fence. The men faced a large pasture that was occupied by a single, black colt. Catrin was shocked to see a bow at Rolph's side, and she moved in to investigate, Benjin hobbling along at her side. Their stomachs rumbled with hunger, but her curiosity won out over her appetite.

"Ho there, Rolph," Benjin said. "You don't mean to shoot that colt, now do you?"

"Aye, Cannergy. If we can't catch 'im any other way, I'll have to wound 'im. No one's been able to catch 'im so far, and his time's a-runnin' short. He still wears his yearlin' halter, ya see, and if'n we don't get it off soon, he'll be ruined. The armies left us only three horses, and I need 'im for breeding. T'will be a blasted shame if I have to shoot 'im, but what else can I do?"

Catrin could not believe her ears, and she could sense Benjin's inner struggle. He could catch the colt, but it would reveal his deception, for he could not do it while faking his limp.

"May I try?" Catrin asked, and all eyes turned to her.

"She's good with animals," Benjin added.

"We've nothing to lose, lass. But don't get yerself hurt. He's a feisty colt, and you'd not be the first to be injured by 'im. T'be honest, I don't hold out much hope for it. No offense to yer skills, but in a field that big, it's dern near 'mpossible."

Catrin was not offended by his lack of faith, but she did not intend to chase the colt around the pasture; all that would do was wear her out.

"Have you a length of rope and some soft cloth?" she asked, and her question raised more than one eyebrow.

Obviously intrigued, Rolph nodded and went to retrieve the items for her. When he returned, he handed them to her with a curious look, but he did not ask what she would do. He and the others chose, instead, to simply watch in silence.

Catrin walked the fence, inspecting the posts. When she found one that did not wiggle when she pushed on it, she tied one end of the rope around its base. After a few tugs to ensure its stability, she tied a noose and stop-knot on the other end. The blanket she used to pad the noose, and she tested it by looping it over her own head several times. Once she was confident she could quickly secure it over the colt's head, she climbed through the slats of the fence.

The colt watched her enter his pasture, and he raised his tail as he trotted in a wide arc, challenging her to catch him, but she did not even look at him. Ignoring him completely, as if he did not exist, she walked into the pasture and sat on the ground. With the noose in her lap, she picked blades of grass and inspected them as if that were her only reason for being there. The men stood at the fence, and no one spoke a word. A tense silence hung in the air.

For a while, nothing happened, but Catrin was in no hurry; she had all day if that was what it took. After she picked the spot in front of her nearly clean of the coarse grass, though, the colt became curious. He approached her from behind and nipped at her shoulder before charging away. Again, Catrin ignored him. He returned two more times, and each time he stayed longer and became bolder. At one point, he put his head over her shoulder and nudged her with his nose, but an instant later he wheeled and snorted.

Catrin hoped his inquisitive nature would continue to get the best of him, and so it did. On his next return, he stuck his head into her lap and nearly knocked her over, which was the exact moment she had been awaiting. Quick as a striking snake, she looped the noose over his head and rolled away from him as he panicked. She was not quite quick enough in her escape and received a clout on the head for her troubles.

Her goal, though, had been achieved. The colt fought, wide eyed, against the rope that held him fast. The stop-knot prevented him from crushing his own windpipe, and the post remained firmly rooted, much to her relief. She watched and waited as his struggle became wild, and he threw himself against the restraints with abandon, but still the post held, though it did begin to move a bit more with each yank.

In a desperate move, the colt tried to get a running start, but when the rope went taut, it knocked him from his hooves, and in that moment, Catrin sprang, leaping onto him and straddling his neck. With her weight firmly settled just behind his ears, the colt could not get enough leverage to stand. He continued to flail, but Catrin spoke soothingly into his pinned ears. After a few more moments of struggling, the colt surrendered and stopped fighting.

The yearling halter was already cutting into the colt's growing flesh, and Catrin could see that Rolph was right: left on any longer, the flesh would have grown around the overtight halter. As gently as she could, she undid the buckle and pulled the halter from his head.

"Have you a halter?" she shouted, and the stunned men sprang into action. Rolph returned moments later with a much larger halter made of leather and brass. He handed it to her and let her do the honor of placing it on the colt. Careful to avoid the newly exposed flesh, she slipped the halter on. The colt struggled under her weight but was still unable to rise.

"Lead line," Catrin said, and it came out as an order, but Rolph didn't flinch. He just handed her a lead line. Once she had it secured to the halter, she pulled the noose from the colt's head. "Have you a stall ready?"

"Yes'm, and I'll have the aisle cleared," Rolph replied, and Catrin prepared for the most dangerous part of her task. Using her hand to keep weight on his neck, she climbed off and stood. As soon as she took her hands from his neck, the colt stood. He tried to fight her for a time, but she was skilled at avoiding his kicks and strikes, and she refused to let go. They spun in circles, and she slowly edged him toward the gate.

The men backed away and allowed her room to move as they left the pasture and entered the barnyard. Still they spun, and still Catrin moved him toward the barn. When she tried to get him through the open doors, the whites of his eyes showed and his panic increased, but much of the fight was out of him.

"First stall you can get 'im into will be fine," Rolph said, and she made for the first stall on the right. The door was narrow, and the colt balked. He strained against the lead line and halter, which Catrin knew must be painful on his raw flesh, and the pain increased his frenzy.

"Smack 'im on the rear," she shouted, and Rolph rushed to comply. In an instant, the colt went from resistance into a leap. He struck his hip on one side of the doorway and nearly trampled Catrin in the process, but he was in the stall. With a quickness born of skill and fear, she unhooked the lead line and fled the stall. Rolph slammed the gate shut behind her. The colt paced the stall restlessly, still blowing from the workout, and Catrin dropped to the floor, blowing nearly as hard as the colt. Benjin and Rolph reached her side as soon as she hit the ground and checked her for injury.

"I'm fine," she said. "Just winded."

"We owe you a great debt, Elma. You saved that colt, and you've given us back hope. With 'im available for breeding, we can replenish our stable yet. Didn't even have to shoot 'im," Rolph said with a broad smile. "Never seen the likes o' that, I tell ya. Yer a clever girl indeed."

Catrin blushed at his compliment, and her stomach practically roared in hunger.

Rolph heard the rumble and seemed to recall himself. "Ye've not even eaten yet; shame on us. Come, let's feast to yer success," he said, and she gladly followed him inside.

As Rolph entered the cottage, ducking his head under the low door, Collette stepped in behind and cuffed him on the back of his head. "You great oaf, how could ya let that poor girl catch yer colt on an empty stomach." Rolph made no argument, and Collette turned to Catrin. "I saw what ya did out there, Elma. Yer brave and smart as can be. Couldn't be more proud of ya. To celebrate, I pulled out our last cured ham. We'll eat well this day, for ye've given us back our livelihood. Ya don't even know how many times those men tried to catch that rascal, and here you pluck 'im in a single mornin'. Tickles me," she said, and she gave Catrin a warm hug.

"Did ya see that, Gramma?" Jessub asked as he stormed into the house, and rather than wait for an answer, he acted out the entire scene. His antics sent laughter into the air, and it was one of the most joyful moments of Catrin's life; she had truly helped these good folks, and it warmed her heart. Still she felt guilty eating the last of their meat.

"Are you certain you wish to serve the ham? Soup would be fine."

"Nonsense! Ye've earned a good meal, and I'd say the first foal born should be yers as well," Collette said in a tone that left no room for argument.

The meal she served was nothing short of spectacular, given the circumstances, as she broke out the best of their stores: ham, bread, and cheese were accompanied by sugared nuts and apple cider. Very little was said as everyone enjoyed the meal, but it was a merry silence. A weight seemed to have lifted from Rolph's shoulders, and he looked younger than when they had met.

"Ye've got to name that colt now," Collette scolded Rolph. "I don't think 'No-good rotten son of a common hussy' suits him anymore."

Rolph laughed from his belly, and his laughter was contagious. Catrin's full belly soon hurt, and joyful tears ran down her cheeks. "I think I'll call 'im Elmheart. What d'ya think of that, Elma?"

"I think that suits him just fine. I'll take pride in his naming."

"That ya should. That ya should," Collette said, nodding her head.

"As much as I hate to leave your hospitality," Benjin said with a hand on his full belly. "We should be on our way. We've a long way to go."

"I'll not send y'off on foot. No sir, I won't. I may not have a horse to spare, but I've an ox and an old oxcart. If ye'd be willing to help me fix up the cart, I'd say ya more than earned it," Rolph said, and Catrin's jaw dropped open.

"That's far too generous a gift for us to accept," she said, and Benjin nodded his agreement.

"I'll not hear it. No, I won't," Rolph insisted, and Collette added her vote to his.

"Are you sure you can do without?"

"Ah, I must admit our gift is not all it'd seem. Curly's no prize. He's cross-eyed and unp'dictable, but he'll pull a cart. B'sides, in a few weeks, the colt'll be broke, and I can use 'im to pull the plow if'n I needs to. We'll be fine."

* * *

Rocks tumbled into the ravine as Lissa tried to regain her footing, the heels of her sturdy boots finding no purchase amid the brittle layers of shale. Using her gloved hands, she slowed her fall and eventually came to a stop. Before her stood only open air, below a sheer face that raced to meet the river valley far below. Using the skills Morif had taught her, she climbed slowly back to safety.

He'd always been a mentor to her and had listened when no one else would. She wished he were with her now, but she knew even he would make her go back, make her face what everyone seemed to think was her responsibility--her duty. No one could make her face that--no one. Instead, she made the choice for her people. She would rather they perish as free people than survive as slaves to the Zjhon and Kytes.

Better to be free, she thought as she searched for food and shelter. Better to be free.

Chapter 19

If you wish the devout to ingest poison, wrap it in pomp and seal it with ideology.
--Von of the Elsics

* * *

Catrin, Rolph, and Benjin worked on the oxcart in the afternoon sun. The cart was in poor condition, and one of the wheels was seized. After they removed the wheel and greased the hub, it moved more freely, but was still less than perfect. Catrin was glad to have the cart as it would make their travels much easier, and she hoped it would help them appear more like locals. Collette folded the blankets from the loft and insisted they would make a good cushion for the splintery wooden seat. Their kindness in such a trying time spoke volumes for their generous souls, and Catrin vowed to never forget them and all they had done for her.

When the cart was deemed ready for travel, Rolph led them to a pasture on the outskirts of the farmstead. On his way, he retrieved a bushel basket of hard corn still on the cob, and he handed an ear to Catrin.

"Take this out to him. Hold your ground now. He's harmless," Rolph said with a mischievous grin, and Catrin reluctantly slipped through the fence.

Curly stood at the far end of the field, tall as a horse, half again as long, and twice as big around. His shaggy coat added to his girth, making him look like a barn on legs. As soon as Catrin stood within the fence, he turned and charged, building momentum as he came. Afraid she would be run down, Catrin did as Rolph had instructed: she held her ground, albeit with her eyes closed.

Heavy breathing and the pounding of his hooves grew closer, but just before she thought Curly would trample her, he stopped. When Catrin opened her eyes, he stood before her, eyeing her with one eye; the other stared off to her right. He snorted and nudged her with his broad head, and only then did she recall the ear of corn she held at her side. As she extended it to him, he grabbed it greedily from her hand.

He shoved his ear into her hand as he chewed, nearly knocking her over. She scratched behind his ear, and he leaned into her, groaning with pleasure.

The ear of corn kept him busy for only a moment, and he nudged her hands for more. As she turned to walk back to the fence, he followed on her heels, occasionally nudging her from behind.

"I think he likes you," Rolph said with a chuckle, and Catrin stuck her tongue out at him, which set him to laughing from his belly.

"He seems like a friendly beast," Benjin said. "We can't thank you enough for your generosity."

"It's the least we can do."

Catrin slid back through the fence, and they retrieved the oxcart. Rolph brought a yoke and lines from the barn, and Curly paced the fence excitedly, rattling the gate as he passed it. But as Rolph opened the gate, a bell rang out in the distance. Its peal sent a chill down Catrin's spine and raised the hair on her arms.

"Citizens call!" echoed across the distance. "Citizens call!"

Despite Curly's protests, Rolph closed the gate. "Well, let's see what news the crier brings," he said, and Benjin nodded, showing no signs of concern. Catrin followed nervously as they crossed the fields to a small town. The call for citizens continued even after they arrived, giving those in more remote areas the chance to congregate with the rest. A large crowd had gathered around the crier, who stood atop a stage of crates draped with a red cloth.

"Good citizens, I greet you with news both grand and dire," the crier said with a dramatic flourish. "In the south of Faulk has been found the likeness of god and goddess, the very symbol of the Zjhon, with a life its own. It glows from within, proof it is a divine gift from the heavens, and we rejoice!" His words were met with a muted hush, but he continued on, apparently undaunted by the lack of applause.

"The faithful are called to the great city of Adderhold to gaze upon god and goddess, to worship in person. Failure to do so will be considered insult and heresy. Prepare yourselves, pilgrims, for Istra and Vestra call you to them, and only the masses can assuage their thirst for worship."

A louder murmur rushed through the crowd. Few seemed pleased by the prospect. Angry and frightened faces surrounded them, and the air grew foul with tension. The charge of it weighed on Catrin as the masses broadcast their anxiety, and waves of it battered her senses. She breathed in deeply to stave off the nausea, and the crier waved his arms for silence.

"The next is sad beyond reckoning, and I ask that the weak of heart be seated," the crier continued, waiting it seemed more for dramatic pause than anything else. "The armies have returned from the Godfist with only three ships. The rest were lost. The Herald Witch laid waste to the armada, killing our people and her own without discretion. She has betrayed god, goddess, the Greatland, and the Godfist with her actions, and her own people have cast her into exile. The remains of our armies took mercy on the good people of the Godfist and helped in what ways they could before they left in pursuit of the renegade Herald Witch."

Catrin swayed on her feet, along with many of those around her, but for different reasons. She knew it to be false--all of it--and she was appalled by the depth of the Zjhon's deceit. They lied to their own people because they feared the truth. Rolph leaned on Catrin and nearly fell, and she supported his weight. His face was contorted into a mask of pain and grief, and Catrin's fury rose higher. The crier's lies caused him needless pain, and she resented it deeply. She had set the armies free, but the crier's words made it sound as if she had slaughtered everyone.

"Go, citizens. Prepare yourselves for the final triumph of the Zjhon. Together we shall beat back the Herald Witch, and we will prevail. To Adderhold with you, one and all! The divinity shall arrive at Adderhold by spring, and all are required to attend. In their light shall the rifts in the Greatland be healed and the enemy crushed. Until I see you there, I bid you blessings in the light of Istra, Vestra, and the Zjhon Church."

"What do they expect us to do? Eat stones?" someone in the crowd asked. "How can we leave our fields and homes and expect not to starve?" The crier had no answers for them; instead, he just packed his stage cloth and moved on to the next town. The crowd milled in confusion. No one seemed to know what to do, and some seemed on the verge of panic. The false news of the armies' losses had the most devastating effect. Many wept in mourning for family members they presumed dead.

Catrin, Rolph, and Benjin walked back to the farmstead in oppressive silence. Rolph's shoulders occasionally shook with sobs, and Catrin sensed that he dreaded relaying the news to Collette. She stood in the barnyard when they returned, and she dropped to her knees when she saw Rolph's face; she had no need to hear the words from him. He ran to her, and they clung to each other for support. It was a gut-wrenching sight, especially when one knew the news was false. Catrin had an enormously difficult time holding her tongue, but Benjin's pointed stare urged her to do just that. Rolph helped Collette into the house, and he returned a moment later.

"Mother needs a rest," he said, his voice heavy with emotion. "Let's get you settled while I've still the energy to move." They opened the pasture gate, and Curly nearly charged to the oxcart. "Thinks he's going to town. He's well known, and the children always bring him corn. It can make fer a wild ride, but he does no harm," Rolph said, and while Benjin loaded their gear, he pulled Catrin aside. "I've one last gift for you." He led her into the barn and pulled a heavy coat from a hook in the feed stall. "This belonged to one of m'sons, Martik," he said, his lip quivering. "He was studying arch'tecture before the Zjhon came. He used to say he'd one day be the builder of great things. He won't be needin' this jacket anymore, and I want you t'have it. Keep the hood up, and it'll be harder to guess yer age. I hope it helps to ease the troubles of yer journey in some way."

"Will you go to Adderhold?" she asked.

"Not me. Boil the Zjhon fer taking m'boys, and boil the Herald Witch for killing 'em. Boil 'em all," he said, his face going crimson.

His words struck Catrin like a physical blow. Though she understood his reasons for saying them, they stung and shamed her. She longed to tell him the truth, to tell him his sons most likely lived as citizens of the Godfist. Would he even believe her if she told him? Tortured by the sight of his tears, she could take it no longer. "Do you trust me?" she asked, and he appraised her with his eyes.

"Aye, Elma. I trust you," he said, and the use of her pseudonym shamed her; he trusted her despite her deception, and she wondered if she deserved his trust.

"The words you heard today were false. The Herald did not kill all the men who did not return; she freed them. Most of them still live. Though they face a harsh winter with little food, I expect the majority will survive," she said, and she felt as if a vice had been released from her chest; the giving of truth allowed her to breathe again. Still, she knew she had just risked everything. Rolph's face was almost impossible to read as he contemplated her words, and she waited anxiously for some response.

"How do you know this? Tell me true."

"We've not been completely honest with you about our origins, I admit, but I would not deceive you about such a thing. I know these things because I was there. I saw it with my own eyes."

"So you're saying m'boys live?"

His simple question impaled her; she could not have felt his pain more keenly, and it left her rattled. "I cannot say for certain. Some men were killed during the invasion."

"I thank you for your words, Elma. You'd best get going," Rolph said as he noticed Benjin with an angry look on his face, and Catrin wasn't even certain he believed her. Acting as if nothing had happened, she and Benjin left as quickly as they could, which turned out to be faster than Catrin had expected. As soon as Rolph untied Curly, the ox charged toward town. Catrin and Benjin bounced along in the oxcart, barely able to keep themselves from flying off. The charge did not last long, though, and Curly slowed, unable to maintain the pace for a long distance. The jostling became bearable, and Catrin glanced at Benjin, who had not said a word.

"You are your father's daughter, of that there can be no doubt," he said, shaking his head.

"He was in so much pain because of the crier's lies. I couldn't let him believe his sons were all dead at my hand when they most likely live; it would've been too cruel."

Benjin didn't harass her any further about it, and they rode in silence for a while, heading on a westerly course.

"Do you think we should make for Adderhold?" she asked, if for no other reason than to break the uncomfortable silence.

"I suppose we haven't much choice. There's little chance of us getting anywhere near the statue while it's being transported, though I'm not sure we have any chance of getting near it when it arrives at Adderhold either. We'd have to pass through lands held by your family and those held by their rivals, the Kytes. A more dangerous path I cannot imagine. Do you know what you will do when we get there?"

"I have no idea, but I must try. It would be cowardly of me to turn my back on these people. The people of the Greatland would pay the greatest price for the Zjhon's folly, and I cannot allow that to happen. I just hope we're right about the true nature of the statue. I can find no way to prove our beliefs or disprove the beliefs of the Zjhon. I suppose I'll have to act on faith alone."

"Blind faith," Benjin said.

"Blind faith, indeed," Catrin said. She hoped some other solution or some bit of proof that would allow her to believe more firmly would present itself, but none came.

Following a narrow cart path, they passed local farmers on their way. Folks waved as they passed, and they returned the waves, trying to appear as if they belonged there. Benjin urged Curly to pick up the pace. Curly would have none of it, though, and set his own pace, despite Benjin's clucks, chirps, and more than a few smacks on the rear with the lines.

As night fell, they entered more heavily settled lands, and the lights of a distant town shone on the horizon. Reflections of the lights could be seen in the wide river that lay on the far side of town. A copse of oak and elm stood on a nearby hill, and Benjin steered Curly toward it as best he could. Curly resisted his direction, and they nearly rode past the trees, but Benjin managed to get him stopped. At the bottom of the hill, Benjin handed Catrin the lines and climbed from the cart. After retrieving an ear of corn, he lured Curly into the trees.

Curly chewed noisily on the corn while Benjin tied him off to a tree. Once Curly was unhooked and taken care of, they set up a small camp and ate sparingly from their provisions. They lit no fire, for fear of drawing attention to themselves, and they spent a long night huddled together for warmth.

* * *

The following day was bright and clear, and the morning sun warmed the air enough that they could no longer see their own breath before them. The road into town was congested with wagons, carts, and hundreds on foot. Catrin and Benjin blended into the crowd as best they could and eventually made their way into town. The streets were jammed with pedestrians and roaming vendors. Curly was ill suited for such tight quarters. He stepped on toes and knocked over vendors' carts, leaving behind a trail of angry people wherever they went. Benjin sought out the market proper and spotted a man selling livestock.

"It'd be nice to ride all the way to Adderhold, but I think we should sell Curly while we can. Major bridges in the Greatland bear a toll, and we'll need coin to cross," he said.

Catrin didn't like the idea one bit, but she could think of no other way to get coin short of stealing, which she was unwilling to do. They approached the livestock vendor, and he appraised them as they moved closer. Catrin suspected he saw an easy profit as he moved into the crowd to great them.

"That beast has lived beyond its years, Yusef would say," he said, shaking his head. "Not fit for plow or plate. Don't think he can use that one. No, Yusef doesn't."

"These days there's little to be had," Benjin replied. "Most would be glad to have such a fine beast. P'haps there're others here who'd be more interested," he said, casting his gaze around the market. Catrin searched for other vendors selling livestock, and while she saw a few goats and a handful of chickens, no one else had large animals for sale.

"Try if you'd like, but anyone here'll tell you that Yusef is the man t'see," the vendor said as he spread his arms wide and bowed deeply.

"And what would Yusef offer for this fine beast and cart?"

"Yusef has no need for the cart, but he supposes he could dispose of it without a great deal of trouble. Yusef offers a silver."

"Good luck to you, Yusef," Benjin said, and he chirped to Curly, who completely ignored him.

"Don't be hasty now. A silver for a beast that appears to be deaf as well as blind is a fair offer, but Yusef is a generous man. A silver and two coppers."

"Three silvers."

"Three silvers! Why that's robbery, friend. Surely, Yusef deserves to eat. Two silvers."

"Three," Benjin said, and Yusef appeared wounded by his firm stance. He made no counteroffer; instead he just shook his head as if in deep thought. "Perhaps now is not the time to sell," Benjin continued. "Prices will only go higher as the pilgrimage begins, and we've nothing but time. Perhaps the traders in the next town will be more generous."

"Thieves, they are. Why, you would have to travel all the way to Adderhold to find a better offer, and even then you take your chances. You seem like good people, and Yusef has a soft place in his heart, he does. Three silvers."

Benjin climbed from the cart and shook his hand. "Deal."

As soon as the coins were in Benjin's hands, Yusef seemed to forget that he and Catrin existed, and he began hawking Curly as if he were a prize bull. "Who will give me five silvers for this fine beast? Full of vigor, he is, and Yusef'll even throw in this finely crafted cart," he shouted into the crowd even as they unloaded their packs.

While Catrin stuffed the blankets from the seat into her pack, the wind blew the hood away from her face, and she hastily pulled it back up. She and Benjin shuffled through the crowd, and Benjin continued to affect his limp and lean on the staff. It did him little good in the jostling crowd, and they were nearly knocked off their feet several times within the sea of people. The lack of respect these folks showed one another was remarkable. It was as if they were so great in number that none of them mattered as individuals. Each person was just another body congesting the streets.

A long line snaked away from the base of the bridge, and a dozen guards stood at the height of the span, holding up the mass of people crossing. Fear gripped Catrin at the sight of them, and she cast Benjin a furtive glance, but he seemed unconcerned.

"Toll collectors," he said, and his statement was confirmed as she watched the soldiers accept coins from each person who passed. They waited as patiently as they could in the line, but it moved dreadfully slowly, and Catrin began to see the wisdom in Benjin's decision to sell Curly. It would have been difficult to maneuver him through the crowd, not to mention the coin they needed to pay the toll.

When they reached the highest part of the span, they were packed tightly against the other people waiting to cross. The stone beneath Catrin's feet seemed to move from side to side, and she feared the bridge would collapse from the weight of so many people. Her feet sore from standing so long, she shifted from one to the other to ease the pain, but it provided only a small amount of relief.

The line continued to move inexorably forward, and the scrutiny of the guards drew ever closer. Catrin felt trapped. If the guards somehow realized who she was, she would have no way to escape. The crowd packed tightly on all sides, and panic threatened to relieve her of her sanity.

Benjin must have sensed her distress, for he took her hand and gave it a small squeeze. "Just a little farther, li'l miss. Hold on for a while longer, and this'll all be behind us. Try to imagine yourself in the middle of an open field," he said.

Catrin tried to take his advice, but the mass of energies around her assaulted her even with her eyes closed. She could sense them. She could feel their impatience. Their smell filled her nostrils, and she thought she might be sick. In an effort to stem off the nausea, she concentrated on her

217

breathing, which had become short and rapid. Deep breaths probably would have settled her stomach if it were not for the smell of unwashed bodies.

When they finally reached the guards, Catrin's hair was soaked with sweat, and her hands trembled. Benjin approached a guard, who gave him a bored glance.

"Copper apiece," he said.

Benjin handed him a silver and pointed to himself and Catrin, as if he were mute. The guard was obviously disgusted to have to make change, and he sighed heavily as he dug in his pouch. After a moment, he produced a handful of coppers and shoved them into Benjin's hand.

"Next time bring coppers," he said and turned his attention to the next in line.

The line on the far side of the toll moved rapidly, and within a few short moments, they gained the far shore. Catrin sucked in the cool air as if she had been drowning, and Benjin dragged her off to one side.

"Calm yourself. We're not out of danger yet. There're more soldiers about."

"I'll be fine in a moment," she said, and she felt her panic begin to recede. They were across the bridge, and though she felt she was stepping from one precipice to another, she was almost accustomed to it; it had begun to feel normal.

* * *

Rats scurried at the edge of the torchlight, and the shadowy form of Chase's guide filled most of the dank tunnel they were following. The land surrounding New Moon Bay was riddled with sewers and passages, and this one was supposed to take Chase to a ship. After days of hiding in cellars and crawling through sewers, Chase was looking forward to being back at sea.

Very little had been said during his travels; Brother Vaughn had made most of the arrangements. Chase didn't even know the name of his guide or what ship he was being taken to, but he made himself keep walking despite the uncertainty. Catrin needed him, and he would not fail her.

The air became less foul as they walked and began to smell more of salt than sewage. When they reached the end of the tunnel, his guide simply pointed to a familiar-looking ship in the harbor and turned and walked back into the tunnel.

The water was far below the tunnel exit, and Chase stared down at the waves crashing on the rocks, hoping the water would be deep enough where he landed. Before his courage fled, he took a running leap into the harbor and struck the water hard. As he reached the surface, wiping the water from his eyes, he heard voices.

"Who goes there?" barked a gravelly voice.

Coming toward Chase was a small rowing craft filled with uniformed men. Taking a deep breath, he slipped beneath the dark water.

Chapter 20

Evil exists only in the hearts of men.
--Ain Giest, Sleepless One

* * *

As he climbed back to the chamber atop the mountain, Nat's legs trembled from exertion as well as fear. Only the hope that he would learn something important kept him moving. Within the chamber, his visions became absolute, blotting out his current reality and showing what he thought were vivid glimpses of a likely future. Though they left him feeling nauseated and abused, he kept coming back, drawn by morbid fascination and the quest for knowledge.

Beside him, Neenya climbed, and her presence bolstered his confidence. Never before had someone shown such faith in him. As he slowly learned her language, all barriers between them seemed to fall. To trust someone so completely was a thing Nat had never believed himself capable of, but Neenya's unwavering dedication and loyalty made it impossible for him to feel otherwise.

Concern was clearly visible in her eyes as they reached the final stage of their climb, but there was something else there, something Nat could not easily define. It was acceptance, he finally decided, and he sighed. Though endeared by her devotion, Nat also felt the weight of responsibility. The Gunata, as Nat now knew the villagers called themselves, believed in him. They believed he had been sent to them to do something special, something important. Neenya had given her life over to him, leaving behind whatever it was she had done in the past, and Nat prayed he would not fail them.

When the chamber entrance came into view, Nat quailed. Only the needs of those who were depending on him drove him forward, and he practically fell into the chamber. As he crawled forward, drawing ragged breaths, the power of premonition obliterated all other thought.

Neenya held him in her arms, and when the vision finally released him, he looked into her eyes, tears streaming down his face. No words could express the horrors he'd seen, and as he pulled Neenya closer, he squeezed his eyes shut, praying that, just this once, his visions were untrue. "I'm so sorry," he whispered. His body shook in grief as his mind reconciled what he'd seen. As he wept, Neenya sang softly, rocking him to sleep.

* * *

The days merged into one long, miserable blur. Catrin could not recall how long it had been since they sold Curly, but the blisters on her feet spoke of more days than her memory could reconcile. They trudged along, surrounded by pilgrims who marched in morose silence. It wasn't a joyful journey for any of them; it was more like a death march. Like sheep to the slaughter, they put one foot in front of the other and nothing more. The people seemed to know they were going to their deaths, yet they continued.

Catrin despaired and wondered why they would leave their lives behind to seek out an idol. Even if the archmaster had mandated their presence, he was certainly in no position to enforce his edict, but they seemed not to care. From what Catrin sensed, most simply wished the misery to end.

The roads were churned to mud, at least until the snows came; then they froze, their texture sealed by frost. Ruts and frozen footprints threatened to turn their ankles, and illness began to spread. Catrin could not breathe through her nose, and a cough rattled in her chest. Benjin did what he could to secure dry places to camp and wood for fires, but the landscape was usually picked clean long before they arrived.

Large groups huddled together at night for the protection in their numbers, but Catrin and Benjin kept to themselves. They had no desire for the company, and those around them seemed to have no desire for the fellowship of strangers.

Occasionally they passed an inn, and the rosy glow that came from within beckoned to them, but Benjin insisted they save their coin for food, which was becoming increasingly expensive. Vendors took advantage of the massive migration and inflated their prices. Perhaps the

221

shortage of food could explain away the cost increase, but Catrin resented it. She felt as if they preyed on the poor and hungry, and she detested them for it. Anger and spite were all that kept her going at times, and she used her fury to stay warm.

"You've not lost hope, have you?" Benjin asked at the end of another silent day.

Catrin remained mute for some time before answering. "Hope," she said. "Hope for what? A quick death? An end to the misery? I've no idea what to hope for. I cannot hope to save these people, and they cannot save themselves."

"Such thoughts will get you nowhere. There's always a chance that things will work out, and you're not the only one attempting to stop this madness. Others labor toward the same end, and we can only pray they've not given up," he said, but she continued to spiral into her own personal nightmare.

"Even if the statue is destroyed, what then? There are no crops in the fields. The food supply is already growing scarce, and disease is sure to follow. I begin to wonder if saving these poor wretches from a quick death is the right thing to do. If they'll only suffer slow deaths, then what good will I have done?"

"You act as if all is already lost, but the sun still shines and we still live and breathe. I, for one, plan to do whatever I can. I'll not give up until my last breath leaves my lips."

"Good luck to you, then," she said. "I'm tempted to simply lay down and die. I've no more to give, and this dreadful march will never end."

Benjin stopped and yanked her aside by her arm. His face was crimson, and she had never seen him so angry; he frightened her, and his grip was painful. "How dare you give up! Did your father teach you nothing? Anything worth doing is difficult, and this could not be more worthwhile. How could you expect it to be easy? You shame me." At one time, those words would have stung, but she simply shrugged.

"Who knows if my father is even alive? I doubt it. I'll never see him again, and if he wants to be disappointed, then let him. And that goes for you as well. Perhaps you would rather walk alone."

"It's tempting, but I'll not allow you to give up so easily. If I have to drag you by your ears, you'll fight, and you'll win, if only to spite me," he said, and a crooked smile actually tried to form on his lips.

Catrin couldn't fight him; he was right, and she knew it. That didn't make it any easier, but it did keep her moving. "You're right. I know, but I'm tired. So very tired."

"I know, li'l miss, but I'm here to help you. I'll always be right by your side. You can count on that," he said.

She leaned against him for support. "You amaze me. How can you stay positive amidst this horror?"

"It's not easy, and I'm not saying it is, but it's all in how you look at it. We could've been hung, or drowned, or burned a dozen times now. How did we survive those things? How are we still here to try? Hope, determination, and in some cases, sheer stubbornness."

"Well, that's one thing we have in abundance. If only we could eat it," she said and actually chuckled.

"There, you see? I told you we could do it. Laughter keeps the world alive, you know." And with that, they stepped a little lighter, marched a little faster, and the pain seemed to ease in Catrin's feet, as if it had been imposed by her despair rather than the endless footsteps. When an inn appeared on the horizon, Benjin led her toward it.

"But we should save our coin," she protested.

"One night's lodging won't break us, and I think we've earned a bit of respite. I'd also like to look for signs of the Vestrana." Their hopes were dashed when they arrived, though.

"Full up," the innkeeper said when they inquired about rooms, and the sheer number of folks jammed into the common room gave her statement credence. The rotund woman turned to tend other customers.

"Please miss. A stall in the stables, a bit of floor in the kitchens, we'll take whatever you can offer." The woman looked disgusted, but Benjin pleaded with his eyes.

"Two coppers and you can sleep in the loft with the rest of the fools," she said, and Benjin quickly pulled four coppers from his pouch.

"Might we get a bit of food to go with our lodging?"

"You're a pushy one," she said, but she accepted the coin. "Potato broth is all we have left, but this'll get you two bowls."

A thick layer of grease was congealed on top of the broth, and it tasted little better than laundry water, but it was warm and it felt good in Catrin's belly. They drained their bowls in short order, and the innkeeper had the stable boy show them to the loft. At the top of the ladder, they found mounds of flea-ridden straw, and there was barely a spot to be found that did not harbor a sleeping body. People cursed them as they wandered through the disorganized mass of humanity, but they eventually found a corner in which to lie down. Catrin pulled the blankets from her pack and prepared the best bed she could for them, and they laid themselves down to rest.

"You get some sleep," Benjin said. "I don't trust these folk not to rob us. I'll keep watch for now. I'll wake you later."

She would have argued, but his words were muffled by her wide yawn, and she let sleep claim her. When she woke, sunlight streamed through the cracks in the walls, and Benjin slept beside her, his belt knife still in his hand. When he woke, she saw that his purse and other valuables were beneath him. He was an intimidating figure, knife in hand, and she supposed that had been enough to keep any would-be thieves at bay.

The sun already high in the sky, they left the inn long after most of the others who had shared the loft with them. A small town lay ahead, and in many ways, it looked the same as every other town they had already passed. It made Catrin feel as if they had been walking in circles.

"We're nearing the western border of Astor," Benjin said as they entered the dirty little hamlet. "Soon we'll be in Mundleboro, the lands ruled by your mother's family. We'll have to be extra careful when we get there. Keep your hood up at all times. I've been searching for signs of the Vestrana, but the signals I've seen are conflicting. They are close to correct but include subtle warnings. I'm afraid to seek their aid since it seems they fear they've been infiltrated."

Walking past the smithy and shops, Benjin stopped at a storefront that displayed cured meats. Salted hams, smoked fish, and several strange reddish sausages hung under the watchful eye of the storekeeper.

"What'll you be needing?" the beady-eyed man asked, and it was clear he did not trust them. His look urged them to buy something or move on.

"How much for the pepper sausage?" Benjin asked.

"A silver."

"Why, that's robbery. Surely you cannot expect to get such a price?"

"Already have and will again. Take it or leave it," the man said, and he cleared the sword at his waist from its scabbard, daring them to steal it. They did not intend to stoop so low, but that price would consume most of the coin they had, and they still had a long journey ahead of them.

"Come on, li'l miss. Let us find a more pleasant thief to steal our coin," Benjin said.

The storekeeper spit at them as they left. The argument drew unwanted attention, and several people among the crowd stared at them as they turned away, as if they hoped for a fight to break out, if only to break the monotony.

At that moment, a chance wind gusted through the streets, and the hood was pulled from Catrin's face. As she rushed to pull it back up, she saw a woman who was as wide as she was tall, and she was walking toward them.

"Lady Lissa! What in all the gods' lands are you doing here? You were to be at Ravenhold weeks ago. And what have you done with your hair?" she asked as she approached, and Catrin looked about to see who she addressed, but then the woman stopped abruptly and her eyes went wide. She leaped across the short distance that separated them and grabbed Catrin by the arm.

"If you make a move," she said in a low voice, "I'll shout for the guards and label you thieves. Come with me quietly, and no one gets hurt. Understand?" Only then did Catrin feel the pressure of a cold blade against her back.

Benjin stood, frozen, seemingly afraid the woman would run Catrin through. Without a word, they let the strange woman lead them into a nearby inn.

The common room was crowded, but no one paid them any mind except to curse them for pushing through the throng. The knife at her back urged her up the stairs, and they stopped before a sturdy wooden door at the end of the hall. This door was the only one to bear a lock, and the woman produced a key from the folds of her shawl. Within a moment they were inside, the door locked securely behind them.

"Don't think to lie to me. I'd know you even if you were burned from head to toe. You're Mangst as sure as Vestra shines," she said.

Benjin let out a heavy sigh. "Who are you?" he asked, and the woman wheeled on him with her knife.

"The questions are mine to ask. Never you mind who I am. The question is who are you, and what are you doing here?"

"That's a long story and not one easily explained," Benjin began, but the woman cut him short, literally; she sliced the air before him as if to demonstrate her skill with the knife.

"Shut your mouth. I'm not asking you. I ask her. What is your business here?"

"We're bound for Adderhold," Catrin said, unsure of what else to say. She decided a small bit of truth was all she was willing to give. She didn't even know who this woman was or what evil deed she suspected them of committing, but her patience was already worn thin.

"Lies," the woman said, and she punctuated her statement by tapping her slender blade on Catrin's chest. It was a move meant to threaten and cow her, but Catrin had had enough. She and Benjin had done nothing to deserve such treatment. With a quickness she didn't realize she possessed, she clasped the woman's wrist and twisted hard, driving her knee into the woman's groin. By the time the woman hit the floor, Catrin had the blade wedged between the woman's multiple chins.

"Easy now. Easy. Let's not get too excited. Let her up, li'l miss. We mean her no harm, and she means us none. This is all just a misunderstanding," Benjin said, but his words were ignored.

Catrin snarled at the woman, who now became the target of all her anger, all her resentment. Suddenly this woman was the source of all their troubles, and with one twist of her wrist, she would be gone. It would be so easy. The woman's flesh was soft and pale and would part easily before the razor-sharp blade.

Benjin grabbed Catrin's arm and pulled the knife away from the woman's throat, but he got no gratitude. The woman pulled another blade from her belt, and they all stood in suspense, assessing one another.

"Please, both of you. We can solve this peacefully. Put the blades away. Shedding each other's blood will help no one," Benjin said.

His words penetrated the haze of fury that still gripped Catrin. With obvious reluctance, she reversed the blade and handed it back to the woman, who seemed surprised.

"Now let us begin again. I'm Benjin Hawk," he said, and the woman's eyes grew wide again. "And this is Catrin Volker, daughter of Elsa Mangst."

His words might as well have been a physical blow for the effect they had on the woman. She fell back against the far wall, and her breathing became rapid. Catrin was shocked by his honesty.

"By the gods, it's true. Isn't it?" she asked with a hysterical glance at Catrin.

"He speaks the truth," Catrin said, and it was as much an accusation against Benjin as it was an affirmation. The woman sat down heavily and stared at them as if they were beyond explanation.

"You don't mean to kill me," the woman said, making it more a statement than a question, but Catrin felt the need to respond nonetheless.

"We never intended you any harm, but you certainly scared us," she said, and she was surprised to see the woman relax a bit and actually sheathe her blades.

"I am Millicent, maid to the Lady Mangst," the woman said, and now it was Benjin's turn to appear shocked.

"Millie? I didn't even recognize you."

"You need not tell me the years have been unkind; I am aware, but they've touched you as well," Millie said.

"You know each other?" Catrin asked.

"It's been many years," Benjin began before Millie cut him short.

"Since you and that scoundrel, Wendel, stole Elsa away from us."

"After all these years, you are still shortsighted, I see," Benjin said, but Millie ignored him.

"Let us speak no more. This matter should be taken up with the lady, not her lowly servant. I'll arrange for passage to Ravenhold. Be warned, if you try to escape, I'll have you hunted down and killed. Do I make myself clear?"

"You do, but your threats are unnecessary and insulting," Catrin said with an arch look, daring the woman to question her integrity again. Millie gave her a sidelong glance but said no more. Instead, she walked out the door, leaving them alone.

"This is not going to go well," Benjin said almost to himself.

"I assume my family will not be happy to see me?"

"Or me," he said, shaking his head.

"Well, let them be unhappy. I've no intention of staying long. You don't think they'll try to stop me, do you?"

"I don't know, li'l miss. I'd hoped to avoid them completely. They're not fond of me to begin with, and I have no idea how they will react to you, but I doubt they'll welcome you. Your mother's family are not the most forgiving people I've ever met."

Catrin asked him no more questions, knowing he would not have the answers. She supposed she would just have to take it up with the Lady Mangst--whoever that was. It bothered her a great deal that she didn't know, yet she decided not to ask. She would find out soon enough.

The room began to feel very small as she paced back and forth, and the air felt thick and heavy, as if she were breathing water. She did not know how long Millie had been gone, but it seemed like days, and when she finally returned, Catrin's patience was lost to her.

"We must leave at once," Millie said. "I was not to return for three more days, but this'll not wait. I've arranged a carriage for you. It waits in front of the inn. Come."

"Will you be joining us?" Catrin asked, uncertain of what exactly was taking place.

"I'll be traveling in a separate carriage, but they will travel together. So, yes, in a sense. Morif will act as your bodyguard and assure your safety."

In other words, Catrin thought, he would be their jailer, there only to make sure they did not try to escape. The fact bothered her greatly, but she put no voice to her misgivings, for she doubted it would do any good. Without another word, she and Benjin followed Millie from the inn.

As promised, two carriages waited, and they were like no carriages Catrin had ever seen before. Completely enclosed, with small doors in the side and smoky glass windows, their black finish shone in the sun, and even the wheels were spotless. Each one was drawn by a team of four horses, which appeared to be more for show than out of need. The carriages were large but not so large as to require more than one horse. The horses were obviously bred for looks; their coats gleamed, and their manes flowed. Their forelocks were so long that it was a wonder the horses could see anything. These were nothing like the horses her father raised, which were primarily workhorses, bred for power. And these were far showier than the horses of the Arghast tribes. It reminded Catrin of the townies, who used their horses primarily as a display of wealth, and the thought left a foul taste in her mouth.

Morif proved to be an imposing man. He was missing one eye, but his movements spoke of death. His muscles were well defined, and the cords of his tendons stood out in relief. He gave them a baleful stare as they climbed aboard the carriage, and Catrin returned it, which seemed to surprise him. She would show him no fear, and for once, she felt none. Let him try to hurt them, and she would show him just how dangerous she was.

The interior of the carriage was opulently appointed with deeply cushioned seats and smoky glass windows framed by frilly curtains. The journey to Ravenhold took four days, and they spent their nights in the best rooms the inns along the way had to offer. The common rooms were always full when they arrived, but somehow Millie always managed to secure not one, but two rooms each night.

Morif kept watch outside their door, and the tension between him and Catrin grew as time passed. She knew she should leave the man be, but his very presence annoyed her. At every opportunity, she let him know she didn't appreciate his watchfulness, whether it was something as small as stepping on his toes when she passed, or something as overt as spilling her dinner down the front of him. It was clear he struggled to restrain himself, but Catrin didn't care. She almost wished he would provoke her so she could take out her fury on him.

When she was honest with herself, it was not him she loathed. It was the thought that her family was automatically distrustful of her. It went against everything her father had taught her, and she resented the fact that they used his name without any trace of respect. She'd had her fill of people looking down their noses at her, and she thought she might bite the nose off the next person who did it.

Strange sensations crossed her mind, though, as they moved closer to Ravenhold. She was farther from the land of her birth than she had ever dreamed she would be, and yet, in some small way, she felt as if she were coming home.

Chapter 21

The souls of heroes are forged by the gods and tempered with the pain of life.
--Matteo Dersinger, prophet

* * *

Ravenhold proved to be an impressive sight. Larger than the Masterhouse and constructed with far more decorative appeal, it appeared to have been built more for show than strength. The land surrounding it was fancifully landscaped, and even in the dead of winter, there was color everywhere from the scarlet berries on the holly trees to the orange and yellow leaves of the sprawling oaks. Rose bushes lined the roadway, and Catrin knew they must be gorgeous in springtime.

Despite its beauty, the place filled her with dread. She was but a simple farm girl. There was no place for her here. The grand facade included bas-reliefs and statuary, and all of it lent to the air of superiority, as if the people who dwelt there were of a higher race. The closer they drew, the smaller Catrin felt, and it was a feeling she liked not one bit. Benjin tried to start a conversation a number of times, but her irritation would not allow for it. Instead, she brooded in oppressive silence.

No one greeted them at the gate except stable hands, and Millie instructed them to follow her. Morif shadowed them, and Catrin cast him baleful glances, but he ignored her completely. A subtle sidestep nearly tripped him, and she smiled--ignore *that*. He didn't lay a hand on her, but the look in his eye conveyed his thoughts.

As they climbed the wide marble stair that led to a pair of oak doors twice Catrin's height, she forgot about Morif and took in all the details. Carved from the white stone, a pair of roses presided over the entrance. They twined around one another, their thorns curved delicately away from the stems, and the name *Mangst* was engraved in an arc over them. It seemed an arrogant display, but it was overshadowed by what lay within. Thick carpets covered the center of the wide halls, leaving only a couple of hand widths of polished stone visible along the edges.

The walls were adorned with likenesses of those she supposed were her ancestors, for they all bore the family resemblance. Small gold plates at the bottoms of the portraits gave the names of those depicted, and Catrin tried to memorize each name as she passed them. There was a regal-looking man with gray hair only over his ears--Rasmussen Mangst--and a stern-looking woman in her middle years--Marietta Mangst. Their stares seemed to follow her, accusing her of besmirching their name. She was a ragamuffin among nobility, and her leathers and homespun seemed rags amid the glory of these trappings.

Millie led them to a side hall decorated with finely carved tables that bore elegant pottery and dried flowers--mostly roses. When she reached a set of oak doors, Millie ushered them inside.

"Please wait here while I alert the lady to your presence."

"I'll do no such thing," Catrin said, her hands on her hips. "You've dragged me here against my will, and I'll either see the lady now or be on my way."

Morif crossed his arms over his chest as if to bar her path, but Catrin pushed him out of her way. He glanced at Millie, obviously looking for direction, and she sighed.

"Very well," she said. "Suit yourself."

"I believe I'll do just that," Catrin replied with venom.

Millie jogged ahead, but Catrin refused to be rushed. She let Millie gain distance on them as she strode with feigned confidence through the hallowed halls of her ancestral home. She felt no more comfortable, but she refused to let her insecurity show. Morif followed them with a scowl, but she pretended he wasn't there. Instead, she acted as if she were the one who ruled this house.

Benjin walked beside her and matched her step. He didn't appear happy about her outbursts, but he supported her nonetheless. They were in this together for right or wrong, and she appreciated his not chastising her when it was obvious he didn't approve.

A pair of young men in rose-embroidered livery flanked doors no smaller than those at the main entrance. Millie rushed toward them. The men did not stall her, and she scurried inside. When Catrin and Benjin arrived, however, they barred the way. Catrin didn't attempt to force her way past them and instead stood in as regal a manner as she could muster. She listened intently but could hear only muffled conversation at first.

"What?" came a louder voice from inside. "Here? Now? Why did you not leave them in an audience room?" This was followed by more low conversation. The two young men exchanged puzzled glances but remained at attention. "Insisted, did she? Well, bring the whelp in. Let us see what she has to say for herself." Catrin heard the disdain in the lady's voice, and her mood worsened.

Millie was pale and shaken when she reappeared, and she motioned for them to enter. Catrin waited a moment, just for the sake of being contrary, and the two young men wore their shock on their faces.

"Let's not start things off badly, li'l miss. We've been summoned," Benjin said, urging her inside.

"I'll enter when I'm good and ready," Catrin said, and a tense silence hung over the hall. After a very long moment, she strode into the room as if it were her own, and Benjin followed closely.

"So, Benjin Hawk, you darken my doorway once again, after all these years. What do you plan to steal this time?" asked the elderly woman who waited inside. She was petite and her skin hung on her like an overlarge garment, but her eyes bored holes into whatever met her stare.

"Lady Mangst," Benjin said with a slight bow, but he said no more, as if he had not heard her question.

"And who is this waif at your side? Someone posing as my granddaughter?"

"Catrin Volker, Lady. Daughter of Wendel Volker and Elsa Mangst," he replied in a polite tone even as Catrin's anger flamed higher.

"Do not speak that foul name in my presence. That man stole my daughter, and his get is not worthy of my name."

"If you wish to address my Guardian, you will do so with respect. And with regards to my father, you are not fit to speak his name, for you would only foul it with your forked tongue," Catrin said as she stepped between Benjin and her grandmother.

All the color drained from Millie's face, and she eased into the shadows, but the Lady Mangst drew herself up, and a fire to rival Catrin's burned in her eyes.

"Respect is earned, not given."

"Every creature deserves a basic amount of respect. Unless, of course, you consider yourself better than everyone else," Catrin replied.

"Insolent child."

"Self-righteous wench," Catrin parried, and the air between them was charged with hostility.

"Now, ladies, surely we can be civil," Benjin interjected, and both women wheeled on him.

"Stay out of this," they said in unison.

"At least you two can agree on something," he mumbled as he took a step back.

"So what brings you here, sweetling?" the Lady Mangst asked.

"Your serving woman dragged me here on the threat of my life. I had no desire to come here. In fact, I believe I'll be leaving now," Catrin said as she turned to leave, but she was shocked to hear a slap echo through the room. She turned to see Millie with tears in her eyes, holding a hand to her face, and the Lady Mangst turned from Millie to face Catrin once again.

"You expect me to believe that you were not bound here anyway? Where else would you be headed?"

"Adderhold," Catrin replied.

The Lady Mangst spit on the floor. "What would you want in that house of vipers and vermin, to worship idols perhaps?"

"I don't see where that is any of your business."

"I'm your grandmother."

"You certainly don't act like it," Catrin said, and she realized this argument would get them nowhere, but she refused to back down, refused to show weakness in the face of one so pious. And she was surprised to see her antagonist reappraise her.

"So you ask nothing of me? No coin or lands or titles? You do not claim your birthright?"

"As I said before, I wouldn't have come at all if not for your underlings," Catrin replied, and she felt a little ashamed for being obstinate when her grandmother seemed to be warming to her, even if only slightly. "I ask nothing of you but my freedom."

The Lady Mangst said nothing for a few moments as she considered Catrin's words. Benjin and Millie exchanged furtive glances, but Catrin ignored them all. Her thoughts were muddled by her emotions, and she struggled to focus. So much had happened in such a short time, and she felt she was reacting poorly rather than using the situation to her advantage. It was possible her family could aid her in her quest, if only she could prove herself in their eyes.

"You've not told me why you were traveling to Adderhold. May I ask why?" the Lady Mangst asked in an almost conciliatory tone, but Catrin judged it genuine.

"I've no desire to worship the Statue of Terhilian. I wish to destroy it."

Her grandmother's eyes bulged. After a sharp intake of breath, she broke into a fit of coughing that threatened to claim her completely. Millie rushed to prepare her tea, but the spell passed long before the water was heated. Still Millie brought her the tea, and she sipped it with tears in her eyes. Catrin could not tell if the tears were from the coughing or something else entirely, but she waited patiently for a response.

"I truly do not mean to be rude this time, but I must ask. What makes you think you're capable of such a thing? Though, before you answer, I will add that I think it a noble goal and one I wish I could do myself."

Catrin cast Benjin a querying glance, but he only shrugged in return. The decision was hers.

"I'm not only your granddaughter. I am also the one they call the Herald of Istra."

This statement brought on a new fit of coughing, and Millie looked as if she would faint. Benjin gave Catrin no

235

indication as to his feelings on her decision, but it was done now, and she couldn't take the words back. She would simply have to live with the consequences. The Lady Mangst slowly recovered, and after sipping her tea, she met Catrin's gaze.

"You don't really expect me to believe that, do you?" she asked, and Catrin sensed no sarcasm. She decided to take no offense and drew a breath to answer, but Benjin could no longer hold his tongue.

"Please don't ask her to prove her powers. It's far too dangerous, and I don't want to see anyone get hurt."

"It's not a problem, Benjin. I will do this for my grandmother as a sign of respect," Catrin said, and Millie nodded firmly, as if this were how it should be. Catrin closed her eyes and focused her mind on the one thing she shared in common with the lady: her mother.

She focused on memories of her childhood: her mother's scent, the feeling of her gentle caress, the warmth of her embrace, the safety and security she had always felt in her mother's presence. All of these she poured into her meditation, not allowing the startled gasps to disturb her. She added the tinkling laughter and the love her mother had always shown for her and her father. Lastly, she added the sorrow, grief, and loss brought on by her mother's death. It was painful to recall, but she felt it necessary to convey the full truth. With the kindest and gentlest of intentions, she sent her focused thoughts to her grandmother.

When she opened her eyes, she saw Millie kneeling on the floor, her jaw hanging slack. The Lady Mangst had her back to Catrin, but her shoulders shook and her voice trembled with anguish when she finally spoke. "Leave me now, I beg of you."

Catrin was startled by the request, but the trembling of her grandmother's shoulders gave further evidence of the impact of her demonstration. Millie slowly drew herself up and motioned for them to follow her. Catrin and Benjin did so without question, for the lady's distress was plain to see, and they left her to grieve.

"My dear Elsa, why did you leave me?" they heard her wail as the doors closed behind them. Catrin felt no joy at

236

bringing her grandmother pain, and she walked in subdued silence. Millie wobbled as she walked, and it was obvious that the day's revelations had been hard on her as well.

"I want to thank you for the kindness you showed our lady, despite your disagreements, and I apologize for my actions. I have wronged you, and I hope you'll forgive me," she said when she stopped before a set of doors.

"We all make mistakes. And since I have already forgiven you, I must ask you to forgive me for my insolence and rudeness. Had we met under better circumstances, I'm certain we could have been friends."

"It's kind of you to say, Lady Catrin," Millie replied, and Catrin felt she was sincere, though the title still seemed ill fitting.

"Please accept our hospitality. You'll find the apartments within well appointed, and I'll attend to your needs personally."

"Your kindness is appreciated. You have my thanks," Catrin said, and Millie bowed deeply before her.

"I'll send for food and bath water."

Catrin nodded her thanks. Her efforts and emotions had taxed her, and she was grateful for the respite. Benjin joined her as she entered the apartments, and he whistled as he looked about.

"Millie has honored you by bringing us here," he said. "If I am not mistaken, these quarters are reserved for their most respected guests."

Catrin was not surprised by his words, for the apartments were lavishly appointed. Deep carpets cushioned her feet, and beautiful works of art adorned the walls, depicting scenes of nature as only the most talented artists could render them. Elaborately carved chairs bore soft cushions, and a fire burned in the fireplace. Two doors led to private sleeping chambers that were not much smaller than the common room. Within she found a delightfully soft feather mattress shrouded by a canopy of sheer material.

Though the bed was inviting, Catrin could not bear the thought of soiling the linens; she needed a bath desperately. A parade of liveried servants arrived with steaming basins of water and washtubs that required four men apiece to carry.

The men placed the tubs within the private rooms, and they filled them with water and rose petals before departing with respectful bows. Others followed with soft towels, robes, and a bounty of exotic foods. Catrin thanked them for their efforts, which seemed to confuse them more than anything, but she was truly grateful for the gifts.

Heat soaked into her bones as she slid into the scented water, and she allowed herself to remain in the tub until the water had gone nearly cold. She dried her wrinkled skin with the plush towels and donned a robe that bore her family sigil.

Sitting by the fire, she sampled the array of delicacies. Deep red wine cleansed her palate as she ate both sweet and salty, and soon her hunger was sated. Benjin joined her, looking completely out of place in his robe, which made her giggle, but he ignored her jibes as he attacked the food with vigor. With surprising speed, they finished every morsel, and they settled into the cushions with their bellies full. The fire lulled Catrin into a deep trance, and she soon forgot about the bed as the chair cradled her like a pair of loving arms.

When Millie returned, Catrin stirred from her stupor, and she was unsure if she had been sleeping or simply in a daze.

"The lady wishes to speak with you now. Will you follow me?" Millie asked.

"I should dress first," Catrin said.

"You're fine as you are. The lady's private apartments are but a short walk from here."

She followed Millie into the hall with Benjin in her shadow. True to her word, Millie led them only a short distance before they arrived at another grand entranceway, flanked by a pair of guards who nodded to Millie and immediately allowed them to enter. The apartments within were not much more grand than those provided to Catrin and Benjin, which only served to confirm the honor that had been granted to them.

"Come, my dear. Please sit beside me, and we'll let the fire warm our bones," the Lady Mangst said. "As I grow older, the cold does pain me so." Catrin moved to the seat beside hers. "Come, Benjin, do not be shy. I promise not to bite--this time."

Benjin sat on the edge of a nearby chair, and Catrin was struck by the changes in her grandmother. She was no longer hostile, and Catrin sensed deep-seated pain, both physical and emotional.

"By the gods," the Lady Mangst said, "I don't know why you wear your hair so short, but you look exactly as your mother did at your age, more one of the boys than one of the girls. You have her look about you, but mostly, it's in your eyes." After wiping away a tear, she turned to Benjin. "Please, tell me how my daughter died."

"I'm very sorry. Elsa was murdered."

"In what manner?"

"As far as we've been able to figure, it was a large dose of mother's root concealed in sweet buns from the local bakery, which was run by Baker Hollis. I know of no reason he'd commit such an atrocity, but I mean to find out."

"The Kyte family put him up to it, of that I can assure you. Catrin's aunt was killed in the same horrible manner. They are a despicable lot," the Lady Mangst said.

"How did you know about my aunt's death?" Catrin asked, confused.

"How would I not? I was by her side during the entire ordeal."

"Wait. I don't understand," Catrin said. "My aunt died on the same day as my mother, on the Godfist. How could you have been there?"

"I'm very sorry, dear, but it seems you've lost two aunts to the Kytes. I assume you speak of your father's sister?"

"His brother's wife. I had another aunt?"

"Your mother's sister, Maritza. She was killed some fifteen years ago. It seems they've taken both my daughters from me, but not before each bore me a granddaughter. You and your cousin, Lissa, are my only living descendents."

"I'm very sorry, Lady," Catrin said, sincere. The pain of her mother's death had faded with time, but it was fresh for her grandmother, like an open wound, and now knowing she had lost another aunt made her heart ache.

239

"Please, call me Grandma, if you would. That's what Lissa has always called me, and it would please me greatly if you would do the same."

"Thank you, Grandma."

"It must've been difficult for you, growing up without your mother."

"My father and Benjin always cared for me, and I wanted for nothing. Though, I miss her dearly."

Her grandmother raised an eyebrow and seemed to reappraise Benjin. "It would seem I owe you a debt of gratitude, Benjin Hawk. You and Wendel have raised my granddaughter as a fine and strong young woman."

"Wendel deserves more credit than I, but I did what I could, and I'd do it all again if given the chance," he said, and the lady nodded, tears in her eyes.

"The darkness of these days has soured my disposition, and I was angry with Elsa--so many years she had been gone without a word. Now, of course, I understand the reason, though it makes it no easier to bear. I thank you for coming and for not leaving. You would've been entitled given our treatment of you."

"Let's put that all behind us. I forgive you for any hostility you expressed, and I forgive myself for reacting poorly. I hope you'll do the same," Catrin said as she took her grandmother's hand in hers.

"Yes, dear, of course," she responded, patting Catrin's hands lightly. "Now tell me. How do you plan to destroy the Statues of Terhilian?"

"Statues?" Catrin said, swaying in her chair.

"Oh dear, you didn't know. I'm sorry to give such dire news, but a second statue has been discovered in the Westland."

Catrin sat back heavily in her chair as desperation clutched her, and she found it difficult to breathe. What had started as a nearly impossible quest had just become completely hopeless. There was no way she could destroy two statues; she wasn't sure if she could even disarm one of them. She cradled her head in her hands as a cloud of impending doom threatened to crush her under its weight. "I don't know, Grandma. I honestly don't. When I heard of the first statue, I simply had to try, but now . . . now I see no hope at all."

"Nonsense, child. There is always hope."

Chapter 22

Darkness, no matter how powerful it may seem, can be driven back by the tiniest spark.
--unknown soldier

* * *

"There is perhaps a way you could travel safely to Adderhold, but I doubt very much you will like it. Before I tell you what it is, there are some things you must know."

Catrin wasn't certain she wanted to hear what her grandmother had to say, for fear of more bad news.

"When the Zjhon forces attacked us, I knew we could not resist. If we had, we would've lost far too many of our good subjects. Instead, I negotiated terms that would allow the subjects of Mundleboro to remain mostly unmolested, though under Zjhon rule. In truth, the Zjhon did not wish to depose us; they simply insisted we adopt their religion and support the efforts to spread the teachings of their Church. It wasn't something we wished for, but it was far less disruptive than a full-scale invasion would've been; thus, we surrendered.

"The conditions of our surrender were unpleasant, and we still lost a large number of able-bodied men to conscription, but for the most part, life went on as it had before. This kept the majority of our subjects happy, and they paid the increased taxes with little protest. Things have changed since then, though. Now the Zjhon are demanding higher taxes and something far more sinister. They've demanded a marriage between the Mangst and Kyte families. While they claim the move is intended to strengthen both lands and reduce border conflicts, it'll surely weaken Mundleboro and Lankland alike."

Darkness clouded the periphery of Catrin's vision, and flecks of light danced before her eyes as the words sank in. A less desirable union she could not imagine.

"Your cousin Lissa is to wed the youngest grandson of Arbuckle Kyte, but she has defied me. I've no idea where she is hiding. This is another reason I was so wroth when you arrived. I make no excuses, mind you; I simply need you to understand the dire circumstances that we find ourselves in.

"If Lissa is not within Adderhold by the appointed time, our family will forfeit our hold on these lands. The Zjhon will descend upon us, and there is little we can do to stop them. The only solution I can find is to send you in her stead."

The words were like a blow to Catrin's stomach, and the air left her lungs with a whoosh. She attempted to respond several times, but her tongue refused to form the words. Benjin appeared as dumbstruck as Catrin, his jaw hanging slack.

"You wish me to marry into the family that murdered my mother and both my aunts?" she asked finally.

"I've not asked it of you. I said it was the only solution that I've been able to find. I know you have no reason to love the people of Mundleboro, but it seems their fate lies with you, as your blood right would have dictated anyway. You have the opportunity to make this sacrifice for them, and they would love you for it. But, again, I don't ask it of you. This is something you'll have to take on willingly, for I'll not force your hand."

"If Catrin traveled under the guise of Lissa, we would be granted access to Adderhold, which is our main goal, and that would put us far closer to the statue than we would have been able to achieve on our own. Perhaps this is a boon, li'l miss," Benjin said, appearing thoughtful.

"Have you lost your senses?" Catrin asked, appalled that he would even consider it. She had no wish to be married, let alone to one of her family's mortal enemies. However, while she knew nothing of the people of Mundleboro, she did feel responsible for their safety, if for no other reason than because she felt her mother would have wanted to spare the innocent. She'd been a kind and loving woman, and Catrin could not imagine her leaving thousands to die when it was within her power to save them, but the thought of sacrificing herself made her physically ill.

"Don't feel pressured to make your decision now, dear, but the appointed day is rushing toward us, and by the new moon, we must either comply or prepare for war. I've considered offering myself up, but I have already been married, and they would surely decline. Unless Lissa finds it in her heart to return, I'm afraid we have no other options. Millie, please bring Catrin a calming elixir, she looks as if she's going to faint."

Indeed, Catrin found it difficult to remain upright as she was faced with responsibilities she'd never imagined. She was but a simple farm girl; certainly she had not the makings of a ruler, even a powerless one.

Benjin came to her side and placed a hand on her shoulder. She supposed he was trying to reassure her, but it felt like compulsion, as if he were trying to persuade her to make the sacrifice. She wanted to rebel against him and her grandmother, to lash out and make them regret asking this of her, but a vision of her mother came to her. Strong and proud, she said nothing, but her eyes commanded Catrin to be noble, to take the lives of her subjects in her hands and cradle them, just as she had cradled Catrin those many years ago. And mostly, she seemed to ask Catrin to do that which her mother had failed to do: accept the responsibility of her birthright and protect those who needed her.

It seemed strange to Catrin that being born of noble blood would carry so much weight and onus. She'd always thought the nobility leeched off those who worked the land, but now she saw an equally daunting encumbrance. Perhaps the true role of those with power was to serve those who toiled for the sake of their brethren. No longer did the scales seem tipped in the favor of nobility; now they seemed to almost balance one another. The common people needed the nobility as much as the nobles needed them. Like the cycle of life itself, if one component failed, all would perish.

Ignorance had been so much easier to bear.

"It's my duty to protect those who cannot defend themselves, and if that means I must sacrifice myself for the greater good, then so be it," she said before the courage to utter the words left her. She hadn't known what kind of reaction to expect, and in truth, she hadn't even taken the time to consider how her words would be received, but the sobs that wracked her grandmother's feeble form nearly made her weep.

"You are truly my granddaughter," her grandmother said when her emotions subsided. "I couldn't be more proud of you, and I know your mother would approve."

"You have her strength and the beauty of her heart," Benjin added. "She would, indeed, be proud . . . just as I am."

Their words would have warmed her soul if not for the icy fear that threatened to consume her. She trembled as she imagined herself surrounded by those who'd attempted to kill her when she was only a babe. They must be monsters, these Kytes, and she envisioned herself within their houses, like a lamb surrounded by hungry wolves. The visions terrified her, and she nearly fled. It would be so much easier to disappear into the masses, to become anonymous and unimportant, as she had been when she was just the daughter of a horseman. Perhaps, she thought, that was what Lissa had done.

Deep in her heart, she knew running away would bring her no happiness. Images of those she failed would haunt her, not the least of which would be her father, the man who had taught her right from wrong, who had instilled his values in her, and who had trusted her to do what needed to be done. She could not let them down; her conscience would simply not allow it.

"I don't know if I'll be able to neutralize the statue, but I still plan to try. The marriage is within my power, and despite my misgivings, I will do it. I set out to save as many people as I could, and though this is not how I intended to do it, it serves the same purpose. Perhaps, with the luck of the gods, I'll find a way to achieve both," she said.

"You are a courageous young lady," Millie said as she approached with a lightly steaming mug that she held in trembling hands. "Your bravery makes me proud to serve your family. Here, sip this. It will help to calm you."

"Thank you, Millie, but no. I need my wits about me," Catrin said. Millie nodded and downed the contents of the mug in only a few gulps before she walked away, looking dazed.

"I'll not yet hold you to your word, Catrin, for I feel you should take the rest of the day to consider carefully. You may return to me on the morrow," her grandmother said, and it was obvious that her words were a dismissal. Millie led Catrin and Benjin back to their apartments, and not a word was spoken. It seemed no one would try to influence Catrin one way or another on this matter. Secretly, she prayed Lissa would arrive and relieve her of the burden.

* * *

In the days that followed, Catrin firmed her resolve, and Lissa remained absent. Though she'd never met her cousin, Catrin began to loath her. What kind of person could abandon her responsibilities? The fact that Lissa was said to resemble Catrin in almost every physical way did not sit well with her, and she resented someone else bearing her likeness but not her morals.

Millie had taken to dressing Catrin every morning, and each day brought a new affront. Frilly dresses and lace-trimmed petticoats were anathema to her. She was uncomfortable no matter how hard she tried to get used to the attire she was expected to wear. She knew she could not arrive for the wedding dressed in her leathers and homespun, but in the evenings, she often donned them for the solace they brought her.

It was on one of these occasions that she suddenly grew panicked as she realized the gilded box that held her noonstones was missing. She could not bear to think of Millie as a thief, and she supposed they might have fallen out when her garments had been taken for cleaning. Benjin was nowhere about, and her anxiety increased when she realized her staff was also gone. After a frantic and futile search of the apartments, she sat down and cried. The stress overwhelmed her, and she hugged herself in an effort to stave off a massive wave of depression. Her entire life was in disarray, and she could no longer take it. The fact that she needed to leave for Adderhold in the morning helped not at all. When Benjin and Millie entered, all smiles, she did what she could to hide her distress, but it was of no use; her anxiety was plain to see. "I've lost my staff and my stones," she managed to say.

"I know you're upset, li'l miss, but everything is going to be fine. I promise you," Benjin said. "Right now, I want you to take a deep breath and dry your eyes; we need to visit with your grandmother."

"I need to change back into something more suitable," Catrin said, and her face flushed with embarrassment.

"You look just fine to me," Millie said and, taking Catrin by the arm, led her from the room.

Millie propelled her through a number of halls that Catrin had never walked before, and she began to get a cold feeling in her stomach. She couldn't have been more surprised, or more mortified, to be led into a cavernous hall, filled to capacity with well-dressed strangers. At the far end of the hall, behind a table laden with fine foods and colorful pitchers, sat her grandmother; beside her waited a single, vacant chair. Unerringly, Millie's course led to that chair.

Every eye upon her, Catrin felt vulnerable, and she wished for Benjin to sit beside her. Instead, he stood directly behind her in the ceremonial role of her Guardian. His presence was one of the few things that kept her from crawling under the table to hide; her grandmother's warm and welcoming smile was another.

"Why did you let me come dressed like this?" she asked Millie with an accusing look.

"It'll be good to let them see you as you are. These are good people. They'll not judge you poorly. Most are simple folk, and your attire may very well endear you to them even more. Don't be embarrassed. You're beautiful no matter how you dress, and these people owe you a great debt. They've come this day to honor you."

"Citizens," the Lady Mangst said in a bold voice that carried across the hall, and a hush fell over the assemblage. "I present to you my granddaughter, Catrin Volker-Mangst, daughter of the late Elsa Mangst."

The crowd raised a cheer, and Catrin was honored by the use of the Mangst name, though it sounded foreign to her ear. At the same time, she was honored that her grandmother had chosen to use the Volker name as well--a show of respect for her father. She blushed furiously as the crowd erupted in a cheer, and some even called out her name.

"The Lady Catrin has offered herself for service to her land and her people, and she will depart on the morrow for Adderhold." This statement was met with less enthusiasm, and Catrin assumed the people knew she was to wed a Kyte. "But this day bears another significance; one that I think Catrin has forgotten under the weight of her responsibilities. On this day, the Lady Catrin reaches her majority, and I ask you to celebrate with us."

A deafening roar erupted in the hall, and Catrin's knees nearly buckled. She'd forgotten, and the sudden remembrance nearly overcame her. She had dreamed of this day for years, but all of her visions had included her father. He was supposed to be there to accompany her as she left childhood behind and entered the world of adulthood. His absence brought her physical pain, and only the reassurance of Benjin's hands on her shoulders prevented her from breaking down completely.

"One and all, raise your glasses and join me. Drink to the honor of this brave and glorious child as she begins her new journey."

A great clatter followed as all the people in the room held their goblets aloft.

"To Catrin," they shouted on her grandmother's cue, and Catrin could no longer contain her tears. Never before had she been given such an honor, and the significance of it was not lost on her. Quietly, in the shelter of her mind and soul, she thanked her mother and father for bringing her into this world, and in that moment, she felt them with her. The vision of them raising a glass to her brought her strength, and she stood on shaking knees.

"I thank you, one and all," she said, and the room shook as the crowd chanted her name.

Her grandmother stood by her side and gave her a smile. "Let us feast," she said, and the room was soon filled with the sounds of revelry.

Food and drink were served to Catrin first, and she declared it the finest feast she had ever attended, which was not an embellishment. Roasted duck was served alongside glazed ham and sugared beets. The finest wine filled her goblet, and it gave her a heady rush as she drank it too quickly. No one was denied their fill, and liveried servants rushed to fulfill the whims of every guest. Amid the din, Catrin turned to Benjin, tears welling in her eyes. "Thank you," she said.

"I'd not forget such a day, and I know your father would give anything to be here. I can only hope that I can fill the void in some way," he said, and she took his hand in hers.

"I'm so glad you're here. Thank you for always being there for me," she said as she squeezed his hand softly.

After the sweets were served, musicians played merry tunes, and every member of the crowd lined up to greet Catrin. Many approached with trepidation, but Catrin decided to discard all propriety, and she embraced each of them as if they were family. She hugged, kissed, laughed, and cried with them, and in doing so, she won their hearts completely. They lavished her with gifts of flowers and gems, and Millie stood behind her, taking each gift and treating it as if it were the most valuable treasure. The table became a monument of their gratitude, and Catrin could hardly believe their generosity. Behind her was amassed more wealth than she had ever expected to see in a lifetime.

It was a young boy who gifted her with the finest thing of all, though, and his gift came in the form of a request. "Will you dance with me?" he asked, his cheeks flushed with excitement, and his mother appeared mortified by his bold request. She grabbed him by the arm and scolded him, but Catrin smiled and spread her arms wide.

"I would be honored," she said, which brought a shocked look from the boy's mother and a beaming grin from the boy. "What is your name, sir?"

"I'm Carrod Winsiker, Lady Catrin. You honor me," he said as seriously as if he were courting her, which brought a prideful smile to his mother's face, and the crowd erupted as Catrin allowed him to whirl her around the center of the hall. The musicians played a joyous tune with a fast tempo, and soon everyone in the hall danced. It was the most wonderful night in Catrin's life, and she wished it would never end.

When Carrod was exhausted, he bowed to Catrin and thanked her for the dance, but before he could walk away, she kissed him on the cheek. He blushed and held his hand over the spot where she kissed him, and as he ran to his mother, she beamed at Catrin. Benjin remained at his place behind her seat, and Catrin led him to the dance floor. He surprised her completely; he danced wonderfully.

"You never told me you could dance."

"It's a closely guarded family secret," he replied as he whirled her through the crowd of dancers.

Like all good things, the celebration had to end, and as the night grew long, the crowd began to disperse. When all the revelers were gone, Catrin rubbed her aching feet and stifled a yawn. The servants cleared the remnants of the meal, and only Catrin, her grandmother, Benjin, and Millie remained in the hall.

"You're an amazing woman, Catrin," her grandmother said, and the title did not escape her notice. "I was afraid our subjects would reject you, but in a single night, you made them your own. I believe they'd follow you anywhere."

With that, she bade them a good night and retired to her chambers, obviously taxed by all the excitement. Benjin and Catrin followed Millie back to their apartments, and she closed the door behind herself as she left. Catrin was about to seek her bed when Benjin emerged from the other room looking like the cat that caught the bird. He carried her staff behind his back and approached her.

"Before you go off to sleep, there is one more gift for you. This is from your grandmother and I," he said as he presented the staff to her. She was uncertain why he would gift her with her own staff, but then she saw the noonstones gleaming in the eyes of the serpent. "I hope you don't mind. I knew you needed some way to have the stones accessible, and this seemed fitting."

Indeed, it was as if the staff had been waiting for the stones, and together, they completed the whole.

"It's perfect," she said.

Chapter 23

To persevere when all seems lost is the most courageous act.
--Wendel Volker

* * *

Dressed as a peasant, Lissa watched as the parade of carriages prepared to leave Ravenhold, and she could barely contain the growl that threatened to escape her throat. An imposter, a usurper, and worse was riding in *her* place to Adderhold. Only days before, Lissa had returned to overhear tales of Catrin, the savior of Mundleboro. Unable to bear the taste, she spit.

How could her grandmother betray her in such a way? She had run away to prevent the marriage between the Mangst and Kyte families. Why would her grandmother send a stranger in her place?

"Pure madness," she muttered through clenched teeth. Torn, she tried to decide what to do next. If she let this Catrin go in her stead, all she had gone through would be for naught. Yet if she tried to stop it, she would reveal herself, and Morif would probably take her to Adderhold in chains.

Lissa did not relish the thought of their next meeting, certain he was furious with her for leaving. He was always going on about how her actions hurt Millie. Lissa didn't care about Millie at that moment, though, as the carriages began to roll. Her last chance to act was at hand and she stood, frozen. Unable to move or speak, she simply watched until the carriages disappeared from view.

* * *

The journey to Adderhold was only slightly less miserable than it would've been on foot. The carriage jostled constantly over the uneven roads, or it sat waiting for the crowds of people clogging the roads to disperse. Catrin was struck by the resentment her passing brought about. People cursed them, rotten vegetables were thrown at the carriages, and murderous looks followed them. These people had not

251

been at the celebration, and they had no reason to love her. The dozen guards assigned by Catrin's grandmother did what they could to control the situation, and Catrin insisted none of them harm any of the people, but it was difficult for them to comply as many altercations broke out.

Her people's despair brought Catrin physical pain, and she found the yoke of responsibility terribly difficult to bear. She had almost grown accustomed to feeling responsible for the people of the Godfist. It was a natural role that any citizen would feel compelled to fill, but her responsibility for the people of the Greatland was suffocating. The entire known world's future depended on her actions, and it appeared many would die no matter what she did.

Shifting in her seat, she adjusted the folds and layers of her skirt, which seemed to bunch under her no matter how she sat.

Benjin scowled, as he had been wont to do of late.

"What are you thinking?" Catrin asked.

"Hmm. Well, I was just trying to understand the relative disappearance of Vestrana agents across the Greatland. Of the inns we have encountered, only two offered any indication of the Vestrana, and even those signals were mixed. I suppose the times are much more dangerous these days, and it may be that they have become more secretive because of infiltration. It's mostly unimportant now since we've secured our entrance to Adderhold."

Adderhold. Catrin imagined a place crawling with snakes and scorpions, a dark and evil place that waited to consume her. She knew it was foolish to let her imagination run wild, and the visions were probably far worse than what actually awaited her, but a contagious dour mood blanketed those around her. Millie rode in a carriage with two other serving women, but each time they were together, she seemed more nervous and fretful than the last. She feared everything from an ambush to poisoned food, and the fact that her fears were plausible put their entire party on edge.

Along the Inland Sea, the lands were clogged with ragged campsites, and a foul stench hung in the air. The roads impossibly jammed, their caravan was forced to move overland through a maze of disarray. The twined roses on

252

the doors of their carriages became a liability as angry mobs, made up of those from Mundleboro and Lankland alike, left their bonfires to express their displeasure to the exposed nobility. Scuffles broke out between the mobs and her guards, but mostly cold iron kept the peace. As they neared the docks, though, the mass of people became denser, and the spaces between campsites were not wide enough to admit them passage.

A writhing mass of humanity stood between them and the road, which was as impassable as the clogged meadows, for it was jammed with people. They were only a short distance from the dock, but reaching it seemed impossible. One brave guard rode ahead to seek the officials at the docks; he was hard pressed, but he rode aggressively. Most moved out of his way; those who moved too slowly he pushed out of the way.

An uproar rolled across the meadows, and many shook their fists in the air as a mounted detachment plowed through campsites on their way to the carriages. Men became bold and rocked the carriages back and forth, and one man was fatally kicked by one of the horses drawing Catrin's carriage. Visions of assassins closing in around her gave Catrin the chills, and she clutched her staff, ready to defend herself. Within the confines of the carriage, though, there was no room to maneuver. Catrin felt trapped. Benjin's short sword was cleared from its scabbard, and he'd already reached for the door at least a dozen times, but he remained within the carriage.

Surrounded by guards and dock officials, they began a painfully slow procession through scattered remains of campsites, and Catrin doubted these people would love her as those at her majority banquet had. How could she blame them? She'd always disliked those who thought themselves more important than she. Her passage was a necessity, though, and this affront was simply unavoidable. The gathered crowd booed loudly as Catrin and her guards were escorted onto a waiting ferry. No one else was allowed to board with them, and hundreds were forced to wait for the next ferry.

Glad to be gone from the unruly crowd, Catrin relaxed a bit. Through the overcast skies, she could feel the energy of the comets above her, and she knew the next time the night skies were clear, she would see them. The energy bolstered her strength, and she let it calm her stomach as the carriage rocked along with the ship. It was a strange feeling, to sit in a carriage while aboard a ship. The horses had been unhooked for safety's sake, and the carriage's tongue was firmly secured, yet she felt as if she were perched on a branch in high wind, as if the carriage would slide from the deck and into the sea.

"Can we take a walk on deck?" she asked, but Benjin shook his head.

"Can't risk an ambush. Nearby ships could harbor assassins, and given the family history, I'd be surprised if they didn't. Best to stay in here until we reach Adderhold."

"Lovely."

Benjin tried to make the time pass more quickly by quizzing Catrin on her etiquette and ceremonial duties. While it took her mind from the motion of the ferry, it also reminded her of what lay ahead. Her role in this wedding was small. She need only show up and say a few words. Under no circumstances was she to look a man, especially a Zjhon holy man, in the eye. The restrictions on her behavior were ridiculous and triggered deep-seated resentment. Even as a member of a royal family, she was forced to endure the rules of others. The thought of kissing the archmaster's ring made her want to retch; she hadn't forgotten about his letter:

". . . My emissaries will remain on the Godfist until you have presented yourself to me personally. This matter must be settled between you and me. It would be a pity if your countrymen and mine suffered needlessly as a result of your selfishness. I beg you to put away your ego and do what you know is right . . ."

Even after so much time, his words rang in her memory and raised her fury. Belegra had caused hundreds to die then laid the blame at her feet. Trying to contain her rage was like standing before a flash flood, and despite her efforts, it threatened to consume her. Only the reason in Benjin's voice kept her from succumbing. His logic and planning gave her something to hold on to, something to believe in.

"After the exchange of names," he said, "you'll each carry a torch to a pile of kindling. You'll kneel and then light it with your torches. I'm guessing they'll place the kindling near the base of the statue for effect. That'll probably be your best chance to reach it," Benjin said.

"When I stand from the fire, toss me the staff. I still have no idea what I will do then, but I'll think of something . . . I hope."

Benjin seemed unable to formulate a proper response to that statement, and they spoke little more during the crossing. A tailwind drove the ferry toward the island that cradled Adderhold. The citadel rose on the horizon, and the closer they got, the more intimidating it became. The island was not small, yet Adderhold dominated it as if the man-made structure were larger than the land that held it.

Parapets reached so high into the sky that their tops were lost in the clouds, and the wall that snaked around the hold seemed impossibly thick. The buildings within were oddly shaped; nothing seemed squared or even at right angles. Instead, the city seemed to writhe, all curves and gentle sweeps. As they neared land, she saw that the structures, in many cases, were shaped like serpents, their fanged jaws forming entranceways and windows. The beaches resembled the far shores in many ways except that there was nowhere for the pilgrims to go. The island constricted them.

Alerted of their coming, Adderhold's guards created a narrow avenue through the knot of pilgrims. Those on the island were more subdued than those on the far banks; here there was no place to hide, and cross words could get them killed. Still they cast venomous glances toward the lace curtains that were pulled over the windows of the carriage. Fear was not all-powerful, though, and one man had the courage to throw a rock at them. His aim was uncanny, and the window shattered, the rock landing on Catrin's lap. The residue of the angry energy still clung to the rock, and she flung it to the floor. After brushing the reddish slivers of broken glass from her dress, she sat in a state of readiness, prepared for whatever assault might come next.

Amazingly lifelike carvings of serpent heads protruded from the walls that surrounded Adderhold, and the largest ones guarded a towering archway. No gates barred the entrance. A large structure stood atop the arch, looming above the massive tunnel. Darkness enshrouded the carriage as they entered, and a deep chill set into Catrin's bones before they emerged from the other side.

Adderhold was a bizarre mixture of the hideous and exquisite. Lush gardens were inhabited by ghoulish statuary and serpentine themes. The way they were crafted made them appear as if they would reach out and strike anyone foolish enough to come close. The buildings were constructed of a grainy, white, stonelike material that Catrin had never seen before. It sparkled even in the dim light, and it had allowed the architects to create wonderfully flowing lines.

Beyond the shops and homes that ringed the city stood the keep. Carved from the side of a mountain, it looked as if it would consume the city, so aggressive was its stance. Coiled and focused, the keep was formed to resemble a single serpent of such stature and ferocity that most could not enter without fear of being devoured. Elite guards lined the cobbled boulevard that led to the keep, and their embossed plate gleamed. Their helmets were fashioned in the likeness of pit vipers, giving them an inhuman appearance.

No one spoke, and no trumpets blared. Catrin's party entered the gaping maw with no welcome waiting within. Stables stood to their left, and they moved in that direction. Benjin disembarked first, checking for danger, then helped Catrin from the carriage. As her feet touched the reed-covered flagstone, a hooded man approached in a steady, measured pace. He seemed to be trying for the gliding effect mastered by the Cathuran monks, but he could not complete the illusion.

He said nothing when he stood before them. He just nodded and turned back the way he came, departing with the same unvarying gait. Catrin and her attendants followed him, and it seemed to her that the mood was more suited to a funeral than a wedding; anxious tension thickened the air.

Atop a grand stairway stood another facade with bas-reliefs in the form of Istra and Vestra. The archway was unguarded, and the halls were empty. Their boots echoed loudly, and she felt as if the oppressive stone would close in upon her and grind her to dust.

Slender windows filled with multicolored glass provided meager light, which was supplemented by firepots that hung from ornate chains. The polished flagstone ended at a recessed stair, which was guarded by the most fearsome serpent carving yet. This one struck a primal fear in Catrin, for this was no glorified snake. Furrowed ridges protruded over the eyes and emerged from flesh as horns, which gave it an air of intelligence, and one other feature distinguished this beast: wings.

So cleverly had the carving been created that the feral stare seemed to follow Catrin, stalking her every move. Recalling the skeletal remains found near the statue, she needed little more evidence to believe the old tales. Dragons had once roamed the land and flown the skies. Atop all her other problems, it seemed a bad omen, and dread filled her as they moved deeper within the keep. The place seemed designed to take the spirit from all who entered, and the builders had done their job well. Each step seemed to take her closer to her death.

The robed man abruptly stopped in front of an archway that opened into what appeared to be a temple since it contained nothing but rows of bare benches. More colorful windows adorned the far wall, and one window in particular drew Catrin's eye. Beyond it was the glowing silhouette of Istra, Goddess of the Night. Only part of her visage was visible through the slender opening, but it was exactly as she had seen it during her astral travels; only now, it glowed more brightly.

The somber procession filed into the room. They tried to make themselves comfortable on the unforgiving benches, but it was impossible.

"These accommodations are an insult," Millie said with her hands on her hips, but their guide simply turned and left the room.

"This will be fine, Millie," Catrin said, hoping to lessen the tension. "I've no desire to stay here long. We'll do what we came here to do, and then we'll leave. Until then, we'll just have to accept whatever hospitality is offered."

Benjin nodded his agreement, and Millie mumbled something unintelligible that Catrin doubted was complimentary toward the Zjhon. As evening came, the skies were afire with color, and the eerie, greenish light of the statue grew brighter yet. Sleep was impossible, and Catrin ignored Millie's protests that she couldn't be married with sagging eyes. The wedding was a farce, and everyone knew it, bride and groom included.

For two days, they were left with little more than broth to sustain them. Millie paced the floors, casting furious glances at anyone who crossed her path. The waiting was dreadful, and no matter how hard she tried, Catrin could not make the days fly by any faster than they would. Even Benjin became snappish.

* * *

Atop Limin's Spire, the winds gusted, and even within the shelter of the stone walls, it was painfully cold. The structure's lack of a roof helped not at all. But the skies were clear, and Milo was convinced he had the focusing mechanism working properly.

"I have only a few more parts left to assemble," Milo said. "Then we will see things no one has seen in thousands of years."

Strom and Osbourne watched, waited, and shivered.

"I just want to get this done and get down from here. Heights make my head spin," Strom said.

"The view is incredible, don't you think?"

"I try not to look at it."

"That's it," Milo said. "We're ready."

Strom and Osbourne wasted no time. After wrapping the looking glass in leather, they picked it up and began climbing to the top of the pedestal. There was no railing; nothing stood between them and a terrifying drop. Tears streamed down Strom's cheeks from more than the wind stinging his eyes; he feared that same wind would blow him from the spiral stairway.

Not long after they passed what Strom considered the halfway point, his arms began to quiver from the exertion, but he was determined to keep going, and he gritted his teeth.

"I'm not going to make it," Osbourne said. "I need to put it down now."

Frustrated, Strom eased his end of the looking glass down. Leaning against the pedestal, he closed his eyes and waited for his arms to stop tingling. Osbourne moved around him, walking up and down stairs. It made Strom want to scream. How could he not realize how close they were to falling into an abyss? Milo, at least, had the sense to remain still.

When Osbourne announced he was ready, Strom stood, planted his feet, and opened his eyes. After a deep breath, he bent down and picked up his end of the looking glass. As they neared the top, the climb seemed a bit easier, and they soon reached the mounting bracket. With one final effort, they lifted the looking glass and gently set it in the bracket. Milo slid the pins into place, and finally Strom and Osbourne could relax.

"This thing better work," Strom said.

"That's what you said last time," Osbourne said.

"Yeah. I know."

Milo aimed the looking glass away from the morning sun and began turning the large ring he said would focus the lenses, but his arms weren't long enough to reach the ring while looking in the eyepiece. "Osbourne, my boy, I need you to turn the adjuster while I look through the glass."

With slow and tentative movements, Osbourne turned the adjuster and, by the look on his face, feared the whole thing would come apart in his hands.

"Wait. Stop," Milo said. "Go back. Stop! That's it!"

"It really works?" Strom asked, unable to believe what he was hearing.

"Strom, come here. You're eyes are better than mine. Help Osbourne adjust it."

His excitement finally overcoming his fears, Strom gazed into the eyepiece, but all he saw was the blue of the midmorning sky, and there was nothing to focus on.

"It will be easier at night, but do the best you can. This is important," Milo said as Gustad arrived with a leather satchel. "I'll be back." Both Gustad and Milo climbed down, wanting to look at their books and calculations somewhere more sheltered from the wind.

"Turn it some," Strom said, and the image grew fuzzy. "Go back the other way." This time the image became clearer, but then it grew fuzzy again. "Go back just a bit. There. Stop. That's the best I can do without something to look at. Let's swing this around and see if we can find anything."

"I don't think that's a good idea."

"Come on, Osbo. We did most of the work on this thing. I think we've earned the right to take a look around. Besides, Milo and Gustad are hiding something. Look at them down there. Did either of them tell you what this was all about?"

"No."

"Then let's find out. We just push here, and it should swing right around."

"Don't look at the sun!" Osbourne yelled.

Strom aimed lower, closer to the horizon, looking for something and not knowing what. But then he saw something strange and stopped. "Turn the ring," he said. "Back the other way. Stop!" Unable to believe what he saw, Strom just stared in silent awe for a moment. "By the gods. What *is* that?"

"What is what?" Osbourne asked as Milo and Gustad started climbing back to the top of the pedestal. Strom stepped back and let Osbourne look for himself. He didn't need to look again, the image was imprinted in his memory.

". . . should be visible by now," Gustad said as they reached the top, but then he looked Strom in the eyes and ran to the looking glass. Osbourne stepped away, bereft of speech.

"The charts we found in the lost library are real,"
Gustad said as he stepped away from the looking glass. Milo
rushed in for his chance to see. "Istra has arrived."

* * *

Catrin and all the others stood when a soldier entered
the hall. Millie blocked his path and looked him in the eye.

"Be ready by midday," he said, casting a cold and
disinterested glance around the room.

Millie controlled her anger enough to nod and only
turned her back on the man. She fussed over Catrin's hair for
an impossible amount of time, most of which Catrin spent
staring out the rose and chartreuse windowpanes. The sky
beyond was clear, but she could feel the comets coming; they
were close. She felt as if she could reach out and touch them.
Though there was little evidence to support her feelings, a
cloudbank on the eastern horizon seemed strange to her--
unnatural.

She was to wed this day, and she'd never even seen the
face of the man who would be her husband. When she
turned her thoughts to the wedding, her anxieties brought
their full weight to bear. She didn't even know if she'd be
able to gain access to the statue, let alone destroy it. Feeling
like a prisoner, she doubted she'd be free to do anything
beyond take the vows. As her mind went in circles, she
resigned herself to the uncertainty. She'd know what to do
when the time came--she hoped.

As the sun moved toward its zenith, when Vestra was at
the height of his power, a dozen robed men arrived to escort
the bride. Benjin took his place behind Catrin as she
followed her guards from their cell, as she had come to think
of it. Like a funeral procession, they walked in silence, and a
pall of sadness hung over them, one and all. Tears were shed,
but none were tears of joy. Catrin missed her father dearly
on this day, a day he should have shared with her, and she
wiped her eyes with the sleeves of her flowing dress. Millie
cast her a sideways glance but said nothing.

At the turn of a corner, the sound of a large crowd
carried through the halls, and a sunlit field became visible in

261

the distance. At its center stood the Statue of Terhilian. Though only its base was visible from their current vantage point, there was no doubt as to what they saw. The land surrounding the level field angled upward in all directions, like a giant bowl, and ascending rows of stone seats had been carved from the mountainside. In only a few places was the stone still visible; most seats were already taken, and the rest were filling quickly.

Primal fear struck Catrin's heart. Not only must she face her new husband and the Statue of Terhilian, she must do it in front of the largest assemblage she'd ever witnessed. Only one thing consoled her, and that was the location of the altar, which was scant paces from the base of the statue. Her guts twisted into knots when she saw another procession coming from the opposite direction. In the lead came a proud young man who walked with his chest out and his head tilted slightly back.

It was not his physical features that intrigued her, though; it was the nimbus that surrounded him. Unlike the auras described in the old tales, it had no color and was only clearly visible when she squinted. But when she did, she could see an area around him that distorted whatever was behind him, like the heat of a fire only less fluid.

He ignored Catrin completely, and she felt her face flush. Surely he must be curious about his new bride. How could he not even try to see what she looked like? Perhaps, she thought, he had already decided she was a monster, a hideous and undesirable wretch not worthy of his blood.

In a moment of sudden clarity, she realized she had done the same to him. No matter how kind or polite he was, he'd always be a Kyte, one of the people responsible for the deaths of her mother and aunts, and who knew how many others. She made herself look anywhere but at him, knowing he would sense her stare. She looked beyond the statue to the towering archway that dominated the eastern end of the arena. It was twice as large as the one at the main entrance, and Catrin guessed it was the only opening large enough to admit the statue.

In the skies beyond, the strange thunderhead grew larger and uncharacteristically bright, as if illuminated from within. But Catrin soon reached the raised dais, and the statue blotted out the rest of her world. The energy radiating from it felt unclean, nothing like the waves of energy that descended from the skies. Like a kernel of hard corn held over a fire, its inside boiled, and at any moment, it could release all its energy in a single, devastating flash. Standing before it took much of her willpower, and her knees felt untrustworthy, as if they would buckle in the slightest breeze.

When the groom stood directly across from her, she looked skyward once again, and the heavens were aglow. The storm was no storm. It was a comet scudding across the skies. Grinding against the air, it erupted into a conflagration the likes of which had not been seen in thousands of years. Its energy slammed into Catrin, and combined with the noxious charge from the statue, it was more than she could handle. She swayed on her feet, and Benjin supported her from behind. As he held her, her staff pressed against her bare forearm. The feel of the polished wood was comforting, and she took solace from it.

"Behold, the eye of Istra," a voice boomed, startling Catrin. She had no doubt it was Archmaster Belegra who spoke, but she could not make herself look at him, afraid of what she might see. "This day she has come to witness the union of Lankland and Mundleboro under her light and likeness. Vestra joins her, high in the skies, and we ask for their blessings. Give us a sign, and we'll rejoice!"

Catrin waited along with everyone else for some sign, and none were disappointed when red lightning spanned the eastern horizon, cast out in all directions from the raging comet. The distant rumbling did not fade like natural thunder; instead it grew steadily, intensifying, but no one was prepared for the blast that knocked them from their feet and seats alike. A wave of fetid air roared from the west, and the ground shook.

The western horizon took on its own eerie glow, one that matched the light of the statue. And Catrin knew, in that instant, without any doubt, the Statue of Terhilian that had been found in the west had just detonated, and she shrank away from the realization that tens of thousands had just perished in an instant. A new cataclysm had begun, and the

263

next component of destruction stood within throwing distance of her. Zjhon guards formed a ring around the dais and effectively barred her path.

Most people had regained their feet, though the moans of the injured could still be heard, and angry voices protested from the crowd.

"The other statue has exploded!" someone shouted, and many looked about to see who it was, but no one laid claim to the statement.

"The Herald Witch has attacked the Westland," a woman shrieked, and Archmaster Belegra jumped on the opportunity.

"Friends, we are besieged. The Herald Witch has brought war to the Greatland, and we are all in dire peril. We must stand together and face our common foe as one unified nation. If we remain separate, surely we will perish," he bellowed, and the acoustics of the arena carried his words to even those in the highest rows. Ragged cheers broke out, but many within the crowd seemed unsure, as if their faith had been something of little consequence in the past but was now coming to haunt them. They would need to quickly decide what they believed, for now their lives depended on it.

"Can the Herald travel a third of the Greatland in the span of just one breath?" a familiar voice asked, and Catrin searched for the speaker without success.

"Of course not," Archmaster Belegra replied, seemingly outraged by the notion. "No one can do such a thing. The Herald Witch is powerful, but she's not unstoppable. We have but to join with one another, and we can defeat her. We must do this before she brings any more evil into our world." He seemed pleased with his words.

"Could the Herald cause such destruction in the Westland if she was here, within Adderhold?" the same voice shouted from the crowd, and the speaker became easy to locate, as just about everyone in his vicinity moved away. He stood proud and defiant, and Catrin could hardly believe the cruelty of fate when she recognized him: Rolph Tillerman, one of the few people in the Greatland who might guess her identity. She cursed herself for her own stupidity. She should

264

never have let her tongue slip, but the damage was already done, and all she could do was wait to see how dire the consequences would be.

"There's no way the Herald Witch could cause such damage from a great distance. We are safe here," Archmaster Belegra replied.

"Then the attack on the Westland could not have been committed by the Herald," Rolph bellowed triumphantly.

"How could you know such a thing?" Archmaster Belegra asked, clearly confident that Rolph would only prove himself witless, but Rolph's response stirred the frightened crowd into frenzy.

"I know this for certain, since the Herald of Istra stands before you," he said, and Catrin leaned heavily on Benjin as Rolph's eyes turned to her. "In a wedding dress."

Chapter 24

Death, like life, is part of the natural cycle. To fear one is to devalue the other.
--Manul Praska, shaman

* * *

Time slowed and Catrin swung her head in a wide arc, taking in every detail as she spun. All eyes were on her, and she felt every stare acutely, especially those from within the hoods of the men surrounding Archmaster Belegra. Hostile energies gathered there, making ready the attack, and Catrin was jolted by the recognition of one.

Prios.

The pattern of his energy was unmistakable, and she sensed his recognition of her even without being able to see his face. He gave no outward sign save a small twitch of his hood. But then her gaze moved to the very close face of her betrothed. His eyes were filled with rage, and his aura reached out for her like fingers of flame. For a moment, time accelerated; then he was leaping for her throat with deadly quickness.

Instinct drove her, and the heady abundance of energy she'd been absorbing made her off-balance parry a massive blow that sent him tumbling through the air. Even as he spiraled into a crowd of those attempting to flee, she wondered at the fact that she didn't even know his name, this Kyte whelp, and she wondered if it wouldn't soon be a name she'd wish to forget. For the moment, though, he'd pose no more threat; his limp form was dragged from the field by his guards. The flesh of her neck and throat stung, and when she ran her hand over it, it came away covered with blood. Had he raked her flesh without ever touching her? She wondered at that, but her attention was required to stay alive, and the world rushed around her again.

Her momentum carried her, and she found herself facing Benjin, who tossed her staff into the air between them. Catrin leaped to meet it halfway and caught it deftly. She rolled over it and sprang into a fighting stance only to

find no one between her and the statue. One man moved to
bar her path, but his eyes bulged, affixed to the heel of her
staff, and he fled. She risked a quick glance at her staff. The
serpent head stood out in bold relief, outlined by pulses of
liquid energy, and, for the first time, the true nature of the
serpent was revealed. Tendrils of liquid fire clearly showed
the outlines of wings, but Catrin could look upon it no more.
The noonstone eyes shone bright white, and blue spheres
obscured her vision long after she looked away from the
blinding glare.

The comet above seemed likely to destroy them all as it
moved in front of the sun and was spectacularly backlit
during the eclipse. Deep shades of purple and amber rolled
away from the massive sphere of ice, and a towering cloud of
vapor trailed behind it. The air sang like an anvil rung by a
thousand hammers, accompanied by the monotonous
thundering that threatened to vibrate everything into
oblivion.

So quickly did Catrin propel herself to the statue that
she had to let her body catch up. The thrumming air seemed
to suspend her flesh, and her spirit barely clung to it. Her
hands fumbled as they gripped the staff and prepared for
impact. With all the force she could muster, she struck the
glowing base of the statue. The energy trapped within pealed
and flowed through the staff, through Catrin, and into the
land itself. She could do nothing to stop it. Every muscle in
her body contracted, and her face contorted in a twisted
rictus.

Immediately she realized her mistake. The statue
contained a small but highly charged core of noonstone
opposite some other type of stone she did not recognize,
one that stored a massive negative charge. Only a thin layer
of dense metal separated the two charges. If that insulating
barrier broke down, the resulting chain reaction would be
monstrous, just as the one in the Westland had been. The
explosion would be felt all the way in Endland, which
seemed almost unfathomable to Catrin, having struggled to
cross the massive expanse.

The men rushing toward her and those with bows
drawn compounded her problems. Missiles were already on

267

their way to meet her when she flung energy about her for protection. An angry sphere of red and lightning formed a shield around her. Arrows and spears burst into flames as they struck the wall of plasma, falling away harmlessly. But Catrin's resolve nearly faltered when men dived upon her sphere, hurling themselves against her energy flow. She felt their energy clash with hers and their spirits released by the impact. Each one was like a knife to her heart, and she wept.

"Please stop! I cannot keep you safe if you attack me. The energy has me trapped. Please stop! Please," she wailed, but Belegra urged more men to assault her defenses. He showed no regard for human life as he chided those who would preserve themselves. Those who stood around him, those hidden within the depths of their robes, seemed compelled into action. Each had access to Istra's power, but they were bound by Archmaster Belegra's will--slaves. As the archmaster moved his arms in wild and rigid gestures, the robed figures attacked without moving.

Hot, fetid rays of adulterated power emanated from them. Each of the energies merged with the others and was orchestrated by Archmaster Belegra. Somehow, he exerted nearly total control over these men, with the exception of Prios, who was clever. His energy separated itself once beyond Archmaster Belegra's field of influence and only brushed across the surface of Catrin's sphere, whispering to her, over and over again.

"You gave me a name. You gave me power."

Archmaster Belegra was completely consumed in his machinations and seemed unaware of the communication between Prios and Catrin. The remaining mixture of energies, however, slammed into her sphere, and she reeled. The impact was worse than the time she had been kicked in the chest by a plow horse, and she wondered if her ribs were broken. Archmaster Belegra continued to pummel her with the twisted energies, but it became obvious he would not be able to do so much longer. His breathing was ragged, and beads of sweat raced down his mottled flesh.

Without so much as a twitch, Catrin sensed Prios separate himself from the twisted flow completely, and he lashed out at Archmaster Belegra. Like a striking snake, a

268

thread of energy arced between them, and they both collapsed. The others swayed on their feet as the compulsion ended abruptly, and two fell to their knees, leaving only two standing.

Catrin took advantage of the respite and desperately reached into the statue, casting her senses over the deadly charges. There seemed an impossible amount of energy still trapped within, considering what had already been released, and she despaired. At the rate it was draining, it would take days if not weeks to deplete, and the insulating barrier was rapidly breaking down. It writhed and bubbled, boiling. Desperate, she tried to draw the scorching heat out of the core. Slowly the barrier cooled to a near-solid state, though the ground around Catrin's feet caught fire.

With the insulator stabilized, she returned her efforts to draining the excessive energy stored in the noonstone core. After the initial shock, she became desensitized to the massive energy flow, and though she felt as if she were slowly melting away, she could control herself and the flow of energy much better.

"Good people of the Greatland, flee!" she shouted. "I fear the statue will explode no matter what I do, get as far away as you can. I'll hold it as long as I am able."

"Don't listen to her," Archmaster Belegra shouted as he pulled himself from the ground. "Attack! Avenge your brethren! The Herald Witch is the true cause of these evils. Destroy her! Any who flee are traitors, and their lives will be forfeit."

His words rang discordant over those who still milled about the arena, and only a few fought to reach Catrin. The majority continued to flee, but some rallied together and advanced on Archmaster Belegra and his supporters. With his time undoubtedly short, Archmaster Belegra launched a desperate attack. He tore the energy from those who surrounded him and thrust at the Statue of Terhilian itself.

In one motion, he undid all that Catrin had accomplished. The barrier began to vaporize, and she knew it would soon break down completely. She attempted to divert his continued onslaught, but the mass of wild energy was beyond her control. As she tried to influence its course, it leaped out in all directions and struck down men and women without discretion. Even as she pulled away from it, lesser bolts of energy blasted Benjin and several of her guards. Their smoking forms lay frighteningly still where they landed, and Catrin nearly lost consciousness.

Breathing became almost impossible in the overheated air, and she drew ragged gasps. The arena spun before her as her vision clouded. The world was collapsing around her, and there was nothing more she could do. She'd given all she could give, and it hadn't been enough. Doomed to failure, she wondered why she even bothered to continue struggling. It would be so much easier to just give up, to lie down and die, but some inner fire still burned, and while any chance existed, she would fight.

After sucking in the deepest breath she could manage, she prepared to launch her final assault on Archmaster Belegra. Her skin grew taut and her fingernails peeled back as she gripped the staff, drawing more energy than she'd ever tried to contain before. She drew not only from the statue, but also from the staff, the noonstones, and the air itself. The natural energy helped to balance the wild forces trapped within the statue, but her exhaustion threatened to claim her. She walked a knife's edge between delivering a mighty blow and succumbing to it.

The polished surface of the staff bubbled, and her fingers bit into its flesh. Blistering sap raised welts on her hands, and she could draw no more. Fear gripped her as the reality of her situation set in. She was about to die, and so was everyone nearby. She could not hope to deliver this much energy and still remain standing; the statue would run its course, and with the comet still grazing the atmosphere, it wouldn't be long before it was all over.

Resigned to her death, she peeled her hands from the staff, and for a moment marveled at the imprints of her fingers carved deep into the wood. Turning to face Archmaster Belegra, she drew herself up. He was not unprepared, though, and launched an attack of his own. Green and yellow flames roared from his fingers as he drew upon the remaining members of his cadre, which included

Prios, who seemed to have no more fight left in him. His form slumped forward as his life's energy was drained.

Enraged, Catrin delivered her blow, hurtling a rope of fire and lightning at Archmaster Belegra's head. He ducked under the assault, but the heat took his hair and blistered his flesh. With a terrible cry, he fled, and Catrin wobbled. She spun and reached about her, searching for something to hold on to, and her hands landed on the staff, still protruding from the statue's base. Her fingers settled precisely in the same place that bore their recessed imprints, and the energy surged through her again.

Without even understanding exactly what she was doing, she tugged on the energy and pulled it to her, embracing it. Her body thrummed, and she felt her spirit becoming free. She watched with a sense of indifferent attachment as she hung in the air above her physical form.

Before her, the statue glowed so brightly that it was blinding, and beyond it, the remnants of the crowd parted like the sea before the hull of a fast ship. Catrin barely heard the howling that split the air, but she saw an enraged bull of a man charging the statue.

"Do not despair, heart of the land! I've come for you," he bellowed, and Catrin recognized him at last.

Barabas.

"Abomination, be gone!" he roared as he closed the gap, and Catrin drifted closer to her body, intrigued.

Barabas struck the statue at a full run, and the arena was rocked with the concussion. The Statue of Terhilian trembled on its base, and Catrin felt Barabas as he was freed from his body. His spirit sang as it blasted free, knowing his sacrifice had not been in vain.

Some force moved Catrin's ephemeral spirit, and she slammed back into her body. Though she felt as if a part of her were lost, she became, once again, constrained by her physical form just as it hit the ground, and her breath whooshed from her lungs.

The statue was no longer a viable weapon. Barabas had done that which Catrin had not thought to do. Rather than deplete the positive charge, he had neutralized the negative charge by hitting it with his own positive energy. The

271

noonstone core still stored a tremendous charge, but the reactive agent was gone.

An ear-shattering crack brought her out of her stupor. The Statue of Terhilian split down its center. Istra and Vestra were parted from their eternal embrace and sent crashing to the ground. Large pieces fractured into smaller sections, and it rained stone. Rough hands grabbed Catrin by the back of her dress and dragged her away from the disintegrating leviathan. She floundered, her limbs leaden and unwilling to respond to her command, and she let the darkness claim her.

Before she drifted into oblivion, a warm and bright spirit visited her, and Barabas spoke one last time before he departed the world of the living.

"Be strong, heart of the land. Your work is not yet done."

Epilogue

Hunching his shoulders over the massive crystal he carried, Prios struggled to keep his grip. Heavy and slick, the ebony stone's sharp edges bit into his hands, but he made no complaint. He'd spoken out once, when he was younger, and Archmaster Belegra had ordered his tongue cut out. Even deprived of speech, he could communicate well enough with those sensitive to Istra's power. Archmaster Belegra and the others of the cadre had little difficulty understanding the mental images he sent them, and Catrin had understood him even when their bodies had been leagues apart. It was the memory of her that kept him going.

She gave me a name. She gave me power.

It was his mantra, and he repeated it to himself over and over. Prios. She had named him Prios. The name gave him pride, and he built his identity around it. He was no longer a nameless slave child, powerless and weak. He was Prios, and he was the master of his own destiny.

After the destruction of the statue, he had expected to be killed for his betrayals, but the archmaster acted as if he were unaware. Prios still couldn't believe it, though, and he dreaded the moment when Archmaster Belegra unleashed his fury. Surely he was not so blind that he hadn't noticed. Even if he were truly ignorant, what of the other members of the cadre? How long until one of them revealed his deceit? They had no reason to love him, yet they, too, had reason to hate Belegra. He had enslaved them all and used them without mercy. Prios could not know if the others were aware of his actions or if they would remain silent, and his life hung from the thinnest thread. All he could do was move on and hope for the day he would be reunited with Catrin. His dreams were full of her, and the thought of joining her was like a beacon in the darkness. It guided him forward and kept him from despairing.

Nearly losing his footing on the slippery gangplank, he thought a moment about letting himself fall into the dark waters, taking the precious crystal with him. It was so tempting. He would be free of his bonds at last, freed from the cruelty of his existence. Again, a vision of Catrin came to

273

his mind. She glowed so brightly, and she lured him, just as the scent of roses draws the honeybee. She was brave and powerful, beautiful yet humble. He drew strength from her and climbed aboard the ship determined to find her. He would join her, and together they would be free.

She gave me a name. She gave me power. And, one day, I will be free.

About the Author

Born in Salem, New Jersey, Brian spent much of his childhood on the family farm, where his family raised and trained Standardbred racehorses. Brian lives with his wife, Tracey, in the foothills of the Blue Ridge Mountains. After years in the world of Internet technology, the writing of this trilogy has been a dream come true for Brian and what feels like a return to his roots.

For more information, visit http://BrianRathbone.com

Be sure to grab your copy Dragon Ore, the exciting conclusion to The Dawning of Power trilogy.

If you enjoyed this book, please consider leaving a review, rating, or even just "liking" it on the retailer of your choice or on Goodreads. Thanks!